The appearance of the raving stranger and the flight of the hounds were but the first two mysteries to arise in Blackstone on this night of dire portents. They were not the last nor, to the lord of the manor, the most troubling. Instead, Earl Blackstone found the third mysterious occurrence to be far more sinister, its portents more evil.

Like the other two, the third was a puzzle that developed during the darkness of the night of the full moon, though it was not discovered until the morning.

This was when a guard, patrolling the outside of the great manor house, came upon the body on the ground. It lay face-down below the third-floor window leading to Currag's chambers. When the stunned guard rolled the corpse over, it proved to be that of the young heir to the noble house.

There was no mark to be found on him, no sign of any physical injury—except, of course, for the brutal impact of the forty-foot fall into a stone-paved courtyard. Despite that impact, the features on the face, the expressions of the mouth and eyes, were still visible.

It remained for his father, the earl, to wonder at the thing that had come to Currag Blackstone in the depths of the fatal eve. Yet this much he knew: The visage of his son at the time of his death was a mask of almost unimaginable horror.

FANTASY ADVENTURE

Prophet of Moonshae
Douglas Niles

The Druidhome Trilogy: Book One

PROPHET OF MOONSHAE

First Printing: March, 1992
Printed in the United States of America
Library of Congress Catalog Card Number: 91-66509

9 8 7 6 5 4 3 2 1

ISBN: 1-56076-319-1

TSR, Inc.
P.O. Box 756
Lake Geneva, WI 53147
U.S.A.

TSR Ltd.
120 Church End, Cherry Hinton
Cambridge CB1 3LB
United Kingdom

To Jim Ward,
for all your advice and
inspiration through the years

Prologue

The dragon was very old and very evil. For centuries he had dwelled on the fringes of the Realms, preying across continents and oceans, passing countless decades of rapacious existence. No longer could he remember all the villages he had ravaged, all the damsels devoured.

Great knights rode against him, as often as not perishing within their plate armor from the heat of the creature's fiery breath. Those who survived the killing fireball succumbed to jaws studded with scimitar-like teeth or claws that could rend a war-horse with ease.

And when the knights failed, the wizards came to slay him. But the shrewd wyrm met them, spell for spell, with fire and ice—and dark, pernicious magic of even greater scope. Wrapped within a protective cocoon of sorcery, the serpent deflected lightning bolts back at their casters, sneered at spells that meant certain death to lesser creatures, and then spewed a seething, hellish cloud of infernal flame at the few surviving mages who dared persevere.

But ultimately, after more than a millennia and a half of monstrously evil existence, the great dragon confronted an enemy he could not defeat in battle nor deflect with sorcery—the measured passage of time itself. The massive eyes, with their cruel, slitted pupils, began to cloud. Muscles and joints, though still knotted with awesome and deadly power, grew stiff, supple movement impeded by the effects of dampness and chill.

Within his mountain, curled upon a vast pile of treasure, the dragon, called Gotha by those of his slaves and captives who had lived long enough to converse with their lord, pondered. A hateful life lay in the wyrm's wake, and all that hatred coalesced now into something made even more vile and spiteful by the crippling effects of age. Shrieking suddenly, unable to contain his rage, the monster lurched to his feet. Dripping, fanged jaws gaped, and the hissing roar of a fireball exploded inside the lair, searing dampness from the walls and incinerating a small mound of priceless antiquities.

Smoke wafted through the enclosed air as the dragon's hooded lids sheltered his eyes. Gold, from statues and coins, flowed from the treasure in liquid streams, melted by the infernal blast to finally collect in heavy pools on the rough, stone floor.

Ancient one . . .

The dragon froze, startled as a disembodied speaker projected a message into Gotha's mind. He immediately recognized the voice as belonging to a god. Though he didn't know the identity of the deity, it could only be one of most sinister chaos and evil, else it would have no business with Gotha.

"Speak to me," said the serpent in a deep, rasping voice. Settling back, catlike, onto its trove, the creature waited.

I am Talos, the Destroyer.

"A god of evil and violence."

A god of ultimate destruction—and one who has observed you for many, many seasons. Though you have not labored in my name, your works have added mightily to the workings of chaos.

The dragon said nothing. The facts spoke for themselves.

I speak to you now because I have something to offer—something you desire very much.

Gotha pondered, puffing a blast of smoke to screen his sudden anxiety. The monster knew of Talos the Destroyer, also called the Raging One. He was a god who used the destructive force of storms to lash the world—lightning, tornadoes, cyclones, blizzards—for no other purpose than his own vicious whim. Talos was a god of vengeance and evil, not to be trusted, but he was also powerful—very powerful indeed. And he offered something the dragon desired, and that could be only one thing.

"Continue," the dragon said, holding his deep voice steady.

Swear yourself to me, and you shall never die. Your power, already awe-inspiring, shall rise to heights you have not imag-

ined. The centuries, the ages shall pass, and you shall remain.

"Swearing what in return?"

You will perform a task for me, a task of violence and destruction.

"What is the task?"

I cannot say, for I do not know. It may not occur for hundreds, perhaps thousands of years. After you swear, I shall call you when the need becomes apparent.

"Your powers shall preserve and prolong my life?" Intrigued in spite of himself, the dragon crept forward, raising his sinuous neck as if the presence of the god shared the lair with the serpent.

You shall not die.

Gotha was an intelligent creature and had proven to be a shrewd negotiator during those rare previous instances in his life when dialogue had seemed advantageous. Under normal circumstances, he would undoubtedly have noticed that the god did not, in fact, reply affirmatively to the serpent's question.

But the situation had tempted the ancient creature beyond his natural caution, for the inevitable onset of decay and, ultimately, death terrified the wyrm such as nothing ever had. And now, through the intervention of a god, a greater power of the Realms, even that final disaster might be overcome.

"I accept. I shall swear to perform a task for you when you summon me. I commend myself to your power!"

Excellent. You must now fly to the great north, to an ice cave that you will find there, for I shall guide you. There you shall be granted that which you desire.

The serpent slithered from the trove, creeping through the long network of caves that honeycombed the mountain lair, and finally burst into the night air. Under a nearly full moon, Gotha soared to the north, crossing the desert of the Endless Waste, cresting the jagged teeth of the Icerim Mountains, and finally soaring across a seemingly limitless expanse of ice and snow.

Directed by the persistent images of the god, the wyrm settled to the snow beneath a gaping chasm in the face of a glacier. Creeping inside, the monster pressed ever deeper, seeking that to which the god directed him.

That god, Gotha noticed idly, now seemed to be strangely absent.

The collapse of the cavern roof came suddenly, with no warning. Millions of tons of ice crushed downward, smashing the monster to the floor, pinning the scaled flesh, crushing bones, pulverizing the immensely powerful wings, compressing the dragon into a brutally mangled form. The thunderous avalanche continued for many seconds, and when eventually the ice settled, there was no sign of movement in the vast chamber.

But the god had spoken the truth, for the dragon did not die. Instead, the serpent lay there, alive, hateful, and trapped. Years passed into decades, and decades into centuries, until more than two hundred years had elapsed, and still the dragon did not die. Constant pain wracked his great, immobile body, and a mind that had always flourished upon evil now learned even greater depths of loathing.

Time became a doleful march. Corrupted by the fiendish influence of Talos, the monster became a twisted and horrifying image of himself. Gotha's body remained frozen in its crushed shape, but his nerves grew taut with fury. Still alert, he felt pain even through the numbing chill. Gradually his life evolved—and if he did not die, neither did he remain fully alive.

The dragon became a dracolich, an undead creature of base, unadulterated evil. Frozen, the flesh did not rot from his bones, nor did the leather folds tear from his massive wings. His eyes shrunk and shriveled, but in the two sockets, as large as bushel baskets, two spots of hateful crimson grew, developing into a terrifying mirror of the creature's life.

And then, after two hundred and thirty-seven years of decay and imprisonment, Gotha once again heard the voice of Talos.

The dracolich learned that it was time to perform his task.

❧ 1 ❧

The Prophet

The old man pressed through the underbrush, unaware of the thorns, the slashing branches, and the thick, wet foliage. Rain drove into his face—it always rained these days—and he bared his teeth, relishing the force of the weather.

Overhead, the full moon reigned in the night, but no clue showed on the land below. Heavy clouds blanketed the land, and the lashing rain further masked visibility.

Indeed, the storm masked more than this locale. For a distance of more than a hundred miles to the north and the south, the entire island of Alaron suffered the drenching of downpour and the cruel scouring of wind. And beyond this great island, the rest of the Moonshaes quaked amid blackened seas and the raging press of the heavens. Hail and lightning, floods and stark, killing cold alternated in their onslaughts, but never did they cease entirely.

The figure now pushing through the bramble looked upward, his face split by a grin of exultation. His eyes shined whitely, even in the darkness, and if they didn't seem to focus clearly, neither were they blind. The darkness did not impair him. Indeed, the man wrapped it around himself like a protective cloak that insured his safe and undetected passage.

In the distance, hounds wailed. Whether the full-throated cries honored the unseen full moon or heralded the presence of this strange figure in the brush did not matter. As the old man pushed forward, the baying increased in frenzy until a harsh voice commanded the dogs to silence.

Finally the figure broke free of the brambles to stumble onto an open lawn of grass. Flaring lanterns of golden light sparkled across a wide courtyard before him. They hissed and sputtered beside a great oaken door, casting a yellow wash that outlined the metal-shirted figures of two brawny men-at-arms.

Around the door towered a great manor house of stone, with a high, peaked roof that vanished in the darkness overhead and long, dark beams framing the outline of the walls and windows of its three great wings. Blackness swallowed sprawling gardens to either side, as well as the stables and kennels and other outbuildings.

The storm swallowed the sounds of the old man's passage, concealing it, at least, from the guards, though the hounds once again took up their howl. Now, however, the figure raised his head to stare at the doorway and the glaring lantern light reflected from his bright, widely set eyes.

The men-at-arms stiffened as they beheld those gleaming spots of light, like supernatural apparitions come to haunt them. They felt no relief when they realized the glow came from the eyes of the trespassing figure. A twenty-foot palisade of sharpened stakes surrounded the grounds and manor of Earl Blackstone of Fairheight, with a single gate that remained closed and guarded. There was no simple explanation for the presence of this bizarre and apparently maddened intruder.

"Who are you?" demanded one of the guards, reflexively lowering his long-shafted halberd. "What do you want?"

"How did you get here?" demanded the other, driving more directly to the point. The second guard drew his narrow longsword and held the weapon at the ready.

"The power shall rise! You know your folly!" The voice pierced the gloom like the strike of lightning. Harsh and clear, it wasn't hysterical, but—also like lightning—it commanded attention. The guardsmen instinctively tightened their grips on their weapons, gaping at the stranger as he slowly advanced into the circle of illumination.

"*Flee!*" cried the old man, his voice rising. "Flee before it is too late!"

The shambling figure waved his arms over his head. His eyes darted madly, first at the door, then at the lanterns, and finally along the high wall overhead. He moved closer, into the full lamplight.

The stranger's bald crown glistened, soaked by the pounding rain. White hair encircled his scalp, a stringy fringe that covered his ears and straggled in mats onto his shoulders. A long beard of the same color as his hair, also soaked, framed his wide mouth. He wore a shabby robe of wool, with a belt of ratty rope. Toes jutted from ragged things—they had long since ceased to be boots—that covered each of his wet and muddy feet.

Around the corner of the great manor house, the barking of the hounds rose to a frenzy. The wooden gate of the kennel crashed under the repeated assaults of huge canine bodies. But it was the intruder's eyes that commanded the attention of the two watchman. They stared into those gleaming spots of light and knew they confronted a madman.

"Call the lord!" cried the halberdier, lowering his weapon protectively to block the door.

His companion wasted no time in hammering against the portal with his mailed fist. "Open up! Summon Earl Blackstone! Quickly!"

His voice nearly cracked. The guard was a steadfast fighter. He could have faced the charge of berserk northmen or the attack of a raging firbolg giant with steadfast courage. Yet this deranged man, with his matted beard and wild, staring eyes, disturbed him in a way that no merely physical threat could.

"How did you get past the wall?" demanded the other guard, the halberdier. Frantically the man wondered, Did we leave the gate unlatched? Had the guard fallen asleep? The palisade had no breaches, and the noble lord would tolerate no lapse in the vigilance of his guards.

The bearded man came closer, dragging his feet along the ground, practically stumbling with each step.

Abruptly the door swung open. The black-bearded figure standing there, strapping and unafraid, was not the lord of the manor—instead, it was Currag, Earl Blackstone's firstborn son.

"What's the commotion?" he demanded, his eyes immediately fixing upon the intruder.

"This fellow—he must have climbed the wall! He's talking crazy, ranting about doom and despair!" The halberdier's mind still raced. If a gate *had* been left unlocked, his own neck would be all but forfeit.

"Set the hounds on him," growled young Currag Blackstone, spitting toward the white-bearded man.

The guards blanched. The Blackstone moorhounds numbered nearly two dozen. Huge and savage creatures, they were kept hungry by the handlers for just such eventualities.

"But he—he hasn't attacked," objected the swordsman. "He might be harmless, merely lost."

"You are *doomed!* Accept the power *now*, you who have forsworn the light! It is your only hope of survival!" The madman shook his head, and the white hair and beard bristled, casting droplets of water in a glittering ring around his face.

In that instant, a flash of lightning hissed across the sky, illuminating the courtyard and its surrounding woods. The shadow of the intruder stood out clearly, etched upon the ground for one brief moment.

"Get out of here, old man!" growled Currag, stepping between the guards. He advanced and shouted into the intruder's face. "Go now, or by the gods, the hounds will tear you to pieces!"

"*Fool! Imbecile!*"

Currag shoved the intruder, and the figure toppled backward to sit heavily in the mud. The young nobleman stalked to the corner of the great house, where the hounds shrilled and slavered. In one gesture, he pulled the latch from the cage door.

Huge, shaggy beasts surged outward, baying frantically. The moorhounds were huge dogs, their backs reaching the height of a man's waist. Long legs carried their muscular, powerful bodies with astonishing speed. The pack raced toward the white-haired man in full cry, fangs glistening in the darkness. Their vibrant howls rang throughout the yard, intermixed with low snarls as they neared their victim.

The white-bearded man climbed to his feet with a smoothness that belied his apparent age. Then he stood strangely still. His eyes, for once sharp and well focused, fastened upon the face of the leading moorhound.

The lead moorhound, called Warlock by the Blackstones, was a splendid example of the breed. Tall and muscular, sleek sinew rippling beneath a shaggy coat, Warlock belled his outrage at this intrusion of his master's precinct. His powerful haunches flexed, driving his body, which was the color of rich, moist soil, through soaring, graceful bounds. His shoulders tensed, reaching forward and pulling the dog at a steadily increasing speed. Long, curved teeth gleamed like ivory beneath his snarling jaws as, frenzied and slavering, he leaped for the throat of the white-bearded man.

"Halt!" The intended target of the leap raised a hand.

To the astonishment of Currag and the two guards, Warlock's legs stiffened, and he came to an abrupt stop, dropping to sit attentively before the intruder. The rest of the pack immediately ceased their barking and howling. Ears raised curiously, the hounds stood in a semicircle and stared at the stranger.

"Seat yourselves, my creatures, my children!"

The dogs, in perfect unison, sat upon their haunches, still staring with rapt attention into those wide-set, gleaming eyes. Instead of bared fangs, the hounds' slack jaws now revealed long, pink tongues. The animals sat with ears pricked upward and eyes alert as they regarded the white-haired man.

"*Kill him!*" Currag, sputtering in outrage, commanded his hunters. When they didn't respond, he waded into the pack, kicking the hounds with his heavy boots. Suddenly he halted as Warlock turned and glared balefully at his master—his *former* master.

The nobleman took a step backward toward the safety of his two stalwart men. The dog watched him go silently.

"*Flee!*" The old man's voice, piercing and full, broke the spell.

With another rough bark, Warlock sprang past the intruder, the rest of the pack on his heels. They belled again, as if they followed the fresh spoor of a stag, or even a bear. In moments, the dogs vanished into the darkness, crashing into the same thicket from which the raving madman had emerged.

"There is hope for them! The children—yes, the *children* will be saved!"

His eyes closed, his face locked in an expression of fierce joy, the bearded man threw back his head, allowing the rain to wash across his cheeks and his chin. Grimacing from the strength of his rapture, the old man remained rigid, as if listening.

Currag stared in hatred at the intruder. He heard the dogs plunging away, knowing they would soon reach the palisade. The sound of the pack rose to a fevered pitch of excitement and frenzy. Then abruptly the sound faded. It could still be heard, but as though it came from much farther away.

"They've gone over the wall," said the halberdier, his voice full of wonder. Even a nimble man, they all knew, would need a rope to scale the twenty-foot palisade with its top of sharply pointed stakes. For a dog, it must certainly be impossible!

"You're insane!" snapped Currag, not even convincing himself. Indeed, there could be no other explanation for the suddenly fading sound of the chase. The young noble knew sorcery when he saw it, yet he was a cool and steady warrior. He did not fear this wild stranger.

"They *know!* They *understand*, and now they are safe!" The intruder, momentarily forgotten, opened his eyes. Once again the passion glowed there.

"Safer than you, lunatic!" Currag's rage shifted instantly to the man. He slapped the guard on the shoulder. "Your sword—give it to me!"

The man-at-arms did not hesitate. The young laird of Blackstone raised the blade, stepping toward the still figure of the prophet. Currag's eyes held murderous purpose, but the old man's lip curled back in a caricature of a sneer.

The blade darted forward, oddly liquid in its movement, and thrust through the old man's ribcage. It met only slight resistance. A spot of crimson spurted through the robe.

"Madman!" cried Currag, his own eyes burning fiercely as his victim fell on his back, rigid, eyes bulging toward the dark skies. Then an expression of peace, as if he but slept, crossed the stranger's features. He sighed softly.

Raindrops spattered in the growing pool of blood, and soon the water washed the thicker liquid away.

* * * * *

The appearance of the raving stranger and the flight of the hounds were but the first two mysteries to arise in Blackstone on this night of dire portents. They were not the last nor, to the lord of the manor, the most troubling. Instead, Earl Blackstone found the third mysterious occurrence to be far more sinister, its portents more evil.

Like the other two, the third was a puzzle that developed

during the darkness of the night of the full moon, though it was not discovered until the morning.

This was when a guard, patrolling the outside of the great manor house, came upon the body on the ground. It lay face-down below the third-floor window leading to Currag's chambers. When the stunned guard rolled the corpse over, it proved to be that of the young heir to the noble house.

There was no mark to be found on him, no sign of any physical injury—except, of course, for the brutal impact of the forty-foot fall into a stone-paved courtyard. Despite that impact, the features on the face, the expressions of the mouth and eyes, were still visible.

It remained for his father, the earl, to wonder at the thing that had come to Currag Blacksmith in the depths of the fatal eve. Yet this much he knew: The visage of his son at the time of his death was a mask of almost unimaginable horror.

* * * * *

From the Log of Sinioth:

I walk among men, but I am not a man.
I have a name, but it may not be spoken.
I serve my master, Talos, and his power makes me strong. I labor in his name, and the Raging One grants me the will and the means to grow, to gain mastery in the world, and to spread the word and the truth of his power.
Now my god has chosen this place called Moonshae. Here the name of Talos will be made great—and I, the Priest With No Name, shall rule in the shadow of my lord.

Coss-Axell-Sinioth

❧ 2 ❧

The House of Kendrick

The chariot thundered across the vast expanse of grass, effortlessly cresting the frequent rises in the moor, then plummeting with dizzying speed into the bowls between. Two magnificent horses, a gray mare and an auburn gelding, drew the small two-wheeled platform with bounding ease. The stocky, nimble creatures darted this way and that, responding instantly to each of the driver's commands.

The charioteer carried no whip, but held the reins with strong, sure hands. Insulated against the morning chill by leather leggings and a woolen cloak, the nimble figure balanced lightly on the tiny, lurching platform, springing into the air each time the chariot skipped over a rise. A stout cap of leather covered the rider's head, slight protection in the event of a hard fall.

To the east, the waters of Whitefish Bay gleamed in the morning sun. That brightness also etched the craggy highland of the Fairheight Range in vivid detail. The crest sprawled the length of the western horizon while blue sky—the first cloudless weather in months—domed overhead. Only beyond the mountains, far to the west, did a fringe of clouds linger along the horizon.

Before the chariot stretched a seemingly limitless range of rolling grassland. The rider directed the racing team with confidence, often darting onto the narrow pole between the horses. There the charioteer perched, exhorting the steeds with encouragement and praise. The small vehicle, careening behind the horses, followed the creatures into a gully, splashed through a gravel-bottomed stream, and then bounced up the steep bank.

The driver held on, guiding the twin wheels around boulders, up a barely discernible path, and once again onto the freedom of the moor.

"Geddaway there, now! C'mon, Brit! Run, Mouse!" The voice was intense, and the rider's eyes stared toward the sea. The horses bounded forward with renewed intensity, clods of dirt flying beneath the thundering hoofbeats. The wind whipped the crouching driver, who once again perched on the bar between the straining beasts. They crested a steep rise and the chariot left the ground, soaring like a flying thing.

Caer Callidyrr came into view then, its alabaster walls gleaming in the sun. The haze had burned from the hills, and the castle stood out clearly as the dominant feature of the panorama. High ramparts stretched across three small hilltops over the town that clung to the edge of the bay. Towers soared, a dozen of them higher than any other man-made structure in the Moonshae islands, fitting grandeur for the palace and castle of the High King, ruler of all the Ffolk.

The team began the long descent with a staccato gallop, but gradually the driver pulled them into a canter, slowing to an easy walk by the time they rolled toward the stable building along the outside of the castle wall.

Here the charioteer's strong hands revealed gentleness as they tugged the reins slightly, bringing the two frothing steeds to a rest. Reaching upward, those hands lifted off the driver's leather helm, releasing a cascade of hair the color of rust. Curling slightly, as thick as a lush stand of wheat, the locks wrapped like a full blanket, trailing behind the lithe figure halfway down the slender, proud back.

Alicia Kendrick, Princess of Moonshae, returned to the castle, her cheeks stung red by the breeze, her heart pounding.

"By the goddess, what a ride!" She made the announcement to the liverymen who already moved out to tend the exhausted horses. She stepped smoothly to the ground and shrugged off her cloak, which was quickly caught by an attendant. Jauntily Alicia strode toward the door of the stables. Though the castle was huge, the Kendricks maintained their stables outside the walls for convenience's sake—and because, in Alicia's lifetime, there had never been any threat to those high walls or indeed to any other portion of her father's kingdom.

Any military threat, she corrected herself. She couldn't forget about the scourge of weather that seemed to constantly afflict the Moonshaes, the reason today's warmth had been such a compelling summons to the outdoors.

For the last five years—fully a quarter of the young woman's life—the Moonshae Islands had suffered the onslaught of terrible violence, but it had been the violence of nature run amok, not of man. Winters of deep frost, broken only by the blizzards that howled in from the great Trackless Sea to bury the land beneath tons of wet, clinging snow, had marked each of those five years. Then followed spring, such as the one just passing, with days of torrential rains, pounding hailstorms, and winds that seemed determined to rip the outposts of land from their precarious perches in the sea, all combining to blast the beleaguered isles for months on end.

But the summers, perhaps, were worst: searing weeks of blasting heat, unbroken by cloud or even the hint of rain, would yield to periods of violent thunderstorms. Lightning slashed the land, and towering, moist cyclones blew in from the sea to uproot trees and smash houses. The storms lasted into the autumn, until the cycle of ice resumed.

Then today, as they neared the start of the fifth summer of this ruinous pattern, the weather had paused, as if marshaling strength for the next horrible wrack. The skies remained clear for hours, and the winds mellowed enough to allow one to enjoy the warmth of the sun, a warmth the princess had been unable to resist.

Alicia stopped abruptly when she saw the tall, thin figure standing in the stable doorway. He was a young man who wore a long brown cloak. His narrow face wasn't displeasing, though it bore an unhealthy-looking pallor. He was cleanshaven, but his brown hair tumbled over his ears to the height of his narrow shoulders. Now, unaccustomed to sunlight, he squinted at her.

"Hello, Keane," she said, offering her most winning smile, a look that was very dazzling indeed as her green eyes sparkled. A whisper of freckles marked her cheeks and her nose, and these seemed to dance across her face, expressing her joy.

The tall man, however, did not share her pleasant mood. His heavy eyebrows dropped as he made an attempt to glower menacingly. Though older than Alicia, he was still too young to effectively look the part of the displeased senior.

"Your lessons!" he reminded her sharply. "Your father will have my head if you cannot recite the Tale of Cymrych Hugh at the councils of midsummer!"

Alicia sighed. "I'm sorry, Keane—I really have been working on them, every day but today. But this morning, for the first time in weeks, the sun was shining. Mouse and Brittany were as frantic to get some exercise as me!"

"*I*, not *me*," the tutor corrected automatically.

Then Keane, too, sighed. "I really can't blame you. These storms of late—they've gotten to all of us, the gods know! What with black clouds and rain and hail, even I might welcome a chance to spend a day outside."

Indeed, the weather had lashed the lands of the Moonshaes with unaccustomed sharpness during the past winter and spring. Even among the savage pattern of storms, the droughts and floods and cyclones that had plagued the islands for the past six months, ruining crops, freezing livestock, and destroying homes and buildings, had been particularly grueling.

"And even you used to be young once, didn't you, Keane?"

The tutor grimaced, and Alicia felt a twinge of guilt. He wasn't that much older than she. He had passed his twenty-seventh winter, while Alicia would be twenty in the fall.

"I'm sorry," she added hastily. "That wasn't fair. But I wish you'd understand—on a day like this, I didn't have a choice."

"I know." Keane shook his head. "I wonder if the king will have me beheaded or simply hanged."

Alicia laughed, knowing her teacher's displeasure had passed—at least, to the point where he could joke with her.

"Tell me which you'd prefer, and I'll see if I can use my influence with him. I *am* his firstborn child, you know."

She followed the man into the castle, knowing that Keane was in no danger from her father. Indeed, the regard felt by the king and queen for the tutor was the reason he had been entrusted with the education of the princesses.

Once Keane had been an apprentice to a powerful magic-user, but Alicia had gotten the impression that sorcery had proven beyond his skill. He had abandoned the study of spells, eventually, to devote all his time to the education of the royal daughters. Tristan and Robyn Kendrick could afford the finest tutors in the Realms for their children, and they had chosen Keane.

"Ah! That reminds me," said Keane. "Your father sent for you. He's meeting with the Earl of Fairheight and the Lords Umberland and Ironsmith in the Great Hall. By now, doubtlessly, he wonders with some annoyance what has happened to you."

Alicia laughed again, not worried. "No doubt he'll have both of us drawn and quartered," she teased, enjoying the look of exasperation that Keane gave her as they passed through the high castle gatehouse.

* * * * *

Angry pressures mounted in the icy depths, emerging as heaving waves across the storm-tossed Sea of Moonshae. Like the terrain of a jagged-toothed mountain range, monstrous swells loomed in all directions. But they were crests in motion, with living summits rising, then toppling to cascade into the next liquid massif. Overcast skies darkened the water to charcoal shades, and rain lashed the peaks and valleys of the pounding swells.

Below the storm-tossed surface, the world did not warm, though it became more still . . . and more dark. The gray depths became black, and even if the sun had broken through the clouds, its rays couldn't have penetrated this far below the chill surface.

Yet still farther into the depths the pressure grew and the blackness closed in like a cloak of icy ink. Fish dared not swim so deep, and the beds of kelp remained far above.

Finally came the ocean bottom, a wasteland of silt-strewn plain dotted with the occasional skeleton-like framework of a ship or the bones of some great sea creature. The plain of the ocean's floor stretched, featureless and flat, for many miles. Then yawned a place where the descent plunged still farther as a great chasm cut like a raw wound through the flatness of the seabed. Sheer walls plummeted into the unimaginable deep, farther still below the realms of light where the fish and the fauna dwelled. Yet even at this frightful depth, under the burdens of pressure and darkness, there was life.

Within this undersea canyon, occupying both sides of the steeply sloping walls, the sahuagin had built their city of Kressilacc. The aquatic humanoids were constantly vicious and hungry, the mortal enemies of air-breathing humankind. Covered with hard scales and, on the males, bristling dorsal spines, the fish-men formed a horrific army when they ventured forth. They carried bronze weapons, wore shell shields, and swam in great, swarming companies.

From Kressilacc, twenty years earlier, the Deepsong had thrummed, luring hordes of the fish-men into war with the Ffolk and northmen of the surface world. It had been a war during which the sahuagin armies fared very badly indeed.

After the battles, their ranks decimated and their pride savaged, the proud warriors of this evil submarine race had returned to their remote city, there to lick their wounds, to praise their dead, to punish their clerics . . . and to let their hatred fester.

The clerics had been followers of Bhaal, and it had been their exhortations that had led the sahuagin into the ill-starred war. Bhaal was now a vanquished god. And so the priestesses had died—slowly, with much suffering, which is the way the sahuagin prefer to dispose of their enemies.

The king of Kressilacc, a great bull of a fish-man called Sythissal, had barely escaped the slaughter wreaked upon the clerics—indeed, it had only been his vehement cries for vengeance, claiming that he himself had been dazzled by foul sorcery, that had shifted the rage of the sahuagin away from the one who had led them to disaster.

Thus King Sythissal's hatred of the surface dwellers was even more profoundly rooted than was the vengeful bloodlust of his subjects. And yet, though he loudly declaimed human treachery and greed and often sent his leanest warriors forth to harass and sink the ships of men, the king had never returned to the surface since the last battle, a disaster that had culminated with an abject collapse of morale. His army fled in disarray from the base of Caer Corwell back to the sheltering darkness of the sea.

This defeat had done another thing to King Sythissal. It had inflicted upon him a deep and vengeful mistrust of all things clerical.

Temples to gods of chaos and evil had long stood in the wide galleries and long, curving balconies of the cliff-wall city. Images of Bhaal, and Malar the Beastlord, and Talos the Destroyer and Auril Frostmaiden and many others had occupied these holy places for untold centuries, but the king ordered them all cast down. Thus at the same time as the New Gods secured their grip upon the worship of the Ffolk, the evil gods worshiped in the deep were cast aside, abandoned by their followers, their power spurned with them.

All except one, that is. The faithful priests and priestesses of Talos the Destroyer foresaw, quite accurately, the day when the power of their god would gain prominence in the Moonshaes. With a surface world swept free of interference by the gods of good and their pitiful human tools, these scaly priests understood that the sahuagin would be able to attain ultimate power. Mastery of the isles was a dream that could soon become real!

The key to the future of the sahuagin race, Sythissal knew, lay in defeating the hated humans and the air-breathing dwarves, elves, and halflings who were their allies. His loathing of the surface peoples grew into a palpable abhorrence, a hatred so strong that, for the King of Kressilacc, it became a reason for living.

The clerics of Talos prepared their king for the coming of their god. They sent to him nubile priestesses for the Great Spawning, and these pleased him well. While the king rested, the priestess fish hissed premonitions to the piscine monarch, and Sythissal dreamed of a great messenger. That one would come with word of a plan, the king saw, wherein the humans would bring about their own destruction. Talos and his faithful would rule!

Sythissal saw one whose skin had scales like his own. But this messenger claimed all the skies as its sea and moved through those lofty heights with the same ease that the king glided through brine. Sythhissal saw that the messenger was a thing of death, but also of unspeakable power.

To prepare for this messenger—one the king did not yet know as the harbinger of Talos—the great sahuagin desired gifts. He wished to meet this great one in a fashion that would indicate the might and richness of Kressilacc. Thus Sythissal decided to personally lead a war party to the surface, reveling once more in the taste of warm human blood.

The sahuagin city lay in the Sea of Moonshae but wasn't far removed from the trading routes connecting the eastern cities of the isles—most notably Callidyrr—to the wealth of the distant Sword Coast. Instinctively the king desired to strike at the Ffolk for his treasure raid; a lingering sense of vengeance required it. Too, their vessels tended to be slower than the longships of the northmen, making easier targets for the swimming fish-men.

For the first time in two decades, King Sythissal led a great host of his warriors forth from the city, upward and eastward toward the realms of sunlight and air. He would find a prize, he knew, and claim it for his own. Then when the messenger of the gods came to them, the sahuagin would be ready with appropriate offerings.

Soon now, the priestesses told the king, that messenger would come to the Moonshaes. Then the sahuagin vengeance could begin.

* * * * *

Following Alicia to the council, Keane understood why the princess felt no concern that her father would punish her tardiness. The king indulged the whims of Alicia and her sister Deirdre in a manner that the tall tutor often found annoying. As High King, Tristan Kendrick was the mightiest ruler in the Moonshae Islands, yet still his daughters had always been uppermost in his thoughts and cares, to the point where both of them had become somewhat spoiled, in the opinion of their hardworking teacher.

Keane watched Alicia walk. The princess moved with the confident swagger of a warrior, inexplicably coupled with an alluring sensuality that allowed no mistaking her for a man. He shook his head, embarrassed but not surprised by the awareness of her femininity. It was a knowledge that intruded into his consciousness with disturbing frequency. For years he had quashed it, but now that she had reached full adulthood, Keane found it harder to stifle.

Alicia trusted him and usually treated him with respect. Of the two girls, she was the more enjoyable to teach, though days like this made him wonder. But whatever Alicia did—even when it was simply to complain about her tasks—she did with energy and enthusiasm and humor.

A perfect counterpoint to Alicia, Keane knew, could be found in her younger sister, Deirdre. Born barely a year after Alicia, Deirdre seemed to be her sister's opposite in every way. She was dark and quiet, even sullen, where Alicia was fair and outgoing to the point of boldness. They were tutored by the same man, but Keane felt none of the rapport with the younger sister that he knew with the elder. Indeed, sometimes Deirdre disturbed him, for she seemed to remain completely distant from any of his attempts at friendship, at the same time absorbing completely whatever information he happened to be imparting.

In their studies, he had to admit that Deirdre outshone her older sister in every category. Always focused and intent, the dark-haired girl would brusquely confront him if he tried to short-cut an argument or present as fact some knowledge not fully documented.

In an earlier decade, perhaps, Deirdre would have followed the druidical calling of her mother. Now, however, the druids who still lived served primarily as caretakers of the shrinking tracts of wild land that could still be found among the kingdoms of the Ffolk. Their powers of magic, which had allowed them great control over aspects of nature, had been broken by the passing of the goddess Earthmother twenty years earlier.

Keane often reflected on, and taught, the great irony: It had been the great victories of Tristan Kendrick that brought the Ffolk to a pinnacle of unity and power they had not known for hundreds of years. Bearing a blade of legend, the Sword of Cymrych Hugh, the young king had used the aid of the druids and the ancient folk of the isles, the dwarves of Mountainhome and the Llewyrr elves of Synnoria.

Yet the price of that victory had been a change in godship, from the hallowed nature worship of the goddess Earthmother to the agricultural domination offered by Chauntea, a goddess of crops, irrigation, and tamed, quiet pastures. The great mother had perished at the moment of the Ffolk's ultimate triumph, and now Chauntea and the other New Gods ruled the land.

Keane's reflections were interrupted as they reached the doors to the Great Hall of Caer Callidyrr. The huge oaken panels loomed and then swung outward, opened by a pair of blue-cloaked guardsmen.

King Kendrick chose to hold counsel in his Great Hall more often than in his imposing throne room. He said that his visitors showed a greater tendency to talk when gathered around the huge hearth with its perennial blaze.

"Hello, Father," said Alicia, ignoring the king's brief look of annoyance.

"Come in," Tristan said impatiently. "You, too, Keane."

Tristan Kendrick, High King of the Folk, was a man who had grown into the role. He sat in a huge armchair, his long brown hair still thick, though streaks of gray lightened its fringes. His beard, worn full in the traditional manner of the Ffolk, covered the upper half of his chest.

Emblazoned in silver on his blue tunic was a lone wolf's head, the king's personal crest. Over the hearth, snarling from the wall, was mounted the head of a great bear, symbolizing the unity of the four lands of the Ffolk.

Another man sat in a nearby chair, and raven-haired Deirdre almost disappeared into a small sofa a few feet back from the fire. Overhead, the heavy oaken support timbers crossed back and forth, soot-covered and stained. The dark wooden ceiling was lost in the overhead shadows, though long, slitted windows along each side of the room stood open, admitting the fresh air for once instead of sealing out the perpetual storm.

"You know Earl Blackstone, Master of Fairheight," began the king, gesturing toward the visitor. "The Lords of Ironsmith and Umberland were here briefly to discuss their iron and coal production. They have gone to attend to business in the city."

"My lord." Alicia nodded politely to the black-haired, stern-visaged noble, wishing privately that she had arrived while the other two lords were still present. She knew Umberland and Ironsmith to be unprepossessing rural lords, neither of them too bright but both loyal and direct.

Not so the Earl of Fairheight. She looked at him surreptitiously as she seated herself. The earl's thick eyebrows grew together over his great beak of a nose, and his full black beard parted in a smile that sent a slight shiver down Alicia's back. As always, she felt an uneasiness when she was around Blackstone that she could not totally explain.

Among her father's subjects, Angus Blackstone was the most powerful noble in all Callidyrr, presiding over the cantrevs of the Fairheight Mountains. These were the towns of miners and smelters, the Ffolk who had supported the kingdom during these years. Yet whenever she was forced to be in the same room with him, which was blessedly rare, she felt a sense of menace that made her want to pull a cloak tightly about her shoulders and keep her eyes watchfully upon the swaggering earl.

"To business." Tristan spoke brusquely, and Alicia sensed that the king was annoyed by Blackstone. "Continue your tale," he instructed the brawny nobleman.

Blackstone's demeanor grew grim. "He came out of nowhere, raving like a lunatic. My son set the hounds on him, but he worked some kind of sorcery. The hounds ran, leaping the palisade, and disappeared into the night."

"Have you had sign of them since?" inquired the king.

"No, sire. They may as well have chased a shadow off the face of the earth! Then the madman went berserk, in a fury. My son Currag had to slay him to defend himself!"

"The body?" asked the king.

"We burned it—like a witch, or any other foul sorcerer! The bastard claimed the life of my oldest son!" fumed Earl Blackstone. "It *was* sorcery, Your Highness. I know this!"

He finished the gruesome tale of the discovery of Currag's body the following morning, smashed on the stones of the courtyard, and how, even after the brutal force of the fall, his face retained that hideous, tortured grimace of terror.

"You have two sons remaining, I believe?" Tristan ventured sympathetically.

"Aye. Gwyeth and Hanrald. The former, Gwyeth, is my heir now. He's a good knight, Your Majesty."

Alicia thought it curious that he said nothing about his

youngest son, Sir Hanrald. She wondered about a knight who could be a disappointment even to one so base as Blackstone.

"The ravings." Deirdre, out of the shadows, surprised them by speaking to the earl. "What did the lunatic say?"

The nobleman turned toward the younger princess, his dark brows knitting in concentration. "He came out of the storm. He hollered about doom, I recall. And he told the guards to flee . . . said it was their only chance of survival. To escape the power that would rise, or some such idiocy."

"What *else?*" persisted Deirdre, her voice sharp. "There must have been more."

Blackstone bristled. "I don't know! I can't remember!"

"Enough." King Kendrick spoke to the lord. "When my envoy reaches Fairheight, you will make your guards, and any other witnesses, available for interview. That is all."

"Yes, sire." Blackstone nodded in assent.

"Now," Tristan continued, "tell me of the matter that brings you all the way to Caer Callidyrr."

"Certainly, sire. It is a matter of some good news, I should think. Naturally you know of the wealth of gold my miners have pulled from the Granite Crest."

"Indeed. It has given me the profits to purchase food for years—food without which thousands of my people would have starved."

"Well, Your Majesty, it appears that the vein extends for a greater extent than we had any previous right to hope. Our initial explorations indicate a find of more vast and wealthy extent than any previous gold mine in the islands."

"Splendid! The additional tariff shall do much to see that our coffers can be filled by winter. Is it simply this news that brings you to the castle? Or, as I suspect, is there more?"

Blackstone sighed, apparently in real regret. "A small thing . . . trifling, really. I regret to trouble Your Majesty with it."

"A Moonwell." said Keane, speaking without thinking.

"I beg your pardon?" King Kendrick scowled, turning toward the young man who had spoken. Even his favored young tutor had bounds of propriety to observe. Lord Blackstone, meanwhile, glared darkly at Keane.

"It's the reason he comes here," Keane blurted, as if regretting his earlier remark but now determined to amplify his decision. "Gaining access to the new vein will require him to destroy a Moonwell."

"Is this true?" The king turned to regard the lord.

"Yes—if you can call the stagnant cesspool a Moonwell!" Blackstone forged ahead, his anger toward Keane thickening his voice. "We all know that the power of the Earthmother is gone, and with her went the enchantment of her pools—*all* of them! I know that some wild-eyed druids still tend them, but just to keep the waters free from weeds! Their power exists only in memory!"

"We have always honored the custom of leaving her Moonwells undisturbed. The Great Mother is the symbol and the heritage of the Ffolk!" Keane boldly countered the duke's arguments. The king appeared content to let the two wage the verbal battle; he remained silent, watching each speaker in turn.

"No one would question the wisdom of that policy." Blackstone's tone was not as sincere as his words. It sounded as though he wanted very much to question the policy. "But this is different. Exception is called for!"

"The site is sacred!" Keane persisted.

"Enough." King Kendrick silenced the debate. He looked at the participants and then at his daughters. For a time, no one said anything, sensing that Tristan was about to speak.

"I debark for Murann, on the coast of Amn, in one week," he said. "Regardless of the weather. The storms scattered half of the last fleet of merchant vessels, and we lost much badly needed sustenance. Lord Pawldo already engages in a mission to Waterdeep, but even with his bargaining skills to help us, we shall need more!"

The king's voice thickened, and he suddenly seemed very tired. "In addition, our coffers have fallen dangerously low. The grain merchants of Waterdeep and Amn remain agreeable only so long as the gold in my hands is pure."

Tristan sighed. For a brief moment, he looked very old. "My next voyage will deplete the treasuries to dangerous levels. I cannot, in good conscience, allow the kingdom to face the prospects of starvation so that we can preserve sites to the memory of a vanished goddess."

Keane's eyes dropped to the floor. Alicia felt a surprising

surge of outrage at her father's swift capitulation. Even more disturbing was his casual dismissal of the Earthmother as a "vanished goddess."

Yet as a retort formed upon her tongue, she looked at King Kendrick and realized that the burden of his decision already weighed heavily upon him. She would do him no service by adding to his woes.

Instead, she turned toward her sister. Deirdre seemed to be paying no attention to the discussion, but Alicia knew this was not the case. Her sister's dark eyes were half closed, her heavy black hair—the hair Deirdre had inherited from their mother—veiling her cheeks. She feigned disinterest now, just as she feigned so many things of her life, perhaps feeling that the less people knew about her thoughts, the greater advantage she could gain over them. And Alicia knew her sister was a young woman who looked for advantage wherever she could find it.

Alicia suddenly realized that the men had risen to their feet. She hadn't heard the rest of the conversation, but it seemed to have ended. Blackstone left, and Deirdre followed, walking slowly, deep in thought. Alicia paused at the door, wondering about Keane's role in the meeting.

The princess wanted to talk to him, but then the king gestured to the lanky tutor. "Stay a moment, Keane," he commanded. At the door, Alicia fussed with her boot, curious to overhear.

"How did you know they wished to excavate a Moonwell?" asked the king. His tone was understanding.

"A lucky guess, I suppose, sire."

Tristan Kendrick chuckled softly. "Not if I know you."

Keane lowered his eyes, then looked back up at the king. "Perhaps, Your Majesty, it's because Blackstone takes so many liberties. He exploits his power to rule like a king in his own earldom! He will do as he pleases, for the most part. So it was a simple matter of elimination, sire. The Moonwell is the only part of his estate where he still feels bound to consult you."

The king nodded, not offended. "May the gods curse it, but I need him right now. Without Blackstone gold, the kingdom couldn't support itself for another six months."

"I know, sire." For a moment, Keane felt a flash of sympathy for the monarch. It was a revelation to see how neatly the king was caught in this trap borne of necessity.

Tristan clapped the younger man on the shoulder. "You're important here, Keane. What you did in there, pointing out arguments to me as well as to the earl—I need you to keep doing that." The king paused reflectively for a moment, a soft smile playing upon his lips. "When you came to the castle—what was it, seventeen years ago now?—and asked to apprentice yourself to my council of mages, I had little thought for what you might become."

"I shall always be grateful, sire, for that first chance."

"No—*I* should be grateful." The king spoke with sincerity. "You're more than an adviser to me. You've given my daughters an education that far surpasses my own, and I well know they're not the easiest pupils to teach!"

"I make every effort," replied Keane, coughing awkwardly as he gave Alicia a sideways look. At the door, the princess hastily fixed her lace and left.

King Tristan smiled and clapped the tall mage on the shoulder. He raised his head, looking absently past the younger man. "I know that, my boy," he said gruffly, affectionately. "I know I can count on you."

Keane thought, as he saw the king's eyes focus on some distant scene—something far beyond the Great Hall—that the monarch seemed sad.

* * * * *

Alicia hurried down the hallway, strangely agitated. She caught up with Deirdre as her sister neared the library of arcane materials where the younger princess spent so much of her time.

"Deirdre?" Alicia called as her sister slowed and turned toward her, eyes still cautiously hooded. The dark-haired woman looked once, anxiously, at the library door. Then Deirdre turned back to her sister, regarding Alicia with a blank stare.

"What do you think?" asked Alicia. "Should they dig up a Moonwell for gold?"

"The goddess has gone. Those wells are nothing more than

muddy ponds," Deirdre retorted.

"But . . . doesn't it seem sacrilegious?"

Deirdre shrugged and looked back to the door. Alicia turned away, knowing that her sister's mind was elsewhere.

The younger princess disappeared behind the shelter of the dark-paneled door, and Alicia drifted aimlessly through the hallways, beneath their towering ceilings. Wandering up the grand stairway, vaguely remembering the morning's fine weather, she walked through the crystal doors that led to the high courtyard.

This courtyard was actually the roof of the Great Hall, throne room, royal kitchens, and other rooms that made up the heart of Caer Callidyrr. Surrounded by a stone battlement, it was a vast open area with a good view to all four sides. Indeed, only the castle's towers could bring one to a loftier height.

She saw the blue waters of the bay and noticed them turning gray. With a sigh, she looked upward at a wall of storm clouds rolling toward Callidyrr, darkening the sky over the Fairheight Mountains and promising soon to cast all the rest of the island under bleak shadow.

Suddenly angry, Alicia turned around and went back inside. Here it was, barely noon, and the first hours of good weather in nearly six months had already come to an end. She couldn't begin to guess how many more days might pass before she would again see the sun.

* * * * *

Musings of the Harpist

My dreams are troubled, and so I rise and walk the parapets of Caer Corwell. Earl Randolph, the king's trusted regent here, has graciously allowed me the freedom of his castle, and his hospitality has warmed me through the long winter and chill, windy spring. (Indeed, the earl, a handsome widower, has found many ways to drive the ice from these old limbs!)

Too, Lord Pawldo is a delight, as always. I shall never tire of his company. Even now, after all these years, he spins tales I have never heard, makes me laugh in ways I once took for the giddiness of a young girl.

And only in Corwell can I behold the wonder of Caer Allisynn. The castle was miraculously moved here by the goddess
Earthmother twenty years ago, a sign that she favored the
reign of the then-young king, Tristan Kendrick. Even as the
power of the Mother faded from the land, the tall castle stands
as a proud symbol of her memory.

But beyond that memory, so much has vanished. I miss the
magic of her presence in the strings of my heart and in the
empty hopes of our age. I have always missed her, but now,
for the first time, I am also afraid.

Soon, with the approach of summer, I leave Caer Corwell,
taking ship for Alaron, to the palace of my king. Yet it is not
time for me to depart—not quite. I do not know for certain
why I wait, but I sense this need to delay as strongly as any
premonition I have ever known. I await some symbol, some
sign. I must be here when it happens.

When what happens? I do not know . . . cannot even guess.
But I will remain in Corwell till it is time to learn. Then I shall
carry word to my king.

❦ 3 ❦

Deirdre

The black-haired princess closed the door behind her, welcoming the sheltering confines of the palace library. This was the only place where she felt that she was truly her own mistress. Often she buried herself in the great works here. She loved the histories of peoples and nations, the subtle mysteries suggesting powers great and deep—knowledge that lurked discreetly amid the volumes, waiting only for the one who had the patience to seek it out.

Now, however, she felt tense and impatient, finding it impossible to sit down and read. She paced the wooden floor over boarskin rugs and finally found herself before one of the three narrow windows in the library's outer wall. As usual, it was shuttered against the weather.

Now Deirdre threw open the shutters to reveal a landscape of moors and hills, all blanketed by a heavy overcast. No rain fell—at least, not for now—so she left the window open and then cast open the other two pairs of shutters. Finally she turned to regard the room in the increased illumination.

Several heavy tables stood between the boarskins, as well as soft chairs that formed a casual semicircle before a fireplace and hearth of heavy, rounded fieldstone. Oil lanterns occupied each of the tables, as well as the mantel over the hearth, but the princess much preferred the natural lighting, even filtered as it was by the charcoal-colored clouds.

Dark boards paneled the walls of the library, framing the great shelves with their rows of scrolls and tomes of arcane or historical import and the thoughts of learned sages—the most extensive library in all the Moonshae Islands.

Many sources, Deirdre knew, had been added to the royal collection only during the last twenty years. These tomes and volumes had been discovered in Caer Allisynn, the tall castle that now rested on the shores of Corwell Firth beside Caer Corwell, her father's home.

The tale of that castle had become a common legend in the isles, the topic of numerous ballads. The tomb of Queen Allisynn, bride of the hero, Cymrych Hugh, it had been built centuries ago to serve as a resting place for the young wife upon her untimely death. Bereaved, Cymrych Hugh had used the power of his druidic council to send the fortress into the sea, where for hundreds of years it had rested on the bottom, secure from trespass and plunder. But then, at Tristan Kendrick's hour of greatest need, the goddess had sent the castle forth from the depths. Its magnificent presence had helped to place him on the High Throne.

Upon the King's ultimate victory over the forces that threatened to drag the Moonshae Islands into darkness and chaos, the castle anchored itself upon the shores of Corwell Firth. There it remained proudly, a sign of the Kendrick reign. The fractious nations of the Ffolk—Moray, Corwell, Callidyrr, and Snowdown—had, for the first time since the rule of Cymrych Hugh himself, united under a strong leader. Together they formed a kingdom strong enough to stand against their traditional enemies to the north.

The northmen, savage warriors who had long ago sailed into the islands upon their sleek longships, seeking war and plunder, instead found homelands and farmsteads. Since well before Tristan Kendrick's birth, fully half the islands' land was controlled by the sea raiders. King Kendrick, however, had forged a lasting peace with their neighbors to the north. While the northmen swore no fealty to the High King's crown, they had nonetheless ceased raiding the lands of the Ffolk. In this state of truce, with the two cultures standing side by side, the isles had no cause to fear any outside threat.

All of this, Deirdre knew, was her father's legacy. His reign had changed the face of the Moonshaes and given the Ffolk the hero they had sought for centuries. For fifteen years, the promise of that gleaming coronation had been sustained. It was an auspicious start, she thought bitterly, to a reign that had slowly degenerated into a struggle for the Ffolk's survival. The threat to the people had come from an unexpected source: the skies, and the clouds, and the sea. The Ffolk had always lived as a part of their land, using the earth and her fruits as a means of prosperity, but never vanquishing the elements of nature and beauty. Led spiritually by the druids, who formed the staunch spine of their religion, the Ffolk had cared for their wild places with all the devotion they had given to their pastures and fields.

The first clerics of the New Gods had journeyed to the Moonshaes several centuries before the reign of Tristan Kendrick, and their words had been filtering through the cities and towns through all those years, enticing and converting many of the island people to the worship of deities such as Chauntea, Helm, Selene, and Talos. And though they welcomed these New Gods, and many people took them into their homes and their hearts, always the Ffolk remained rooted firmly in the earth—and the benign goddess who was the land's true mother.

But with the epic battle waged by Tristan Kendrick against the dark and warlike Bhaal, a transformation had come over the land. The Moonwells, once the lustrous sources of power for the druids, had faded to mundane ponds. The druids themselves had lost their powers. Although many of them still survived, dwelling hermitlike among the oaks, aspens, and pines of the Moonshae forests, their magic no longer flowed from the earth. Many of the Ffolk blamed the last five years' onslaught of storm, drought, blizzard, and hurricane upon the loss of this faith. They had called upon the druids to save them, to plead with the goddess for a return of her power, her benign influence and protection.

These prayers had gone universally unanswered.

Even years ago, at the wide-eyed age of fourteen years, Deirdre had known they would. She could not have explained then, nor could she now, the source of this knowledge. She only knew it to be a fundamental truth that she sensed in the deepest core of her being.

The goddess was *dead!* The Ffolk would turn to the New Gods and bring them into their hearts and souls. Only then would the storms cease and bounty once again return to the land. Yet the young princess inherently mistrusted gods and considered dependence upon them to be a mistake.

Still impatient, Deirdre tried to force herself to sit at the table. Opened there was a rare volume she had been perusing, *The Military History of the Sword Coast*, by the famed sage, Elminster of Waterdeep. She had spent more than a week with the volume and had come to the conclusion that the famed scholar was in reality a pompous old windbag. There was perhaps an element of parochialism in her opinion—the ancient authority had spent little space on the wars waged in the Moonshaes or the southern realms of Calimshan and Amn, preferring instead to prattle overlong about the crucial role of Waterdeep and Baldur's Gate to the advance of civilization in the world.

Angrily she pushed the book aside, knowing that it didn't contain the things she desired to know. She paced before the great shelf, examining scrolls—*The Ballad of Cymrych Hugh*, by the famed Greater Bard Dolsow . . . *Mastery of Arcane Transformation*, a stack of parchments containing essays by many of the mightiest wizards of Waterdeep . . . a fresh scroll, barely ten years old, containing the epic poem called *The Darkwalker War*, by the bard Tavish of Snowdown.

Deirdre knew Tavish well, having called this loyal friend of her parents "Auntie" since the days she could say her first words. This, the bard's greatest ballad, related the tale of Tristan's rise from the small kingdom of Corwell to his status as High King. Several years ago, Deirdre had confounded and embarrassed her parents by analyzing the structure of the verse and comparing it—unfavorably, and in Tavish's presence—to Dolsow's earlier work on Cymrych Hugh.

But none of these volumes, nor any others around her, answered her purpose of the moment, for in truth Deirdre sought neither knowledge nor wisdom. Her hunger was simple and well focused in a fundamental craving for *power*.

Anger flared within her—the old, familiar anger, mostly directed toward her older sister. Alicia was flippant and irresponsible, far less diligent than Deirdre. Yet one day Alicia would be queen! The bitter injustice rose like gall in her throat, and she paced the library, unable to contain her agitation. Power! That was the door, and knowledge was the key that would open it.

For a time, Deirdre had sought this power through the mastery of sorcery. She studied the tomes of the mages. She pleaded and begged with Keane to teach her the beginning elements of sorcery, enchantments she had mastered with an ease that had amazed her tutor.

Then suddenly Keane had told her that he would teach her no more. He offered no acceptable explanation, making some lame excuse about "time away from her serious studies," which she knew to be a blatant falsehood. Yet the man had evaded her every attempt to draw an answer from him, all the while refusing to aid her in any further development of her magic-using skills.

This had left Deirdre to labor on her own, and to this end, she used the library. For long hours, sometimes all through the night, she squinted at sorcerous sigils, straining in the light of a sputtering lamp to decipher the instructions left by some long-dead practitioner of enchantment. This was where Deirdre had found her solace—and where also, she sensed, she would discover her future.

Still, she couldn't bring herself now to sit and read or even to meditate. She continued to pace the room, crossing to each window in turn and gazing across the moor, seeing the rain falling in sheets, still miles away but creeping inexorably closer.

Finally her pacing worked some of the tension from her muscles and she collapsed into a soft chair, facing the open window. Slowly, reluctantly, she closed her eyes. In a few minutes, she slept, but it was not a restful slumber.

Instead, she twitched in the chair, clenching and unclenching her hands, groaning between taut lips or kicking restlessly with her feet. As she slept, the storm crept closer, and tendrils of mist reached forward like clutching fingers, struggling to pull Callidyrr into the clouds' rain-lashed embrace.

One of the tentacles probed at the castle wall, swirling like a miniature whirlwind beyond the open window of the library. It probed inward, wisping around the sleeping princess, caressing her long black hair. It poised there only for a moment as huge gray clouds massed, and then the rain swept across the city and the castle and bay, swallowing the small tendril. Yet, as proven by the thunder and by the exultant, battering rain, the storm was well pleased.

The opening of the library door startled Deirdre awake, and

she sat up quickly, rigid, prepared to rebuke whoever dared enter without knocking. She paused when she saw who was there.

"Hello, Mother," Deirdre said quietly.

Robyn Kendrick, High Queen of the Isles, nodded wearily at her younger daughter. It seemed, Deirdre thought, that her mother did everything wearily these days.

"Are you reading, Daughter?" she asked. Robyn's black hair, unlike her husband's of brown, showed no trace of gray. It fell straight and full over her shoulders and back, past her waist, to the level of her knees. Her eyes, of deep green, were bright and alert, though lines of care now spiderwebbed outward from the corners. She walked with all the grace of her station, but Deirdre suspected that her mother sometimes wanted to cast that mantle aside and return to her life of simple tenderness and care, the life of a druid.

Twenty years before, Robyn had been the most accomplished member of that order, studying under the Great Druid, Genna Moonsinger herself. With the passing of the land from the hands of the Earthmother into the watchful protection of Chauntea, goddess of agriculture, Robyn—unlike most of the other druids of the Moonshaes—had changed her faith to the worship of Chauntea.

Deirdre thought that perhaps, unlike the bulk of her compeers, Robyn had sensed the truth of the Earthmother's passing and had turned to a living deity to pursue the pathway into the future. More likely, thought Deirdre, she had understood that her role as queen would take her from the lands and wilds she had grown to love. Her daughters sensed that this choice of their mother's—to take the hand of the man she had loved, at the expense of the places she had sworn to tend—was a burden that she carried with her to this day.

"Did you meet with your father and the lords?" inquired Robyn, sitting in one of the chairs before the cold fireplace. Though the hearth was bare, she leaned forward, as if seeking some sort of residual warmth.

"Yes. Earl Blackstone, as always, was quite persuasive."

Robyn sighed. "We need him, now—you know that. Without the gold he mines and pays in tribute to the king, we wouldn't be able to trade for even minimal goods. His efforts keep thousands of Ffolk from starving each winter."

"I know. You don't have to convince me of that." Deirdre didn't particularly care about the lord and his mines, or the trading needed to sustain her people. She did, however, know that Lord Blackstone was the most powerful lord on the island—after her father, of course—and thus, on his visits to Callidyrr, she made every effort to impress him with her acuity and intelligence. She remembered that he still had two sons and had determined that one day she would meet them.

"And you know that your father sails for Waterdeep in a week?"

"Yes. You were to remain here in his place."

"But now I am needed in Blackstone to inspect the new mines our esteemed lord wishes to open—to sanction the violation of a Moonwell." Robyn's voice remained quiet, her manner somber. Nothing in her tone betrayed other than the logical necessity of the mine, yet her daughter saw a deep bitterness in her mother's eyes.

Robyn looked out the open windows, her expression wistful. The rain did not enter the room but lashed against the courtyard beyond the window. They could feel the moisture on the freshening wind. The queen wished to close the windows, Deirdre knew, but the princess stubbornly remained seated. Something about this storm appealed to her, and it if caused her mother to leave her alone, so be it.

Surprisingly, Robyn rose and crossed to the windows herself, pulling each shutter closed and latching it in turn. When the last shutter was closed, a cloak of semidarkness pervaded the library.

"Mother," Deirdre said, suddenly bold, "what does Chauntea tell you of these storms? Does she offer us no succor? Should we not pray to a different god for deliverance?"

She expected her mother's response to be anger at her sacrilege. Indeed, that was part of the reason she had asked the question. Instead, Robyn surprised her again.

"We can pray to whatever gods we like," she said, her voice level. "But I am beginning to think that they have all forsaken us."

Dierdre looked at her mother in surprise. The princess was startled to find the queen's eyes boring into her own, flashing with an emerald intensity that the young woman found unsettling. Immediately Deirdre cast her eyes down to the floor, her face flushing. She felt guilty, as though she had been caught doing something wrong.

As softly as she had entered, Robyn left the room. Deirdre, standing in the center of the dim library, looked after her mother and wondered.

*   *   *   *   *

The expanse of ice stretched to the encircling horizon, and for uncountable leagues beyond. Windswept, so bleak it was almost featureless, the glaciers and snowpack would have glared beneath rays of bright sunlight. But so far north did they lie that even now, in late spring, the sun was a pale sphere climbing through a shallow arc, never moving far from the southern limits of view.

Winds moaned, breathing frost across snowdrifts and jagged shards of ice. No other sound disturbed this region; no wolves howled, no birds cried, nor seals barked, for the glacial waste was utterly devoid of life.

Then one day, after eternal seasons of lifeless chill, something moved. It began as a patch of ice buckled, sending shivers across the face of whiteness. Cracks appeared, and light snow puffed away, flying from niches and crannies where it had escaped from the wind.

Then a great sheet of the surface pitched into the air, toppling to the side, crashing into a million pieces. Below, a vast chasm lay revealed, and in the depths of that chasm, a presence stirred.

Gotha moved for the first time in more than two centuries. Talos the Destroyer had summoned him to his task and imbued the dracolich with the strength to free himself from the crushing tons of ice.

The creature that emerged from the depths of the glacier resembled only superficially the powerful wyrm that had come here more than two hundred years before. The scales, blood-red chips of plate as hard as bone, still coated the serpentine crimson body. Yet now, as the monster moved, many of those scales cracked and fell away, revealing flesh that had long since frozen and organs that had ceased to serve any purpose, for the dragon was now a being of the undead.

The huge wings unfurled, and they, too, cracked and splintered, grown brittle from the long generations of frozen inactivity. When they finally reached their full span, they looked more like spiderwebs than wings, for most of their leathery surface had broken away.

Yet, when Gotha pressed them downward, he flew, borne aloft by a dark power that transcended the mere pressure of wing surface against air. He sprang into the air and gained altitude slowly, driving the great limbs against the wind and feeling the air pass through the shattered membranes. And then he knew: It was the power of his undeath that supported him, the might of Talos coursing through the corrupt body.

At the thought of that capriciously malevolent deity, Gotha raised his head and uttered a bellow of rage. His hatred, having festered for centuries, now spewed forth, and all of it exploded toward that hated presence, the whispering voice in his brain that he had known as Talos the Destroyer.

Yet now, as he flew, Gotha sensed the god's will, a compulsion that came into his mind. He struggled to resist, but he could not. The vow he had made so long ago still bound him. He would do the task toward which Talos compelled him.

Deep in the dragon's mind, however, hatred and resentment seethed, building into a volatile compulsion for vengeance. Someday, somehow, the dracolich would strike out at the god who had betrayed him, but having passed so many centuries already, he would remain patient.

After hours of flight, the ice fell behind, breaking into a fringe of alabaster chips bobbing in the storm-tossed waters of the northernmost oceans. The vista below evolved from the unending, still, and lifeless white of the icecap to the constantly pitching and heaving surface of gray water, flecked with foaming whitecaps. For long hours, the monster passed no island, no settlement, human or otherwise, in its great southward flight.

The seascape below held no fear for the dracolich. Indeed, Gotha felt as though he could fly forever. But he also knew that he would not have to.

The first spots of rock showed as little more than bald

crowns thrusting up between the waves like desperate swimmers struggling for air. When the gray water rose, it often buried these tiny bits of land, too small, really, to be called islands. Nevertheless, these rocks were important, for they confirmed to Gotha that he followed the right course.

Indeed, shortly afterward, the dracolich saw larger rocks, some with patches of green showing on narrow shelves perched high on steep shoulders, out of reach of the grasping brine.

The Korinn Archipelago.

The name entered the creature's mind unbidden, and again he felt the hateful presence of Talos. But Gotha couldn't resist the compulsion in his master's instructions. His vow, made in good faith to the god more than two centuries ago, bound him to obey until he had performed the task commanded by Talos.

On some of these islets, Gotha saw houses, with chimneys that puffed smoke into the air and fields speckled with white dots—sheep! Every fiber of the great monster's being urged him to swoop down to ravage these settlements, destroying the houses, slaying the humans, and devouring the sheep.

But such was not the will of Talos, and reluctantly the flying creature veered away. It suited his master's will that Gotha remain undiscovered by the island's inhabitants. Now the dracolich swerved to the west, once again over gray open water.

Something disturbed the water's surface, arrogantly carving a course through the tossing waves, leaving a foaming wake in its path. A single tall mast stood in the center of the sleek, narrow vessel, and from that mast a proud sail billowed. A long, slender hull trailed from an elegantly curved figurehead of a blond-haired goddess. The sleek craft flew over the sea, running before the full power of the wind.

Here Gotha could fulfill his master's command and also slake his expanded thirst for blood, for he knew there would be no survivors to report his presence.

Diving, the dracolich swooped toward the ship. He saw humans scurrying about in the shallow hull, heard their screams and even saw them raise bows and swords and axes, mere stinging annoyances to the monstrous apparition that settled toward the stern of the vessel.

Gotha's wings expanded, and the dracolich settled his rear

legs on the transom, feeling the ship rock and groan under the massive weight. Two brawny warriors wearing horned helms sprang at the creature's momentarily exposed belly.

The beast slashed out with a single forepaw, pitching the shredded remains of the two northmen over the side as bait for sharks . . . or worse. Massive jaws gaped, and Gotha belched a searing cloud of fire straight into the bulging pocket of the longship's sail.

The canvas flared briefly and then collapsed, still flaming, onto the sailors crowded amidships. But these men of the north now rushed at the horrific thing that pressed the stern of their vessel into the brine. Gray water roared over the gunwales, each wave carrying the craft a little lower in the heaving swells.

Gotha met the attackers with his foreclaws, ripping their heads away or tearing open great wounds in their chests and bellies. The hull filled with blood and water as more and more corpses joined their fellows among the planks along the keel. Flames, meanwhile, coursed down the mast and spread through the forequarters of the vessel, hissing upward and greedily consuming the seasoned timbers that held the ship together.

More of the fierce northmen hacked at the monster that threatened their ship. One veteran succeeded in reaching the beast, driving a gleaming battle-axe against the decaying chest, but the axe bit against one of the exposed ribs, and the keen blade shattered into a thousand shards. Gaping jaws closed about the head and torso of the axeman, lifting him from the hull. His exposed legs kicked madly for a second, until the monster bit down. The severed limbs toppled into the sea.

Gotha knew a fierce joy that he had all but forgotten. The smoke wafting past his nostrils, the taste of warm blood, the sounds of shrieks and screams of terror—all of these combined to vitalize his undead heart, to feed his evil soul.

Finally he sprang back into the air, the force of his upward leap shoving the flaming vessel's stern beneath the waves for the final time. The bow, with its elegant female figurehead, loomed in the air for a moment, and then, with a sizzling hiss, the once-sleek ship disappeared beneath the waves.

Gotha flew onward, fiercely exultant. His hatred for Talos

remained, but now it was easier for the beast to hold the emotion in the background of his awareness. Indeed, he had already begun to serve his new master, and that service had given the monster pleasure.

Ahead, another block of land rose from the water, a larger island than those the beast had first encountered in the archipelago. This rocky shore was bleak, all but uninhabited, and here Gotha settled to earth.

He dove toward the breakers erupting against the shore, knowing that he had arrived at the place where he had been sent. Here finally his work could truly begin.

* * * * *

Musings of the Harpist

Today I embark for Callidyrr. I knew when I awakened this morning that the time had come, for I saw the evidence of mighty portent before my very eyes.

Is it the power of the goddess, somehow miraculously resurgent? Or the presence of evil, once again threatening these shores? I cannot say for certain. Even a bard must sometimes stick to the unadulterated facts!

Yet the significance is great—as great as anything in the past twenty years. For as I look to the west this dawn, along the mist-shrouded shore of the firth, I see that Caer Allisynn is gone. The proud castle has silently vanished into the mist, sinking back beneath the sea. Its absence casts an unsettling pall over the town of Corwell.

Now I must take word to the king.

❧ 4 ❧

Storms Over Callidyrr

Rain swept across the town, forming rivulets down the few cobbled streets, turning the bulk of the avenues into morasses gummy with thick mud. Most of the inns and houses and shops huddled against these lanes and alleys, and here dwelt the populace of the city.

Paved roads ran through the grand center of Callidyrr, however. Here, in the heart of the largest city on the isles, a quadrangle of large stone merchant houses stood like gray blocks, solemn and aloof, as the humans scuttled about in their shadows. Vendors of gems and gold, of wools and iron and coal—each had his mercantile castle, with the stone avenue leading past its door.

Beyond these imposing edifices, the lowest portions of the city huddled against the shore of Whitefish Bay. A network of docks and breakwaters extended into the water, meshing the land with the sea. Long buildings of wood stretched beside the quay, stinking of fish. Narrow alleys twisted between shoddy buildings, where sailors visited and whores, alchemists, and smugglers plied their trades.

The harbor vanished into haze as the downpour drummed on the hulls of the sturdy curraghs and square-sterned cargo haulers at rest in the placid water. Against the wharf stood a ship that dwarfed all the others: a tall Calishite galleon, hired into the service of the High King.

Disdaining the royal coach, King Kendrick rode to the waterfront on horseback, accompanied by his wife and daughters, as well as their tutor Keane, and trailed by a score of his royal guard. The latter wore blue capes and feathered helms, and each was a master of the crossbow and longsword. Vigilant even in these times of peace, they rode behind their king while their eyes searched the buildings and alleys around him, seeking any hint of a threat.

No dangers appeared today—only the relative disinterest of a populace who had grown used to watching their monarch sail to the Sword Coast, bartering the gold and iron of the isles for the food that they must acquire in order to survive.

A collection of merchants gathered at the waterfront, awaiting the king's arrival beneath dripping awnings. They raised a listless cheer as the royal procession passed them at a slow trot. A dreary lethargy seemed to linger about them, gray Ffolk before gray buildings in a gray city.

Alicia felt a sense of dismal loneliness that had grown heavy during the long downhill ride from the castle. It was a mood uncharacteristic for her, and though she tried to blame it on the weather, combined with her father's imminent departure, she suspected that its true roots lay at a deeper, more unconscious level.

She looked at her mother, riding next to the king, the two of them leading the small procession. Think how she must feel! Though Tristan had journeyed abroad many times during the last few years, Alicia doubted that the absences had become any easier for her mother to bear.

Finally the king reined in, dismounting on the dock beside the looming galleon. The queen joined him, while Alicia and Deirdre stood to the side. The older princess cast a sidelong look at her sister and saw that Deirdre's face was blank. Her mind might have been a thousand miles away.

Tristan turned to address the Ffolk who had ridden with him and those who now gathered to see him off. Perhaps two hundred citizens stood around the fringes of the long wharf, watching and waiting quietly.

They stood, ever patient, and Alicia thought that they reflected the faces of the Ffolk across all the isles. The men were bearded, muscular and strong, but not tall. They wore boots of leather and tunics of wool, with leggings of either dark woolen cloth or tanned animal skin. Some of the women wore leggings as well, though many were clad in colorful skirts. Their hair grew long, and those who had married kept it bound at the back of the head or the neck.

All of them were people of peace and hope. Perhaps that

explained their interminable patience, Alicia reflected. Unlike the volatile northmen, the Ffolk were generally content to make do with what they had and to exert themselves as necessary to gradually improve the lot of their children.

Startled by a voice, the princess looked up to see that the king had begun to speak.

"My journey may extend up to a pair of months," he announced. Later his words upon departure, witnessed by all those present, would become the public record of the decrees made in his name to govern during the king's absence.

"Until such time as I return, the High Queen shall rule in my stead. She is in all respects mistress of the realm."

He paused, his listeners remaining silent.

"In my name, she will journey henceforth to Blackstone, attending to the business of the crown. For the duration of that travel, I hereby appoint Keane of Callidyrr acting seneschal for all matters of local importance until the return of the queen to Callidyrr."

The tutor looked at the king, nearly dropping his jaw in shock. Alicia blinked, surprised and—even more surprising—a trifle jealous.

"Good-bye, Alicia," said Tristan, clasping his daughter in his arms and kissing her forehead. She returned his hug, but at the same time, she felt hurt and rejected. Why had he appointed Keane to oversee the castle's daily affairs? Surely she was capable of that!

Her father embraced Deirdre and then Robyn while these thoughts chased through Alicia's mind. She said nothing as he climbed the gangplank, turned once to wave, and then stepped out of sight onto the galleon's high deck.

* * * * *

Thunderheads loomed into the heavens, columns of darkness that seemed to erupt from the ground, expanding upward into the limitless expanse of sky. Sunlight faded, and the darkness of the clouds intensified a hundredfold. Swirling into a deadly vortex, they centered themselves over a certain place.

Callidyrr.

The god who lay at the heart of the storm, Talos, knew that

the white castle below him represented the greatest obstacle to his object: the reign of chaos upon these isles.

Throughout the Moonshaes, in secret shrines and dark temples, clerics of the Raging One worked their charms, pleading for his violence to continue. These clerics responded to the will of their dark-robed master, called the Priest With No Name. This priest gave to his minions gold and encouraged them to pray and pray some more.

Nevertheless, Talos the Destroyer sent his storms against the Moonshaes not because of prayers but because it pleased him to do so. He furthered the cause of chaos, driving a wedge into the peace that threatened to pacify the isles for all time. He would use his agents, the dracolich and the sahuagin and the clerics, to maintain the pressure of the assault.

Now Talos pored over the walls, swirled about the towers, and sifted through closed shutters, even into the deepest sanctums of the castle. He looked, and he listened, and he learned.

He would be patient, for he knew that he would not have to wait for long.

* * * * *

Supper that night in the palace dining hall was a quiet affair, especially compared to the gala dinners that had marked the spring court. Earlier this year, as during every spring, the noble lords and earls of the kingdom had attended Tristan's hall in Callidyrr. The High King presided over contests, feasts, and bouts, and often several hundred people would laugh and chatter in the Great Hall over a dinner that would last for many hours.

Now only the queen, her daughters, and Keane supped here at one end of the lone table that still remained. A fire blazed in the huge hearth, attempting with limited success to combat the unusual chill.

The venerable servingwoman, Gretta, who had left the Kendrick family estate on Corwell twenty years before when Tristan and Robyn had moved to the castle of the High King, served them their meal, producing from the kitchen a roast haunch of lamb, with a pudding of corn and a beverage mixed from the rare beans just now entering the markets of the Sword Coast. They were called "cocoa" and originated in the land known as Maztica, discovered at the western shore of the Trackless Sea.

"You know, my Queen," Gretta said as she moved around the table, pouring steaming cups of the delicacy, "the cook tells me we're completely out of salt and fruit, and low on bacon as well. . . ."

"Perhaps, with Lord Keane's permission, we can shop the markets tomorrow?" asked Deirdre with a raised eyebrow. Her mouth twisted in a wry smile directed at Alicia.

As quickly as that, her father's slight came back to Alicia— *Keane* appointed as seneschal of the realm! Her face flushed, but then she felt Deirdre's eyes on her. The intensity of her sister's gaze made Alicia squirm in her seat. She glared back at her sister, but Deirdre had already turned back to her meal.

"Yes, of—of course," stammered Keane finally, nonplussed by the young princess's sarcasm.

They had begun to drain the last of the hot, spicy drink when the palace sergeant-at-arms, after knocking respectfully on the great wooden door, entered. They all knew the bowlegged, gray-mustached old war-horse who—to Alicia's amusement—was called Young Arlen. He had been one of Tristan's youthful recruits during the Darkwalker War.

"A visitor, Your Majesty," announced the bearded veteran. "She has just arrived at the castle and begs leave to enter."

"Of course," replied Robyn. "Her name?"

"It is the Lady Tavish, Bard of the Isles, Majesty."

"Auntie Tavish!" Alicia sprang to her feet and ran toward the door as the guard bade the visitor to enter. She called the harpist by the name she had always known her, though no blood ties existed between them.

The merry bard swept the princess into a hug, beaming her broad smile across the room. Though Tavish neared sixty years of age, she had all the energy of a young tomboy.

"Greetings, my Queen!" she boomed. "And a thousand thanks for the warmth of your hearth and the protection of your roof!"

"Oh, stop it!" chided Robyn. "You know that you're always welcome here!"

"Nevertheless, I welcome the shelter—especially in these times, when traveling is such a chill, soggy affair. I saw no banner of the wolf above the gatehouse. Does the king travel away from the castle now?"

"To Amn," Robyn explained. "He left but this morning."

"Rot my timing, then, though it is indeed a pleasure to end a trip with the company of the Kendrick ladies!"

"Have you journeyed far?" inquired Alicia. She always enjoyed the bard's tales of the far islands of the Moonshaes and even the Sword Coast.

"Always, lass—always! But not so far as sometimes, if the truth be told. I last hail from Corwell."

"Corwell!" Robyn's face lit, and then her joy faded into a wistful remembrance. "Tell me, how is life on that fair island?"

"I have news," said Tavish. All the listeners detected a slight cautionary note to her voice. "But perhaps it can wait until I've had a bite . . . or two."

It was more like three or four, but none of them begrudged the woman the time to fill her ample stomach. As the premier Greater Bard of the Moonshae Islands, Tavish enjoyed certain privileges akin to nobility—the shelter of anyone's roof should she but ask, and the hospitality of their table. These boons were never resented, for a visit from the bard was always an entertaining and informative affair.

Indeed, only recently had the knowledge of printed history come to the Ffolk. Always before their bards had maintained a pure oral tradition of lore, and thus the story of that people's history was told and preserved. And via the hearts of the harpists, from one generation to the next, those tales continued to flourish and grow.

In Tavish's case, however, her bonds to the Kendrick family extended beyond these conventional courtesies. As the author of the ballad telling the tale of Tristan's wars, she had spent years in Callidyrr during Alicia's childhood, asking questions and beguiling them with her own interesting stories.

As she had aged, the harpist had grown more, not less, active. She could ride a horse like a warrior and throw a punch that would deck most brawlers. Her ribald songs and the boastful tales of her own presumably exaggerated amorous exploits had been known to make the queen blush and the princesses stare in wide-eyed wonder.

Now, after she mopped up the last bit of gravy and pudding with the final crust of bread, she removed her lyre from its traveling pouch. The others waited expectantly as she tuned it carefully, finally stroking her fingers across the instrument and calling forth a series of bright ascending chords.

"It's been too long since we've had the sound of your music within these walls," Robyn said, leaning back in her chair to listen.

Tavish made no reply, instead strumming a series of powerful notes that faded into a mournful, minor key.

She began to sing, and her voice held them all in its grip. Tavish played a ballad of a farmer's son, a poor lad who had served his lord in the wars, winning glory and horses and treasure. The tale was a long one, and the listeners thrilled to the farm lad's exploits, shared his grief at the passing of his lord, knew his joy upon winning the love of a maiden's heart and claiming lands awarded him so that he could make himself a freeman's homestead.

Then, as in the way of such ballads, the man perished, not in the thick of some raging battle, but slain by a boar that rushed him as he began to clear his fields. The final notes, heavy with deep, minor resonance, seemed to swirl about the listeners, first bringing them to the verge of tears and then ultimately washing away their sadness in the totality of a life well lived, and well told.

"Beautiful," Alicia said quietly, several moments after the bard had finished her tune.

"Indeed. A moving ballad, and one we have not yet heard in Callidyrr," noted Keane.

"Well, I should hope not!" Tavish feigned high dudgeon. "I composed it during my winter's rest in Corwell."

"Oh, yes," Robyn interjected. "Now, tell us—you said you have news!"

Tavish's face grew serious. "Aye, Lady. Some of it, perhaps, is familiar, for Corwell and Gwynneth suffer the same from flood and storm as have the rest of the Isles these past several years. Fortunately they have not so many mouths to feed, and the harvests from the sea have been good on those days when weather permits the fisherffolk to sail."

"That's some welcome news," Robyn allowed. "It's good to see more of the Ffolk take to the water that surrounds them. We have always been such a land-bound people."

"Indeed. But with the keelwork that was laid by the shipwrights of the northmen as a personal favor to His Majesty, the Ffolk of Corwell and Moray have considerably improved the seaworthiness of their craft."

"And Earl Randolph?" inquired the High Queen. The earl had once been captain of Corwell's castle guard, advancing to the earldom when Tristan came to rule in Callidyrr.

"He is well, and sends my lady his good wishes. The steading of the Kendricks is in good hands, you may rest assured." Tavish paused, looking past the others, pondering before she continued.

"Much of the time I spent there, the fog lay thick across the town and the moor. It rolled into Corwell Firth before dawn and stayed till dusk. On many days, you couldn't see Caer Allisynn where it stood, a bare half-mile up the shore."

They all remembered that towering castle, anchored upon the gravelly bed of the Firth for twenty years.

"Finally came a day when the fog lifted, opening again to firth and moor. Then it was that we saw, and I left in haste to bring the news to you."

"What?" Robyn's face had grown pale. "*What* did you see?"

"It's what we did *not* see," the bard replied, softly. "Caer Allisynn. It was gone. It may as well have sailed with the midnight tide."

Alicia sat back in her chair, stunned. She heard a sound to her side and turned, gasping, as her mother groaned and slumped back in her chair. The others looked at the queen and then sprang to her side as they saw that her face was locked in an expression of deep, supernatural fear.

* * * * *

The storm pulsed as Talos became aware of a sudden vulnerability. Power flowed between the thunderheads, arcing across with sizzling explosions. Lightning flashed earthward, heavenly javelins of deadly force.

And while the crushing fists of the storm beat about the walls of the castle with lightning and hail, sinister fingers of mist penetrated the closed shutters, slipped beneath barred doors. Those perilous tendrils trickled along the floor, seeking the place of weakness that the god had sensed.

When those fingers of fear felt the nearness of the High Queen, they clutched forward, eager to clasp their chill grip around the faintly beating heart.

They grasped, and then they squeezed.

* * * * *

Robyn's head tossed on the pillow as Alicia patted her brow with a damp cloth. Suddenly the queen's eyes opened, but they did not see her daughter. Instead, they stared at something Alicia sensed was far, far away.

Then Robyn fell back, limp again, but this time her eyes remained opened. Alicia saw, with profound relief, that her mother's gaze now seemed to focus.

"Don't try to talk, Mother," she soothed. "It's been a terrible shock. Just rest."

"No." Robyn shook her head weakly. "It's a sign! We forsook her, and now, one by one, she takes our lives and our lands from us."

"She? Who?"

"The goddess!"

"Please, Mother—you've got to rest." Frightened again, Alicia wished someone was here with her.

"Summon Keane and Deirdre."

"What?" Alicia, startled, felt as though her mother had eavesdropped upon her thoughts. She rose and went to the door, speaking to one of her mother's ladies-in-waiting.

"They'll be here in a few minutes," she said, returning to sit upon the edge of the bed.

"Help me sit up." Robyn wiped her hair from her forehead and leaned forward so that Alicia could arrange her pillows. In moments, she looked strong again. Only after careful study did the princess realize that her mother's eyes had sunk deep in their sockets, and her cheeks remained drawn and pale.

In a short time, Deirdre and Keane arrived, and Robyn bade

all three of them to take seats near the bed. She took a breath and began to speak.

"I was seized by a spell of weakness. It lingers, though the immediate onslaught has passed. Nevertheless, I shall not be able to journey to Blackstone as I had planned."

Alicia blinked. She had forgotten that her mother had been requested by the king to make that journey.

"My daughter," the queen continued, addressing Alicia, "you must make the trip in my stead. And after the news that Tavish has brought, you must reconsider your father's decision regarding the Moonwell."

Keane spoke. "Lord Blackstone should be instructed not to disturb the pool?"

Robyn smiled wanly. "I cannot make that decision from here. But neither can we dismiss the portent of Caer Allisynn."

"I don't understand," Alicia balked. "What *do* you want me to do?"

"You must see if there is anything—anything at all—that the miners can do to avoid the well. There *must* be a way to save the sacred pool!"

"I'll do my best," Alicia pledged, deeply frightened. Suddenly she wished she had paid closer attention to her lessons. She listened to her mother's next words.

"Sir Keane," the queen continued, "I must beg a favor of you. We know my daughter is wise, but she is also young."

"Indeed, Lady." Keane suppressed a smile, but the tightening of the tall man's lips annoyed Alicia.

"Will you journey to Blackstone with her? This, her first task in the name of the crown, is a matter of delicacy and importance. Your help would be very useful, I am certain."

Now it was the princess who smiled privately. Keane's aversion to travel, indeed to anything of the outdoors, was well known. To his credit, the tutor concealed his dismay. "Of course, Your Highness. It shall be my pleasure."

"Good. Now." Robyn turned to Deirdre. "The clerics have told me to stay in bed overnight, so I'll need your help with some things for the next few days. The ambassador from Calimshan is coming to dinner tomorrow."

"Of course, Mother." There was nothing private about

Deirdre's pleasure. She had longed for such a chance and felt no reluctance to accept the reins of responsibility.

Robyn leaned back against the pillows. Her face was drawn, her brow once again spotted with perspiration. She sighed weakly and then spoke. "I will sleep in a moment, but please, one more thing. Will you send for Tavish? I'd like to speak with her in private."

"She's right outside," said Keane, not surprised that the bard had earlier anticipated the queen's request. They filed quietly from the room and Tavish entered.

"My Queen," the bard said, grieving, "it is to my wretched shame that the news I bring should cause such a heavy burden."

Robyn waved her hand, impatient. "It is not just the news—and by the goddess, am I an ignorant war queen who knows no better than to hold her messenger responsible for the news she bears?"

"I should hope not, Lady."

"Well, of course not! The news is grievous, of course—all the more so because it confirms that which I have feared."

Tavish waited expectantly before the queen continued.

"These curses, the misfortunes that have befallen our lands, are not simply the effects of dire weather. We are being punished! Punished for our faithlessness."

"Would that I could argue with you, for I should not hesitate to do so," replied the harpist. "But, alas, it is a feeling that I have come to share as well."

Robyn reached out and took the older woman's stronger hand in both her own. "That is why Alicia's journey is so important. I don't believe we can afford to lose a Moonwell, stagnant and lifeless though it may be!"

"There, too, I must agree."

"Then please, Tavish, go with them. Go with Keane and Alicia to Blackstone and see that their counsel is wise . . . and prudent."

"Of course." The bard bowed her head, humble before her queen.

"There is one thing more." Robyn gestured toward a dark hickory chest near one wall of her bedchamber. "You will find the key in my nightstand. Please open it."

Tavish did so, inserting the tiny golden tines into the keyhole, turning it to release the catch, and then lifting the heavy lid with both hands.

"The staff—take it out." Robyn's voice was a command.

Tavish saw that the chest contained several felt pouches of rich cloth as well as a pair of scrolls, a metal torque that she recognized as having graced the queen's neck at her wedding, and a long stave of smooth, white ash.

The bard lifted the staff out and closed the lid. Turning, she offered it to Robyn.

"No." The queen shook her head. "It is the Staff of the White Well, the tool of a druid, not a cleric—nor a queen. Take it with you on your journey. It may be that you will come upon one who shall use it."

"Very well, Lady," Tavish replied, bowing deeply. "I am honored by the trust."

Robyn leaned back again, her face grown shockingly pale. "You do me honor if you help my daughter succeed."

* * * * *

He presented himself as a cleric, and how else were the men to take him? His powers were real enough: They had all seen him materialize in their midst, along the storm-wracked shore of Whitefish Bay. When he spoke, his voice was full of power and promise, sweeping the hundred or so ruffians in his audience to a pitch of enthusiasm and loyalty. They had gathered from the slums, from the waterfronts and garrison quarters, of the worst dives along the Sword Coast.

There were also the matters of his robe and his identity. The one who had summoned these men—bandits, mercenaries, and outlaws, from Gnarhelm and Callidyrr and places beyond—was robed from head to foot, revealing only his hands. The latter were pale and spotted, almost skeletally frail, but supple and quick of movement.

And not one of the men summoned here knew the name or the identity of the robed man. Yet he spoke of the gods like one who knew their ways, and his gold was real. Finally, his promise of gold answered the important questions.

Lost in the mist and rain, the white towers of Callidyrr

thrust skyward no more than five miles away, but they might have been across the world for all they could be seen. The band of scoundrels gathered here secretly, coming from the cities and forests and highlands—wherever the robed man had found them.

He divided his recruits into two companies. Those of the north he outfitted with helms and weapons of the type used by northmen.

"You, Kaffa, will be my captain," said the robed man, addressing a huge, one-eyed northman. "You will take seventy men to the longship I have provided. It is anchored in a cove along the north shore of Whitefish Bay. I have the location sketched on maps, which I will provide you when our business here is concluded. Also, I have affixed a talisman to the ship— a thing that will protect you against sorcery."

"You don't lead us there?" inquired Kaffa, with a spit.

"I have other, equally important matters to attend to. But listen to me carefully, for here are your orders:

"Sail swiftly down the coast of Callidyrr," the mysterious priest ordered the crew in that dry voice that discouraged questions or debate. "Strike all the major cantrevs—Blythe, Dorset, Kythyss. Land quickly and burn what you can, wherever you can. Take treasure and captives only as it does not jeopardize your mission. Then, when you reach Southpoint, pass to the western shore and continue your raiding along the western shore of Alaron."

"Aye, Master," replied the one called Kaffa.

"And you, Larth," the priest continued, now speaking to a strapping outlaw known to be skilled with sword and shield. "You will lead the other thirty men. I have collected horses and armor in a barn beside that same cove. You will don them and ride, as knights of Callidyrr, against the lands of the northmen. Kill and burn as you ride. Take what treasure you will, but I want no prisoners!"

"As you wish, great one," replied Larth, grinning easily as he contemplated mayhem.

"Both of you, my captains, must remain alert for a message from me. When that comes, I want you to join me as quickly as possible. I will need you without delay!"

Standing on the gray shore of Whitefish Bay, the men nodded and then turned to their tasks. They would move north in small bands, agreeing to gather at the appointed cove in four days' time.

Watching them go, the robed figure allowed himself a shadow of a smile beneath his masking robe. The mist parted as a sudden gust drove the rain momentarily inland. The man glimpsed the towers of the great white castle.

He thought of one who dwelled there, who dreamed of the robed man, though she did not know it yet. Still, her dreams were a summons, an appeal to him, and soon she would know his presence. To her, he would become more than the impersonal figure who had just sent these raiding parties on their missions. Indeed, she would need to call him something— though, of course, he could not let her know his real name. The faint smile played with his lips as he thought of the young princess and her naive welcome.

"She will call me Malawar," he whispered to himself with a soft chuckle.

* * * * *

From the Log of Sinioth:

The pieces of war are gathered. Talos awaits the rise of chaos, when the armies shall march and his power shall rule over all the land!

Of course, I do not control these armies, but through the wisdom of my master, I do not have to. The mere triggers of war, prodded by the agents of Talos, will be enough to sweep away the fragile framework of twenty years' peace.

And in its place, once again the isles will tremble before the thunder of war, raging conflicts of men and of gods!

❧ 5 ❧

Road to Blackstone

Gotha finally touched claw to land upon an islet that stood in lonely isolation, rising a little higher than the gray seas about its bleak shore. The barren rockpile was crested by a low hill, and near the rounded summit, Gotha discovered a cave. The natural cavern did not approach the grandeur of the magnificent lair he had once claimed, but it was a dwelling that would serve him well for the task at hand.

Next he went about exploring the islet, knowing that it was not huge but having earlier seen evidence of human habitation. The beast prowled the rock in the dark of the night, stalking the land like a huge hunting cat. Wind howled, and sheets of rain drenched him, but Gotha pressed on, unmindful of the weather.

The dracolich came upon a small pasture of sheep and gleefully slayed the stupid creatures. When their bleating brought a shepherd forth, the hideous monster disemboweled the wretch with one quick slash of his foreclaw, deriving even more pleasure from this killing.

Creeping across the fogbound isle, the dragon-beast found more huts—dwelling places for lone shepherds and fishermen mostly, though in one place, he encountered a dozen or more buildings clustered together, forming the beginnings of a town.

Gotha's eyes—red orbs that seemed to float in his deep, black sockets—glowed fiercely at the discovery. Slinking silently along the ground, sheltered by the heavy mist and the thickness of the night, the beast coiled in the center of the rude buildings. The structures employed, for their walls and roofs, the wreckage of ships that had been cast upon this lonesome rock, giving each a temporary, haphazard appearance.

From several, Gotha smelled odors that would have once

been pleasant: a kettle of boiling fish, a leg of mutton sizzling over a driftwood fire, even the sweet scent of tobacco wafting through the dusk. Now these spoors triggered nothing beyond memory, for the undead dragon no longer felt hunger.

He still, however, lusted for the savage joy of killing.

Gotha raised his gaunt head to the sky like a spearhead thrust upward into the night and uttered a bellow of fierce challenge. The force of the sound rang through the night and brought the northmen stumbling from their huts, peering in terror through the mists, trying to see the nature of that which had inspired such deep and primeval dread.

And even as they learned, they died.

Carefully, methodically, Gotha set about making the island his own. The huts and houses of the inhabitants he left intact, save in a few cases in which a desperate human—as often as not, a male with female and young to protect—barricaded himself in his dwelling.

These Gotha dealt with directly, spreading his jaws and belching the murderous gout of flame. His metamorphosis from dragon to lich had not impaired this ability, he swiftly realized. Indeed, it seemed that, if anything, the power of his deadly attack was increased, for the monster blasted six or eight structures in this manner. Previously half this number of explosive fireballs would have exhausted his belly until he had fed well and rested.

The seasoned wood of walls and roofs burned quickly, and in minutes, the inhabitants ceased their pathetic wailing. Those courageous enough to break from their shelter met a faster and more merciful end that was nevertheless just as fatal and violent.

Satisfied that no more humans survived on the small island, the wyrm went to each corpse and tossed it into the sea. The sheep, too, he gathered and killed and tossed into the brine. It wasn't that the gruesome bodies would have affected the dragon in any way. It was simply that this, too, was part of the plan of Talos. Once again Gotha could do naught but obey.

Next he followed the shore of the islet along its full circumference, noting several wooden-hulled fishing boats pulled up beyond the reach of high tide. These he punctured, driving one sharp claw through each keel and then pushing the vessels into the surf, where they quickly foundered and sank. One cove held several slightly larger craft, bobbing at anchor, and these too he sank, crushing the hulls with forceful blows of his massive foreclaws.

Finally the serpent returned to the cave. The rock-enclosed cavern sprawled beyond a narrow niche that cracked the top of the island's tallest summit. Gotha pulled and tore at the rock, widening the entrance and clearing the field of view down the slope. Using the strength of his massive forelegs, he excavated parts of the shelter that did not meet his fancy.

In the course of this quarrying, he collapsed a thin shelf of rock that separated his cave from a lower network of passages. Delighted, he pressed forward in eager exploration. The lower tunnels led to a vast sea cave, where salt water splashed in a great pool. It was low tide, and Gotha could feel the wind scouring past. The tunnel was open to the sky!

This was a splendid discovery, for one of the finest features of any lair was the existence of an escape route to the rear. At low tide, at least, the dracolich would be able to sally forth at sea level.

Gotha crept upward again, toward the large chamber he would claim as his sleeping room and, perhaps later, the site of his hoard. More of his flesh and scale had fallen away during the exertions of his journey and the claiming of the island. His wings were bare outlines of bone, and his ribs showed as white streaks on both sides of his wretched, decaying body.

Yet he felt no weariness, none of the stiffness nor sore muscles that would have plagued him five hundred years ago should he have attempted such a vigorous campaign. No hunger gnawed at his belly. The bites of meat he had taken during the killing had been enough, apparently, to maintain his fiery breath weapon.

Neither did he feel any need to sleep. This, too, he marked as an advantage, since a dragon was always most vulnerable during the time he lay curled in sleep.

Gotha coiled himself, awake, and lay still for a time. His flesh continued to rot, but his evil soul remained as vital as ever. He needed only to wait now for the inevitable commands from his god.

The Raging One spoke to Gotha, then, in the midst of the

rain-lashed night.

You have found your lair, my wyrm.

Instantly the dracolich tensed, hissing smoke from his gaping nostrils and fixing his crimson eyespots on the opposite wall of his cave. "Give me my task, treacherous one."

The god may have chortled internally at Gotha's insolence. In any event, Talos did not punish his servant. *You will participate in a mighty triumph of chaos, for we shall bring down a kingdom that has been founded upon law and justice! In its place, we shall set a reign of unadulterated evil and corruption.*

"What reign is this? How do we destroy it?"

Several kingdoms shall fall—one of the Ffolk, and others of the northmen. We topple them by bringing about that which the humans will gladly do on their own—we sow the seeds of war and allow the realms of men to reap its harvest.

"And my task?"

It involves many steps, which you will learn as you need to. We shall have powerful allies, but we must work with subtlety as well.

The time we begin is now.

* * * * *

Talos the Destroyer was the subject of attention in another part of the isles on this same dark night. To the south of Gotha's isle and a little to the east, the great island of Alaron darkened the surface of the sea, forming the eastern bulwark of the entire Moonshae group.

The southern portion of Alaron, mostly rolling hill and fertile dale, fell under the dominion of the High King himself, for this was Callidyrr. The Fairheight mountains formed the northern frontier of that kingdom. The remainder of the island, a rough and tumbled expanse of rocky crag and icy fjord, fell under the sway of the northmen of Gnarhelm.

In the heights of the range, farthest cantrev to the north and west of Callidyrr, was the Earldom of Blackstone, and here met two men to whom the workings of Talos were very significant indeed.

They gathered in a darkened hall at the heart of Caer Blackstone, the earl's manor. The Earl of Fairheight himself leaned forward, his scowling features etched in the light of an oil lamp as he listened earnestly to the hoarse whisper of the second man's voice.

The latter sat in the shadows, visible only by the soft outlines of his dark cloak and the hood that fell far forward on his head, masking his face.

"The money, then?" inquired the cloaked figure. His voice was like the rasp of a file on coarse wood. "Have you the coin for my labors?"

"Of course." Blackstone, too, whispered. He hefted a sack from the floor—the brawny lord needed both hands to lift it—and grunted as he set it on the table.

"Excellent. My apprentices maintain their charms and beseechments. It pleases Talos to continue his onslaughts against the farms of the Ffolk, and your payment has ensured that we can purchase the necessary components to extend the castings indefinitely."

"With a little extra, no doubt, to compensate for your troubles," growled Blackstone, his humor very dry.

The nameless robed figure made no response, nor indeed was any reply necessary. For five years this man had represented himself as the agent of Talos the Destroyer, claiming influence over that capricious god. Supported by the wealthy coffers of the earl, he had exhorted his vengeful god to smite the Moonshaes with all manner of storm-wracked violence.

"My god works his violence against the farms, while you get rich from your mines. It is a fair trade," suggested the stranger.

"Aye—satisfying to both, as long as your god does as he is bid!" grunted Blackstone, his mind already considering other problems.

The other man looked at the earl, his eyes hooded but blazing scorn at the man's arrogance. Blackstone missed the expression, but undoubtedly he wouldn't have noticed even had he looked up.

"And the queen?" The stranger asked the question. "When do you expect her?"

"I don't." Blackstone shook his black mane of hair. "I received word today. The elder princess, Alicia, journeys here in place of the queen. I took it as good news." The black-maned lord nodded his head. "The High Queen was once a druid. I'd rather she not be the one to have to condemn a Moonwell."

"Do not be too delighted," cautioned the robed figure. "The daughters of Kendrick are not without capability."

"Do you mean that we should fear her?" asked the earl in disbelief.

"It is a wise man who practices eternal vigilance. Now, I must make haste to Callidyrr. I, too, have a meeting with a princess of the isles."

The lamp still flickered, and the shadows remained thick, but even in the darkness, the earl could see that his robed visitor had gone.

* * * * *

The party of Alicia, Tavish, and Keane rode alone, since the reign of Tristan Kendrick had seen a virtual end to banditry and danger on the highways. At first the queen had planned to send along an escort of the king's guards, but Alicia had convinced her, with little difficulty, that this was unnecessary. Indeed, the road was well traveled and passed through many small cantrevs, and every few miles in the countryside, a cozy inn offered shelter to the weary traveler.

The smooth-paved King's Road connected the towns of Callidyrr and Blackstone, twisting and climbing around the foothills that lay between the two communities. As far as Keane was concerned, this avenue was the only thing that made the trip—a two-day ride through lashing rains and winds that howled like dervishes—remotely possible. Alicia and Tavish, however, seemed to take no note of the weather, and their high spirits taunted the teacher for every league of the ride.

Consequently Keane went to great pains to point out that he was an educator and scholar, not an adventurer.

"Ah, but you studied the spells of sorcery," Tavish pointed out. "And at a very young age, as well. I should think you'd have a wanting to test those in the real world, wouldn't you?"

"The world of my library and study is quite real, thank you," Keane sniffed, responding to Tavish. "And one can sample it without suffering the constant thrill of water trickling along one's spine!"

"You gave up those studies when I was still a girl," Alicia reminded him. "Why?"

Keane shrugged, frowning. As always, this was an issue he preferred to avoid. "Wisest thing I ever did," he grunted finally. The princess continued to wait for an answer. "Some people are suited to magic, and others very definitely are *not!* Now, can we stop somewhere for a cup of hot tea before my teeth chatter to nubs?"

"Stop complaining!" Alicia cried, finally exasperated. "We've slept indoors every night. We've even stopped at inns for our midday meals! The horses move at a walk along this smooth road. This is *not* an adventure!"

"It's plenty of adventure for me," retorted the tutor, wrapping his scarf tightly around his face and sinking into his saddle, a ball of misery.

For a time, the rain lifted enough that they could see craggy foothills around them. The road followed the winding floor of a wide, flat-bottomed valley, twisting through long and gradual turns as it led upward into the hills. Patches of pine and newly leafed aspen swathed the slopes, looking as soft as down in the distance. A shallow, gravel-bottomed stream rumbled and spumed beside the road, carrying off the excess water delivered by the heavy clouds.

Finally the highway veered from the stream and crested a low rise between a pair of blunt, rocky tors. The gray clouds hung overhead, but for the time being, they held their moisture intact, so the trio saw the valley before them unobscured by showers or mist. They reined in, sharing a mutual but initially silent reaction.

Despite the absence of rain, the air of Blackstone was far from clear. A dark, smoky haze thickened the atmosphere, obscuring the view of the far side of the vale. A mixed stench of sulfur and coal and other, more acrid, odors swept upward, encircling them as they passed the rim of the valley and started the gradual descent toward the cantrev.

From this distance, the dark spots of tunnel mouths were visible near the bases of the slopes that ringed the valley. Black chimneys jutted into the air from a long row of large, sooty buildings. From many of these, fresh gouts of thick smoke belched forth, adding to the haze that lay in the air.

"Kind of takes your breath away, doesn't it?" Tavish observed wryly as their noses and throats stung from the bitter air.

"I was here years ago," Keane noted. "It was always dirty, but never like *this!* Of course, it was just an iron cantrev back then. They discovered gold here only five or six years ago."

Alicia looked around in sadness. She knew that the gold, and to a lesser extent the iron, from these mines and forges was the lifeblood of the kingdom, but the extent of the devastation sickened her. She felt somehow that this was wrong.

The feeling lingered during the final walk to, and through, the cantrev itself. It was late afternoon, and raucous laughter erupted from many of the countless saloons, brothels, and taverns on the town's main street. Though this avenue had once been part of the same King's Road that had brought them from Callidyrr, in the town, the graveled surface had long been trampled into an all-encompassing sea of mud.

The earl's manor house was in reality a small castle perched on a low knoll on the far side of the cantrev. A wall of stone, topped with a castellated rampart, encircled the great structure, while the Blackstone banner—a midnight-black background, bordered in gold, emblazoned with a crossed pattern of swords and shields—sagged limply in the windless air over the gatehouse.

They felt a growing sense of oppression as the road climbed toward the great structure of Caer Blackstone. Passing underneath the gray gates, Alicia felt an urge to whirl her horse around and flee. She would have been comforted to know that her two companions resisted the same compulsion.

The house loomed before them as they halted their horses and dismounted. It shambled off to the sides and towered overhead, with a stone parapet ringing the flat roof and several towers jutting upward from the corners. The grounds within the walls were spacious, with stretches of lawn, paved courtyard, and thick brush and foliage.

"Greetings, royal visitors!"

It was the earl himself, standing with outspread arms on the great steps of the huge stone house. His thick black mane of hair spiraled outward, giving him the likeness of some great bear. His smile was friendly, though his eyes remained hooded and narrow.

"I request the shelter of your walls and the warmth of your hearth," announced Alicia, responding formally, although she did not curtsy in her leather riding breeches. She remembered her discomfort at Blackstone's earlier presence and realized that the feeling was only amplified now that she was his guest.

"It is granted, my Princess. Come, you shall have the shelter of your rooms and a bath, and then we shall dine. I am anxious for you to meet my sons!"

Alicia couldn't shake off a vague feeling of alarm, though her companions quickly relaxed under the auspices of the earl's hospitality. The rooms, in fact, were splendid: three adjoining bedchambers with private dressing rooms and a central parlor. All were furnished in the most elegant style, with silken canopies over deep feather beds. They equalled in every way the sumptuous guest quarters of the grand palace at Callidyrr.

Only the view from the window, in the fading light of the late afternoon overcast, showed them the truth. A small lake, perhaps half a mile away, lay stagnant and brackish. No vegetation grew around it, while the mouths of many mine tunnels trailed red tailings to the water itself. These rusty scars showed the progress of Blackstone's excavation. Never, thought Alicia, had she seen such a lifeless scene.

When they had washed and dressed for dinner, they descended the stairs to find that the Great Hall, too, boasted of the earl's wealth and grandeur, if not his good taste. Blackstone had set out a massive table for the royal party, decked with white linen and plates of burnished pewter.

Alicia felt something scrutinize her from above. Startled, she looked up to the top of the dark-paneled wall. A great bear leered down at her, widespread jaws gaping in a soundless expression of lasting hatred. Only as she gasped and flinched away did she realize that it was merely the head of a bear. Looking along the wall, she saw the mounted heads of wolves, deer, several smaller bears, and—across the hall, above the massive hearth—a green dragon.

Below the grim trophies, the walls proudly displayed an assortment of finely crafted weapons. A great double-bladed axe hung near the dragon, its smoothly curved head of gleaming, highly polished steel. The weapon, like many of the swords, halberds, and spears mounted beside it, showed nicks and scrapes obviously inflicted during hard use.

Blackstone noted her reaction with a hearty chuckle, and Alicia felt a hot surge of anger. She took a deep breath, as her mother had taught her, bringing her temper under control while the earl blabbered about this stalk and that kill. Though she held nothing against hunting—indeed, with her own bow she had brought down many a deer, rabbit, and bird, whose meat had gone to the palace table—she found something vulgar, even sacrilegious, in the ostentatious display of the earl's trophies.

"Ah, my sons!" Blackstone's voice boomed as two men entered the hall. "Come and meet the Princess Alicia, heir to the crown of the isles."

The sons were even larger men than their father, one dark of skin and hair, the other fair. Their beards hadn't grown in so full as the earl's. The dark one wore a green tunic, the other a cloak of deep blue. Together they advanced and bowed.

"This is Gwyeth." The earl indicated the son in green, who had hair as dark as his father's as well as the same glowering eyebrows.

"And Hanrald," Blackstone concluded. The latter, who bowed with a shy smile, was not so huge nor so hairy as Gwyeth. His hair and beard were speckled with cinnamon-colored strands.

Alicia nodded her head politely as she watched the pair. "We have met, Lady," announced Gwyeth, rising and grinning crudely at her. His dark eyes flashed, and she suppressed a sudden urge to back away from him.

"It was our honor to be knighted by your father some years back, in the Great Hall of Callidyrr," Hanrald added quietly. The younger son seemed embarrassed by his brother's rude stare, but he finally met her eyes and smiled tentatively.

"Oh, yes—of course," she said, smiling in return. She did not in fact remember, for King Tristan had dubbed a good many knights during the last ten years or so.

Other guests filed in—a royal visit was cause for no small celebration—and Alicia and her companions saw the bald, pudgy Lord Ironsmith, who had accompanied the earl to Callidyrr before Tristan's departure.

"Who's that with him?" asked Alicia, indicating a large-breasted young woman a good foot taller than Ironsmith who clung protectively to the lord's arm.

"His wife," replied Blacksmith. He chuckled lewdly before remembering that he spoke to a maiden princess. He tried to swallow his humor by clearing his throat.

Others came, too, mostly wealthy merchants who had gained huge profits from the mines and forges, though a smattering of local nobles showed up as well. Blackstone introduced Alicia's party to Lord McDonnell, who was the mayor of Cantrev Blackstone and a loyal follower of the earl's, and to Lord Umberland, owner of extensive holdings in the mountains.

Alicia admitted to herself that the earl set a fine table. His wife had died years ago, at the time of her third son's birth, she recalled. Still, he maintained a kitchen full of servingwomen—young, beautiful servingwomen, the princess noted. Blackstone himself filled the role of the gracious host. He seated the princess to his right, while Keane and Tavish were placed farther down the long table. His two sons sat at the two places to his left. He made sure they would have the opportunity to speak with the royal daughter.

But the younger, Hanrald, spoke barely a word during the meal, preferring to remain silent. Alicia found him almost sullen, but nevertheless she liked him better than his brother, who proved vain, vulgar, and boastful. Gwyeth spent most of the meal reciting his own feats of arms or loudly exclaiming about his many quests and accomplishments.

The princess noted Keane, within earshot, listening to the young man. Finally the tutor could hold his tongue no longer.

"It's a wonder there are any firbolgs left in the hills. It sounds as though you have driven the race to extinction," he remarked dryly. Ironsmith's large-bosomed wife giggled hysterically at the comment, but the rest of the table fell silent.

"Do you call me a liar?" growled Gwyeth Blackstone.

Keane looked shocked. "Did I say *that?* Why, my lad, it was merely an observation—nay, an expression of gratitude—that you have made this country safe for those less accomplished than yourself to travel."

Gwyeth squinted, all but mouthing the teacher's words as

he tried to follow Keane's response.

"Why—you *mock* me! A man who spends his days indoors, like a woman! I see those hands, far better fit for spinning wool than for holding a man's weapon. Come, sir. Dare you raise steel against me?"

Before anyone could react, Gwyeth kicked his chair over backward and stood to his greater than six-foot height. In his hand, seemingly from nowhere, appeared a long, steel-bladed dagger.

Keane blinked, nonplussed. He looked at Lord Blackstone, apparently wondering if that noble would rebuke his son's poor manners, but the earl remained silent, scowling at the two men.

"Come, I say. At least *pretend* you're a man!" Gwyeth took a step forward.

"My lord!" Alicia said firmly. "Is this the hospitality of an earl?"

But Blackstone appeared not to hear. Carefully sliding his chair backward, Keane stood. His face was calm. "I have no wish to fight you. It would be ungracious, in light of your father's hospitality. But you shall not insult me!"

Gwyeth's face lit in a fierce grin. "Hah! Frail as a girl, he is, and now he tries to hide with a woman's talk!"

Keane seemed to stretch—at full height, he was an inch or two taller than even Gwyeth, though the burly knight outweighed him by perhaps a hundred pounds. Still, something in the thin man's gaze gave his opponent pause.

But Gwyeth had staked too much of his manhood on this confrontation. He could not back down. He lunged sharply at Keane.

The teacher snapped his fingers, and Alicia saw something like dust or sand puff into the air from the thin man's hand. At the same time, Keane waved his other arm toward the charging figure of Gwyeth.

In the next instant, the burly Gwyeth tumbled face-forward onto the ground. He lay still, only the rapid pulsing of his torso showing that he still breathed. After a moment, he found his voice, croaking a hysterical shriek amid a spattering of drool on the floor.

"Remove him!" barked Blackstone, gesturing to four men-at-arms, all of whom were required to heft the huge man and cart him from the hall.

"Sorcery!" The whisper passed around the great table, and the guests looked at Keane with new, appraising eyes, their expressions a mixture of respect and fear.

"I beg my lord's pardon," Keane said, bowing to the earl before reseating himself. "He shall recover free movement in a matter of minutes."

"Pah!" growled the lord, returning to his meat. Alicia sensed that he was disappointed in his son's embarrassing performance as much as anything else.

The remainder of the meal passed in somewhat stilted conversation, mostly concerning the past five years of weather. Finally the dinner guests made their way to the doors, while Alicia and her two companions bade good night to the earl and retired, with a feeling of relief, to their chambers.

Tomorrow morning, after breaking fast, they would journey with the earl to the Moonwell.

* * * * *

The oil lamp flared and smoked as the wick soaked up the last of the fuel, but Deirdre took no notice. Instead, her pulse quickened with excitement as she read the pages of the tome before her. It was an obscure volume, the *Origins of Arcane Power,* by one Dudlis of Thay, but it provoked within her feelings that she had never before tapped.

She had stumbled upon the tome almost by accident. She had been browsing among the titles along several high shelves that she had not previously investigated, when the glint of candlelight along the book's golden spine had attracted her eye. At the time, she had laughed at the fleeting suspicion that the book was calling to her, asking to be read.

Now she wasn't so sure that her reaction had been caused by her imagination.

The mind must open to the power that would flow, and the power itself must be fed and nurtured. It is a matter of diet, of meditation—and of joy.

This writer, this wizard—he *understands!* She felt a kinship to the long-dead author, for this was the power she had long felt within herself. Keane had touched it for her when he had begun to show her simple enchantments, but then the tutor had stopped, almost as if he had been frightened.

When one has the power, it may be a matter of fear to others, even close friends. . . .

That was it—Keane *feared* her! The thought gave Deirdre a little thrill of pleasure. Her lip curled in scorn as she thought of Keane, of Alicia and all the others who dwelled smugly, secure in their stations. What did they know of courage? Of determination? Only one such as Deirdre, born to nothing by a second child's status, could truly grow up to be strong.

As always, the envy in her heart coalesced into hard anger, growing colder and more firm as she delved further into these works of power. Unaware of the omnipresent power of the storm that still lurked about the castle, Deirdre allowed her mind to wander. Her frustration, her resentment, grew to an almost palpable force, sailing forth from the library into the dark and windy wastes of the night.

And as these thoughts surged forth, they served as a summons to one who had been waiting long for just such an opportunity. A form sifted through the shutters of the window like air, swirling through the shadows of the room, gathering in a darkened corner, behind the back of the brooding princess. When finally the shape had gained substance, it moved, causing a soft scuffling of boots across the floor.

Deirdre gasped at the slight noise, standing suddenly and knocking over her stool as a figure advanced from the shadows in the corner of the library.

"Who *are* you?" she demanded, her voice steady despite her fear. "Where did you come from?"

"Fear not, king's daughter," said the man. His voice was rich and deep . . . and soothing.

"How long have you been there?"

"But a moment, no more—though, to be sure, I have heard you from afar many times these last few years. You must realize that. After all, it was you who summoned me here."

"I?" Deirdre stared, more astonished than ever. No longer, however, did she feel any fear of this strange intruder. "I *summoned* you?"

"In a manner of speaking." Now the visitor flung back his

robe. His golden hair lay full, well combed and hanging past his ears. A smile, sincere yet somewhat pensive, curved his mouth. Deirdre thought he was the most handsome man she had ever seen.

"Please explain," she requested, gesturing him to sit as she, too, took her chair. She very much wanted to listen to him.

"Your mind was freed by your reading, by that tome before you. I sensed your need and came here quickly."

"From where?"

"Callidyrr. I have a small shop in the alchemists' lane, though I am seldom there."

"Tell me of this need of mine—this thing that you sensed." Deirdre spoke calmly, wanting very much to appear in control. Inside, however, her heart squirmed like a worm on a hook.

"You possess the potential for great power," he said. "You simply need someone to teach you the secrets of that power, the means of unlocking those doors."

He *knows!* Deirdre had felt a rush of relief and gratitude and joy. The way before her—the secrets of her own power—suddenly seemed to beckon, a path that was wide and sunlit and smooth.

"Who are you?" she asked suddenly. "What is your name?"

"I cannot tell you—yet," the man said, softly waving away the question. And indeed the matter no longer seemed important. She realized that he spoke to her again.

"I must take care in my comings and goings. Besides, I know that you have done well with your studies, even without me here to guide you."

"You *know?*" she asked wonderingly.

"Remember, my little blackbird," he replied, "you summoned me. Yes, I can feel your progress, and I know that you progress very far."

Dierdre tingled to his praise. She would have clung to him in her joy, except he broke away to step over to the table. There he looked at the volume by Dudlis she had been reading.

"See—you make excellent headway, even in the advanced works. That is a very good sign."

"But where does it lead?" she asked petulantly. She immediately regretted her tone when she saw the look of mild reproach he gave her. "I'm sorry," she whispered.

His look became a soft, sympathetic smile. "I know your impatience as well, my dear. But you will need to wait for some levels of knowledge."

Hesitantly she approached him, knowing the rightness of his words yet wanting to disregard them.

"But how *long* must we wait?" she asked.

"Already you learn great things and do not even realize it," he said reassuringly. "Here, let me show you."

Her visitor went to one of the great tables and picked up a long taper. "This is a power I'll wager you do not even know that you possess." He drew a knife and whittled some shavings from the candle onto the stained planks.

"Come, girl. Sit beside me here," he encouraged as he touched the flame to the shavings. To Deirdre's surprise, a cloud of dark smoke spurted upward, floating as a circular mass in the air.

"Now," said the golden-haired man, "think of someone you know—your mother, for example. Call a picture of her into your mind."

Deirdre imagined High Queen Robyn as she had looked at dinner that night.

"Pass your hand through the smoke."

She did so, then gasped as the thick cloud slowly seethed and coalesced, until at last it formed the image of her mother, floating in the air before them.

"Did *I* do that?" she gasped, amazed and delighted.

"Of course. This is just one proof of the things you are learning, the powers that will become yours."

Deirdre wanted to question him further, to learn more about the things she would know, but suddenly he seemed strangely preoccupied. He scoured the tomes and scrolls and the shelves while she followed eagerly behind.

"Here," he said, finally drawing down another book, also bound in the red leather that signified a tome by one of the wizards of Thay. "When you have finished Dudlis, you should read this. I will return when you have completed it."

Dierdre's heart quickened. "This means you'll be back soon?"

He smiled patronizingly. "This one, I suspect, will take you a good while to read. But fear not, dear child. I shall return when you are ready."

"Please!" she cried, her voice louder than it should have been. He raised a hand, his expression pained, as she continued. "Can't you stay for a little longer? We have to . . . to talk. I need to know more about you! Please stay!"

But the wind puffed through a window that was already empty.

*　*　*　*　*

Deep within the darkened confines of Kressilacc, the weight of the sea fell so heavily that the press of the storm was as nothing. Yet even here, far beyond the reach of sun and air, the coming of Gotha was seen. The priestesses of Talos knew this, and so they told their king.

"The treasures—take them forth!" commanded Sythissal, waving a webbed hand tipped by five claws. Each of the talons was a foot long and studded with rings. He gestured at the gold-encrusted swords and jeweled shields his warriors had claimed by plundering a trading vessel of the Ffolk.

"No! We must choose carefully!" Nuva, his favorite of the yellow-tailed priestesses, argued persuasively. "We should not give all the treasures—not in our first offering."

"But how shall we choose?" The great king, reclining in his throne made from the bow of a shattered longship, scowled, his long, fishlike mouth twisting downward. His eyes, milky and opaque, gaped dully at the slender female who coiled affectionately in liquid circles around him.

"It has been given me to see in a vision," she whispered, her voice like oil on the turbulent waters. "We should take these swords, these that bear the sigil of the King of Moonshae, and place them on an island to the north."

"Which island? Do we meet the messenger?" Sythissal disliked these instructions, feeling himself once again drawn into the schemes of the priestesses.

"I will show you where. I do not know if the messenger of Talos will be present, yet the placing of these items will commence the plan of our god."

When Sythissal remembered the vividness of his own

dream, the premonition of a messenger's arrival, he could only agree.

Thus it was that, hours later, King Sythissal emerged from the surf at the shore of Gotha's island at the head of a column of his warriors. They bore with them several swords from the Ffolks' merchant vessel. Oddly, the priestess had compelled them to break the blade of one of them.

The sahuagin cast the weapons among the ruins of the huts and homes there. Then, like silent ghosts, they slipped back into the sea.

*   *   *   *   *

The High Queen of the Isles, Robyn Kendrick, removed the wet compress from her head and leaned back, deploring the weakness that sapped her spirit. The news about Caer Allisynn had struck her like a physical blow, and she couldn't help believing that its departure represented another disastrous portent in these years of catastrophe.

She felt desperately alone and sorely missed her husband, the king. Though he had left her often before, never had she felt such a looming presence of despair.

Finally, late in the night, she fell asleep in her great chambers, the rooms she shared with the king when he was present. Now she slept alone.

She didn't notice the black, vaporous form that slipped beneath her door, having drifted through the castle halls all the way from the library. Nor did the queen's sleep suffer disturbance as the cloud gathered over her bed, once again shaping itself into the image of the queen that her daughter had so delightedly created earlier that night.

When the cloud sank onto the bed, growing dense upon her face, she started and struggled for a brief moment. But when she drew her breath to scream, she inhaled the dark vapor and grew suddenly rigid.

In another moment, she grew still, beset by a darkness that was much deeper than slumber.

*   *   *   *   *

Musings of the Harpist

Are we too late? Or even worse, do we travel in the wrong direction entirely, misguided by whim and hope away from any real prospect of success? What is the true path? Where does it end?

Are we three striving to save a lone Moonwell, while the surging seas of chaos and destruction batter against the full circumference of our shores? Or as I suspect, does our destiny involve far more than this single pond?

One thing above all else gives me hope—the growth of the Princess Alicia. In the year since I have seen her, she has come into full womanhood. She regards the challenge with the optimism of youth, and she will face each obstacle with fortitude.

I will do what I can to embellish this fortitude with wisdom.

❧ 6 ❧

A Moonwell Dying

As the first son of a young monarch, Brandon Olafsson stood one step removed from the kingship of Gnarhelm. Indeed, there were those among his people who whispered that he would make a better ruler than his father, Svenyird, ruler of the northmen occupying the rugged northern portion of that greatest island of the Moonshaes, Alaron. Brandon was young, of proven courage and keen wit. And no one could deny that the old king's step had slowed, his eyes grown cloudy and his brain, all too often, confused.

Yet Brand would have been the first to whip the speaker of such treason, for he was a loyal and trustworthy prince of these hardy seafaring people. He was content to champion his family, and, as his nation's most accomplished sailor, to sally forth on whatever missions his father might deem necessary.

For a long year, however, there had been no such journey. The young warrior had become irritable, feeling his skills growing stale, his muscles stiff. Though these afflictions occurred mainly within his mind, they were nonetheless real. To a young man, leader of a warlike people, times of peace were trying. Brandon—bigger, faster, and stronger than any of his countrymen—felt this tension more than most. He was a caged animal, restlessly pacing before his enclosing bars.

He had found some small amusement in hunting the great white bear of the northern coasts. Together with the other young men, he gathered to tell stories during the long hours of winter darkness and the slow spring awakening. Nevertheless, they had been seasons of almost maddening monotony for Brandon and his warrior kin.

Thus it was that when Sigurd the fisherman returned from a voyage that had taken him far beyond the sheltered waters of

Salmon Bay, frantically racing ashore and shouting an alarm, Brandon had been among the first to gather in his father's great lodge. Soon the rest of the warriors gathered, and the king had taken his great oaken throne, the chair that was cloaked in bearskins and stood beneath the head of the sea dragon Svenyird had slain in his younger days. Heavy beams supported the wood-shingled roof, and thick traces of smoke curled eternally among the rafters. This was a dark and sweat-stained place, a manly place.

The northmen waited impatiently as Sigurd cleared his throat, timing the opening of his tale with meticulous care.

"I set sail, near a fortnight hence now, to catch the salmon schools," Sigurd began, finally satisified that he had his audience's attention. "Followed the coast north, I did—but the gales! They came and they swept me from the bay! My friends, I fought those waves as our great king must once have struggled with yon sea dragon!"

The fisherman paused to allow his listeners to look at the mounted dragon head. He waited, allowing the heroic image to form in their minds.

"I ran before the storm—used nothin' more than a coupla scraps of canvas on my mast. Before I knew it, the rocks of the archipelago loomed ahead of me—gray death, as you all well know! But if I passed them, nothing but two thousand miles of ice-flecked water waited for me.

"Well, my brave friends, my choice was simple, and it was no choice at all. I ran for the lee side of one of them rockpiles and just managed to slip into a tiny cove. There, I tell you true, I thought my troubles were over!"

Once again Sigurd paused, his last words hanging in the air. Now the northmen leaned forward with almost palpable tension.

"I know the isle. So do many of you. We have kin there, and I thought sure someone would come to meet me. But no one did, and at last I set out to look around. Near to where I touched shore were several huts, and these I went to visit." Sigurd looked full into the eyes of the king.

"I approached with caution, sire, feeling the presence of a great evil lurking somewhere within the mist and fog," Sigurd explained carefully.

"Yes, man—tell the tale!" barked the king, sharing the tension that had spread about the room like a smoky incense.

"Strangely, the door of the hut stood open. I entered, calling aloud for one who might live there, but there was no answer."

Sigurd cast his pale eyes, set in the midst of a face weathered for many years by the lashing of the sea, around the room. The northmen's attention was rapt.

"Each of the houses, sire, I entered—and found no one. Finally I came upon a dwelling—I had previously thought it to be a pile of wreckage—and discovered charred timbers. Within, there were four bodies—a man, a woman, two children."

A growl passed around the lodge, rumbled from a hundred warlike hearts. Sigurd paused again, his expression smug.

"Well, my lord, caring little for my own safety, I pressed onward. I found another village—a dozen houses by a larger cove. These, too, were empty, several destroyed. I noticed other things, then. Their boats were still there, apparently at rest along the shore. When I looked closely, I found that the hull of each had been holed. They were useless!

"Here, too, I found bodies in the burned huts. But more—at one of them, I found these!"

Now Sigurd raised the pouch he had worn at his side throughout his tale. Reaching within, he pulled forth an object of steel and several circular shapes of bronze.

"A broken sword, sire—and see, here? The hilt bears the mark of Callidyrr!"

The growls surged upward in force, becoming hoarse cries of outrage. Some warriors stamped their feet, while others shouted their fury.

"Treachery!"

"Betrayal!"

"War!"

"Aye!" Sigurd continued, raising the bronze circles. He had one other bracelet, of gold, but that he would keep hidden from the eyes of all the others, knowing his king would claim it as his due if he but saw it.

The fisherman concluded with a dramatic flourish. "A neck torque and a warrior's bracelet. They bear the symbols of the Ffolk!"

Now Brandon of Gnarhelm stood on his feet. In his hand, he

held his keen steel axe, raised high over his head. "Northmen of Gnarhelm!" he cried. "We cannot let this treachery pass unavenged! Follow me to war! We shall take this butchery of the Ffolk and return it to Callidyrr tenfold!"

The rest of his words vanished, lost in the thunderous accolade of his warrior kin.

* * * * *

Earl Blackstone led them into the mountains on horseback, up a winding and rock-strewn trail. Alicia, Tavish, and Keane accompanied the nobleman and his second son, Sir Hanrald, as well as a squad of mounted men-at-arms. Sir Gwyeth, the elder son, had not ventured into the hall that morning. Alicia thought that the bluff knight still suffered from the humiliation of the previous night. In any event, she had not minded his absence in the slightest.

The day was chill, the sky leaden, but at least there was no rain.

"Why such protection?" Alicia had asked, indicating the dozen swordsmen.

"Gold," the earl replied simply. "It does strange things to men. Though we carry none with us, the effects of its presence in these hills cannot be ignored. The hills aren't safe from bandits now that there is wealth about."

"Besides," Hanrald added, with a gruff look at Keane, "despite my brother's boasts, a few trolls and the like remain at large in these hills."

"Yes, well—that bit of knowledge should keep me from slumbering in my saddle," Keane said, acknowledging the obscure apology. Alicia decided that perhaps Hanrald was not quite the boor that his brother was.

She rode beside the earl's son on the trail, and as the horses carried them easily along, she turned to him. "Your father told us in Callidyrr about the madman that came to your estate. I wonder—had he ever been seen around here before?"

Hanrald shook his gruff, black-maned head. "Not before that night. The raving fool was some dark sorcerer, I think. May the gods curse his . . ." He stopped suddenly. "Forgive me, Princess. I am not used to polite conversation."

"You don't offend me," Alicia told him. "I know, too, that your brother perished on that night."

"Aye. Currag and I had our differences, but he didn't deserve that! I believe it was the stranger's sorcery that drove him to his death!"

Alicia thought Hanrald's remark about his brother a curious one. She remembered the young noble's earlier answer. "You said he hadn't been seen before that night. Do you mean that he *was* seen prior to his arrival at the estate?"

"Indeed, Princess." Hanrald gave her a gruff smile. "In the cantrev itself—Blackstone, as we learned later. He shuffled along the main street and went into each of the taverns there. Got himself thrown out of each one, too!"

"What did he do to bring that about?"

"The same thing he did at Caer Blackstone—he threatened everyone with doom, told them they were all going to die. Called these miners 'corrupters of the land,' or some such nonsense. I don't know if you've seen the men and dwarves who work our mines, Lady, but they're a rough and snarly lot. Talking to them like that is asking for a beating, or worse."

"Did they? Beat him, that is—or just throw him into the street?" Alicia was curious about this mysterious stranger, and Hanrald seemed to know more about him than anyone else she had talked to.

"Kind of funny, that. From what I hear, no one hurt him— just 'encouraged' him to move on. You know, it never struck me before how odd that is, but some of those fellows would just as soon slit a man's throat as talk to him."

"Does anyone know where he came from?"

Hanrald shrugged. "Not as I've heard. I suppose he could have been a deranged hermit come down out of the mountains. The gods know that a solitary life up there, watching for trolls and firbolgs around every hill, would be enough to drive a man to madness!"

"Lady Princess," called Earl Blackstone, turning to look over his shoulder at her from his position at the lead of their column of horses. "I would speak with you if that meets your pleasure."

"Certainly, my lord." She turned to Hanrald. "Thank you. It sounds a most mysterious circumstance!"

"Aye—mysterious, and fatal," replied the young lord as Alicia's mare trotted forward to Blackstone's side.

"This whole block here is the Granite Ridge," the earl said, gesturing to a huge gray mass of rock that rose to their right and extended along the horizon like the backbone of some spiny lizard. The trail had gradually climbed away from the cantrev and the earl's estate.

All along the ridge, the riders saw the black mouths of tunnels, all leading toward the interior of the great block of stone.

"Where you found gold," Alicia added.

"Indeed." The memory obviously pleased the earl, and well it should, for the discovery of the yellow metal had made him the wealthiest man in the kingdom.

The trail took them around a great shoulder of the ridge, and all at once Alicia felt the onslaught of a great sadness, like a heavy cloak that fell across her shoulders, one that she was unable to shake free. She noticed at the same time that none of the tunnel mouths, with their rust-colored drool of tailings spilling downward in wide fan patterns, marked this face of the rock-studded landform. It looked oddly barren, in contrast to the heavily excavated slopes they had passed, yet Alicia knew that this was in fact its natural state.

Granite Ridge reached out, as if with a protectively curled arm, to wrap around a small pool of water in a narrow swale. Steep slopes, rocky but climbable, rose upward on three sides of the pond, while the trail approached from the fourth. Stunted cedars sprouted, apparently from solid stone, around the stagnant surface.

The path curved downward, over erosion-smoothed boulders, to the shore of the brackish-looking water. A small shelf of level ground surrounded the circular pond, though much of the shore was choked with bracken and willows.

"The Moonwell," breathed the princess. This was not the first of these once-sacred pools she had seen, but never had one affected her like this. She felt within her the birth of an almost hopeless sense of despair. The water lay placid, deathly still, the surface too dingy to reflect an image of the encircling rocky height. She saw a speckled pattern across the surface where weeds flourished in the liquid that had once been as sacred as the blood of the goddess herself.

"Not much to look at, is it?" inquired Blackstone gruffly.

"Ah—beauty lies not always on the surface of the view," Tavish pointed out.

"No, this surface seems to be mostly algae and other such scum," observed Keane dryly.

"Shhh!" Alicia, not knowing why, hissed for silence. The others ceased speaking, though the clopping hooves of the horses intruded loudly. Abruptly she looked at her companions, all of whom studied her curiously. The scrutiny annoyed her. There was something here. Perhaps the others didn't feel it, but she most certainly did.

"Let's dismount," she suggested, though they were still a hundred paces from the well.

The others obliged, though Blackstone bade his men-at-arms to remain astride their horses and alert some distance away from the princess and her party.

As if sensing that Alicia saw something they did not, Tavish and Keane held back as the princess started slowly toward the shore. Blackstone would have lumbered at her side, but the bard laid a restraining hand upon his arm and, with a scowl, he slowed his pace to remain with the pair.

Alicia noted other details: the perfection of the setting, with the bluff curled protectively around the pool; the symmetry of two waterfalls—little more than splashing rivulets, actually—that spilled toward the well, one from the right and the other from the left. Among the cedars, she noted a flat-topped stone arch, symbolic gate to this sacred place of the Earthmother's.

Once again the young princess tried, unsuccessfully, to shrug off the bleak feeling of sadness. The Moonwell seemed like an open wound, crying out for some kind of salve. In that instant, she knew that the mine could not be allowed to corrupt it.

Reverently she passed beneath the arch and approached the shore. The placid water swirled slightly as a gust of wind eddied in the circular valley, and then the surface fell still. Alicia walked until her boots rested on two low stones that jutted from the shore into the water. She couldn't see the bottom through the murky stuff, though it must have been a mere foot or two deep here.

She stood there in silence for some time. It might have been hours, though more likely only a few minutes passed. She felt herself drawn deeper and deeper into the *soul* of the water before her.

"Lady Princess, what do you see?" Blackstone couldn't help himself. He clumped forward on the rocks to stand at her side, not waiting for her to answer his question. "The vein of gold extends at least through that height . . . there." He pointed to the shoulder on their right.

Suddenly Alicia had a picture of those tunnel mouths, dripping tailings down the slope, into the well. She immediately understood the desecration that would be.

"The well must be preserved," she said quietly, turning to look at the earl.

Blackstone's dark eyebrows came together in such a ferocious scowl that his anger felt like a slap across her face—and that, too, was an abomination in the sacred place of holiness and peace.

"You can't be *serious!*" he insisted. "It's *dead! Look* at it, for the sake of the gods and the Ffolk! It stands here useless, while above it lies gold, millions of coins worth!"

"Enough!" Alicia barked her command, not in her role as a princess but in the voice of something deeper, more abiding. It was a power that filled her words, as proved by Blackstone, who blinked, biting back his anger, and held his tongue.

Abruptly a wave of weariness swept over Alicia, and she staggered on the rocks. She would have fallen but for the arm of Tavish as the bard reached out and helped her back to the dry shore.

"What is it, child? What happened?" asked the older woman, her voice soft and concerned.

Alicia looked at her and at Keane in wonder. "I don't know. . . . Something, a feeling, came over me—a knowledge that this place is still important."

"For the sake of the gods, *why?*" demanded the earl, his fury once again forcing him to speak. In his mind, he saw a stream of gold flowing away from him, just out of his reach.

"Perhaps you should leave her for a while," Keane suggested, his voice low.

The earl whirled on him, and for a moment, the full force of his fury threatened to explode against the thin tutor. Then something—perhaps the memory of Gwyeth's humiliation at Keane's hand—gripped his tongue. Still furious, he stomped away from the trio at the edge of the pool.

"Thanks—thank you both," Alicia said. She felt shockingly weak, as drained as if she had just undergone a long and arduous training session with horses or arms.

"Now, tell us, what did you see?" Tavish persisted. Alicia noticed that the bard's eyes flared brightly, as from the heat of some private excitement.

"Nothing—not really. I didn't *see* anything, but I had a feeling here. First, of sadness—a sadness so bleak that I feared my heart would break. Then when I approached the water, it was as though I heard a soft voice counseling me, warning me. I *knew* that it would be wrong to let any harm come to this well!"

"I fear yonder earl does not share your conviction," murmured Keane, with a sidelong glance at Blackstone. The earl had rejoined his men-at-arms and now glowered darkly at the trio on the shore of the pool. His son Hanrald said something to the earl, but the noble brusquely gestured the younger man away.

Alicia looked up in alarm. "He *must not* destroy the Moonwell! We—*I*—have to make him understand and obey me."

"It won't be easy," Keane observed. "The king has already given him virtual agreement to go ahead with his plans. Remember the meeting in Callidyrr?"

"Agreement pending the approval of King Tristan's envoy—of me!"

"He may dispute that, claiming that the envoy was originally announced as the queen."

"She would understand. My mother would know if she could but come here!" Alicia exclaimed. "But even without her presence, I don't believe Blackstone would disobey an order backed by the authority of the High Crown of the Isles!"

"Shall we make our way back to the manor or give the earl the good news right away?" wondered the tutor.

Alicia thought for a moment. "Neither. A delay of a day or two will not harm our purpose, and I would spend some time beside this pool." She looked at the sky, which, though still gray, did not show the heavy darkness of impending rain.

"My friends," she said, looking back and forth from Tavish to Keane. "I wish to stay here through the day and the night. Will you remain here beside me?"

Tavish chuckled. "Your mother's daughter, that you are! Why spend the night in a comfortable lodge, with cooked food and a warm bed, when a mattress of the goddess's own boulders beckons? Of course I'll stay."

Alicia thanked the bard and turned to look at the tall young mage. She was surprised by how much she wanted him to agree. For some reason, she realized, Keane made her feel surprisingly safe—not because of any warlike prowess, but for his alert mind and his steady presence. And, too, his display against Gwyeth had been impressively effective. While she knew that, as princess, she could command him to stay, that felt like a very unsatisfactory alternative to her.

Keane cleared his throat awkwardly. "Outside? Well, for one night, I suppose I could manage. . . . Do you suppose we could ask the earl to send up some food?"

"And bedrolls, too," laughed Alicia, suddenly relieved.

"Surely you wish me to leave men to guard you!" objected the earl, after Alicia had explained her intent.

"That won't be necessary." The princess felt that the absence of Earl Blackstone's swordsmen would enhance her security far more than their presence.

Grumbling something under his breath about scatterbrained girls, he finally agreed to send up food, wine, and some furs for sleeping. He rode away at the head of his guardsmen, and Alicia watched them until the winding trail carried them out of sight. Only then, and despite the stagnant water and the high, barren rocks looming overhead, did she feel the first stirrings of peace descend over the Moonwell and its little vale.

* * * * *

Once again the cloaked stranger came to Blackstone Manor in the dark of night, and though the man had been many miles away in Callidyrr that very day, the earl did not question his means of transport. He met him alone, in the privacy of his personal chamber. Even his sons would not know of this dark, nocturnal visitor.

"The younger sister, I believe, will be pliant to our will," said the newcomer, speaking from beneath his drooping hood.

"Good," growled Blackstone. "The older one is going to be trouble." He told of Alicia's intransigence in the exploitation of the well.

"She *is* an obstacle," agreed the dark one. "But such obstacles can be overcome."

Blackstone glowered, his eyebrows meeting in a bushy ridge of darkness over his eyes. He stared, as if his gaze would penetrate that cloth enclosing the serenely hooded figure. "What do you mean?" he asked carefully.

"You couldn't have arranged the situation better had you planned it. Of course, no harm can be offered the girl—not while she is your guest. But has she not herself foresworn your hospitality tonight?"

"Indeed." The earl continued to study the cloaked figure.

"In fact, you tell me she declined your offer of a protective escort—guards to keep her safe against such threats as lurk in the hills."

"Aye—and those threats are real, but they do not materialize at my beck and call. And I cannot risk sending some of my own men, however well disguised. What we speak of is treason against the family of a very mighty High King. The loyalty of even my most trusted sergeants would be strained by such a task."

"There is another way." Now the hooded man leaned forward, clasping his hands over his knees. They extended from the sleeves of his robe, and Blackstone saw that they were slender and frail, almost womanly. The blue of veins showed through the pale skin.

"Continue," said the earl quietly.

"You remember, I am certain, the choice portions of iron and steel I have claimed from you these past years?"

"Aye . . . and gold aplenty, too!"

The stranger laughed mirthlessly. "Even gold. All of these are materials that have enabled me to complete a task."

"What task is this?"

"There is a thing I have made—an iron golem. It is completed, hidden in a cave in the hills not far from here—and not far from the Moonwell."

"What is it? What can it do?"

"It is a mighty creature, more powerful than a dozen giants. It is immune to weapons and capable of killing with a single blast of steaming breath. But more than this, it is capped with the horned helmet of the northmen. It will be taken, by whoever sees it, as a great icon of the raiders, sent to inflict harm upon the Ffolk."

Blackstone scowled more fiercely than ever. "Why should I seek war with the northmen? My manor sits astride the border with Gnarhelm. We would be the first to feel the scourge of battle!"

The deep hood shook slowly back and forth. "There need not be war, but there will be suspicion. If the golem continues its rampage, perhaps destroying one of your own mine shacks, that suspicion will fall away from you. The princess will be an unfortunate casualty to an arcane threat, that is all."

"Can this . . . creature accomplish this task tonight?"

"It is not a creature. It is a *thing*, created by myself!" snapped the visitor somewhat peevishly. "And, yes—within two hours of my leaving you, it can reach the Moonwell."

Blackstone sat back and looked upward, uncomfortable. He contemplated doing a thing he recognized as monstrous treachery. Though he had always been ambitious, he had come to his position honestly—by an accident of birth, true, but nonetheless the earldom of Blackstone was rightly his.

Now, with the failure of crop after crop of the Ffolk's harvest, the wealth of his holdings had made him foremost in influence among the king's advisers. This position was his, regardless of the activities of tonight.

Yet deep within himself, the Earl of Fairheight admitted that he wanted more . . . much, *much* more. This princess of Callidyrr, a mere babe, would stand in the path of his ambition, and his anger seethed.

And, the truth be known, Blackstone worried more about escaping the blame for his treason than he did about any moral qualms of his action. This concern was mollified by the promises and the plans made by the hooded visitor whose name the earl had never learned. Yet always before, the man's counsel had proved profitable. Had he not been the one who had first encouraged him to begin the excavations in Granite Ridge?

"Very well," he grunted, in the end reaching the decision that had been inevitable. "Go now and awaken your golem."

* * * * *

"This is the place," suggested the one-eyed pirate called Kaffa.

"Right you are," agreed Larth, for the isolated coastal farmstead matched up perfectly with the map given to the two outlaws by the nameless cleric.

Indeed, a brief search revealed Kaffa's longship, concealed amid a dense coastal thicket. A sail was carefully furled alongside the mast, and the ship was provisioned with food and water for a long voyage, as well as an assortment of fine steel weapons.

"As soon as the tide's high, we can put out to sea," muttered the grizzled, one-eyed northman with a snap of his fingers. He pointed to the prow of the sleek-hulled vessel. "Aye, and look: She's got a right proper name, at that!"

"The *Vulture*," read Larth. "She'll carry you to some ripe carrion, I'll bet!"

Kaffa gestured to the mast, where a triple-bolted image of lightning, made of steel, was fastened. "And here's our proof against sorcery," he noted, well pleased.

Already the coastal towns of Callidyrr seemed to beckon the piratical captain, offering the promise of plunder and other amusing diversions to the unscrupulous captain and his crew. The ship was long and sleek, easily capable of carrying a seventy-man complement.

"And here," added Larth, a few minutes later. "This will outfit a steadfast company of knights." He had discovered the barn where the unnamed cleric had collected armor and weapons, as well as horses, for Larth's thirty-man company. Heading north, Larth knew, they would soon enter the kingdom of Gnarhelm, and there they would act out their part as invaders from the south.

"The guy gave me the spooks," admitted Kaffa, reflecting on the robed priest who had collected them, given them their orders, and then paid them. "But he's got his organization down pat. He had everything here we could possibly need!"

"Aye," agreed Larth. "And not poor horseflesh, either."
The veteran rider had just completed an inspection of his war-
horses. "These steeds would do a king's guard proud!"

"All right, then!" Kaffa chortled. "We'll sail with the dawn
to make war on the Ffolk!"

"And we ride at the same time to invade the north!" added
Larth with a grin.

Then the two men bellowed their laughter, delighted, as if
they had just made a great joke.

* * * * *

From the Log of Sinioth:

*It is with a feeling approaching disbelief that I speak the
command words. Breathlessly I await the results, watching.
And then it moves! It rises!*

*It is the child of five years' labor, but now the child looms
high over the parent. Like a gargantuan of destruction, it
leaves this lair—this sheltered cave where I have so carefully
crafted it over this half decade—and marches into the night.*

*Go now, mighty slave, and do the bidding of your master!
Stalk your royal prey beside the once-sacred pool. There you
shall slake your thirst—and there will Talos begin his climb to
ultimate mastery!*

❧ 7 ❧

A Golem of Iron

"Gather the tribes!"

"War—there must be war!"

The cries of hatred and rage resounded through the lodge of King Svenyird Olafsson as the northmen decried the treacherous attack on the island of their kin. None questioned the perpetrators as other than the Ffolk.

Finally, however, the king raised a hand. The rumbling in the great, smoke-filled lodge died away as these savage seamen waited to hear what their monarch would say.

"Know you all, as do I—for most of our history, the Ffolk have been our implacable enemies. In the wars between us, quarter has not been asked nor given. I myself earned my first battle scars in raids against the west coast of Alaron!"

A chorus of assenting cries, muttered in unison, echoed the king's words.

"But for these past two decades, there has been no war between northman and Ffolk. Their king seemed to my father an honorable man." All knew it had been King Olaf himself who had represented Gnarhelm in the treaty talks with the new High King within a year after Tristan had assumed the mantle of rulership over his people.

"And King Kendrick still reigns, and reigns well. What cause should he have now to break this accord—an accord which he labored so hard, together with my kinsman Grunnarch the Red, King of Norland, to bring about?"

No man could supply a satisfactory answer.

"But the proof!" cried one.

"A talisman of the Ffolk, found at the scene of butchery!" Brandon, son of King Svenyird, shouted his own accusation. "There is no other explanation!"

"Ah, my son. As always, you are ready to lead my men to war. This is as it should be. But first you must gain the blessings of old men such as myself, and I am not yet prepared to concede that the High King of Moonshae has done us wrong."

"But would you have us absorb the hurts like old women?" Brandon demanded, angry.

"Do not forget yourself in your rage," his father admonished, and the strapping war leader bowed his head in apology.

"Forgive me, sire."

"You are forgiven. But this matter needs debate and investigation, not unproven accusations and wild plans for vengeance."

"But how?" Another gray-bearded veteran, known as Knaff the Elder, now shouted his objection. "What more proof can we gain? Do we ask our enemies for explanation?"

"Our *former* enemies!" barked King Svenyird. "I remind you all that most of the warriors in this council today were but beardless youths when our last war with the Ffolk reached its conclusion."

"What, then?" cried another warrior, hulking Wultha, who, like Knaff and the king, was old enough to remember those wars. Wultha's nose, broken in battle, was flattened across his face. "Surely we must do *something.*"

"Indeed we shall. It is my intent to send an ambassador to Callidyrr, one who knows the ways of war in the event of treachery. He will take a party of men but approach the throne of the High King in peace. He will present our evidence and demand an accounting."

"But it may be a trap!" shouted Knaff. "You could be sending your man to his death!"

"I will make no command. The warlord I name shall be free to accept or decline. If he accepts, he shall know the risk, though I venture it would take more than a simple ambush to place the noose of death around his neck."

"Who? Name the man!" The questions, the cries came pouring forth from the mass of northmen.

Brandon knew the answer, and he stood as his father's old eyes came to rest—with tenderness and pride, the young man thought—on the face of his son.

"Brandon Olafsson, Prince of Gnarhelm, will you accept my

commission as ambassador and journey in peace to the palace in Callidyrr, there to call upon the High King in such manner as we have discussed?"

The young warrior's pulse pounded, and his face flushed with pride. "I will hasten to do as you command, sire. If the Ffolk be honorable, I shall return in peace." He paused, bowing, before he continued with the words that he knew that warriors among his people wanted him to speak.

"But if there be treachery among them, I shall make them regret their betrayal tenfold, a hundredfold, even if it means that I must shed the blood of the High King himself!"

The king sat back in his fur-lined chair, an expression of satisfaction on his gray-bearded face. Brandon's own mind soared, inflamed and encouraged by the accolades ringing from the throats of his countrymen.

* * * * *

Alicia stirred restlessly beneath the heavy bearskin that served as her bedroll. Finally she abandoned all thought of sleep, rising to pace about their small camp. She, Keane, and Tavish had made a sleeping place in a flat clearing among the boulders a hundred feet from the shore of the dead Moonwell.

Now, as the moth is drawn to the light, she felt herself compelled to approach that once-sacred water.

Why had she wished so strongly to sleep here tonight? The question nagged at her, for she had no idea as to the answer—and yet it had been a very compelling desire indeed. Her two companions had seemed to sense this, for both of them seemed more relaxed and comfortable here than they had been when surrounded by the hospitality of Blackstone's hearth and table.

She looked at the water, wondering if she saw a trace of its phosphorescent glow. Her mother had told her that, in Robyn's youth, all of the Moonwells had glowed in darkness with a soft white light widely taken as proof of the benign presence of the goddess. It saddened her now to look at this brackish pond, clearly outlined before her in its circular frame of the boulder-lined shore.

But why could she see it at all? The night was inky dark

around her. Heavy overcast covered the clouds, totally obscuring the moon that somehow she knew waned into its third quarter. That, too, seemed odd. She hadn't seen the moon in weeks, perhaps months, yet within her mind, she had a very clear picture of the exact stage of its phase.

Alicia approached the pond, her feet stepping surely past unseen rocks, until she found a large boulder near the water's edge that would serve as a comfortable seat. She looked upon the Moonwell with a sense of wonder. It *did* glow, very softly.

Lost in meditation, she didn't hear movement behind her. Suddenly she gasped in alarm.

"I didn't mean to startle you," Keane said, almost whispering, "but the night is so still I didn't wish to break the silence."

Alicia moved, making room for him on the rock. "Can you see it?" she asked, indicating the well.

"Yes."

"Is it a miracle?" she asked wonderingly.

Keane laughed, very softly. "There are things in the earth—ores, and minerals—that will emit such a glow when they are properly mixed. The effect has been known to occur in nature. That, I believe, is what we see here."

"An accident of nature? Or perhaps the workings of the goddess."

"Would that it were," he said. "But if the mightiest druids in the land haven't felt her presence in two decades, I doubt that a warrior princess would come upon that discovery here, in the midst of a dark night." Nevertheless, even as he spoke, Keane's voice sounded less sure.

"Tell me," he said, after a brief pause, "why was it so important to you that we remain out here tonight?"

"I don't kno—yes, I do. It was this *water*, the Moonwell. I looked upon it and I didn't want to leave."

"You've seen Moonwells before. Isn't the one in the moors beyond Callidyrr a favorite picnic spot of yours? Have you ever felt such a thing before?"

"Never." Alicia was certain of the answer. The compulsion that had drawn her here was unique in her experience. She sensed that Keane looked at her strangely. "Do I puzzle you, O wise tutor?" she asked, laughing softly. "Well, I puzzle myself as well!"

"Indeed, Princess." The man's voice was strangely hesitant, in a way she had never noticed before.

With a shocking realization, Alicia felt an abrupt awareness of Keane as a man, here beside her in this place of serenity. She liked that feeling but was vaguely frightened by it as well. Disturbed, she lowered her eyes, afraid of what he might see there even in the dark.

And yet the emotion she felt most strongly was a small inkling of delight, of a sweet discovery that came unexpectedly into her life. He did not seem so old now. Indeed, of what real significance were the eight years between them?

At the same time, Alicia realized that she genuinely cared for this man more than any other person outside her family. She trusted him, and his presence made her happy.

Did he think the same thoughts?

Keane stiffened suddenly. "What's that?"

Alicia, her mind wandering, looked at the tutor in annoyance. "What do you mean? What's what?"

Offending her still further, he placed a hand to her mouth to gently silence her. She knocked his arm aside, ready to object, when she heard the noise, too.

"It's coming closer," Keane whispered.

They heard a heavy clank, like a knight in plate mail walking across the rocky ground. Yet the noise was too deep, too resonant to come from plate mail. It was a metal thing that must have been much larger. Like the crash of a great gong, the sound rang through the darkness with vibrancy and power.

"There!" Keane sprang to his feet, staring into the darkness.

Alicia gasped, for she saw something moving along the shore on the other side of the pool. The faint glow cast the object in a soft shade of green, and she saw that it was huge—and it moved, though with an artificial kind of gait, like a poorly controlled puppet.

"A giant!" she gasped.

"*Illuminatus mio!*" barked the tutor. He raised a hand, gesturing to the ground before the looming figure's feet.

A cool wash of brilliance erupted, as if the rocks themselves became crystal lanterns housing wicks of bright, steady flame. The shore, the camp, the well, even the walls of the small valley, stood sharply etched in light. In the midst of it all, the two humans could only stare in shock at the apparition that towered some fifteen feet into the air.

"It's not a giant!" Keane gasped, appalled. "It's metal—a thing made by man!"

Alicia couldn't comprehend a power that could make and animate something so supremely horrifying. The object had the vague outlines of a man, walking upon two legs, with a pair of massive arms swinging at its sides. Atop its metal shoulders rested a round head, with bolted plates forming the grotesque caricature of a mouth and eyes.

A great horned helm capped its iron visage, a helm such as Alicia had seen on some of the northmen warriors who came regularly to Callidyrr. The monstrous thing looked like a giant clad in head-to-foot plate mail, though it moved with a jerking, mechanical efficiency that resembled no living thing.

A huge leg stretched forward, kicking one of the cedars into splinters. The other swung, knocking a boulder out of the way, shattering another rock from the weight of its monstrous step. Huge strides carried the clanking object around the shore of the pond straight toward them.

Desperately Alicia looked toward Keane. He gazed at the monstrosity in stupefied horror, his mouth open. The woman felt for her sword. She had left it beside the saddle up at the camp. She almost laughed aloud at the picture in her mind—her small form bashing the steel blade against this unfeeling colossus until the edge was dented and dull. Suddenly giddy, the princess knew that it was fear that consumed her, threatening to overcome her capacity for reason. The giant loomed overhead, sightless eyes staring past her. She saw the gaping slash of its mouth, the dull red of some internal heat reflecting there.

Alicia felt Keane's hand on her arm. The man had recovered his wits, and now he pulled her from the rock where they had been sitting. The princess stumbled and felt his fingers digging into her flesh, lifting her and pulling her. "Ouch!" she shouted, suddenly furious with him. Moments later, a nearby rock exploded, crushed to gravel by the thing's powerful kick. Stinging shards bit into Alicia's back.

"Run! By the goddess, *run!*" Keane gasped, propelling her

forward, placing himself protectively behind her.

Run she did, blindly scrambling away from the horror. She stumbled and cracked her knee against a rock, she twisted an ankle when she fell a second time, but still she desperately fled, racing away from the well toward the place where they had spread their bedrolls.

For a moment, she remembered Tavish, still sleeping there. The crunching footsteps pursued, slowly but inevitably. She couldn't lead the thing to the bard!

"Tavish!" she shouted, darting to the side, following along the shore of the Moonwell. "Be silent, but *flee!*"

Alicia spun, seeking Keane against the silhouetting effects of the magical illumination. Surely he could do *something!*

Her heart churned in deep panic. She couldn't see Keane anywhere in the small, bowl-shaped vale.

"*Precantos—nimbus. Tu-arlist!*"

There! Suddenly she saw his tall figure, standing like a tree some distance away, shouting strange sounds. Alicia realized, with sharp guilt, that Keane had turned to face the colossal attacker at the same time as she had veered away from the camp, and she hadn't noticed until now that he did not follow her!

The illumination of the light spell still flared, casting its glare across the sloping ground between the iron creature and Keane, uphill slightly from the colossus. The earth there, as everywhere in this little vale, was a mass of jutting boulders and cracked stone.

Keane's magic struck the stones, not with the sudden violence of explosive force but with the slow power of fundamental transformation. The solid nature of the boulders was seized by magic, distorted and adjusted into something much softer, even liquid.

Alicia stared, amazed, as she saw the rocks begin to change shape, oozing flat as if they were soft, doughy mounds, flowing like thick sludge. The rocks melted away, running downhill as thick, brown goop, viscous and soupy. In moments, the area between Keane and the iron beast had become a gooey morass. The tutor's presence taunted the monster, drawing it deeper into the mud.

The sticky stuff flowed around the iron beast's legs, and Alicia saw the gigantic form sink slowly to its waist. It struggled forward, flailing with its powerful arms, splashing gouts of mud with fists that were greater than monstrous hammers. All around them, the rockfield seethed and bubbled, a quagmire. The mud sucked greedily, smacking around the torso and then the shoulders of the animated metal thing.

Finally Alicia saw only its horrible head, capped with the wide, horned helm, and the upward-reaching arms. Then, despite the beast's frantic grasping and thrashing, even these disappeared. Only a thick, bubbling swirl in the sticky surface remained to mark the place where the golem had disappeared.

"Keane!" the princess shouted, stunned and disbelieving. She sobbed and laughed at the same time. "How did you—?"

"*Quiet!*" he snapped, his tone harsher than she had ever heard. She froze, watching as he pointed at the slowly flowing mass.

"*Igneous—layoka!*" he barked.

In that same instant, the movement stopped, and Alicia looked with amazement at a flat expanse of stone, sloping gently toward the water, its surface marked by irregular ripples and folds of odd patterns, but no mark indicating where the iron thing had vanished.

Stepping quietly, Alicia moved back toward the magic-user. Her knees wobbled as she felt the reaction to the shock, and she reached out to steady herself against a rock. She saw Keane standing still, listening carefully.

The rock beneath her hand gave her the first clue when it shook, vibrating in her grip. Sound followed shortly thereafter, a dull rumble that bespoke mighty conflict within the earth itself. Then a crash like thunder echoed in the small valley, and the slab of rock that had so recently formed exploded upward and outward in a shower of stinging fragments and acrid, bitter dust.

A hole gaped in the rippled surface, and in its depths, something moved. The shape crushed and battered the rock, widening the aperture and slowly freeing itself from its tomb of solid rock.

Alicia screamed, not hearing the sound but instead feeling the release of mindless terror. The iron monster still lived—it still *attacked!*

Shaking off rock that had fused around its limbs, the monstrosity bashed with its anvil-sized fists, crushing and widening the hole around it. One arm wrenched to the side as the metal monstrosity climbed upward, and then the twisted limb hung motionless, obviously damaged. But the lone workable hand proved quite capable of bashing away the chunks of enclosing rock.

Another earthshaking rumble wracked the ground as the creature cracked free one leg. Pulling upward, the epicenter of a shower of stone shards, the clanking form lifted itself from the hole, grabbing with its one good hand and lumbering free onto the slab of once-molten stone.

The huge head swiveled back and forth with a dull, creaking sound, as if those steel eyes could see and now searched for prey. Indeed, the view came to rest against Keane, who had stumbled slowly backward as the monster worked itself free of the stone.

The iron mouth gaped, a black hole against the dark plate. A blast of white gas erupted, belching toward Keane. The princess saw the man fall backward on the ground, his body abruptly, unnaturally rigid. The hulking form lumbered closer.

The next sound that ripped through the night jarred Alicia's taut nerves. A shrieking wail rent the air. The noise seemed metallic somehow, as of a great sheet of plate mail ripped across the teeth of many grinding blades.

A surge pulsed in the light spell that still glowed near the shore, and Alicia saw movement there. Tavish! The bard held her harp before her, striking it roughly with her hand. Once again the piercing dissonance jarred their nerves.

Slowly the great head of the iron creature pivoted, coming to rest upon Tavish as Keane still lay immobile before the monster. Alicia held her breath. Would the colossus turn from its helpless victim? Silently she crept forward, trying to reach the magic-user without attracting the attention of the towering mass of iron.

Metal creaked as the monster turned toward the bard, who once again drew the piercing sound from her strings. A great leg stepped toward her, and then another. Keane lay, forgotten for the moment, in the long, menacing shadow.

Alicia darted to his side as the animated metal lumbered

away with surprising speed. She saw Tavish turn and run, her harp bouncing against her back, dangling precariously by its leather strap as she scrambled to escape. The harpist used a long staff to help pick her way through the scattered rocks. She started around the shore of the pond, away from Keane and Alicia. Now the huge form of her pursuer cast long shadows across the bard, outlined by the flaring light of Keane's spell.

"Keane!" Alicia hissed, kneeling beside him, trying to control her panic. "Come on—you've got to get up. We've got to run!"

He blinked at her, the first sign that he still lived. His body lay in that rigid position, his back arched so tightly that it didn't rest upon the ground. Alicia watched in horror as his face began to turn blue.

She smelled an acrid odor and remembered the cloud of gas that had spouted from the monster's maw. Had Keane breathed some of the deadly stuff?

His chest! She saw that he did not breathe, and at the same time, Alicia remembered a thing her mother had taught her. Not all druidical arts stemmed from the magic of the goddess, and now she leaned over the dying man, using a worldly, not arcane, skill. Forcing his clenched jaws apart required all the strength of her arms and hands, spurred on by her desperation.

Finally she took a deep breath and leaned over him, pressing her lips to his. Forcefully she exhaled, feeling his chest rise beneath her hand. She pressed downward, forcing the air from his lungs. Then she repeated the procedure, and again.

Abruptly Keane gagged and coughed, expelling the air by the convulsion of his own body. He pulled in great, tearing breaths, though each seemed to cause further coughing and choking. He doubled over in misery, kneeling on the ground and retching.

"Come on!" Alicia cried, tugging at his arm.

"Wait," Keane gasped weakly, peering across the reflective surface of the Moonwell.

They saw Tavish running, scrambling around the perimeter of the pond. She pushed her way through the brambles along the shore, carrying the staff of ash, using it to help maintain her balance in the treacherous terrain. The bard had made it more than halfway around the pond, leading the monster in a wide circle, but fatigue played a role now as Tavish stumbled frequently and leaned on the staff for support.

Keane suddenly whipped around, taking Alicia's arms in a firm grip. "Flee, Lady Princess—you must! We will keep the thing's notice, but you must escape!"

For a moment, his request beckoned before her like a bright, hopeful beacon, but in the next instant, she knew that she couldn't desert her friends. "No—can't you *do* something? Cast a spell?"

She thought at first he would curse her, so intense was his expression of frustration. He clenched his teeth, almost snarling, and turned back to the pool. Tavish had almost circled the well, and now it seemed that the monster drew steadily closer to the bard with each lumbering step.

Keane ran toward the bard, Alicia at his side. Tavish, they saw as they reached her, staggered from weariness, her face flushed red, her breath coming in ragged gasps. The monster loomed over them, one arm hanging twisted and limp but the other raised menacingly, ready to crush to a pulp any mere flesh found in its path.

"*Incendrius carneto!*"

Once again Keane's voice barked across the still valley. Alicia held her breath, watching a tiny globule of fire pop from his fingertip and float through the air in a deceptively gentle flight until it reached the hulking form of iron.

Then it erupted into an orange blossom of flame, its hot illumination dwarfing the light spell that still glowed among the rocks. Crackling fingers of fire encircled the colossus, grasping it in a searing embrace. The fireball expanded, engulfing the great metal shape until it vanished within the hellish sphere, flames spewing upward like a hungry, growing blossom of death.

For several seconds, the spell blazed. Alicia and Keane felt its heat on their faces as they helped Tavish limp to a flat rock, where she collapsed. Like the seething heart of a volcano, the fireball flared, a perfect circle towering toward the clouds, obscuring all within its infernal center.

"Look! The monster still comes!" Alicia whispered the

words in horror, knowing that Keane could see the black shape emerge from the flame as well as she could. "But how could it stand that heat?"

"Not only withstand it—look, the spell *aids* the monster! See there? The damaged arm?" Keane pointed, and Alicia understood immediately. The mangled limb of the statue, torn as it burst free of the rock, now flexed whole and unmarred.

"*Bulterus!*"

Again Keane barked a spell, and Alicia leaped backward as this time a bolt of crackling lightning exploded from his outstretched arm. Like a giant spear, it sizzled through the air, crushing with explosive force into the monster's chest.

"Look! You stopped it!" Alicia shouted, but then she saw that she was mistaken. The statue stumbled backward under the impact of the blow and shook its head slowly, as if trying to dispel a sense of grogginess. It stepped closer to them again, and though its step seemed less sure, not as quick as before, still it lurched inevitably forward.

"Quick! Get to the horses!" the princess urged, trying to help Tavish to her feet. The bard only groaned and slumped back onto the rock.

"I—I can't move," she gasped, her face flushed and perspiring. "Go—both of you! Go without me!"

"Damn!" Keane snapped, but he didn't leave her side. Alicia saw the white staff that Tavish had leaned on. The bard had dropped it when she slumped to the rock. The iron colossus again loomed over them, but Tavish seemed to lack even the strength to stand.

Desperate for any hope, the princess picked up the shaft of wood and darted toward the lumbering statue. It still lurched unsteadily, as if the lightning bolt had stunned it, forced it to move with the sluggishness of a serpent beset by cold.

"Alicia, don't!" cried her teacher in a voice taut with fear.

But his words came too late, nor would they have changed her course had she heard them sooner. The thing still moved slowly, as if every step required the focus of all its energies. Alicia thrust the stave between the monster's legs as it took a step along the shore of the pool.

The metal being abruptly seemed to break free of whatever lingering restraints remained from Keane's spell. A heavy foot of bolted iron kicked out sharply, striking Alicia in the shoulder. Bones snapped and hot streams of agony exploded through the woman's side. Her arm twisted behind her back, a limp and useless member. Alicia cried out in pain, her scream piercing as she felt herself cast through the air like a rag doll to land, with a chill splash, in the brackish waters of the Moonwell.

The staff twisted under the force of the monster's gait, and for a brief moment, the iron beast paused, as if the lone pole had somehow snared its feet. One end of the rod dropped, touching the surface of the water.

It seemed to Alicia as she struck the water that daylight burst around them with explosive speed, so bright was the illumination that surged upward from the waters of the well, outlining the black and rusty form of the statue in purest white. It was a brilliance that seemed to etch every tiny pebble, every branch of cedar, and each blade of withered grass in acute detail. The light surged upward, higher and higher, into a great column beaming into the night sky, clearly reflecting from the overhanging clouds as if dawn had come early to the Fairheight Mountains.

The beast of iron, bound by light, twisted in visible desperation. Alicia heard a sharp crackling sound as of lightning striking nearby, and then the great metal form toppled into the Moonwell, splashing a huge shower of the milky, glowing water from the pool. The colossus twitched and slowly grew still, lying in the shallows with much of its twisted form above the surface of the water.

Then the liquid—or was it the pain?—closed over Alicia, and she saw no more.

Musings of the Harpist

Within the cycles of birth and death, of winter and summer, of victory and defeat, all things know the Balance. The forces of good and evil remain opposed and taut, and it is this tension that provides support for gods and mortals, for all those who can know the difference between light and dark and can freely choose one or the other.

And if the gods know the cycles of life and the end of life, they also know that the Balance is eternal and that the end of life is no more than the prelude to a new beginning.

So it is with a tiny spark of vitality, the birthing of a new presence, the remanifestation of the great goddess, the Earthmother. Her life has lain dormant for a mere blink of an eye by immortal standards, but this was time enough for great changes to wrack her once-vital body and for a terrible rot to set in, a wasting illness that threatens to complete the task of her death for all time.

The spark of vitality may have been kindled by a mighty staff, once the talisman of the Great Druid herself. Or it may have come from the faith of a young princess, who believed that she beheld the divine might of the goddess in the waters of her well. It may even have originated from the great and arcane power represented by the iron golem, a power that had been fused to the well through the accidental falling of the staff.

Perhaps most likely, the rebirth results from all these things, and more . . . the gradual return of a people to a way of worship that had faded with their mothers, the prayers rendered in the name of the goddess . . . and even the great wheel of the Balance, coming slowly around to the place where a fresh life could begin.

Whatever the source, the effects are real. I have been witness to a miracle, and I know that my life will not be the same.

♥ 8 ♥

Stirrings

The High Queen lay still, her face a pallid white, so pale it seemed that no blood lay behind the skin, no vitality could ever again grace those closed, unseeing eyes. Only the slow rise and fall of the sheets indicated that the woman lived and breathed.

Deirdre stood over her mother, looking down at the queen and wondering why she found it so difficult to feel sorrow or pity. She knew that these would be proper reactions, yet when she was purely honest with herself, she admitted that she did not feel them. Instead, it was an emotion more like scorn that she felt for Robyn as she beheld her mother's weakened condition and understood her helplessness.

This scorn was coupled with a private but very fierce sense of delight that pulsed through her body. For the first time in her life, she was mistress of the castle! Now that joy thrilled her, threatening to break out upon her face, in her posture and words. Quickly she left the room, not wanting to give the nurses cause to whisper.

The princess hastened to the library, where she could unshackle her emotions without fear of interruption or discovery. Barring the door behind her, Deirdre crossed to the window, staring into the darkness.

Would he come to her tonight? With a shiver of delight, she knew that he would. She no longer questioned her certainty. The truth came like a vision of the future to her, and she accepted it as the gift that it was.

And it was *he* who had shown her that truth and that gift! Now Deirdre paced restlessly around the library, cursing the need for silence. It would not do for the servants to hear the king's younger daughter about at this hour!

She wondered again why he would not come to her chambers, but instead insisted upon meeting her here, in this room of dusty tomes and potent, arcane scrolls. Yet of that he had been adamant, claiming that his powers could only bring him to the place where he had first seen her. Although the explanation made a certain kind of sense, something suggested to Deirdre that there must be another reason, but she couldn't guess what it might be.

Then the familiar shape floated in the air, and in the next instant, he stood before her, his hood thrown back, his blond hair gleaming like spun gold in the light of the lone candle.

"My love!" she cried, mindless of the excitement in her voice. His smile was like a soothing fire on a cold night; it warmed and cheered her and seemed to bring a kind of flame to her heart.

"Hsst!" he warned, his tone reproving. "I cannot be discovered here, or it would be my—our—ruin!"

"Oh, I know!" she conceded, mindful to keep her tone low. "But it seems so *wrong!*"

"Come, my princess, my kitten. We must take our lives as we have them now. Soon—perhaps sooner than you believe—our happiness will be full!" He placed his strong yet gentle hands on her shoulders, and she thought that her heart must melt from the surging heat there.

"Yes . . . I'll be patient." In this, however, she did not have so much conviction. She thought of tonight, how she had *known* beyond any shadow of doubt that he would come to her.

Yet when it came to the more distant future, all was a blur. At times a face or an event would crystallize before her, and as often as not these were horrifying, or dark and sinister. No, she could not fully accept his admonishment that soon all would be light in her life.

"Have you attended the passages I bade you to read?" asked her golden-haired lover.

"Indeed. They frightened me in places." She shivered at the memory of dark powers, described in their dwelling places on the lower planes, together with tales of those who had mastered them and of others, far more numerous, who had failed and had perished in pursuit of that dangerous task.

"As they should," he said. He spoke a word and she gasped

as light sprang up in the library, a pale glow that emanated from the chandelier. Deirdre did not have to look up to know that no flame burned in the crystal light. It was the power of his sorcery at work.

His. Another of her nagging doubts returned, and she went to his side as he perused the scrolls that lay along a high shelf—scrolls that had come from the ancient vaults of Caer Allisynn. She took his arm and leaned her head against his shoulder, clinging lightly to him.

"My love, I have need to call you more than that. Can you not now tell me your name?" She spoke softly, feeling him grow tense at her side.

He stepped away and turned to face her again. She saw sorrow and much love in those deep, impossibly blue eyes. "I am sorry, my own love, but you know that I cannot. She who gains my name gains the secret of my soul, and that is a thing I must guard for all time."

"But . . . I must have a word, a name to call you, to know and remember you by."

"Then that is a thing that you must give me." He bowed slightly, a gallant nod of his head.

Did he mock her? She couldn't know and dared not ask him. "I shall call you Malawar," she said, unknowing from where the word came into her head.

"As Malawar I shall hear you," he said, again with that little bow, a smile tugging gently at the corners of his mouth. He proceeded to remove several scrolls from the shelf and place them before Deirdre. "These, now, you must begin. You have learned an awareness of the powers that will serve such as you and I. Now you must attempt to begin their mastery."

Deirdre took the scrolls and seated herself at the great table. She would do as he asked, as she had done before. Gradually the keys to power had been revealed to her, and in this, he showed her the path. Dutifully, knowing that he stood behind her, she began to read.

She felt the words of might wash over her, pulling her upward like a leaf borne on a powerful gust of wind, carrying her above the land, toward the very stars and moon themselves. The power was there, and she would wield it—soon, now, she could see.

For hours she read, and each new scroll took her to a higher flight across the land. Her mind was a hungry thing, driven by instinct deeper than thought to consume the feast he had laid before her. *He* . . . Malawar.

When she finally settled back to the world and the castle and the library, dawn had begun to color the eastern sky. And as she had known he would be, Malawar was gone.

* * * * *

The Earl of Fairheight paced restlessly through his Great Hall. He could not sleep nor even sit still, such was the tension that had gnawed at him throughout this long night.

At times he quailed from the course he had set, a route that might lead him to the mastery of all the Ffolk, to power he had never before imagined. But all too many branches of that path led him toward one end: a traitor's honorless death.

These were the possibilities that tore at his insides, denying him rest and comfort. Did the princess live? Had the mage worked his dark magic? Would his own involvement be discovered, suspected?

For a moment, he regretted the need to have the golem rampage through his own holdings, but he quickly realized the necessity of that tactic. Otherwise, it might prove all too obvious whose hand had orchestrated the death of the High Princess.

A sound disturbed the brooding lord, and he looked up from his pacing. The Great Hall was empty, its row of beastly heads staring down impassively on the great, black-bearded earl.

"She shall be *reborn!*"

The voice, a hysterically pitched shriek that was nonetheless projected with resounding power, echoed through the great room, driving through Blackstone like the slash of an ice-bladed knife.

"Where—where are you? Who speaks?" he demanded, spinning in a great circle. Impulsively he ran to the hearth, seizing the great battle-axe mounted above the mantel. He heard commotion throughout the great house as he ground his teeth together, staring around the shadow-cloaked hall.

"Traitor!" The voice came again, but this time a body materialized behind it, moving forward from the high alcove at the door. "Know ye of the earth's vengeance!"

"Where did you come from?" demanded the earl, gaping in shock at the ragged-robed figure who shambled toward him. "How did you get in here? Guards!"

The intruder's hair and beard flowed in snowy cascades across his shoulders, down his chest. The top of his head gleamed, a cap of baldness, and he hobbled as he walked like a very old man.

But it was the eyes that captivated the Earl of Fairheight, for they were the widely staring orbs of a madman, and they seemed to penetrate into the darkest depths of the earl's soul.

"Repent of your evil! It is not too late—or ye shall know the wrath of she who comes again!"

Other doors burst open as several men-at-arms stumbled into the hall, swords drawn or crossbows at the ready. They paused, looking at the intruder with surprise and at their earl with questioning eyes.

"Now . . . answer my questions!" growled Blackstone, raising the axe menacingly and advancing. "Who sent you? How did you get in here?"

"Hah!" The man threw back his head and cast the mocking shout to the ceiling. "She sends me, who sends hope of the future to us all! I go where I please, and it pleased me to come to you now!"

In the pit of his stomach, Blackstone felt a growing sense of menace from this outwardly frail old man. He remembered the raving lunatic slain by his firstborn son, Currag, and then of Currag's own death, bare hours later. That lunatic, too, had been white-bearded, with a bald circlet atop his pate.

Yet the man had been slain and burned!

"Take him—I want him *alive!*" the earl shouted, his voice uncharacteristically shrill.

His men lunged forward, sheathing their swords and putting up their bows to grasp at the intruder with their gauntleted hands. But somehow the madman slipped away, darting toward Blackstone with such speed that the earl shrieked aloud. His hands lifted the battle-axe over his head, then brought the keen blade slicing downward in a desperate attempt to drive away this apparition of doom.

He felt the metal edge slice into flesh and bone. Only dimly did he sense the blood spray through the air and see the shocked expressions on the faces of his men as they watched their lord succumb to a berserk frenzy.

When the madness finally passed from him, there was not enough left on the floor to prove that the body had ever been that of a man.

* * * * *

Alicia awakened to the soothing caress of a gentle hand across her brow—no, it was the breeze, washing across her skin. She heard the soft noise of water lapping beside her.

Dimly, then, she remembered her broken arm and the stunning kick that had nearly killed her, and she sat up in wonder. Her arm, her shoulder . . . all her body was whole! Or had she dreamed the entire episode, the horror that had stalked them? In truth, there was no sign of a great iron giant, though she sat very near the place where it had fallen into the pool, where the twisted form had jutted upward from the shallow water.

Then she looked around, her amazement growing to a sense of wonder that swiftly became awe.

The vale of the Moonwell had come alive around her! Dewy lilies lined the shore of the pool, with their padded leaves floating on the surface, forming a gentle fringe dividing the placid heart of the pond from the suddenly verdant land. Lush grasses grew away from the water, surrounding cedars that had somehow become tall and stately.

She touched her hand to the water and noticed with surprise that it didn't seem the slightest bit cool to her now, though she recalled a feeling of deep, numbing shock from the icy chill when she had struck the water during the fight.

"Tavish? Keane?" she called, suddenly alarmed.

"Ho, Princess! What say you to this?" She saw Tavish, her face widened by that familiar smile. The bard sat among the rocks nearby, her harp still slung carelessly across her shoulder, and gestured to the soft green flora surrounding them.

"A miracle?" Alicia guessed, hesitant.

"Aye. But look." Ruefully the bard pulled her harp from her back and showed it to the younger woman. Alicia saw that the strings twisted in every direction, broken and bent. The wooden brace of the instrument and the soundboard as well were cracked and splintered.

"The strings went when I summoned that overgrown suit of plate mail to follow me around the pond," Tavish explained. "Then I fell and smashed the frame. It's beyond hope, I'm afraid."

"I'm sorry," said Alicia, feeling sudden melancholy. "Where's Keane?"

"That 'failed apprentice' of a magic-user?" inquired the bard, gesturing to a nearby patch of smooth ground. "He's over there. I tried to make him as comfortable as I could, as I did with you."

A groan from a pile of rocks nearby told them both where Keane lay, and that he lived. The tall man raised himself from the ground stiffly, kneeling for a moment and blinking while he looked around, as if he sought to restore his equilibrium. Though he must have landed very roughly indeed, his skin was unmarked by bruises or abrasions.

For the first time, Alicia noticed that it was daylight. The sun even broke through the eternal clouds for several seconds, casting warmth and brightness on the sacred well before the familiar overcast closed in again.

"That thing—the monster," Alicia wondered, climbing to her feet and walking over to her friends. "What was it? Where did it come from?"

"A golem," Keane supplied. "Of iron—the most difficult type to create. Whoever sent it after us is a sorcerer or priest of great might."

"Speaking of that," Alicia said, diverting attention for a moment away from the question of the identity of their attacker's maker. "Why have you kept your own ability such a secret? Your magic saved our lives last night. Never would I have believed you could wield such power!"

"In truth," Tavish agreed. "That was a display the like of which I've not seen in twenty years—not since the Black Wizards fought to place their own puppet on the throne of the High King."

"My predecessors." There was no humor in Keane's laugh. "It is at the High King's own request," said the young magic-user. "He would not have it known that his own advisers are wizards of any notable power."

" 'Tis true the Ffolk have always had an aversion to magic," Tavish noted.

"And with the trouble brought upon the realm by the Black Wizards, King Tristan preferred to keep my role a secret."

"And all those years you taught me," Alicia said, wonderingly. "I never had any clue, any suspicion that you could do more than light an oilless lantern, or put the dogs to sleep if they barked overmuch!"

"It would seem that your father saw you placed in very good care," observed Tavish to Alicia. "And thank you, mage, for our lives."

Keane blushed, obviously embarrassed. Then he shook his head. "We all took risks, and we all fought for each other. Lady bard, your diversion, leading the creature around the pond, was one of the bravest—and most foolhardy!—acts I have even been witness to. But that's just it. You and I didn't kill that thing! It was when the princess struck it with the staff," he told them.

"No—it was when the staff touched the water," Alicia disagreed, and then turned to Tavish. "Where did you get it, anyway? I've never known you to carry a stave before."

Tavish looked at them both, her face awestruck, her voice unusually somber. "It was your mother's—the ashen staff of the Great Druid. She gave it to me . . . said that I would know when to use it. No, actually she told me I'd know *who* would use it, and use it well."

"Me?" Alicia wondered. She looked around the shore, saw the smooth shaft of blond wood, and went to retrieve it. "A *druid's* staff? But how? All my life I've studied as a warrior!"

"Still, you are your mother's daughter," Tavish reminded her.

"And my father's, too!" the princess snapped, more fiercely than she intended. She felt something vaguely threatening about the long staff in her hands and quickly put it down. "Besides," she continued, tempering her tone, "the faith of the goddess has passed from the Moonshaes. The druids have no might, no power."

"Ahem," Keane cleared his throat. He nodded at the thick,

lush verdure around them. Wild flowers, brilliant blossoms that they knew had not been there when they had awakened minutes earlier, danced among the trees, brushed by the light morning breeze. "Perhaps your last statement is no longer the obvious truth it has been for so long."

"Indeed, this is nothing short of miraculous," agreed the bard. "It is a Moonwell as I remember, in the age before the New Gods ruled the land."

"Wait." Alicia shook her head, stubbornly refusing to accept her companion's arguments. "That iron thing, the golem. You said that it was made by powerful sorcery. Well, now it's gone. All that power must have gone somewhere. Maybe *that's* what warmed the water and brought life to this place!"

Keane smiled with a smugness that inflamed the young woman's temper. He spoke with a patronizing kindness. "It really doesn't work that—"

"How can we know?" she demanded. "Tavish called this a miracle. Doesn't that mean we don't have a good explanation?"

"Well, yes . . ."

"And how do you know what an iron golem can do? Have you ever made one?" She regretted her tone as soon as she saw the hurt look on his face.

"No," he said stiffly.

"Speaking of that," Tavish interjected, "where *did* that thing come from?"

They both looked at Keane, who seemed ready to snap back a reply. Instead, he sighed and pondered for a moment. "I have to admit I don't know. I don't know of a sorcerer in all the isles who could do such a thing."

"It had a helm," Alicia remembered. "Horned, like a northman's."

"In truth," Tavish agreed thoughtfully. "It looked like a northman warrior."

"But there's not a one of them with that kind of knowledge," objected Keane. "The northmen value brawn and courage far above sorcery!"

"And another thing," the princess realized with a sudden stab of fear. "How did it know we were here? Was it random, or directed at us specifically?"

"At you," Keane said softly. Suddenly Alicia was very glad he was here. "The High Princess of Moonshae."

"An *assassin?*" Tavish asked, gaping at the two of them. Very swiftly she, too, saw the likelihood. "That leads us to the next question: Who would send such a one?"

They looked back and forth, not wishing to follow their speculations. It was Alicia who broke the silence.

"I think we had better go see the Earl of Fairheight."

*   *   *   *   *

The crew of the *Vulture* wasted no time in carrying out their orders. The morning following their departure, they made their first landfall, a raid against a small farming cantrev near the southern shoulder of Whitefish Bay's long shoreline.

"Put them all to the sword," ordered Kaffa, without a moment's hesitation. His men leaped ashore, wading through the shallow surf to rush onto the beach. Already the peasants fled their homes, but they would be too slow.

"Spare the comeliest wenches!" Kaffa amended, catching sight of a blond-haired girl who stumbled and fell in her efforts to escape. "We'll bring them aboard ship for the pleasure of the crew!"

Eagerly, like bloodthirsty savages, the outlaws of Kaffa's band raced among the wooden houses and small, neat corrals. Men and women, even children, fell before the slashing bite of their steel. Firebrands were tossed to the roofs, animals seized and butchered, crops trampled in the fields where they had barely begun to sprout.

"No gold, Captain. Nothing much of any value," groused his mate, a mustachioed Calishite named Akwarth, who clutched a screaming red-haired woman around the waist.

"A little souvenir, in any event," chuckled Kaffa, with a nod at the terrified captive. He himself had failed to catch the woman he had spied earlier, but no matter. As captain, he had pick of the booty. Several of his men, he observed, had been more fortunate, or faster runners, than their captain.

Finally all the houses and barns had been put to the torch. Supplies of fresh meat and wine had been loaded aboard. The entire raid had taken less than an hour, yet an entire community had been obliterated.

All in all, Kaffa thought, it seemed like a promising start to the voyage.

* * * * *

From the Log of Sinioth:

My child . . . my slave . . . my creation!

She has destroyed it—ruined my years of effort! In this act, the Princess of Callidyrr becomes my mortal enemy. I must credit her and her companions with more resources than I was prepared to admit. Somehow they bested a creature that should have dispatched them with ease.

Too, there is the disturbing transformation of this Moonwell. I cannot understand its portent, but it is a thing that will bear watching. With some fortune, it is not a matter that Talos will need to attend. The ancient goddess of the Ffolk is anathema to all the New Gods. Perhaps some unwitting cleric of Chauntea or Helm will attend to that problem, leaving the way clear for me to address the young heir of the High King.

❦ 9 ❦

The Younger Pack

Brandon Olafsson, Prince of Gnarhelm, wearing the royal horned helm of his clan, led two hundred brawny northmen on the march to Callidyrr. Normally, though the distance between capitals was eight times as great, they would have made the journey to the neighboring kingdom by sea. To these seafaring people, the length of the shoreline was no deterrent compared to the rugged barrier of mountains that crossed the waist of Alaron.

Now, however, the constant gales and cyclones of late spring made sea travel exceptionally hazardous. Also, in this age of peace, a good road connected the two cities, excepting some steep and narrow stretches through the Fairheight Mountains.

The prince marched at the head of the long file as they started up these approaches to the high pass. Behind him trailed Knaff the Younger, Brandon's best friend since boyhood. Knaff's father, Knaff the Elder, had been Brandon's mentor in all matters of weaponry and seamanship. That veteran warrior now brought up the rear of the column, constantly alert for treachery and ambush.

"I'd rather sail into the maw of the storm god himself than to pretend I'm some kind of accursed mountain goat," grumbled the youthful Knaff. As Brand's chief lieutenant, he had leave to gripe when other men would hold their tongues. Complaints seemed well deserved now as rainwater trickled down the cloaks of the shaggy raiders and made the rocks and trail slick under their feet.

Brandon laughed. "I share your feeling, my friend. I wish we had a pitching deck beneath us instead of these steel-edged rocks!"

Knaff looked suddenly serious. "If it is in fact the Ffolk who make war upon us, we set ourselves at their mercy by this open approach. If they have watchmen on the heights, they'll observe our approach for two days!"

"Indeed," agreed Brandon. "We have to keep our eyes alert and mind our backs."

"Either a man can be trusted to guard your back or he is a threat to it," said Knaff, reciting the proverb of the north as if he read Brandon's mind.

"Would that we knew which place to set the Ffolk."

The prince knew, in fact, that this suspicion was one reason for the overland march. His father had *wanted* them to provide a tempting target to a potentially hostile foe, the better to understand the Ffolk's intentions. Should Brandon arrive suddenly in Callidyrr, it was too likely that the ambassador would get bogged down in tedious discussion and sly, masked propositions and threats.

Far better to a northman to face his enemy with nothing but the keen edge of steel between them. This open march, in plain sight when they were not showered by rain, would give the Ffolk time to prepare a response. If they wanted war, the King of Gnarhelm hoped they would choose to begin it on what they thought were favorable terms.

"Strange people, the Ffolk," said Knaff. "They let their women rule them and counsel them—even fight for them. The men must be very weak!"

"Fight *beside* them," corrected Brandon. "My father sailed with Grunnarch the Red and has many tales of battles against the Ffolk, and with them as allies as well, united against the fish-men!"

Knaff shuddered, and Brandon shared his apprehension. Of all creatures in the Realms, it was the fish-men, the sahuagin, who most terrified the northman warrior. All other enemies could be seen coming, could be fairly met in battle and then chased back to their fortresses or lairs.

Not so with the green-scaled, razor-taloned humanoids who swept upward from the depths, often swarming across a vessel before its crew suspected attack, and then vanishing back into the blue-black fathoms of their homeland.

"Best think about the foes we might meet on land," cautioned the prince. "Even if the Ffolk are friendly, there are firbolgs and trolls in these hills—and bandits, as well, who owe fealty to no monarch, northman or Ffolk."

"Suppose we get to Callidyrr without a sign of threat?" growled Knaff. "I suppose that means we welcome the Ffolk into our arms like brothers!"

"Not only brothers," Brand laughed, remembering their earlier words. "We'll probably have to treat them like sisters as well!"

* * * * *

"A scheme of the northmen!" bellowed Blackstone, hammering his fist on the table. "By the gods, on my own lands, as well! I'll see the bastards burn for this!"

His voice, to Alicia, didn't match the fervor of his words. Indeed, the earl had been slow to greet the three companions upon their arrival at his house, leaving them to wait in his Great Hall for more than half an hour before coming to greet them, then offering his deep sympathies and apologies as soon as they had confronted him with the facts.

The earl's face, the princess saw, was haggard, with great, dark circles gaping under his eyes. Those same eyes darted wildly about, as if the man was terribly afraid of something. Yet she was surprised that the prospect of an enemy attack, while dire, would cause him to display such horror. They had just brought him the news moments ago, yet his face had the look of one who had known real terror through a very long, very dark night.

Penetrating his words to the attitudes of the man himself, the princess sensed that Blackstone was lying. She wanted to get away from him, to confer with Tavish and Keane and see if they had drawn the same conclusion, but she wouldn't give him the satisfaction of witnessing her discomfort.

"We don't know it was the northmen," she objected, her voice cold and, though she did not know this, powerful. "We cannot bring the kingdom into a war based on unfounded suspicions."

You did it, she thought. You treacherous serpent! You're a traitor to your king!

But she could not voice her anger, for she had only her own suspicions at this point, though she felt them very strongly. Still, a charge of treason wasn't one that could be discussed without some modicum of proof. And even the iron creature that had so nearly killed them was now vanished, gone somewhere beyond the depths of the Moonwell!

Hanrald and Gwyeth, the earl's sons, had entered the hall during this exchange. The earl silently bade them to sit, which they did, several feet behind their father. He turned back to the trio of visitors.

"But you yourselves have described this thing's horned helm, such as the men of the north wear! What other explanation can there be?" Blackstone blurted the question, then suddenly scowled. Obviously he didn't desire a great deal of searching for other explanations.

"This is a matter for the High Queen to decide," Alicia announced, unaware of the depth of her mother's malaise. Her tone indicated that the discussion had reached its conclusion. "We shall ride for Callidyrr at once—and, no, we shall not require an escort of your men-at-arms," she added pointedly.

At that instant, the door to Blackstone's Great Hall burst open and a bearded man, covered with the dust and grime of the trail, stumbled into the great chamber to kneel before the earl. He wore a short sword and horseman's boots, and the weariness of a long ride seemed to cling to him like another layer of dirt.

"Your lordship," he gasped. "A column of Northmen march toward the Fairheight Pass! They are armed, and look to be a war party!"

Alicia's first reaction was mildly amused skepticism. How far would this earl go in order to lend credence to his false claim? But a look at Blackstone's face, gone slack with shock, forced her to wonder at her conclusion.

"How—how many? Did you get a count, man? And *where*, for the sake of the gods? How far from the pass are they?" The earl blurted his questions, and the princess realized that either he was a splendid actor, or he was genuinely stunned.

"Two days' march from the summit—perhaps more. About tenscore of them come, led by a great warrior, one who wears the Horned Helm!"

The earl turned back to the princess. Alicia felt the eyes of her companions on her as well. Suddenly she felt very young, very aware of her own inexperience. Yet she was the voice of the High Crown now.

"Well, my lady—perhaps this is the proof!" Blackstone crowed.

"How far is the pass from here?" she asked.

"A day's ride. It is the only good gap through the crest of the range for forty miles in either direction—if we are to meet them in battle, it must be there! If we let them come through the pass, all of the duchy lies open to them!"

"My lady, my lord," Tavish spoke quietly. The bard's voice, it seemed, was a soothing salve laid over the tension that had been building in the room. "While this is a worrisome development, well deserving of investigation, it does not seem that the northmen would commence an invasion of Callidyrr with a mere two hundred men."

"Quite right," Keane chimed in. "I would wager that the earl here could muster a militia that is easily twice that size. Am I correct, sir?"

"Perhaps," growled Blackstone. "Though my men are miners and herdsmen, not the bloodthirsty berserkers that would make up a northman raiding force! If they come through the pass, I daresay they could ransack the cantrev before we could stop them!"

Hanrald, who had observed the conversation silently, raised his head as if he stood ready to dispute his father, but after a moment's pause, he held his tongue.

"Then they shall not do so." Alicia had begun to see the solution. "Summon your militia and post them at the summit, there to stand as need be."

Blackstone looked pleased, but then his face darkened again, his natural suspicions taking over. "Shall we ambush them there? Or does my lady care to meet them with words of peace and kindness?"

"I will meet them before the pass," announced Alicia. "And there find out what they intend."

"What? No!" Tavish, Keane, and the earl all blurted their objections together. Finally the bard made herself heard.

"The risks, my princess, are too great! If this is indeed a

war party, what better hostage could they ask for than the daughter of the enemy's king?"

"Indeed, you'll serve their purposes only too well," added Keane strenuously.

"If this is a war party, I am certain that you will be able to see to our safety," she told her teacher, mindful of his magical powers. "But I am not convinced of that fact, and if my suspicions are confirmed, then the appearance of such a small party before them will do much to allay their suspicions."

After his initial objection, the Earl of Fairheight had quieted. Now he watched the discussion with a sly smile playing across his features.

Keane noticed that smile and spoke directly to the earl. "Perhaps your lordship would be good enough to provide us with one more man."

Blackstone smiled magnanimously. "I fail to see the improvement. Four against two hundred is little better than three, but, of course. I shall send—"

"Your son," Keane finished, cutting Blackstone off and at the same time wiping the smile off his face.

"My son?" inquired the earl, shocked.

"I should be delighted to accompany the princess and her party," announced Sir Hanrald, standing and stepping forth from his brother's side.

Blackstone choked on his objections, but he couldn't banish the scowl from his face as he agreed to the arrangement.

"We'll need fresh horses," said Alicia. "And rations for several days. Sir Hanrald, I presume, knows the path?"

"Naturally, my lady."

"Very well." Alicia turned, relishing her sudden sense of command. Around her stood an earl, two knights, a wizard, and a bard. All of them stood poised for action, sent into motion by her commands. It was a heady sensation she had never known before.

"We ride within the hour," she concluded.

* * * * *

The Earl of Fairheight spoke to his older son in a hushed tone, reluctant to broach even this much of his plans. Yet he needed to take someone into his confidence, and he was glad it would be Gwyeth and not Hanrald.

The princess and her three companions had just ridden from the manor gate, on the road to Fairheight Pass. The earl and his son had retired to the noble's private chambers, where he had chased the housekeepers from their chores so they could have the rooms to themselves.

He had begun by telling Gwyeth of the iron golem and the attempt against the life of the princess. The younger man already knew of the threat posed to the Blackstone fortune by Alicia's insistence that the Moonwell be spared. It didn't take much thinking for the ambitious knight to see the necessity of his father's plans.

"For a moment, it seemed that all lay in disaster," Blackstone explained. "But now—the coming of these northmen is like a gift from the gods! Now all depends upon you."

"I am ready, my father!"

"Pay careful attention, and obey my commands to the letter," the earl stressed. "Assemble two dozen of your most trusted archers. Tell them they will be well rewarded. Take crossbows and gather bolts from the armory—bolts from the royal stock, feathered in the king's colors."

Gwyeth nodded, knowing that his father's arsenal, like the arms of all King Kendrick's vassal lords, included an extensive supply of arrows in the royal colors, for use when the earl's men-at-arms were outfitted for a mission of the king's business.

"Ride along the shepherds' trail. Bring yourself through the pass in good haste, ahead of the High Princess," continued Blackstone. "It shouldn't be difficult. Your party will be young warriors, while they ride with two women!"

"Aye. And then what, Father?" growled Gwyeth. The memory of his humiliation at Keane's hands still burned fiercely within him, and he sensed the approaching moment of his vengeance.

"Find this body of northmen, while yourselves remaining concealed. You'll have the high ground and can look downward from the heights to espy them."

"And when they're discovered?" Gwyeth had begun to perceive the earl's plan.

"You attack from ambush. Remain hidden, and use your horses to escape—but only after several of them have been slain. Do I make myself clear?"

"Indeed, my father!" Gwyeth smiled, his beard split by a cruel leer. "The princess and her companions shall ride into the face of a force enraged by the death of their comrades!" Suddenly his expression darkened. "But, Father, Hanrald rides with them!"

"Aye." Blackstone sighed and straightened his back as if to relieve an ache in his spine. Then he shook his head. "Damn that wench! A keen ruse, to take my son with her. He's all but hostage!"

He turned his dark eyes on his other son, and the hardened determination there was obvious to Gwyeth. The earl grunted awkwardly, clearing his throat, and continued. "Hanrald will have to take care of himself. If he dies, it will be in cause of his family's destiny. No warrior could ask for better."

For a moment, Blackstone's mind wandered back to a night twenty years before. His wife had perished on that night, and the third Blackstone son had been born. Yet even then, he had questions about Hanrald—questions that the woman's untimely death had prevented him from having answered. And as the years had passed, he had seen Hanrald grow, becoming a different sort of person than the earl or either of his older sons.

Indeed, as he thought about it, he was glad that it was Hanrald with the princess and not Gwyeth—Gwyeth, his son who would one day rule as earl!

His mind returned to the present as that same young nobleman rose to his feet and bade his father farewell.

"Aye—good riding, Son," Blackstone said, his voice husky. "And good luck."

* * * * *

"I feel the presence of something up there in the hills." Alicia indicated the high, rock-bound ridges that rose to either side of the steep and winding trail, occasionally visible through the blowing wisps of cloud. The rain varied from drizzle to full downpour, never ceasing entirely, and served to further mask their surroundings.

The cantrev of Blackstone had disappeared several hours before, masked by the enclosing shoulders of mountain and thickening cloud. Now the four riders huddled under their cloaks, yet tried to remain alert.

"You noticed it, too," said Tavish with a frown. "It doesn't seem to be a menace, but I have a sense of eyes watching me."

"There's nothing there!" objected Sir Hanrald, squinting upward and running his eyes across the rocks.

"Always trust a bard when she has a suspicion," warned Keane lightly, and Hanrald laughed.

"True. Indeed, lady, I would apologize for my father's oversight three nights past. Beyond politeness, it would have been a rare delight to hear the music of your harp fill our hall."

"It's nothing," Tavish said with a wave. She looked on the young man with new appraisal, however. "Your father strikes me as a man who has little care for music."

"Aye, or gentleness of any sort, I fear," agreed Hanrald. "Since my mother's passing, at the time of my birth, Caer Blackstone has been a house of manly habits. It could use the brightening of a woman's touch or voice."

"It's hard for me to think of music as a womanly art," objected Alicia. "Have you forgotten the great Keren, who perished during the Darkwalker War yet sent his song to the harp of every bard in the land?"

Hanrald laughed again defensively. "I am corrected, my lady! But, in truth, there is a sound to a woman's voice that can be far more pleasant than any man's, at least in a house that is home to a father and his sons alone."

Alicia, too, laughed, feeling at ease with the good-natured young nobleman. Indeed, she enjoyed a sense of mission and comradeship with these three Ffolk that cast a pleasant shade of adventure over their mission.

"Perhaps I spoke too quickly," the princess replied. "But I rejoice in the fact that we are a people whose women can make themselves warriors, or bards, or farmers, as they will."

"Not like the men of the north," agreed Tavish. "There they place a woman beside the hearth and keep her there lest she cease bearing babes—sons, it is to be hoped!"

"Are there women in Callidyrr—women of the Ffolk?—who practice sorcery?" inquired Hanrald.

Keane answered the question. "There are a few, just as only a few Ffolkmen study the arcane arts."

"How long have you possessed such mastery?" asked Alicia. "Those weren't the spells of an apprentice that you hurled at the iron golem!"

Keane shook his head modestly, and once again the princess sensed that talking about his ability made the mage uncomfortable. Nevertheless, the lanky tutor offered some explanation.

"I began my apprenticeship very young, working for the palace alchemist in Callidyrr. He noted that I seemed to have some aptitude and brought me to your father. That was shortly after you were born," he told Alicia.

"But how did you progress so far?" she wondered. "I didn't think we had masters in the Moonshaes capable of such teaching!"

"We don't," Keane admitted. "But on my journeys to Waterdeep—those periods you and Deirdre refer to as 'days of freedom'—I studied with some of the greatest wizards of the Sword Coast."

Alicia blushed, embarrassed to hear that Keane knew about the sisters' relief when they received respite from their lessons.

Keane continued, smiling thinly at her discomfort. "Because of my, er, aptitude, I have been able to progress smoothly through the studies that, so I am told, generally are the province only of much older magic-users."

They rode along in easy comradeship, concentrating again on the trail as it began to cross back and forth along a steep slope, leading in this zigzag fashion to a notch between two summits high above them.

"There!" Alicia spoke suddenly, twisting in her saddle to look behind them. "I saw something move this time. I'm certain of it!"

"And over there!" Tavish pointed upward, and this time they all saw it: A dark shape moved along a bare slope of rock before darting out of sight.

"Four-legged, I'm certain," Keane announced.

"A wolf?" inquired Alicia, her hand going to the hilt of her sword. She had been weaned on tales of the dire wolves that had long inhabited the wild places of the Moonshaes.

"Can't be." Tavish actually sounded wistful. "The only place they live anymore is the Island of Gwynneth, and even there hunters have killed most of them. They've been rare for many years."

"There's another one—and another," added Keane, pointing to the slope below them. "Why, they're *hounds!*"

"More of them down there," Tavish added. "I should say dozens, and those are only the ones I can *see!*"

"The hounds of Blackstone!" Hanrald cried, surprised.

"What do you mean?" asked Alicia.

Hanrald turned to them, raising his eyebrows. "I would have thought my father had told you. It began the night the madman appeared at Caer Blackstone. He sent the hounds—a goodly pack—running into the hills. They were never seen again."

"But this is more than one pack—even a large one," objected Alicia.

"I said it *began* there. Since then, dogs have run off from their homesteads all through the heights."

For a moment, the young lord remembered the appearance of the lunatic in his own family's hall. He wanted to tell his companions of that incident, but he had vowed to his father that it would remain secret.

"But why do they gather here, in these remote heights?" asked the princess.

"That's only the least of the mysterious occurrences over the last few days," Keane ventured.

The hounds did not close in, nor did they seem to threaten them. Nevertheless, it was disquieting to ride along with the constant silent escort.

Even as the four riders approached the very pass itself, with its steep-sided slopes of rock-studded ground rising to either side of them like watchtowers over a gate, the silent shapes raced and bounded across the dizzying heights above.

* * * * *

"The bastards—to hit from ambush and flee!" Brandon nearly choked on his rage, staring through tear-blinded eyes at the looming crags above them. He cradled Knaff the Younger's head in his arms, holding the body of his childhood friend even as it grew steadily colder.

The arrow that had pierced Knaff's heart still jutted outward from the dead man's chest. For a time, Brand had feared to remove it, sensing that it would inflict further damage to what was already a gory wound.

Now, after the fountain of blood had slowly ceased its steady geyser, it didn't seem to matter anymore. Rain spattered the rocks, already thinning the crimson liquid that had soaked the ground, rinsing it away with a casual ease that further infuriated Brandon.

"See, my prince?" said Knaff the Elder, indicating the feathered shaft protruding so grotesquely through the body of his only son. Brandon shuddered as he heard the cold dispassion in the old warrior's voice. "It is the arrow of the Great Bear, sigil of the Kings of the Ffolk."

"Aye. And a treacherous attack it was, not worthy of a grub-eaten bandit, not to mention a company of king's archers!"

The attack had occurred with shocking, fatal abruptness. The column of northmen had been working its way through a narrow, twisting canyon, still many miles below the summit of Fairheight Pass. The walls to right and left weren't terribly lofty, averaging perhaps forty feet in height, but their precipitous nature guaranteed the failure of any scaling attempt.

Then silently a shower of arrows had fallen among them from the rim of the narrow chasm. A hundred missiles, or maybe more, sliced downward with random accuracy, slaying five of Brand's men and wounding a score more. The northmen caught only quick glimpses of the assailants, and Brandon's two dozen bowmen had barely gotten off one useless volley before the attackers faded back from the canyon's rim and vanished into the twisting maze of slopes, ridges, gorges, and peaks that made up the crest of the Fairheight Range.

Even as arrows still flew, the war chief of the northmen had sent parties of his men racing up the canyon in search of a route to the top. These men had not yet returned, as others of

Brandon's warriors tended the wounded or kept lookout against the rock-edged wall above them. Three clerics, followers of Tempus the Foehammer, performed what healing magic they could, concentrating their powers upon those men who could be returned to battle-readiness with a minor spell.

"Prince Brandon! Up here!" a warrior called down from above. He had obviously discovered a route to the top. "The spoor of horses!"

"And this!" Another man came into sight beside the first. "One of them dropped a dagger as he fled. It bears the Royal Seal of Callidyrr!"

"Damned treachery!" spat Brandon, standing and pacing back and forth before his men. "We'll march with pickets on the heights to right and left."

He cursed himself for not thinking of this elementary precaution beforehand. Though the march would be grueling for those warriors elected to guard the flanks, it would prevent a similar ambush. Before this attack, however, he realized that he hadn't really believed the Ffolk intended to go to war with his people.

The dead were laid to rest in rock biers. On the return march, they would be carried to Gnarhelm for proper burial at sea. Two of the injured, leg-wounded and unable to march, remained behind to hobble as best they could back to the lowlands.

"Any Ffolk we see are to be treated as the enemy," Brandon announced, his grim voice underscoring the mood of his embittered warriors. "Now we march as warriors—warriors on the road to battle!"

No characteristic battle cheer erupted from his men at the prince's words. The campaign had begun in ignominy, and they would not voice their pride until the deaths of their comrades had been avenged.

Slowly now, the column resumed the climb up the long trail. For the men on the heights, the strain increased tenfold, since they had to work their way across rough terrain, often descending from one granite-topped crest merely to pass through a valley and ascend another. Nevertheless, they probed and explored, making certain that no further ambush could menace the column.

The sun drifted into the west, casting the trail in shadow by midafternoon, but the northmen marched grimly onward. Finally the steepness of the grade mitigated somewhat, and they came into a region of high, rolling meadows of heather, broken here and there by copses of cedars and pines.

Here Brandon's caution paid off as one of his scouts came loping back to the main column, having investigated a ridge just ahead.

"Four people coming," he reported. "Two men and two women. They're on horseback, and the men wear beards like the Ffolk. One of the women, the younger one, is a comely wench."

Brandon heard only the one word: "Ffolk." He digested the news and made his own decision. "Prepare an ambush. Slay the men and bring the women to me."

His men, war lust surging in their hearts, hastened to obey.

* * * * *

"All the gods curse this ill luck!" groaned Gwyeth, son of the Earl of Fairheight. He gritted his teeth against the pain as two of his men grasped the haft of the northman arrow that jutted from his shoulder. He couldn't avoid a brief gasp of pain as they pulled the missile free.

"Clumsy oafs! You wish to wound me further?" he demanded, struggling to clench his jaws against a scream of pain.

In truth, it had been poor fortune that had sent this one arrow, blindly aimed against his ambushing force, arcing through the sky overhead to plummet downward and strike the young warrior in the shoulder. Why could it not have been one of his men? Any of the scoundrels should have been glad to offer his life in the name of their earl's cause!

But instead, it was the earl's son who was wounded. Now the blunt-fingered warriors tried to stem the blood that spurted from Gwyeth's shoulder and to lift him back into the saddle for the long ride back to the manor.

When they got there, Gwyeth knew, his father would make ready for war.

* * * * *

Musings of the Harpist

I watch the princess, flanked by the two men, and wonder if she senses her effect upon them. She is a beautiful woman, and bright, but I begin to suspect she may have a blind spot reserved for them.

Hanrald follows her like an eager puppy. Every glance she bestows upon him seems to cause his tail to wag, and should she grace him with a smile or a laugh, it seems the bold knight is ready to perform handstands!

Keane, of course, is quieter in his affections and more aloof. Nevertheless, I have seem him look at her when Alicia's attention is distracted. Unless he is very careful, the true depth of his affection is revealed by the rapt focus of his eyes, the taut set of his shoulders.

And Alicia leads us on, embarked upon what, to her, is a grand adventure. Perhaps it shall fall to me to remind her that we have serious tasks ahead.

❧ 10 ❧

Clash of Cultures

The hounds disappeared as the four companions reached the very crest of the pass, where the two watchtower peaks bracketed a narrow niche. Walls of dark, humid granite loomed on either side, with the route narrowing to no more than ten feet wide at its tightest.

Soon, however, the cliffs parted to reveal a vista of Gnarhelm. Heather-shouldered ridges dropped away before them and off to both sides as the crest of the Fairheight Mountains fell quickly to a realm of rugged foothills. Gray clouds weighted the horizon, and mist filled many of the lower valleys. Their surroundings had a dismal, lonely look, as if they stood upon a massive island of rock that floated through a sea of gloomy ether.

"I never realized that so much of the highlands lie in Callidyrr," remarked Alicia as they rested themselves and their horses before beginning the steep descent.

"Indeed. As well as all the iron and most of the coal. And now the gold as well," Keane explained.

"Do you think that would send them to war?" asked the princess.

"I should think not. The northmen look toward the sea for their sustenance and their treasures."

"And here are our shaggy friends," announced Tavish, calling their attention to the surrounding slopes. They saw a dark shape slide along a rock before quickly disappearing. Another flashed for just a moment, silhouetted against the sky at the top of a ridge.

"I'm glad to see them again," Alicia said. "They don't seem threatening, and who knows? Maybe they're looking out for us."

As if in response to her suggestion, a sharp bark echoed across the rolling heather. It was shortly followed by another, and then a chorus. Hounds sprang from all directions and ran before them, their powerful bodies low along the ground as their legs drove them with easy grace. The full song of their baying resounded across the highland.

"What's that?" Sir Hanrald squinted. The others noticed his sword, held now in his hand. He used it to point. "There. It's a man."

"Several of them—northmen, I should say, by those shaggy cloaks," ventured Tavish. They all saw three men break from the cover of a dense copse, sprinting over a low hill and dropping out of sight. The dogs, still barking, did not follow. Instead, the large pack milled about before the woods, as if they had lost the scent of a stag.

"A trap—it's a trap!" Alicia realized. "Look, warriors could take cover along all those little hills, and we'd ride right into the middle of them." She gestured to the dozen or so knoblike crests that jutted from the rolling countryside surrounding the dirt track.

Suddenly the dogs cried anew, a deep and menacing sound that proved they had located a scent. In a great, flowing mass of dark fur, they surged up one of the small hills, flushing nearly a dozen bowmen from the top, harrying the men down the steep slopes and away from the four Ffolk.

"You were right," admitted Hanrald dryly. "But it seems the danger has been averted." The young noble looked at Alicia with keen curiosity. "I wonder what it is that first brings a Moonwell to life and now brings the hounds of Blackstone to provide us with an escort."

The princess felt uncomfortable under his gaze. Didn't he know that she was as mystified as he? "Should we return to Blackstone?" she wondered aloud.

"I think we've seen what we came here to learn. The northmen are definitely hostile. Why else would they have arranged to take us from concealment?" Keane asked.

"I'm not so sure," Tavish countered. "They might have been there simply to observe us. We could have passed by unharmed and never known they were there if not for the hounds."

The others expressed their skepticism. "That's a spot chosen with an eye toward attack," Hanrald pointed out.

"I think we'd be taking too much of a risk, to ride on alone," Keane said. "We should return to Blackstone and send news of this to Callidyrr."

"I'll ride on ahead and see what I can find out," offered the knight, with a straightening of his shoulders.

"No!" Alicia would not see Hanrald sacrificed for his own bravado. "Keane's right."

The mage's look of relief was plain as she continued. "We should turn about here and thank our stars . . . or thank the goddess, perhaps, that we were not taken in by the trap. When we return to these heights, it should be with a large company of warriors." And myself in their lead, she thought but did not say.

They reined about and kneed their mounts back across the rolling country toward the looming pillars of the pass. No sound gave them warning of chaos as suddenly the ground buckled beside them. The horses reared with piercing whinnies of terror as a great crack split along the earth to gape darkly in the heather. A resounding bellow exploded from the hole, and Alicia felt dire terror in the very pit of her stomach.

"Wait!" cried Keane, trying to control his bucking steed.

A huge shape moved within the hole and then suddenly whooshed upward, soaring in a circle in the sky. A great tail trailed behind the serpentine form, while leathery wings pulled the massive creature higher and higher. Scales the color of fresh blood lined the entire form, which was huge enough to cast a dark shadow on the ground below it, even underneath the charcoal gray of the overcast sky.

Compelled by instinct far more persuasive than the commands of their riders, the four horses bolted away from the trail, streaking across the rolling meadows in dire panic. The humans hung on for dear life as the steeds leaped a shallow ravine and bounded down a steep mountainside.

The red dragon bellowed again, this time belching forth a huge fireball with the sound. The sphere of flame crackled against the overcast sky, though it was so high up that it did not harm them. Indeed, Alicia couldn't even feel the heat of the blast against her face.

Then she saw an awesome spectacle. The beast dove, its wingspan expanding until it seemed to block out the sky, cloaking the entire slope beneath its vast shadow.

"Stop!" she heard Keane cry again, and then he gibbered something that made her think he had lost his mind: "There's nothing to—there—it's—"

The rest of his words vanished behind the blast of another fearsome roar as the great dragon swooped over their heads and started gaining altitude, swinging around for another pass at the helpless humans and their panicked, bolting steeds.

The horses reached the foot of the slope, splashing through a wide, gravel-bedded stream, and then they careened along the valley floor at breakneck speed. Alicia hung on for her life—a fall at this pace onto the rocky ground could very easily prove fatal—and tried to listen to Keane.

For a few moments, the mage was occupied in terrified screams. The princess sensed, however, through her own awe-inspired terror of the dragon, that it was the panicked racing of the horses that frightened Keane, not the dragon.

Alicia herself felt little fear of the ride. She had ridden with great skill since her third birthday. Though she knew that Keane wasn't her equal on horseback, she was nevertheless astonished at the focus of his panic.

"For the sake of the gods," she cried, "hold on! We've got to get to safety!"

"That's *it!*" Keane shrieked, his lips stretched taut across his teeth. "There's nothing to be afraid—*by the Abyss!*" The rest of his announcement vanished in a wail of hysteria as his horse leaped a wide chasm that gaped, perhaps a dozen feet deep, before them.

The dragon swooped past them again, this time so close that they should have felt the thunderous breath of its passage, but there was nothing, not even a slight disturbance of air. Before them now the great serpent spun through a shallow curve, and at last their exhausted horses returned to some semblance of control.

Reining in hard, Alicia studied the great shape in the sky, and as she did, it seemed to shimmer against the gray backdrop of clouds. The dragon whirled and dove at them again, and suddenly it was no bigger than a large crow.

It descended, a serpentine shape of bright colors and gauzy, butterfly-like wings, toward them. The body was first a bright orange in color, but then quickly shaded to blue. The tiny mouth gaped, but instead of a monstrous roar, it uttered a rather ludicrous squeak.

"Stop!" cried the princess, anger suddenly replacing her terror. "Stop right there!"

"What?" The small dragon halted instantly, hovering before them by maintaining the steady beat of its fairylike wings. "Aren't you afraid anymore?" Adding to the incongruity of the scene, the serpentine mouth curved downward in an exaggerated pout.

"What are you doing?" spluttered the magic-user. "You could have gotten us all killed!"

"Oh, bother!" snapped the dragon, its tone petulant. "I can't have *any* fun anymore!"

"Fun is one thing!" Now Tavish joined in the rebuke. "But, Newt, that was downright dangerous! And where did you come from, anyway? What are you doing here?"

"Poosh-haw!" sniffed the dragon, turning to regard Alicia with bright, sparkling eyes. He continued to hover steadily in the air while the four humans dismounted. "You all looked like you could use the run! Besides, it gets so *boring* up here all by myself!"

"Newt?" asked Alicia, recognizing the name though she had never met its owner. "Newt, the faerie dragon?"

"I suppose you thought it was 'Newt the firbolg,' or 'Newt the water snake'?" His voice was still a whine, but he looked at the young woman with keen interest. "And you're the daughter of my friend Tristan, I know."

"Yes, I am. My father has told me much about you—how your courage and ingenuity helped in the Darkwalker War, and how he was fortunate to have a companion as bold as yourself!" She also remembered, but did not remark about, tales of Newt's practical jokes, which several times had come close to getting Tristan or his companions killed.

"He did? I mean, of course he did!" The little dragon's chest puffed outward. "Why, if it hadn't been for me, that lad would have gotten his beard trimmed more than once. Say, did he tell you about the time he was stuck in the mud and—"

"I say," Keane interrupted brusquely, "we should have a nice chance to reminisce, but we have drifted quite far from our trail. If we are to travel back through the pass before dark, we had best be moving."

"Back? Through the pass? Tonight?" Newt digested each bit of news as if it were a tough piece of meat. "But you *can't!*"

The dragon suddenly vanished, popping out of sight with uncanny suddenness.

"Where'd he go?" Keane demanded quickly. "I don't trust that little—"

In that instant, Newt reappeared, hovering in the same place he had been, and then blinked away again. He repeated the process several times as the humans stared.

"He always does that when he's agitated," Tavish explained. "Faerie dragons spend much of the time invisible, and I think he forgets which is which."

"I do *not!*" huffed the dragon, exerting the effort to remain visible. His hover, however, became less steady. Indeed, he bounced up and down like a puppet on a string.

"Tell us," Alicia said, keeping her tone friendly. In truth, she found herself liking the little dragon, despite the shocking nature of his introduction to them. "Why did you surprise us like that? How did you know who I am? And what do you mean, we 'can't' go back through the pass?"

"That's just it. I've been waiting here for you, for a long time. I've got something to show you, but now you're going away before I even have a chance! It's—it's not *fair!*"

"*Waiting* for us? For how long? How did you know we were coming? My parents told me that you lived in Myrloch Vale, on Gwynneth!"

"That was *years* ago," said Newt, a trifle pompously. "When the king moved to Alaron, to the palace in Callidyrr, why naturally *I* moved to this island as well." He looked at the humans as if he was amazed at their stupidity. "But I suppose news travels slowly when you're not of the Faerie Folk."

"Tell us, then—why did you frighten us? One of the horses could have fallen, and the poor beast—not to mention the rider—could have been badly hurt!" Alicia kept her tone friendly but put a note of rebuke into her voice.

"I—I'm sorry," the dragon surprised them by saying. His head drooped, and the color of his scales faded from bright blue to a deep purple, but then quickly brightened again as he smiled. "But I got you to come all this way, didn't I? And I fooled you! It was a good illusion, wasn't it? Were you really, *really* scared?"

"I saw through it right away," Keane pointed out. Alicia remembered the magic-user trying to halt their headlong flight. At the time, she had thought him mad. "Still," the man admitted, "you fooled my horse, and I guess that was enough."

Newt sniffed, cocksure again. "Well, anyway, it serves you right. You're late. I've been waiting here for six winters."

"Six years?" Alicia stared at him, shocked. "But what if we'd never come this way?"

"Oh, you would. I *knew* that. I just don't know why you had to take so long about it! Say, do you have anything to eat? It's been a lot of goat meat and mountain berries for me! How about some cheese? Tristan always fed me cheese, you know. He would bring me the best— Say, you wouldn't have any Corwellian sharp, I don't suppose?"

"Wait a minute," said the bard as the companions looked at each other in astonishment, still reacting to the dragon's initial statement. "You say you knew we were coming. You mean *all* of us? Or *one* of us?"

"Why, *her*, of course. You really are a silly bunch if you didn't know that! I've been waiting here for the princess of Kendrick, daughter of my friends, Tristan and Robyn!"

"Very well," Tavish noted, trying to keep the dragon on track. "Now, *why* were you waiting for her?"

The dragon blinked, as if astounded by her stupidity. "To *show* her, of course!"

"Show me *what*?" demanded Alicia, growing exasperated.

"You'll just have to come with me to find out!" sniffed the dragon, petulant again.

Alicia looked at her three companions, then back to the dragon, who vanished just as she opened her mouth. "I know you're there, Newt, and I want you to listen to me!"

"Hah to you! I'm over here!" The voice chirped from behind her, but she didn't give the faerie dragon the satisfaction of turning to face him.

"We've learned something very important. Our neighbors, the northmen, are going to war against the Ffolk—against the kingdom of your friends, my parents. We must take word of this invasion back to Callidyrr so that the militia can be mustered and we can be ready for the attack when it comes."

"Oh, *that*." Newt clearly was not impressed, though he did reappear to float before Alicia again, his gossamer wings buzzing. "But I have to show you something *important*!"

"Then tell me what it is!" snapped the princess, growing increasingly irritated.

"If *that's* the way you're going to act, I'll just go by myself!" Abruptly the dragon became invisible one more time.

"Ahem!" said Tavish, speaking loudly enough that the dragon could hear if he was still in the area. "If Newt has been waiting here for six years, he undoubtedly has something of great importance to show us . . . to show you, my princess. Perhaps, however, one of the rest of us could carry news of the invasion back to Blackstone and hence to Callidyrr."

"I'll go," Hanrald said immediately. "I'm the fastest rider, and the two of you can remain here to protect the lady Alicia."

The princess scowled at the notion that she needed protection, but then she realized that the duke's son had meant no offense. Indeed, his suggestion made sense, although she realized that she didn't wish to part with any of her companions.

"Very well," she agreed, thinking for a moment. "However, we still haven't gained concrete proof that the northmen intend to attack Callidyrr, and it seems surprising that if this was their plan, they would send a small force rather than their entire mass of warriors.

"Have your father's men stand at the Fairheight Pass and bar the road to the northmen if they should get that far. But don't attack them unless they give you absolute proof that their intentions are warlike."

"Yes, lady," replied Hanrald with a bow.

She felt a sudden rush of affection toward this young nobleman. For the first time, she thought about him as the heir to the mighty duchy of Blackstone, before she remembered, with a bitter sense of regret, that the crude brute, Gwyeth, was his older brother and hence first in line for his father's title. If not for that, in their later years, and with the pleasure of the gods, she would be monarch over all the Ffolk, and Hanrald might become her most powerful subject lord on the island of Alaron.

"May the . . . goddess watch over you," she said.

Smiling grimly, Hanrald whirled his horse through a circle and spurred the steed back toward the path. Riding over the rolling highland in an easy canter, he swiftly shrank into the distance.

"Newt?" asked Tavish as they watched the man ride. "Are you still here?"

"Of course!" Grinning broadly, the faerie dragon reappeared. "*Now* I can show you?"

"If you don't, there'll be trouble," the bard said ominously. "Where is this 'thing' we have to see?"

"Come on!" Newt darted away. Unfortunately he popped out of sight in his excitement, and they couldn't see where he went.

"Wait! Come back! Newt!" A chorus of cries brought the dragon back into sight, and he finally preceded them across the undulating terrain at a more sedate, and visible, pace.

For several hours, they followed the rolling surface of the highlands at a brisk canter. The rugged crest of the Fairheight Mountains loomed to their right as they traveled northward, so they knew that they remained on the Gnarhelm side of the border that bisected Alaron.

Though the ground dipped wildly to the sides, rising and twisting through a chaotic network of valleys and ridges, Newt led them along a path that kept to the high, yet easily traversed, regions of heather.

Eventually their path—it could not be called a trail, since there was no evidence that anyone had followed this route in the memory of man—took them up a soft domed rise in the land. At the top, they found a smaller hillock in the very center of the grassy, rounded summit.

The dragon finally paused, hovering before a square black hole that indicated a passage into the oddly symmetrical hillock. "A burial mound," Tavish said softly. "And a great one, at that."

Alicia, too, recognized the earth-covered tomb for what it was. The grassy dome rose perhaps thirty feet into the air and formed a perfect oval shape. The low door was framed by a heavy timber over the opening, though the weight of years had bent the beam gradually downward.

"But a barrows mound of the Ffolk? Here, in this kingdom of the north?" she asked, puzzled and awed. "And one so huge as I have never seen before!"

"This was not always the territory of the northmen," Keane reminded her in his best tutorial tone.

"It has been for hundreds of years," she retorted. "Since the troubles shortly after the reign of Cymrych Hugh, when the northern raiders in their longships stole half of our lands! And," she added, driving home her points with a certain sense of pleasure, "this cannot be the burial tomb of a northman, for their greatest heroes are always buried at sea."

"Then we know that this is very old, don't we?" her teacher replied, pleased with himself.

"Well, aren't you going inside? It doesn't seem very smart to come all this way and then stand around bickering outside the door." Newt buzzed about the low doorway, lecturing. "Of course, I don't know why I should have expected anything else! You haven't exactly demonstrated your brilliance or anything. I mean, *really!*"

"Let's go," said the bard, swinging down from her saddle. Alicia saw that her broken harp was slung on her back and that she held Robyn's staff in her left hand, leaving her right free to grasp her dagger or short sword.

The princess herself felt the faint stirrings of misgivings, coupled with awe, as she thought of the place they were about to enter. Through the long centuries of their people, the Ffolk had buried their greatest rulers and most honored and wise citizens in such barrows. Yet never had she seen one so large. The remoteness of the location was also highly unusual.

Nevertheless, it was with the caution of a warrior that she approached the dark entrance. Her slim longsword in her right hand, she took in her left the sturdy, albeit small, shield that her father had given her. Crouching, she peered underneath the sagging timber, seeing a rubble-lined passage that swiftly vanished into utter darkness.

"I get to go first!" Newt cried, diving around her and hovering in the passage. "Follow me!"

Alicia came next, followed by Keane and then Tavish. Each of them had to stoop to pass beneath the doorframe, though within the tunnel, the two women could stand upright.

"Ouch!" cursed Keane, as he tried to do the same and crunched his scalp against another low support beam.

As soon as they started to move forward, Alicia tripped over an unseen piece of rubble, nearly falling. The footing proved treacherous, with alternating large rocks, slick pavestones, and patches of thick mud.

"*Illuminatus, dero!*" Keane uttered the barking command of magic. Immediately a warm glow filled the tunnel, and the obstacles stood clearly outlined in the gleam of the mage's light spell.

Newt huffed impatiently but continued to weave back and forth, leading them down the apparently interminable tunnel. None of them made any sound save for the noise of carefully placed footsteps that crunched softly in the dust or gravel.

Abruptly the space around them yawned dark and vast. The light spell seemed to dim. In reality, it was diffused through a much larger chamber. Overhead, massive tree trunks served as beams to support a lofty ceiling. Though mold and rot could be seen on the wood, the beams were all intact and appeared to be sturdy, albeit very ancient.

Columns of great trunks stood along either side of the room. The Ffolk couldn't see into the shadowy niches between the huge posts. The far end of the long, rectangular chamber lay lost in shadow, out of range of the spell.

"Well, here we are!" boasted Newt proudly.

Still silent, the trio of humans advanced slowly while the dragon buzzed in excited circles around them. They approached the shadowy end of the hall, and as the light advanced with them, they began to discern more of its nature.

They saw a great war chariot, gilded around its frame, with huge silver wheels. The skeletons of two gigantic horses stood at its front, still in the traces. The faithful creatures had been buried with their owner, no doubt.

As they moved closer, the light glinted off the facets of many emeralds, diamonds, rubies, and other gems gathered in heaps around the base of the chariot. Somehow, even in this dank chamber, they remained clean and clear, as brilliant as if they had just come from a jeweler's polishing.

The body of the king himself lay upon a high bier of solid gold just beyond the chariot. They came around the vehicle to see the form, still wrapped in the honored silks of his burial robes. A great axe, a longbow, a spear, and the empty scabbard of a sword rested across his chest, seeing him well armed on his journey into the world of death.

"The empty scabbard . . ." said Alicia, awestruck, studying the sigils embroidered in golden thread on the ornate sheath. She couldn't read them, but the thing itself seemed of great portent—more for what it didn't contain than what it did. "A king, but his sword is lost. . . ."

"Indeed, a great king—the greatest of them all," agreed Tavish, her voice as hushed as Alicia's.

"Are you certain?" asked Keane of the bard.

But it was the princess who replied. "Yes—this barrow mound, the place where we now stand, is the tomb of Cymrych Hugh himself!"

* * * * *

Brandon watched in astonishment as the pack of huge, shaggy hounds raced at his men, disrupting the carefully laid ambush. The northmen would fight bravely against any foe they could understand, but there was something unworldly about this bizarre, sudden onrush. Unnerved, several bands of warriors broke from their cover and fled, while others chopped and hacked at the surrounding maelstrom of fangs and stiff-backed hackles.

Snarling and lunging, the dogs ran with their bellies low, their bodies elongated in liquid strides. Thick fur bristled along broad backs, and powerful jaws snapped around the men of Gnarhelm, a more frightening attack in its unnaturalness than any charge of human infantry.

But though they attacked with savage growls and barks, the hounds did not press closely. Several felt the bite of an axe blade or the sting of an arrow, but the dogs seemed content to circle out of reach of the humans' weapons, and their quickness and nimble maneuvering made them difficult targets for Brandon's archers.

Finally, after several minutes, the dogs broke away and vanished into the dips of the rolling highland, disappearing as mysteriously as they had arrived.

"Tempus curse you!" cried the prince of the northmen as those of his men who had fled came shamefacedly back to the band. In truth, he couldn't be terribly angry. This hadn't been the kind of battle for which his men had trained and readied themselves.

"This is an ill-omened march," growled Knaff the Elder, who had stood beside his prince throughout the strange encounter. "Arrows from an unseen foe . . . hounds that emerge from the mist to harry but not attack . . . a dragon that bursts from the ground. And now, see? Our quarry has evaded us."

"Aye," agreed Brandon, with a surly look toward the trail. He had watched with bitter anger the flight of the four Ffolk, first when the ambush had been revealed and then when the great serpent had chased them into the distance. The northmen column, on foot, stood little chance of catching the fleet riders. "Well, with any luck, they're dragon food by now."

He turned back to his old teacher. "Were any of our men hurt?" he asked.

"None." The veteran shook his head. "Mayhaps that's the strangest bit of all. These devil dogs swarm all around and make the noise of a pack on the blood trail, but then they leave us alone."

"What orders now?" inquired Knaff, fingering his huge double-bladed axe. Brandon knew the man still longed to avenge the death of his son.

"We'll scatter into small bands and scour the highlands before we go through the pass. It may be that we can meet some of those Ffolk—if any of them escaped the dragon, that is."

"I'm thinking that stranger things have happened," Knaff agreed sourly. "It wouldn't surprise me to find all four of them curled up as guests in the beast's lair!"

Brandon laughed. He realized it was for the first time since the ambush. But the humor died bitterly in his throat. Their mission was far from complete and even farther from success. Everything that had occurred merely added to the mysteries surrounding them.

Sometime soon, he knew, they would have to find some answers.

* * * * *

The High Queen of the Moonshaes looked like a pale shadow of herself. She lay in the great bed, buried beneath a mountain of quilts. Her long black hair sprawled across the downy pillows, tangled and thin and damp with perspiration. Above her hovered two clerics of Chauntea. They had worked their healing magic to no avail and now resorted to prayer.

But even these beseechments for divine intervention brought no succor to the Lady Robyn. Indeed, she scarcely had the strength to open her eyes for more than a few moments at a time, and she had not spoken for more than a day.

Abruptly the door burst open and the Princess Deirdre stalked into the room.

"Go, you charlatans! Leave my mother to herself for a few moments!" she snapped, her voice low but the anger in her tone still apparent. The two clerics scuttled from the door, their hands passing through rote gestures as if to ward away any insult to their deity.

"Mother . . . can you hear me?" Deirdre sat on the bed and took her mother's hand, noting its cold, clammy feel.

Robyn's green eyes flickered open. For a moment, they held fast to her daughter's face and then widened in . . . what? Deirdre wondered. Was it concern? Fear?

Then the lids drooped, half-closing, and the princess didn't know if her mother remained conscious or not.

Once, two nights earlier, Robyn had shown an abrupt and dramatic recovery. She sat up and spoke with the cleric who had been tending her, and the High Queen had seemed in good spirits. But by the following morning, she had again lapsed into this profound lethargy.

Abruptly the daughter arose and left the room, closing the door softly behind her. She found the clerics and bade them keep watch outside of Robyn's door. Then Deirdre strode purposefully to the library that had become her nearly constant abode.

She felt a torrent of emotion at war within her. Guilt and

anxiety were there, brought about by her mother's condition. But beyond these, dwarfing them in its all-consuming power, Deirdre felt the power of raw, unleashed ambition. All the years of striving in her sister's shadow, of dwelling in a castle where she was subject to the king and queen's wishes, welled up in an explosion of envy. And now no one could command her otherwise.

Once inside the library, she raised the wicks of several lamps, giving her bright light for her reading.

But Deirdre bypassed the musty tome—*Azouns: the Kings of Cormyr*—in which she had been immersed. Instead, she reached for a dark scroll tube, one that Malawar had indicated to her that she should approach with caution and respect. Indeed, her mysterious visitor had instructed her not to read it for some time, warning that although it contained the keys to great power, it also offered its user deadly risks.

Nevertheless, the time she desired such power was *now*. Callidyrr Castle sprawled around her, and within its walls, there was none to challenge her, to interfere with her pursuits. Could that power aid her mother? Perhaps. The fact that it could aid Deirdre herself was to the princess a more compelling motivation.

And the power she desired, Deirdre knew, lay in the hands of the gods. The scroll in her hands gave her the means to reach those gods.

Reverently she removed the tight leather cap from the end of the scroll's ivory container. Withdrawing many sheets of fine vellum, she spread the tissues on the table, between the flames of her bright lanterns.

She began to read. At first the words seemed to dance on the pages before her, swimming just beyond her grasp, always tantalizing her with the promise of knowledge and, more importantly, power.

But then she began to assert her mind, to seize each word, each phrase, and wrest from it the dark truth lying therein. One by one the sigils yielded to her tenacity, and slowly the web of might began to grow around her.

Page after page she read and set aside as she reached for the next. Each seemed to leave her more vital, more alive than she had ever been before. She did not know the source of this power, for the symbols lay as a screen between the reader and the god. They passed knowledge and subtly influenced her mind, while their maker remained secret.

In the background of this tapestry of words, unsensed by Deirdre but very much present—and very much pleased—lurked the dark and looming might of Talos, the Destroyer.

* * * * *

Musings of the Harpist

Newt! I wish I could describe the emotions that his appearance brings to me. He is a courageous little fellow and as bright and cheerful as ever. He knows deep secrets of the isles—witness the Tomb of Cymrych Hugh as one example— and he seems to be genuinely fond of the princess.

Why, then, am I so worried?

❧ 11 ❧

The Beneficence of Cymrych Hugh

Danrak pressed cautiously through the sodden, barren woods. His steps rustled the dead twigs littering the ground, but he knew total silence was impossible in a thicket such as this. Short stalks bristled with dry, leafless limbs, and withered branches lay everywhere underfoot.

Normally such conditions would have held Danrak motionless—at least, until he had carefully studied the terrain. But so great was his current compulsion that he ignored his usual precautions in his urgency to reach the place that beckoned him. Around him stretched the wasteland of Myrloch Vale, a place of swamps and fetid fens, of dead trees and restless, prowling packs of firbolgs. Dire wolves, too, roamed here, and had made Danrak's life a nightmare of constant flight and eternal vigilance.

Yet he had sworn an oath to stay here, and so he would! More than twenty years earlier, he and many other young apprentices had joined the ranks of druidhood. They hadn't been ready to participate in the battles against darkness that had then raged in the vale, so the Great Druid had sent them to places of safekeeping.

Danrak had gone to the idyllic valley of Synnoria, home of the Llewyrr elves. These secretive folk had treated the human as one of their own, and the apprentice druid had learned skills of survival, stealth, and combat. The Llewyrr even allowed him to ride the sleek white horses, among the finest war-horses in the Realms, that were bred in their valley.

The elves taught him the arts of bow and sword until the sister knights—for all the Llewyrr warriors were female— realized that Danrak's aptitude did not lie in the area of combat. Then he had spent much time in the Grove of Meditation, where his alert mind plumbed the mysteries of the earth and its caring mother.

But after the days of the sadness had passed, he knew that he must return to the vale and its great lake, there to await his destiny. Though the great goddess had withdrawn from the known world, Danrak continued to practice her faith, tending the wild places as best he could, caring for creatures that need his aid, even driving away woodsmen and farmers who dared to desecrate the once-sacred vale.

For the first fifteen years, he had lived a comfortable, if hermitlike, life. He ate well, of berries, tubers and fungus, fish and fowl—even, occasionally, venison or boar. He lived in a series of snug, dry caves, and wandered the vastness of Myrloch Vale without threat to his person.

But then, for the last five years, Danrak's existence had changed drastically. It began with brutal frost, so deep that it killed the fish in many shallow lakes and ponds. A late spring, coupled with a summer drought, had altered the balance of life catastrophically. With little forage, the deer and boar and other animals perished in droves, and with no prey, the dire wolves, mammoth bears, and firbolg giants had migrated into the vale, looking for food.

Now Danrak lived in a world that seemed to have lost its fertility, a place of hungry beasts and precious little prey. In winters, he froze, and in summers, he broiled, yet he lived stoically, prepared to grow old knowing no other life.

Until one night, just recently passed.

Then he had the dream, where he saw Myrloch Vale as it had once been: a place of pastoral forests, fresh springs, abundant animal life, and brilliant blossoms. The next morning, he started out, crossing treacherous swamps and oozing bogs, seeking a place he had seen in his dream, a place on the shore of the Myrloch. That great lake was the heart of the once-sacred vale and still a place greatly hallowed by those who remembered the Earthmother.

At times, as he wandered toward the lowlands, he imagined that he had lost his mind. Was it madness to follow the whim of a dream? He couldn't answer the question, but he never wavered from his path.

And now he reached his goal. He approached the great

stone arch beside the vast water with trepidation, but also with a feeling of slowly building joy. Around this one arch were scattered other great blocks of stone. These had fallen and were now half buried by lichen and moss. Within the ring lay a brackish pool of water, covered all over by scum and algae. Beyond, the smooth, flat expanse of the Myrloch stretched almost to the horizon, the surface barely disturbed by a breath of wind. As he watched, a steady rain began to fall, clouding Danrak's vision and closing in his world.

Something moved behind one of the stones and Danrak spun, his hand clutching for the stout cudgel that always, even in sleep, remained tied to his waist. He relaxed slightly when he saw that the form was human, an old woman, clad in tattered leathers and leaning heavily upon a staff.

"Danrak?" she asked. Her voice seemed faintly familiar.

"Meghan?" Remembrance and joy came to him in a warm burst. He reached for her and wrapped her in a hug, recalling an apprentice he had known two decades past. The woman hadn't taken up the mantle of druidhood until after her thirtieth birthday, following the death of her husband in war. Though she seemed ancient now, he knew that she would be little more than a half century old.

"Did you feel it, too?" asked the woman, holding him with soft tenderness. "Did something call you here?"

"*Yes!*" he exclaimed. "You, too? It must have been real, then—not, as I feared, the onset of madness!"

"Oh, to be mad," Meghan sighed sadly. "It has come and gone with me, these past score of years. But, no, my friend, we are not mad now."

Others came forth from the woods—those who had been young druids, who had sworn their oaths and then been hidden away by their masters. Now they sensed the calling of some great portent, expressed to each in a dream.

The druids hoped and believed that the cycle of the Balance was about to begin again.

* * * * *

"Well?" Newt said expectantly. "Aren't you going to *take* something?"

Alicia looked at the faerie dragon in astonishment. "You mean loot the tomb of our people's greatest king? I'm surprised you would even suggest such a thing!"

The aura of Keane's light spell still glowed around them. The three humans stood before the massive treasure trove of Cymrych Hugh's burial mound, while the mummified body of the illustrious ruler lay regally on the high, flat bier. Alicia looked at it nervously, as if she expected the form of the deceased king to rise from the dead and expel them from the barrow. Though he was her family ancestor—"Cymrych" was the word for "Kendrick" in the Old Tongue—the princess felt like an invader nonetheless.

"It's rather amazing that it hasn't been looted before," Keane noted. "I suppose the location explains that, but why would they build him a barrow in these remote heights?"

"Cymrych Hugh's resting place has been a mystery for centuries," Tavish explained. She looked around, smiling dazedly. "After his death, a band of his most faithful followers disappeared with the body. None of them was ever seen again. Rumors said that he had been buried at sea or in the Myrloch, but no one—not even the bards—knew the truth."

"Until now," Alicia said, feeling a sense of reverence slowly overcome her discomfort.

"*I* knew!" Newt said impatiently. "Most of the Faerie Folk do! After all, he was our king too, and *we've* never come here to loot his tomb!"

"So why do you tell us to take things?" asked Keane skeptically.

"Not *things! Some*thing! Each of you should take something! That's why I've been waiting here for so long—to tell you that!" The dragon blinked in and out of sight for a moment, and then, as if by an effort of maximum will, he remained visible for several seconds at a time.

"Us? We should each take something?" asked Keane carefully.

"Yup!" Newt beamed. At least one of these humans seemed to understand a concept after it had been explained no more than five times!

Once again the companions looked across the mounds and stacks of treasures and objects. Light winked, reflected from countless golden coins. A bronze shield had somehow retained its mirrorlike sheen, and now their reflections stared back at them from its smooth surface. Alicia saw a great sword, a dark-hafted crossbow, an iron helm—all the accoutrements of a great warrior.

"A harp!" Tavish exclaimed breathlessly. Gingerly she knelt among the gold and silver coins, scattering several of them to the sides to reveal a small, gracefully curved instrument with a soundboard of wood so dark it was almost black. Reverently she picked it up, letting her fingers trace across the strings.

The sound that filled the tomb was mournful and joyous at the same time, a perfect blending of notes that climbed through the scales in matchless beauty. Though the instrument was plain, with none of the gilded trim or silver keys that were common on splendid harps, the sound surpassed anything they had ever heard.

"It's unbelievable. For hundreds of years, it lay here, and yet it's perfectly tuned." The bard looked at the tiny dragon questioningly. "But such a thing as this—surely it should remain here."

"Nope. It's yours now." Newt beamed happily. "Better to have it out where we can hear it, don't you think?"

"You're right, I suppose," said Tavish. She turned the instrument in her hands, looking over the frame, the silver strings, and the ivory tuning keys. "There are symbols by each of these keys. I can't make them out, though. It's a form of writing even more ancient than the Old Tongue."

"Or of different origin," said Keane thoughtfully. "It's indeed a splendid harp."

"And you?" asked Newt, suddenly popping into sight between the bard and the mage. "Now, *you* choose something!"

"I already have," Keane admitted. He, too, knelt among the coins and reached into the pile. His hand emerged holding a small brass ring.

"How'd you know that was there?" asked Alicia, amazed. The ring had been completely buried beneath the coins.

"I don't know," Keane replied, his tone wondering. "I saw it there—but you're right, it was buried. It's almost as if it called to me. . . ." His voice trailed off as he looked at the plain circlet of brass, or perhaps bronze. The ring seemed pale and ordinary amid the splendors surrounding them, yet there was no hesitation or regret in the mage's manner.

"What is it? Does it have anything inscribed on it?" Alicia wondered.

"No—it's plain and unadorned. Sort of like me." Keane slipped it onto the middle finger of his left hand. "Fits like a glove," he noted.

"Your turn," Newt urged Alicia impatiently. "You pick something now."

The princess shook her head, confused and reluctant. "I can't! It seems so . . . so . . . " Her voice trailed away, though they knew her meaning.

"It seems wrong to you, child, but it isn't," said Tavish softly. "Trust Newt—you must."

"But I don't know what to choose! It's not like you, where something seemed to call and you found it. There's too much here, and it's all so magnificent!"

"Come *on!*" whined the dragon. "Don't you see *anything* that you want?"

Alicia laughed. "That's not the problem." She looked at the great sword and knew that the weapon was too large and heavy to be practical for her. Though she would be a warrior queen, that didn't mean she had to pick a weapon more suited for a brawny male twice her size and weight.

Besides, she reminded herself, the true Sword of Cymrych Hugh had been borne by her father. He had used it to triumph in the Darkwalker War, sacrificing the weapon in the final battle against the beast and its dark god. Any sword found here must be a replacement for her ancestor's legendary weapon.

The axe she also passed over. Like the blade, it was too heavy for her, and her skills leaned more toward the thrust and parry of rapier or short sword rather than the crushing force of hammer or axe.

The crossbow caught her eye and she hefted it. The weapon was large but light, and the action worked with a smoothness and ease she had never before experienced. A good shot with bow and crossbow, Alicia recognized this as a device of precise craftsmanship. Nevertheless, she set it back down, sensing that it was not her destiny to bear it.

She found a golden torque, a ring to place around the neck,

and thought it elegant and bright, possessing an inner strength that seemed to flow into her hands when she lifted it—but that, too, she returned to the pile. A warrior she was, and thus she would find herself a weapon. The torque seemed more appropriate as the badge of a high druid.

Then she saw the silver coils lying beneath the wheels of the chariot. Each was a series of rings made by looping a single piece of metal through several spirals, designed to fit over the forearm. They were identical, each winding through three rings the size of bracelets.

Only as the princess picked them up and studied them did she notice that each bracer was delicately crafted into the coiled shape of a long, wingless serpent. She slid her right hand through the circles of one and found that it rested comfortably on her forearm. The other did the same on her left.

"Bracers fit for a queen," announced Tavish approvingly. Alicia looked at her companions and saw Keane's raised eyebrows.

"I know," she said, understanding his look. "I thought I would gain a weapon here. But somehow these feel right!"

"I don't question that," replied her teacher. She detected an unusual amount of tenderness in his voice. "After all, I dug through a pile of riches to find a brass ring!"

As Alicia looked downward, she thought she saw—or did she imagine it?—lines of silvery light flowing along the serpentine bodies. The bracers seemed delicate, almost frail. Certainly they wouldn't serve as combat protection. It looked as though the bite of hard steel would cut right through argent metal into the flesh beyond.

Why, then, did she put them on with so little hesitation? Alicia couldn't know, but neither did she feel any qualm or question about her decision. As she looked upward to the bier where rested the mortal shell of her great ancestor, she felt somehow that Cymrych Hugh approved as well.

* * * * *

"They left clear tracks through the heath. They rode without time for concealment." Knaff the Elder smiled grimly as he made his report to the prince. The warriors of the north had broken into ten companies, each of about twenty men, and scattered across miles of this rough country. For hours they had searched and explored, but now finally they had discovered a solid and visible trail.

Brandon gestured to one of his own band. The warrior, older and slightly smaller than the average northman, was a barrel-chested fellow who bore a long, curved horn, an artifact carved from the tusk of a great snow elephant.

"Sound the assembly, Traw. Below that peak to the north." Brandon indicated the round dome of a summit that loomed above the surrounding mountains.

Traw placed the end of his great horn on the ground, then put the mouthpiece to his lips. His chest swelled, and a long, low tone resonated through the valleys and across the peaks. It reached the ears of all of Brandon's scattered companies, and with its slow, plaintive notes told them to mark off three leagues to the north of their initial starting place. All ten groups started toward the rendezvous.

More significantly, no one else heard even the slightest hint of the cry, for this was an enchanted horn. It dated from the time when great sheets of ice covered the Realms, and northmen fought for their existence against the continuous onslaught of winter and against the frost-bearded monsters who claimed the icy lands for their own.

The huge tusked beast had fallen to the spears of a half-starved band, and the meat had seen the tribe through the coldest months of the year. In the spring, the men of the cold wastes had asked for the blessing of Tempus, and his might had given the horn its power, for though its sound would carry for many, many miles, it would reach only the ears of those whose blood was of the north.

Now the companies gathered to the sound of the horn, and Brandon led them along the trail of the riders. The trail didn't skirt the high mountain. Instead, it veered back and forth up the long, gradual slope until it reached the crest. Following cautiously, Brandon deployed his men in a long line and moved carefully onto the wide, gently rounded summit.

Here they found the great barrow mound, with its long, dark entrance. Three horses were tethered outside, waiting patiently for the Ffolk who could only be within.

"We'll greet them when they emerge," Brandon decided, ordering his men to take cover out of the entrance's line of sight. He himself, together with Knaff, took a comfortable seat directly above the dark gap. Then, like the three horses of the Ffolk, he settled down to wait.

* * * * *

Gotha grew restless in his cavern, which no longer seemed so massive. He knew nothing of the sahuagin who had come ashore with their gifts, or of the fisherman Sigurd of Gnarhelm, who discovered the items and took them back to his people as proof of a raid that had never happened. Finally his immortal master spoke to him.

Go forth, wyrm, onto the shore of the island.

Gotha crept forth from the cave mouth, his ghastly form emerging segment by rotted segment into the cold, blustery air. His legs creaked as he moved down the steep hill toward the shore where he had ravaged the town. Dark clouds scudded across the sky, and rain fell in spatters, passing for a few minutes and then returning with sudden force. But what did Gotha have to fear from chill?

Then, near the ruined villages, the monstrous dracolich beheld movement—humanoid figures, moving away from the sea toward him! For an instant, the beast toyed with the means of destroying the arrogant trespassers, whom he assumed must be human. Should he burn them with a gout of flame? Or seize them in his great claws, feeling their bodies crushed beneath his might? Or even better, bitten in two by his rending jaws?

But then he blinked and squinted. Dimly he could see that these were not humans. Instead, they were covered all over with green scales, though a few of the creatures, smaller than the others, were yellow. Their faces gaped, the wide slashes of mouths cutting like great wounds across them, widespread enough to reveal rows of sharp teeth.

"Greetings, O most pestilent wyrm!" cried the first of these beasts, throwing himself facedown upon the rain-slicked rocks of the shore.

Gotha paused in surprise as the other strange creatures did the same. He saw still more of the humanoids emerging from the surf, gathering in a semicircle before the dracolich, bowing and scraping and offering gurgling cries of praise.

Red gills flexed at the necks of the things, but they breathed air as well as water, for they showed no inclination to immediately return to the sea. The scaly creatures waited expectantly, as if desiring some sort of command or instruction.

The dracolich saw that some of the beasts wore hard breastplates, apparently made from great turtle shells, or helms made from the carapace of the great sea snail. Many carried weapons—tridents tipped with long sharks' teeth, or swords and daggers of oiled steel that had somehow resisted corrosion in the undersea realms.

These are your warriors. Use them well, my slave.

Gotha started abruptly as the voice of Talos came into his mind. Several of the yellow fish-folk moved forward. He saw breastplates inscribed with coral mosaics depicting the triple lightning bolt symbol of the Destroyer. The dracolich guessed that these were the clerics of that vengeful god.

A sneer of wry amusement curled his rotting lips as the monster considered the irony: He himself, a slave to the Raging One, was given slaves of his own so that he could work his master's will. At the same time, the undead dragon sensed a great deal of use toward which he could put these obviously savage minions.

For one thing, their ability to move through the water gave him great mobility and made his island lair an ideal stronghold—and the perfect base from which to launch assaults against the isles.

"Name yourself," growled the dragon, speaking to the largest and foremost of the fish-men.

"King Sythissal, Monarch of Kressilacc, ruler of the sahuagin, and your most humble slave, O mighty compound of filth and decay!"

The sahuagin raised his head. Gotha saw that the beast's back bristled with long, sharp spires. He was the largest of his band, standing nearly nine feet tall when he was upright.

"Rise," commanded the dracolich. "What know you of the lands around here?"

"These are but small islets, grand slitherer, north of the great islands of Alaron, Gwynneth, and the many Isles of

Norheim," began the king. "But each has a host of humans upon it, except for Dragonshome, which lies to the north of here."

"And the nearest humans?"

"They dwell upon Grayrock, to the south, lying not far beyond the horizon," came the sahuagin's reply.

"Very well," replied the dracolich. "Let us go there and slay them all!"

"We shall kill all humans?" inquired the king hesitantly.

Gotha puffed a cloud of smoke in annoyance. "Not all of them. We shall begin the slaying, but soon they will begin to massacre each other!"

The hissing of the sahuagin, he knew, was their accolade. The dracolich unfurled his broad wings. With a powerful spring, he took to the air even as the troops of his army dove into the surf below.

* * * * *

"It'll be getting dark outside soon," Keane warned. "Unless you want to spend the night in this tomb, we'd better get someplace where we can sleep."

"Let's go," said Alicia reluctantly, with a lingering look at the bier of Cymrych Hugh.

The princess didn't want to part from the wonders around them, yet neither did she feel comfortable with nightfall descending. Like Keane, she felt that their intrusion would somehow be made more severe if they were to treat this barrow as a mere cave, claiming it for a few hours' shelter.

"You don't have to go already, do you?" said Newt, with a pathetic look at each of the companions. "What am *I* supposed to do?" he wailed.

"Well, you could come with us," said Alicia quickly. She wondered if that was a good idea, but she knew that the little dragon had accompanied her father and mother on several of their adventures, and in the tales of those days, Newt's helpfulness had generally tended to outweigh his mischief, though not always by a terribly large margin.

"I *could?*" The dragon beamed, his color immediately shifting to bright yellow. "Oh, but I *couldn't!* I'm supposed to wait here for you . . . but you've already come, haven't you? Why, I must be *done* with that now!" The realization was a great dawning to the dragon. "Sure I'll come! Oh boy, it'll be *great* fun! Where are we going, anyway?"

"We *were* going to meet with the northmen," replied the princess. "I guess we have to make a new plan."

"Let's go, then," Keane said gruffly. Alicia sensed that he was less than delighted with their new traveling companion. "The sunset isn't about to wait for us, I'm sure."

Bearing their treasures—ring, harp, and bracers—the three companions and the faerie dragon carefully made their way down the long, dark tunnel. They emerged onto the mountaintop to see the glow of sunset in the west . . .

. . . and the arrows and axes of two hundred northmen, compelling them to lay down their arms and surrender.

* * * * *

Hanrald pressed forward through the night, though his mare staggered upon weary legs and his own back ached from the strain of the long day's ride. Still, it seemed that news of the ambush needed to be delivered to the manor before dawn and then sent on to Callidyrr as quickly as possible. Now, as the horse lumbered awkwardly down the stretch of the road leading into the valley, Hanrald smelled the familiar and acrid smell of coal smoke cross his nose. As always, the odor depressed and annoyed him.

He thought back to his day's journey and found his mind focusing irresistibly on High Princess Alicia. Stealing glances at her every time he could do so unobserved, he had studied her through the leisurely hours of the morning and during the hectic flight of the afternoon.

By the gods, there was a woman to fight for, to die for—to love! The knight, second heir to the earldom of Blackstone, remembered her cool decisiveness as their ways had parted and the hopeful smile she had given him as he rode away, alone, to bear the urgent news. That smile had lingered long in his memory, steeling his courage as he had dodged the northmen companies that seemed to be teeming through the highlands. Now that same memory kept him riding, pushing resolutely forward as the stars wheeled toward dawn and dead exhaustion strained to topple him from his saddle.

He thought, with momentary annoyance, of the greeting his father had given the princess, so pale compared to what she deserved! Why, if the mantle of Blackstone were his, Hanrald would have arranged a presentation of his honor guard and a festival for the common folk of the cantrevs to come and see their king's daughter!

"Halt! Who rides there?"

The challenge, from the gatehouse of the earl's manor, was Hanrald's first clue that he had arrived at home.

"Sir Hanrald. Open up and awaken my father. I bear important news!"

The steel portcullis started upward with a cranking groan, and a man-at-arms appeared behind it, speaking as the rider dismounted and waited to pass beneath the bars. "Welcome, milord. The earl's already up and in conference with your brother. Sir Gwyeth arrived home not two hours ago, and sore hurt he is, at that!"

"Is his life in danger?" he asked, surprised and concerned.

"I shouldn't say so . . . no more, at least. But his shoulder's broke solid, and the clerics are worried about the arm."

Hanrald left the horse in the care of his groomsman and quickly hastened to the hall, removing only his helm and gloves before he reached the great doors and was announced by the guardsman there.

Gwyeth, seated before the fireplace, grimaced from the pain of his wound as he looked up at Hanrald with sharp suspicion. Indeed, his eyes blazed with a look that seemed nothing less than hatred. Their father stood nearby.

Hanrald saw heavy bandages around his brother's left shoulder. Pryat Wentfeld, a priest of Helm and the leader of the local clerical hierarchy, stood over the wounded man. The holy man had apparently just completed some sort of healing ritual, for he raised his hand in the V-shaped sign of his god and nodded to the duke.

"It will heal well . . . my magic has knitted the bone where it was crushed, and the bleeding has stopped of its own. You must hold the limb still overnight. I shall return in the morning."

"My thanks, good Pryat," said the dark-bearded earl, his voice unusually husky. "Your efforts shall not go unrewarded!"

"The earl's generosity is well known, to the gods and to men alike," said the priest with a tight smile. "Though of course the deed would have been done from loyalty alone."

"Of course. Now I am told my other son brings news. Enter Hanrald, and speak!"

"One more thing, if I may be so bold . . ." The cleric spoke hesitantly, but the earl gestured him to proceed.

"It is this former Moonwell, the pond which the lady's consort has ensorcelled, creating the illusion of a miracle."

"It's a good illusion," countered the earl skeptically. He pointed to the corner of the hall, where a great cedar trunk, freshly cut, lay. The mastlike beam stretched a good fifty feet. "The tallest tree up there was less than half that height yesterday. My men brought me this timber and told me the whole place has sprouted at once.

"Still," Blackstone continued thoughtfully, "perhaps it *is* sorcery. Indeed, there would be no other explanation, would there?"

The cleric nodded in agreement. "But, my lord, there is the matter of the people. They would not understand, perhaps, the power of a spell that could work such a transformation. Word is that a file of pilgrims has already started for the vale— only, of course, to face certain disillusionment."

"This I had not heard." The earl scowled. "What do you suggest?"

"The valley must be burned," said the cleric. "The trees destroyed, the grass trampled. It must be eradicated before the tale spreads and the people begin to believe in a cruel lie!"

"You are correct," Blackstone said, pointedly ignoring Hanrald's expression of shock. "It shall be done in the morning."

The cleric bowed his way from the room as the younger son approached the fire where sat his father and brother.

"Surely you aren't serious," Hanrald protested. "It *is* a miracle—at least, the princess and the bard believe it to be so!"

"We will conclude the matter in the morning." Blackstone

brushed his son's objections away.

"But—" Hanrald persisted.

"Enough!" barked the earl. "Now, what is this news you bring?"

The knight took a deep breath. "A strange tale, Father— more mysterious, perhaps, than anything." Hanrald bit back his objections, telling his father of the ambush and how it had been thwarted by the hounds. Then, with some chagrin, he related the tale of their flight from what had proved to be a faerie dragon. Finally he told of his experiences evading the patrols that had scattered across the highlands after he turned back alone for the pass. His own conclusions, once suspicious of impending invasion, had begun to soften.

"They followed the northward trail of the four of us before I left the princess and her companions. I don't know what they did when they found the parting of our trails. Most, if not all, would have continued north, I suspect."

"Indeed," Blackstone said with a scowl. Only a glint in his eye showed his delight with the news. "So it seems they do not intend to attack us, then."

"That's only a guess, Father," Hanrald countered. "We must be prepared. It is a warlike force!"

"But there's an odd part to this tale, Father," Gwyeth interrupted. "They're not numerous enough to be an invasion army, unless there were many more troops hidden beyond my brother's view."

"Whatever the reason, I suspect they march to Callidyrr for a purpose other than war." The earl decided this point firmly.

Hanrald sat silently, surprised by his father's vehemence. After a moment, he spoke again. "Brother, what of your wound? I'm glad it will mend, but how did you come by it?"

Gwyeth cast a furtive glance at the earl but said nothing. Instead, Blackstone made the gruff reply. "An unfortunate and stupid accident—a careless hunter has already been punished. But we must speak of this crisis."

"Messengers must be sent—I hope within the hour—to Callidyrr," Hanrald urged, surprised his father hadn't already acted upon this point.

"But wait," said the earl slowly, choosing his words with

great care. "Perhaps it is premature to trouble the High King with a local matter such as this. It could well be that this is not the prelude to war. Or if it is, it is a matter that we can handle ourselves."

"Surely you're not serious?" objected Hanrald. "This could be a threat to the whole kingdom!"

"Perhaps father is right," Gwyeth said, his voice purring. "It is a thing that, done well here, can do nothing but bring credit to the great name of Blackstone!"

Hanrald looked from his father to his brother, watching them as their eyes met furtively. Suspicions surged within him, but for now he would keep quiet. He would watch and he would observe, but he would brook no treachery to his king . . . or to his princess.

* * * * *

From the Log of Sinioth:

The seeds of chaos have been planted, and already they flourish. The voyage of one longship, my Vulture, sends frightened Ffolk scattering inland. Panic-stricken messengers ride to Callidyrr with urgent missives for the king. They do not know that he is gone and that his wife lies unknowing, nestled against the bosom of Talos.

My riders cross into Gnarhelm after a hard crossing of the mountains. They are tardy, but I am certain that Larth shall make up in vigor what his company lacks in timing.

All the cogs are in place, and now we only wait for the wheels to turn.

❧ 12 ❧

A Contest of Strength

Their captors herded Alicia, Keane, and Tavish roughly down the winding trail, quickly leaving the barrow behind. The rain poured down, obscuring their surroundings and adding to the prisoners' misery. The horses trailed the column, led by northmen. Newt had disappeared when they were captured.

The gods curse me for a fool! Alicia rebuked herself. She should have scouted the entrance! In the tight confines of the doorway to the barrow, with Keane's power to back her up, the princess could have held off the attackers for a long time. Indeed, her diminutive size would have proved an advantage against the looming men of Gnarhelm!

Yet instead they had blundered into the open as if they had no enemies in all the Realms. Now the treasures—her bracers, Keane's ring, and Tavish's harp—had been put at risk, for surely these plundering raiders would steal them as soon as they noticed their value.

Indeed, the harp, as well as the Staff of the White Well, were now carried by one of the men of Gnarhelm. They hadn't bothered to remove Keane's ring, if in fact they had even noticed it, nor had they taken the silver bracers from her wrists. She had seen several of the long-haired warriors admiring the gleaming coils, however, and suspected that they coveted them.

None of the captors spoke, but a grim anger seemed to pervade them. Once Alicia paused to remove a stone from her heel, and a tall northman cuffed her forward with brutal violence. Sniffling loudly, his huge, flat nose clogged, the giant figure looked at her with narrow, bloodshot eyes when she turned to object. His dirty beard gapped to reveal a sneer, and he loomed high above the princess. The man's size and demeanor frightened her, and she tried to keep well ahead of him on the trail.

Finally they reached the valley floor, where pines covered the flat, fertile ground, and here the northmen made camp in a wide clearing beside a stream. The three captives were rudely shoved to the ground, their hands bound at their backs. Soon one of their captors sat across a campfire from them, while two others stood at the warrior's sides.

Alicia looked at the two who stood. One of these was the huge, surly brute who had cuffed her. He still sniffled noisily and seemed disinterested in the events around him. The other was an older man, wiry strong, though his legs bowed slightly and his hair and beard had gone white. This one looked at Alicia with a scalding hatred that frightened her.

Finally she looked at the man who sat before her. His smooth skin and lithe, strapping physique marked him as younger than either of the pair who flanked him. He had hair the color of gold, and proud, even haughty, blue eyes—eyes the color of deep winter ice. He wore his hair long and braided. Long mustaches trailed to either side of his mouth, though his firm chin was shaved. She sensed, even before he spoke, that this man was the leader of their captors.

"Who are you?" began the seated northman, in accented Commonspeech. "Why do you make war upon our people?"

Alicia paused at his words and suddenly realized that it was her task to respond. "We do not make war against you. Rather, it is you who have attacked us!"

The man sloughed off her reply with an arrogance that inflamed Alicia's temper. "Are you scouts for your army? Or are you spies?"

"Neither!" she snapped. "And why have you taken us prisoner? We offered you no harm!"

"Harm?" This time it was the older man, the one with such hatred in his eyes, who spoke. "Explain how this can fall from the sky and slay my son!"

With an abrupt gesture, the white-haired warrior held out an arrow, and Alicia tried to keep her astonishment from her face. The gold and red markings on the shaft clearly indicated it had come from the High King's arsenal—a fact obviously known to these northmen as well as to her.

"When were you attacked?" she asked. "And where?"

"In the morning of the past day." Again it was the younger man, the chieftain, who spoke. He talked quickly, as if he believed that she already knew the answers to his questions.

"A shower of arrows such as this came from the heights above my column—a treacherous ambush!" Those ice-blue eyes flashed, and Alicia suppressed a shiver of fear. "They slayed five of my men, including Knaff's only son!"

"I can only say that such treachery should be punished, but it was not worked in the name of the High King! Betrayal is done to both our nations in this act. King Kendrick desires peace with the north, as he has for these last twenty years."

"And how is it that a mere slip of a girl speaks for a mighty king?" demanded the old warrior. She guessed the fellow to be Knaff. His eyes burned into hers.

But her own gaze flamed back at him, such that he blinked in surprise and then scowled darkly. Alicia didn't feel Keane's foot nudge her side as, furious, she spat her reply.

"I am the High Princess Alicia, daughter of King Kendrick and heir to the crown of the isles!"

Now the younger northman's eyes widened, and he looked at her with skeptical appraisal. The three warriors jabbered in their thick tongue for a moment, and she saw them casting scornful looks at Keane. Suddenly she realized the warning that had been implicit in the mage's kick, the warning she had ignored when she informed these northmen that they held captive one who could prove to be a very useful hostage.

"Indeed, I have heard that the King of the Ffolk has fair daughters. Now I know it to be true." The chieftain, with a half-smile, nodded his head in a gesture that might have indicated respect. His response surprised her—and annoyed her, as well—but she felt it best to ignore whatever insult might be found there.

"The rulership of my people is a matter of mind and sinew, not determined by fair skin or hair," she pointed out. "But now you have the advantage, sir. Tell me who holds my companions and me so unjustly captive."

"I am Brandon Olafsson, Crown Prince of Gnarhelm," replied the young northman, his face still crooked with that clever half-smile—overly clever, to Alicia's thinking.

"A royal meeting, this," remarked Tavish dryly. "Could it perhaps be accomplished with a bit more comfort for the participants?" She shrugged awkwardly, indicating her bound hands, and Alicia, too, began to realize how the leather thongs had begun to bite into her skin.

The prince nodded thoughtfully, though Knaff's scowl darkened even further. "You haven't answered my questions, but indeed it would seem that you need not be bound for our discussions." Brandon nodded to one of his warriors, who stepped forward with a thin knife.

In that instant, a ripping sound tore through the camp, like the rending of a huge piece of canvas. Clumps of sod flew up from the ground with shocking suddenness, and the northmen recoiled, shouting in alarm. Alicia saw Knaff raise a monstrous double-bladed axe, while Brandon leaped to his feet, barking orders to his men.

The princess watched this hole in the earth with a sense of numb disbelief, for she could see the real ground, still there, even though it had appeared to burst upward.

Beside her, Keane groaned in frustration. "Rotten timing!" he hissed, obviously recognizing the illusion for what it was.

The northmen, however, were fooled to a man. A pointed snout, like a huge rock, jutted from the hole, and then a pair of feet, tipped by monstrous blunt claws, emerged on either side of the muzzle. With a mighty heave, the claws pulled a squat, monstrous body from the ground, dragging pieces of sod on each shoulder. The snout gaped, revealing wicked teeth. Tiny, bloodshot eyes blinked wickedly from either side of the pointed nose.

"Bulette!" cried one of the northmen as the warriors formed a ring around the emerging creature.

Knowing the monster was an illusion, Alicia nevertheless shuddered at the thing's horrifying visage. It was huge, larger than a bull, though its shape resembled that of a monstrous armored badger. A massive shell, like a great sea turtle's, covered its back, and the face and legs were covered all over with armor-hard scales. With a dull roar, it dragged its body from the earthen tunnel and surged toward a northman.

She knew of the bulette, which, though exceedingly rare, was a beast of consummate horror and deadly nature. It burrowed through the earth like some monstrous mole, appearing at moments when it was least expected. Though she knew this one was an illusion, that didn't totally dispel the terror of its violent arrival.

Massive foreclaws reached for a northman, who stumbled backward, slashing with his axe. Both the weapon and the beast's talons missed their targets by inches. Another north- man dodged in to chop into the thing's armored shoulder. Alicia watched in amazement as the man's axe met the illusory sur- face and stopped, almost as abruptly as if it had met a solid object.

The image of the bullette whirled and its jaws gaped before the courageous attacker. He bellowed a cry of fierce and sav- age joy, raising his axe and striking at the grotesque snout. The princess realized that the man fought in a berserker fren- zy. She had heard some northmen were capable of this battle trait, but its reality was beyond her mind's grasp. Howling madly, the berserker hurled himself at the creature again, his blade slashing, his teeth clenched in a murderous grin as the fire of battle lust surged in his eyes.

Suddenly a flash of color popped between them, and she saw the grinning face of the faerie dragon.

"Pretty good, huh?" asked Newt smugly. "But what are you waiting for? Let's get out of here!"

"We can't, you little idiot!" snapped Keane. "We're tied up! They were just about to let us go when your 'friend' arrived!"

Newt pouted. "Oh, bother! Can't you untie yourselves? I mean, you have *fingers*, don't you?"

The answer was lost in a shout as a warrior of Gnarhelm rushed at the beast, but in that same instant, the monster's image wavered, becoming translucent and insubstantial. The charging man plunged through the fading form, stumbling in surprise and then falling headlong into the campfire.

He shrieked in pain as the flames hungrily devoured his beard and the braid of his long hair. Forgetting the monster for the moment, several of his compatriots pulled him from the flames and quickly threw him into the icy stream. When they finally lifted him out, his face was blackened and seared. Ugly red patches showed where his cheeks had been burned.

Two clerics came to his assistance and began to salve his

wounds as best they could. They had no healing spells left, having used their powers to cure the wounds of those injured by arrows earlier in the day.

"Sorcery!" growled the burly warrior beside Brandon, making a curse of the word. Blinking, the gruff warriors looked around, realizing that the attack had never occurred.

"*She* did it!" The one called Knaff pointed a finger at Alicia, the hatred in his eyes flaring to new heights.

"No!" objected Tavish. "It was—"

The three companions looked around then, before Tavish could finish. Naturally Newt was gone.

"Put the witch to death!" shouted another warrior, and Alicia's heart chilled at the chorus of agreement.

"Horac may well lose his eyes," said another, who had tended the burned man. "At least make them suffer the same fate." He fingered a long dagger, and Alicia sensed that he would be only too willing to perform the mutilation himself.

"Hold!" said Brandon, his voice forceful but his manner, like that of his countrymen, taut with rage. He fixed his stare upon Alicia, and once again the ice crackled in his eyes. "Explain this treachery—and quickly!" he barked.

The princess sensed a moment of cusp. The success or failure of their mission, perhaps their very lives, would depend upon her response to his demand and to Brandon's acceptance or dispute with her reply. Why, then, was her mind so gods-cursed blank of anything intelligent to say?

"No treachery," Tavish said smoothly. "A mistake. The enchantment was performed by one who thought he aided us, who believed us to be in danger."

"What one?" Brandon turned his eyes on the bard and again Tavish smoothly responded.

"A faerie dragon. Did you witness the great serpent that chased us today, spooking our horses and sending us far off the pass road?"

"Yes." The companions sensed that, against his more war-like urges, Brandon forced himself to listen.

"Did you wonder how it is that we're alive?" Alicia burst in, exasperated. "How four riders could have outrun such a creature?"

"There are ways a dragon can be bested," Brandon countered, his manner patronizing. He paused for a moment, and then admitted, "Though I have never heard of it being done, nor should I look forward to trying it myself."

"That was Newt, the faerie dragon!" Alicia resumed, but now, remembering Tavish's example, holding her voice low, her tone persuasive. "Now he did this to you, in an attempt to give us a chance to escape. You note, I'm certain, that we did not take that opportunity." Not that we would have gotten very far, she added silently.

Brandon appeared to consider. It was Knaff who next spoke, addressing his prince. "How many hurts must we suffer before we strike back? Good men slain, by arrows of her father! Now Horac, blinded by their sorcery! Surely you don't believe this preposterous story of a dragon trying to aid them? Where is this beast, if he exists?"

"Newt!" cried Alicia. As she had feared, the little creature did not appear.

Keane startled them all by speaking suddenly. "Men of the north, I know something of your ways. I ask you, Prince Brandon, to grant me the Test of Strength."

For a moment, the northmen gaped at the slender mage in astonishment. Then several of them chuckled, making a deep and menacing sound.

"What's that?" Alicia demanded, looking at her teacher.

"Choose a champion from among all your men, and I shall meet him in barehanded combat. If I prevail, you must welcome us as guests into your camp."

Brandon, they saw, did not appear to share the humor of his comrades. He studied Keane, who still sat cross-legged beside the two women, his fellow prisoners. Finally the northman prince nodded his head curtly, and two of his men seized Keane's arms and roughly hauled him to his feet.

"Release him," Brandon ordered.

A knife flashed, and the bonds fell from Keane's wrists.

"Wultha," said the prince, nodding to the second of the two men who had stood beside him during the council, the one who had cuffed Alicia on the march.

The northman called Wultha smiled, his face a cruel and wicked grimace. He clenched and unclenched his clublike fists, which massed at the ends of two lengthy arms. Each of those limbs was strapped with sinew that looked like the gnarled wood of a weathered oak. Wultha's face was flat, his eyes close-set and small, but his chest was as round as a barrel, and his two legs seemed anchored to the ground as firmly as any stone block foundation. He sniffed loudly and wiped a hand across his nose, which spread flat across his face as if it had once been broken. The giant studied Keane, all but smacking his lips in anticipation of the fight.

He stood a full head taller than the lanky Ffolkman and out-weighed his opponent by a factor of twice, or perhaps even thrice. Again he sniffed and spat noisily into the fire.

Now Brandon spoke again. "What is your name, sir?"

"I am called Keane, of Callidyrr."

"Very well." The prince now rose to his feet, as did the other captives. "I grant you the Test of Strength. If you can best Wultha in bare-fisted combat, you and your companions are honored guests at my fire."

Alicia stared in astonishment, appalled. She wanted to shout at Keane, to rail at him for his stupidity. But she understood enough of the northman mind to know that such an act would be regarded as degrading and humiliating to the man, and it would do no good to shame her friend, and now her champion, before his desperate duel.

"Wait!" growled Knaff, suddenly alert. "This reeks of sorcery! What proof they won't use such tricks against us?"

Brandon glared at Keane in sudden suspicion. "What proof, indeed? This is a matter of strength alone."

"You could bind my mouth," suggested Keane, with a casual shrug of his shoulders. Alicia and Tavish stared at him in horror. Any slim hopes they may have held for his ultimate victory vanished at that moment into total despair.

"I have heard that a sorcerer must make sounds to cast an enchantment," muttered Brandon.

"So have I," Keane added wryly.

"It is true, my prince," said a northman, one of the clerics who had tended the injured Horac. "Both the enchantments of the mage's spellbook and those blessings drawn from the gods themselves require a verbal command by the user, else the power is of no avail."

"Very well. Gag him." Brandon spoke decisively, then

looked at the women. "And I will insist that your companions be similarly bound. I know that spells from one can be used to aid another."

Keane shrugged, the picture of cool unconcern. Then he blinked, as if a thought had just occurred to him, and he pointed at the looming figure of his opponent. "In the interests of fairness, of course, he whom you call Wultha should be gagged as well."

"He knows no magic!" objected Knaff.

"That's not the point. We should both be hampered by the same restraints, else where is the fairness?" The tutor voiced his objections to Brandon, not Knaff.

The prince of the northmen appeared to consider the arguments for a moment before turning to Knaff and Wultha. "The tall man speaks the truth. Wultha, I shall not command you to be gagged, yet if you would fight him, it must be evenly matched. If you decline, I shall appoint another champion."

Alicia watched Knaff and saw that the old veteran disapproved of his leader's decision but respected Brandon's authority enough to hold his tongue. Wultha, on the other hand, chuckled evilly. He used his massive hands to rend a strip of cloth from his own greasy tunic and held it out toward Keane with mock formality.

"That will do nicely," the mage said, mocking him back with aplomb. Wultha squinted at the smaller, slender man. Gruffly the bearlike northman pulled the cloth around his mouth while another warrior cinched it tightly at the back of his neck. The princess noticed that the hulking wrestler's breathing came in short, snuffling bursts through his nose. Alicia and Tavish were also silenced by gags.

The northmen formed a great ring around Keane and Wultha, with the fire at one point along the circle. Tavish and Alicia came around the small blaze and sat with Brandon and Knaff the Elder. The princess wanted to stop this grotesque test. Her mind raced, trying to develop a plan with any potential of success, but nothing came to her.

Alicia sneaked a glance at Tavish and saw that the bard, similarly gagged, shook her head in apparent despair. All their hopes rested upon Keane.

A look at the two wrestlers did nothing to fan the flames of those hopes. Wultha loomed over Keane, and even in a bearlike crouch, the northman dwarfed the lanky tutor of Callidyrr. Keane did his best to look formidable, stooping forward slightly, spreading his arms to either side as if he would grapple with Wuthra and throw his huge opponent, but with his long, skinny legs, his brown hair stringing freely to either side of his face, and his wide eyes staring silently above the cloth gag, the overall effect would have been comical if the stakes hadn't been so high.

Then Wultha lunged. The northman struck with surprising speed, reaching out with a hamlike fist to try to catch Keane by the back of his neck. His other hand swung wide, and then both of the trunklike limbs smashed together with a force that could have snapped Keane's spine—if he had been between them at the moment of impact.

But to the astonishment of Alicia and everyone else, the teacher somehow ducked under the blow, rolling backward and bouncing to his feet before the baffled Wultha realized that his opponent had escaped his grasp. Angrily the huge warrior wiped his hand across his nose again, shaking his head like a great bull trying to ward off an annoying swarm of flies. He pawed at the gag in annoyance, then dropped both arms and leaned toward Keane.

The magic-user crouched again, balancing on the balls of his feet. Wultha crept closer, and Keane circled away, trying to stay in the center of the ring. Once again Wultha lunged, sweeping those huge arms like scythes through the air . . . and once again, he clasped his empty hands to his chest as Keane rolled, to the side this time.

Alicia caught her breath, chafing at the gag that prevented her from shouting her approval. A sobering thought reached her: All Keane had done so far was to avoid a pair of blows, either of which could have ended the fight, and his life, in an abbreviated second. Furthermore, there seemed to be no way that he could hope to do anything else.

Indeed, as if reading her mind, the magic-user hurled himself from the side against Wultha's legs, kicking the brute sharply in the knee. Keane bounced away, landing heavily on his back, while Wultha's eyes glittered with delight. If the blow had bothered him in any way, he didn't indicate the fact.

Instead, he threw himself toward the gasping form of Keane, and the wizard desperately rolled to the side. Alicia felt the ground shake from the force of Wultha's landing, but the northman's target managed to evade the blow by inches. Quickly Keane sprang upon Wultha's back, but the northman jumped lightly to his feet and shook himself. Once again the magic-user soared through the air, though he landed in a roll and quickly rose into a wrestler's crouch—or at least, a caricature of a stance that might have been taken by an accomplished fighter.

Wultha shook his head in further annoyance, once again wiping his nose and sniffling. The great barrel chest worked like a laboring bellows—a bellows that did not draw enough air. The northman growled, the sound strangled through the clotting pressure of his cloth gag.

The hulking wrestler lumbered forward with all the force of a charging bull, and when Keane ducked toward the right, Wultha's course veered. A collision seemed imminent.

But Keane's dodge proved to be a ruse, and his following dive to the left was further propelled by sheer panic. Grunting his outrage, Wultha dove into empty air, stumbling forward into the ring of his comrades, who formed the perimeter of the fight. Three cursing warriors went down from the force of the brute's uncontrolled plunge.

"Get him, you lummox!"

"The slippery devil's getting the best of you!"

"C'mon, Wultha. He doesn't weigh more than your breakfast!"

Raucous laughter accompanied the remarks as the northmen took enjoyment from their comrade's discomfort. They jeered, and this inflamed the huge wrestler.

Wultha growled, his eyes wide. Gasping, he lurched to his feet and lumbered back into the ring, peering wildly as if he couldn't see his opponent, though Keane awaited him in the center of the circle.

The northman charged and Keane skipped away. The frail-looking tutor, his eyes squinting in concentration above the tightly bound rag, studied his brutish foe, anticipating each desperate lunge, each clumsy but potentially crushing blow. Indeed, the Ffolkman's dodging grew smoother as the fight worked its way through minute by breath-draining minute.

Keane darted towards Wultha, kicking him in his great belly with no apparent effect. The tutor lost his balance and tumbled backward, but Wultha staggered wildly, unaware of his opponent's vulnerability. The close-set eyes, now bloodshot and unfocused, grew vague as Wultha's heavy lids floated halfway down.

His nose puffed and strained, unable to bring in the air that his lungs required. He wobbled unsteadily, trying to remember where he was . . . what he was supposed to do.

Keane dove at him from the side, once again striking a tree trunk of leg. But this time he timed his attack, watching the knee as it became more and more unsteady. He drove all balance from Wultha, and the northman dropped like a felled log. Keane fell on top of him, clinging desperately as the body flexed spasmodically. Finally Wultha lay still.

Immediately Keane reached around his opponent's head, a dagger flashing in his hand. Brandon stood with a shout, but then saw the Ffolkman slice the gag away. Sitting upon Wultha's chest, Keane forced him to cough and gag. The unconscious man drew in a ragged breath of air, then another. Coughing, he opened his eyes and looked around uncomprehendingly, struggling finally to sit up as the triumphant Keane moved carefully away.

The victor next reached behind his own head and, with the knife he had concealed during their entire captivity, cut free his gag. He looked at Brandon steadily, waiting for the Prince of Gnarhelm to break the silence. The fact that Wultha had been overcome by his own congested sinuses rather than the prowess of his opponent was a fact that had been observed by all.

"You have triumphed in the Test of Strength," said Brandon levelly. His face twisted in a rueful grimace. "Though I admit you have made it more a test of wits than of might. Nevertheless, you have bested our champion."

Alicia and Tavish untied their own gags. The princess warily watched the northman prince, admiring the way he met Keane's gaze squarely. Indeed, she saw, Brandon Olafsson proved to be a man of honor and of his word.

Now the young war chief gestured to a place beside him. "Greetings, guests. Come and join our supper."

* * * * *

Yak of the Great Cat's Head, War Chief of Grayrock, sat before his sturdy home, with its smooth-timbered walls and solid slate roof, reflecting upon the feeling of impending menace that had gnawed at him of late. The great firbolg leaned back, using a short sword designed for a human's hand to pick his great teeth. He looked upward and studied the glowering skies with a cautious air.

Around Yak's shoulders hung the cloak that had given him his name, though the massive, grinning skull currently flopped down his back. He wore it as his helm only at times of great ceremony or in battle, though since coming to Grayrock, he had found no need for combat.

He could never forget, however, that the cloak and its attendant skull had come to him following the most savage battle of all. The sleek black pelt, with its four clawed feet, had once adorned the body of Shantu, the great displacer beast. The tentacles that had grown from the creature's shoulders now served the firbolg as the straps with which he secured it about his broad shoulders. The human king, Tristan Kendrick, had encouraged Yak to skin the beast and to wear the pelt as a badge of honor.

Yet as always, Yak couldn't remember that fight without a tremor of shame and self-doubt. Had he not fled from the enemy, just when his companions' lives were in the greatest danger? The fact that he had fled from an earthly manifestation of a greatly evil god, as had several other of the young king's companions, in no way assuaged the proud firbolg's sense of guilt.

It had been that guilt, even more than the desecration of Myrloch Vale and the waning of the goddess, that had persuaded Yak to break from the usual firbolg patterns of pastoral wilderness existence.

After the battle with Bhaal, he had been spurred by an inexplicable longing. Marching to the northern coast of Gwynneth during the year following the chaos of war, he brought with him his two wives and a half dozen or so other members of his tribe.

They came upon the wreckage of a northman longship on the coast, and, ever skilled woodworkers, the firbolgs took another full year to prepare the craft for sea. As of then, Yak still didn't know where he would take his little band, but the urge to embark had grown stronger in him every day. Finally, the ship completed, they had hoisted a small, heavy sail of deerskin and allowed the wind to carry them.

The memory of that epic voyage still brought a lump to Yak's throat. Never before had firbolgs embarked on such an adventurous quest! The distance they sailed wasn't great by human standards, but they traversed the length of the Sea of Moonshae, from south to north, and came safely and unerringly to their lonely, windswept goal.

Guided by the wind and the tide, the firbolgs reached Grayrock, an inhospitable mass of stone emerging from the pounding surf. A craggy precipice formed the island's shoreline, and a few grasses and shrubs, but not a single tree, withered in small pockets of soil between jagged blocks of granite.

High waves cast the unique vessel into these rocks, but the heavily reinforced keel, a far greater trunk than humans could have employed, did not break. Instead, the firbolgs' ship balanced precariously on a rocky ledge, and the passengers debarked, scrambling upward to the more level ground surmounting the cliffs. Soon the modified longship teetered, and then plunged back into the waves, where the current carried it westward and it vanished into the gray, rolling wastes of the Trackless Sea.

The castaways set about searching their new home and quickly discovered that the level central plateau seemed more habitable than the rocky shore. Finally the truth became apparent—the reason that explained everything to Yak and completed the purpose of his life.

In a grotto at the center of the islet, they found a Moonwell. Like those upon Gwynneth, this pool had no power remaining. Yet it was pristine and clear, a place of sacred purity. The water felt warm to the touch.

It was this remnant of a once-profound power to which Yak would devote the rest of his years. Saddened by the virtual annihilation of his people—for he did not know that firbolg tribes still lived on Alaron, Norland, Moray, and even

Gwynneth—and the supposed passing of the goddess who was part of all life around them, Yak looked with bucolic relief upon this placid duty.

Contrary to most human opinion, especially among the Ffolk, the firbolgs were not, and had never been, the foes of the goddess Earthmother. Indeed, they were among her most ancient followers, and their worship of her—while never formalized nor cultured—remained, in an obscure way, loyal.

Through nearly twenty years now, encouraged by the prayers and ministrations of the giant-kin, the Moonwell showed no signs of decay. The isle grew rich in barley and moorgrass. Drawn by the new fertility, northmen came and settled the rocky shore, and for years, they never suspected the presence of their firbolg neighbors. When members of the two races finally met, it was in peace. Now, when they occasionally encountered one another on the small island, they cautiously avoided giving offense and quickly parted.

But for the first time in two decades, Yak felt a sense of danger, a menace that disturbed his peaceful existence and brought him to a pitch of readiness. Now, sitting in the door of his house, he slowly raised the great cat's skull and placed it upon his huge, shaggy head. The jaw, with its long, wickedly pointed teeth, rested upon his forehead, the fangs framing his eyes. His huge nose jutted outward like a block of granite, and his brown beard flowed down his chest in a lush, rippling torrent.

His small tribe gathered from the nearby houses and the pastures where they tended sheep and goats. A dozen of them assembled, hulking adult firbolgs, each at least ten feet tall. The youngsters they left to play, but Yak fixed each of these full-grown tribe members with a somber glare.

"Danger threatens us," he announced, "of a form I know not what, though it will strike from heaven and sea together. We must go to the humans who live here and warn them."

The others could not question their war chief when he wore the great helm of his rank. The mighty beings dispersed around the island, each going to one of the small collections of hovels and fish shacks where the northmen lived.

Yak himself proceeded to the largest of these, following the rough, downhill trail toward the place where perhaps three dozen buildings huddled together. He was still high above the human habitations when he saw the huge, shadowy form descend from the gray clouds. It was a long beast, serpentlike, with a trailing tail and long, pointed wings—a dragon!

The monster's wings had an odd, insubstantial look to them. As it came closer, the firbolg saw why: Much of the leathery skin had rotted away, yet somehow the beast flew, propelled by a web of bones!

A blast of fire erupted from the serpent's gaping maw, and the watchers saw smoke spew from gaps in the long neck where flesh and scale had rotted away. The cloud trailed in the air behind the monster, like a spoor marking its trail, but that spume was as nothing compared to the infernal blast that erupted before it every time it belched its awful breath weapon.

Then the horror expanded as fish-men, the sahuagin, emerged from the sea, scaling the rocks around the little village and attacking from all sides, trapping the helpless humans within. In moments, the attack became a slaughter as the dragon soared back and forth overhead, rending with its great claws and spewing hellish flame from its awful jaws.

Suddenly the dragon banked, veering toward the highland above the village. Yak ducked away from the trail, diving across the broken ground, racing toward a narrow cave he had discovered years ago. He reached the entrance and crept inside, turning cautious eyes skyward.

Outside, the Claws of the Deep spread around the shore of the island, aided by the death-spewing beast in the skies.

* * * * *

"Lances first, men. We want to make sure they get a good look at our banners." Larth growled the order quietly as he unfurled the silken image of the Great Bear, the royal symbol of the Ffolk.

His company, pledged to the service of Talos, was drawn into a long line. Thirty armored knights sat astride their warhorses, each armed with a long steel-tipped shaft. The long march through the Fairheight Mountains had proved to be a surprising ordeal. Since they couldn't take the main roads, they had been forced to lead the heavy mounts along muddy trails and up and down steep ridges. Only on the previous day had they finally reached lowlands again.

But these were the lowlands of Gnarhelm, and before them was a community of northmen. Larth and his warriors were about to start earning their pay.

The predawn mist swirled around them while the small village of fishermen slowly came awake. Oil lamps winked in some of the windows, and one enterprising sailor was already preparing his boat at the village pier.

"After the first charge with the lance," Larth concluded with a grim smile, "we use the swords."

A horse whinnied nervously somewhere along his line, and in the village a dog began to bark. In a few moments, it was joined by a chorus of other dogs.

"Now—charge!" shouted Larth. "Remember, no prisoners!"

Twenty minutes later, the dogs had ceased to bark.

* * * * *

Musings of the Harpist

I watch the princess and future queen of my people, and again I see her as the little girl I knew so long ago. She possesses an innocence, reflected especially in her laugh, that has quickly won the hearts of our captors. But in her joy and her sincerity, she reveals herself, and she does not know her own weakness.

May the goddess watch over you, child, even though she has not watched over anyone these past twenty years! The hopes of all of us depend on that.

❧ 13 ❧

A Minion of Talos

Deirdre slept but little, her mind surging forward, out of control with ideas and ambitions and new, profound understandings. The power! Never had she imagined such might as now, she knew, lay within her very grasp!

For a few moments, her mind drifted to more conventional concerns. Reports had reached the castle from several different coastal cantrevs claiming that northmen had savagely raided and plundered the Ffolk. This serious violation had alarmed the soldiers and captains of the king's guard. Because of her mother's malaise, the officers had sought Deirdre's permission to muster the Ffolk to arms, but she had not granted them that authority. To her, it seemed that these tales of war and atrocity were unreal. Reality was what she found in her books!

Once more her thoughts turned to those ideas, those powers. She almost laughed out loud in her delight at a re-membered image: She, Deirdre, raising a block of earth into a form that walked, a monstrous slave! Or doing the same with fire, or water, or even air! She knew that she would travel places in the blink of an eye, could gain the knowledge of se-cret counsels, of kings and wizards. . . .

Even of the gods themselves.

And the price, it seemed, was small. The books had shown her the way, and Malawar had been her guide. Now she stood at the brink of might, and it remained only for her to take the final step.

The oath. A pledge to Talos of a life devoted to his cause. But the cause, Deirdre knew, was one much related to her own ambitions. Indeed, she could serve her god well in her high state as princess of the isles.

Finally she closed her eyes in a semblance of sleep. She did not hear the slight gusting of wind that billowed her curtains, entering the room stealthily and gathering as a mist to hang over her bed.

Instead, she dreamed of Malawar—golden-haired, bright Malawar, with his subtle knowledge of her inner self and his soft smile that melted her heart so that she could think, when confronted by its glow, of nothing else! In her dreams, they went through the world together, outside the walls of this room, to everywhere she imagined.

And the cloudy thing in the air above her lithe body coalesced as she dreamed, watching and sharing her vision. It was much pleased, though the ephemeral form gave no sign of the fact. Two spots of red, however, glowed like sparks. They burned side by side, where the eyes might be if it were a human form, and their heat washed crimson across Deirdre's face.

But still she slept, and in her dream, Malawar took her into his arms and held her, and she knew joy. She sensed him beckon to her, and then he stood before a cave, which loomed very dark and gloomy against the ecstatic backdrop of her dream.

Yet Malawar entered that cave, and again he turned to urge her to follow. That smile twisted his face, and for the first time, it frightened her, causing her to clap a hand to her mouth and take a step backward.

But finally he entered and the blackness swallowed him. Standing still for a moment, Deirdre took a step forward, and then another.

She had no choice but to follow.

* * * * *

Alicia knew, as their conversation progressed, that she liked the young northern prince. Sincerity seemed to underline his voice—though the outrage remained present, masked but slightly—when he described the reports of massacre brought by the fisherman to Svenyird and the ambush attack against his column by the arrows of the High King.

"It would seem that someone seeks to indict my father's throne in these crimes, but you have my word, he's blameless!" Alicia was profoundly relieved to see that Brandon believed her.

"In fact, his anger will be as great as yours when he learns what's happened," Keane added. When King Kendrick would receive this information, the mage knew, was an open question. Until then, the queen and her daughters would rule.

The Prince of Gnarhelm had ordered Tavish's harp and staff returned to her, and then the trio of guests had spent the meal hearing Brandon's tale. They learned of the attack on the island and heard the details of the ambush that had slain Knaff the Younger. The puzzle of the attackers' nature grew more and more enigmatic and irritating.

Then Alicia described the attack of the iron golem, with its great horned helm. The princess omitted the details of Keane's sorcery, but she saw Brandon's eyes narrow as the prince studied the magic-user, picturing the enormity and fearfulness of the foe. Obviously he suspected that there was more to the thin man than first met the eye.

"It would seem that someone seeks to bring our two peoples into conflict," concluded Tavish, summing up. "But for what purpose? A vexing question, that!"

Brandon scowled fiercely, and the firelight glinted in his blue eyes. Finally he looked at Alicia, his expression frank. "Will you journey to Gnarhelm with me to tell my father, the king, what you know? It may be that more has been learned there as well. Together, we may put this issue to the test."

The princess felt her heart quicken, not entirely with curiosity. She found this handsome, strapping warrior to be a man of courage, honor, and decision. Here, basking in the warmth of a highland campfire, she decided that these three traits formed the qualities she most admired in a man.

She sensed that Tavish and Keane awaited her decision with some trepidation, but she didn't look at them. This was a decision she was determined to make alone. For a moment, she considered rationally: The kingdom was not in danger from the northmen now that Brandon's force returned to his capital. She had fulfilled her obligation with Blackstone, having ruled that the Moonwell be preserved. And now the mystery of her attackers . . . Could it not be solved as likely in Gnarhelm as in Callidyrr?

"Yes, I'll accompany you. And my companions, if they should so choose."

"Of course," Tavish agreed quickly. "It's been a long time since I've enjoyed the hospitality of a northman's lodge!"

Keane nodded silently, avoiding Alicia's eyes. Instead, she saw him studying the prince of the north, and his expression toward Brandon was not entirely friendly.

They agreed to begin the march northward in the morning, and Brandon showed his guests to a comfortably soft meadow for their rest, near to but not within the camp of the northmen themselves. Here the three companions retired soon, though the early summer sunset still brightened the skies above their eternal blanket of gray.

"Are you sure this is a wise decision?" asked Keane, his tone sharp, when they had passed from the hearing of Brandon's warriors.

"Do you mistrust them?" Alicia shot back. "Didn't he—they—honor their promise when you took the Test of Strength?" Suddenly she felt a twinge of guilt, remembering the risk he had taken on their behalf. Yet the feeling didn't change the fact that she found his manner condescending, and so she said nothing further.

"The prince has proven an honorable host," Keane replied, stiffly. "And I do not suspect him of treachery. Yet what of your responsibilities to the kingdom? Shouldn't you carry word of these events to Callidyrr?"

"What word? We don't know who or what's behind these attacks. Maybe we'll learn more in Gnarhelm! If you want to go back to Callidyrr, you may. Tell them what's happened so far. I'm sure you can pop back there in the blink of an eye or something, can't you?"

The magic-user sighed. "I'll come with you, of course. Now perhaps you'll permit me the comfort of a little sleep before we start out in the morning."

Still angry, Alicia sought out her bed. Some of the northmen had thoughtfully staked a cloak over the ground for her, so that at least her head and torso wouldn't feel the beat of the rain that had resumed a short time ago. Confused, thinking that she should feel happier, she didn't gasp or scream when great snakes started to crawl from the ground around her bed, their ravenous mouths reaching out toward her slender legs.

"Cut it out, Newt!" she snapped, lying down amidst the serpents, which slowly faded to nothing. The little faerie dragon popped into sight behind her, and when she ignored him he curled up at her feet and waited for her to sleep.

Why, wondered Newt, was everyone so peevish around here?

* * * * *

While it was true that teleportation lay within the province of Keane's power, he wasn't about to concede this point to the stubborn princess. In fact, however, if the need was acute, he could have returned to Caer Callidyrr in somewhat less time than the blink of an eye.

Privately, in the silence of the highland night, he admitted that his reasons for objecting to their continued excursion were more personal and selfish.

It was true that he found saddles uncomfortable and nights spent outdoors unsettling—and guaranteed to provide him with a backache upon awakening. He desired nothing so much as a return to his soft feather bed and the warmth and comforts of Caer Callidyrr. Not to mention its kitchens, he reminded himself, as a belch reminded him of the pickled fish he had shared with the northmen this evening.

But none of these factors touched the heart of the reason Alicia's decision bothered him. These thoughts he dared not admit, even to himself, but they concerned the way the bright-eyed princess had studied the rock-chiseled face of Brandon Olafsson.

And the memory was twisted and made more painful by his warm memories of a brief few moments when he had sat beside the princess, watching the waters of the Blackstone Moonwell, and felt her presence as a woman who was near to him in more ways than one.

* * * * *

In Blackstone Manor, Sir Hanrald knew a similar disquiet, though from a somewhat different cause. At its root, however, lay the knight's attraction to the fair Alicia. He had retired early and detected a certain sense of relief in his father's mood at the time. This awareness had tingled his suspicions, which still mused over the memory of his return home and the awkward meeting in the Great Hall. His brother's injury had never been satisfactorily explained.

Even more than this, however, Hanrald had sensed an atmosphere of conspiracy between his elder brother and his father, the earl. This had been the main reason for his early departure from the Great Hall. He did not, however, fall asleep in his chambers.

Throughout Hanrald's life, his father had shunned him when affairs of importance were involved, always welcoming only Currag and Gwyeth to his counsel. At times, Hanrald felt as if he was a mere guest, a traveler who had been granted the shelter of his father's house but not greeted into the arms of the family itself.

For a moment, his mind tugged at the fringes of the stories he had heard . . . rumors, just gossip really, about the mother he had never known. But he rejected those thoughts, as he always did. Now he had important work to do.

His emotions burning with suspicion and fears of betrayal, he rose from his bed more than an hour later and crept to a wall near the back of his room. Here he touched a panel, and a slab of the stone wall pivoted slowly open before him. Seizing a flickering taper, he stepped into the cobweb-draped corridor that vanished into the dusty distance beyond.

The way was known to him, not as an heir to the family home but because he had followed his older brothers on more than one occasion when Gwyeth or Currag had entered these secret chambers. Only those of Blackstone blood were shown the true secrets of the great manor, and yet the earl hadn't chosen to include his third son in these confidences.

Hanrald knew, however, that these passages connected most of the important bedrooms and guest rooms of the house to each other. He also knew that, in the winding catacombs far below his feet, dark torture chambers existed, cells that would never acknowledge the light of day. Until now, he had accepted his father's explanations that such places were no longer used. Now, however, he wasn't prepared to accept anything the earl told him at face value.

Tonight his mission did not call for an investigation of those catacombs. Instead, he followed the narrow corridor for no more than forty paces, coming to an aperture that he knew was concealed on the other side by the back wall of a great fireplace . . .

. . . the fireplace that warmed the anteroom of his father's private chambers. This, he knew, would be the location of any clandestine meeting. He placed his faint candle far back along the passage so that no telltale glow would reveal him through a chink between the stones.

As Hanrald knelt by the secret door, stuffing a hand over his nose to stifle an impending sneeze brought about by the dusty nature of his surroundings, he heard a deep voice that he recognized as belonging to his father, Earl Blackstone.

Gently the knight pushed at the stone slab that formed the door. A faint crack of light washed through the narrow gap, and the voices came to his ears more clearly.

Surprisingly, the first words he heard clearly came from neither his father nor his brother. Instead, a third man spoke, his voice a forceful hiss.

"You yourself must journey to the palace. She will employ your aid, willingly enough I shall ensure, and the furtherance of our plans shall be guaranteed."

"But what of the High Queen? Surely she will not allow her daughter to direct the affairs of the kingdom," spoke the Earl of Fairheight.

"She lies all unknowing," replied the strange, hissing voice. "The younger princess is in fact the voice of the crown in Callidyrr."

"Mayhaps she'll be more of a feminine wench than her sister." This crude growl, Hanrald knew, issued from his brother, Gwyeth. His blood surged at the insult to the Princess Alicia, but he forced himself to restrain his temper.

"She is comely, but you would do well not to press her for advantage," whispered the strange voice, with a strong hint of menace. "For her powers of magic are great, and he who gives her offense will not live to see many sunrises."

Hanrald grinned in silent pleasure, picturing the expression on Gwyeth's face. His brother would surely be displeased by such a warning, yet—especially in view of his humiliation from the magic of Keane—the older son would take no risks where sorcery was concerned.

Then the concealed knight scowled, wishing he dared push the secret portal open farther to catch a view of the stranger who spoke with his father and brother. Yet he had already taken a great risk by opening the small crack, and further movement might reveal itself in the room by sound or even sight.

"I depart tomorrow, after I make arrangements to tend the duchy," continued the earl. "You, Gwyeth, will remain in charge of the cantrev. Also, I place in your hands the matter of this Moonwell's destruction. See that it is accomplished quickly, without fanfare."

"What of Hanrald?"

The eavesdropping knight stiffened as he heard his brother speak his name.

"I don't trust him with knowledge of our plans. I'll dispatch him on a hunt, which should serve to keep him occupied and uncurious. By the time he returns, the thing will be done."

"Splendid." Once again the visitor spoke, and this time his voice was muffled, as if he spoke through a cloth, or perhaps a deep hood. "When you next see me, it will be in the halls of Caer Callidyrr itself!"

Hanrald heard a whooshing sound, as if a wind blew through the room beyond the door, and then his brother cursed. "By the gods! Why can't he leave by the door like a normal man?"

"You have answered your own question," replied his father, his voice once again a low rumble. His tone, however, was not displeased. "Now I must prepare. I have much to do before I ride."

Hanrald heard the door to the anteroom open and close. No further sound reached his ear, and as his taper grew low, he crept back to his own chamber to ponder on what he had heard.

*   *   *   *   *

Followed by the column of northman warriors, Alicia and her companions led their horses at a walk down the steep mountain trails. Persistent rain often covered the trail with spatter-

ing rivulets of muddy water, making the footing treacherous
and the pace slow.

Brandon walked beside the princess, while Tavish and
Keane trailed a bit to the rear. The Ffolk knew that Newt
buzzed somewhere around them, but after a stern rebuke
from the princess in the morning, the faerie dragon had reluctantly pledged to refrain from practical jokes. Instead, he had
become invisible and gave no clue as to his location.

The hulking Wultha walked close behind the magic-user,
squinting at him with his tiny eyes and often scratching his
head, as if still trying the grasp the events of the previous
night. Nevertheless, the huge man's manner was friendly,
even respectful, to the mage, a fact Keane found reassuring in
the extreme.

Brandon had posted scouts on either flank of the column, so
their progress was of necessity slow. Yet this didn't seem to
annoy the prince, for he talked with Alicia of the wonders of his
realm, as if they had all the time in the world.

"The march will take several days," explained the prince.
"We're closer to Callidyrr than Gnarhelm."

"It will be pleasant to see some of your realm," replied Alicia
honestly. She wondered if her enthusiasm came from the prospect of new scenery—especially masked by rain, as it had
been so far—as much as from the company of the rugged warrior at her side.

"You have never been to a city of the north?" inquired Brandon somewhat awkwardly. He didn't know why, but his usual
bluff self-confidence was held firmly in check by the presence
of the beautiful auburn-haired woman beside him.

"No. I have seen Corwell, and Westphal on Snowdown—and
the towns of Callidyrr, of course. I've even seen Waterdeep
and some of the wonders of the Sword Coast. But never have
I been among your people, our neighbors."

"My father's lodge is the greatest building north of the
mountains!" Brandon proclaimed, his arms spreading expan-
sively. "And Gnarhelm has many great captains, each of whom
dwells in his own splendid lodge! But the bay and the shipyard
truly make the city the place that I love."

Alicia, for her part, enjoyed listening to the prince of the
north. She felt a sense of growing peace. The attack of the

iron golem seemed like a distant nightmare, and even the billowing gray clouds overhead couldn't darken her mood. The wind whipped full into their faces, and frequent showers doused them, but she pulled her cloak tightly about her and enjoyed the snug comfort of her wrap. Then, as the latest squall passed away, she uncovered her head again as Brandon spoke to her.

"Your father is a great king," said the prince of the north. "My kinsman, Grunnarch the Red, has spoken very highly of him."

"I know the Red King," Alicia responded, inordinately delighted that she had found some common ground with Brandon. "He has visited Callidyrr several times. My father says that he is a ruler of vision and courage."

"Aye, many times over. It was no easy task to persuade his warriors to go to the aid of the Ffolk a score of years ago."

"But because he did, you and I might be friends—else, for certain, we would have met at sword's point!" Alicia reflected with a quiet laugh.

Brandon looked at her in surprise, at first thinking she mocked him by suggesting that he would fight a woman. Then he remembered that the Ffolk were odd that way. Indeed, this princess dressed like a warrior, and she wore her sword as one who knew its purpose. Interesting, how these features in no way seemed to detract from her femininity. Yet, were a woman of his own people to behave thus, she would have been counted a lunatic or worse.

"I am truly glad, Princess, that such was not the case," he declared, meeting her green eyes with his own of sea blue. He wanted to say much more, but he couldn't.

Alicia met his look, but if she sensed the feeling there, she didn't show it. "And so, Prince Brandon, am I," was all she said.

* * * * *

Yak remained hidden in the cave for several hours, recognizing the futility of resistance against the hideous dragon. Finally, toward dawn, the firbolg emerged into the darkness that was only slightly less complete than it had been within the sheltering niche.

A circuitous route back to his tribe showed Yak that, to the best of his discernment, all the humans had perished at the hands of the savage seaborne attackers. Fortunately the Claws of the Deep and their giant serpentine ally had apparently vacated the isle when their killing was done.

Finally Yak and the other firbolgs headed back toward the pastoral vale of the Moonwell and the small village of his tribe. Though he didn't display his fear, the great firbolg's heart nearly burst from tension as he approached the place. If the dragon had found it, he knew, all of his kin might have perished in the butchery of a few moments. Even worse, to the reverent creature, the Moonwell they had so diligently tended might have been so polluted by blood or soot that it was no longer a fit place of purity and worship.

Yak's sigh of relief was heavy and real when they crested the rim of the little vale, and he saw that the houses and pool remained intact. Sunrise had lightened the clouds, though the gray filter cast everything in a haze, and Yak even saw many of his tribe gathered in the center of the village. They looked expectantly toward him as he trudged down the steep slope and into the little swale.

"What did your searches reveal?" he asked them.

"The creatures attacked all along the shore," said one called Beaknod. "We took shelter as you directed us, for we arrived too late to influence any of the fights."

"Aye," huffed another, Loinwrap, a strapping warrior with a face like a granite cliff and muscles to match. "Though it did not sit well, this cowering and watching a fight. Still," he admitted, "your wisdom cannot be denied. The monsters did not learn of our village."

"Nor," said Yak pointedly, "of the well. *That* is the important thing."

"Why is it so important, if our whole island is sacked in its protection?" questioned Loinwrap, who was no theologian.

Yak sighed. "Why bring children into the world? Why sow grain in the spring? Why do we bother to breathe? You may as well ask me these things, for they are all answered the same.

"I know humans," continued the chief of the village. "They will soon seek one to blame for these deaths, and we must ensure that such charges do not fall against us."

"Why?" countered Loinwrap again. "On our rock, we have naught to fear from humans!"

"Contrarily," disputed Yak, who had indeed learned something of the nature of mankind. "If they decide we are to blame, then we shall have no peace against the numbers of them who come here."

"And how do we change this?" inquired an elderly female, Yildegarde.

"I shall sail to Alaron and speak with them myself," announced the firbolg, enjoying the gaping mouths of his tribe members as they regarded him with astonishment. "You, Beaknod, and you, Loinwrap—you will come, too."

* * * * *

"Whyfor is the sea like a woman?" inquired the painted half-ling, with a sweeping bow to the throne. The bells dangling from his many-pointed cap jingled, and his costume ballooned around him, humorously exaggerating the gesture. Within the lofty seat, Svenyird Olafsson, King of Gnarhelm and Proud Master of the Surrounding Seas, guffawed heartily.

"Tell me, fool. Whyfor is the ocean the same as a wench?"

"Because when once she grasps a man full in her embrace, he will never again be free of her!" The voice, from the door of the great lodge, drew all attention away from the suddenly perspiring halfling.

"Brandon—my son! Welcome!" boomed the king, rising and holding open his arms in an expansive greeting. "But your mission has finished early! Do you bring word from Callidyrr?"

"Far better, Father. I come with an emissary of the kingdom to the south. She is the High Princess Alicia, daughter of King Kendrick and now ambassador to our realm of Gnarhelm!"

The painted jester stepped back, and the prince led his guests to the great throne. The assembled northmen stared at the woman who followed Brandon into the lodge. Though she wore riding breeches and a stout travel-stained tunic, she walked with a bearing that bespoke her royalty. She approached the throne of King Svenyird and performed a gesture that was half bow, half curtsy.

"Greetings, king of the north. I bring salutations and warm wishes from my father and inform you of his own desire that peace between our peoples shall last well past the times of our children's children!"

"Good speech," agreed the king. "And welcome to mine own lodge. Come, we will talk as soon as you have rested. I grow weary of the prattling of my fool.

"We shall make feast tonight!" proclaimed Svenyird, feeling more relief than he cared to admit now that he was reassured the Ffolk did not plan to make war against him.

"We have news, sire," said Brandon, pressing forward and trying to catch his father's eye.

But the king was in no mood for serious talk now. "It shall be our first topic of conversation after we eat! Now, my son, don't be a boor! Show our guests to quarters in my lodge!"

"Aye, sire," agreed Brandon, with a quick look at Alicia. She seemed to enjoy his awkwardness, and he flushed. "Well, let's find some place for you to stay," he grunted, leading the three Ffolk from the Great Hall of the smoky lodge.

* * * * *

"You, Danrak, must be the one." Meghan spoke firmly, the strength in her voice belying her cronelike appearance.

"But there are many more worthy," protested the druid, suddenly frightened. "Mikal, who tamed the great brown bear . . . or Isolde, daughter of the glen! Surely they are wiser than I!"

Meghan's lips twisted, and she allowed her eyes to smile a little. "Wiser . . . perhaps. But you, Danrak—you are elf-reared, and of us all, you have strength enough that you might endure the trials before you. And then there are the dreams . . . the tokens."

The last remark could brook no argument. Danrak bit his tongue, further objections dying unsaid. He looked at the be-draggled Ffolk around him and realized that she spoke the truth. These, the ones who remained of the druid apprentices of twenty years before, made a battered lot, ill-used by the passage of time.

Mikal, whose beard had streaked silver before Danrak

shaved his first whiskers, was indeed too old to make the trip. Now he leaned upon the great bear that, during the last dozen years, he had reared and tamed. It served as his steed, in fact, and was the sole reason the withered druid had arrived at this council. And for the quest before them, Danrak knew that no companion could help.

That was why the druids had gathered here, upon the far northern shore of Gwynneth, where the land reached with rocky fingers into the Sea of Moonshae. Standing at the very headland of Gwynneth, the druids overlooked many miles of gray water. The coasts of Alaron, to the east, and Oman, to the west, lay far over the gray horizons, and to the north lay hundreds of miles of chill, rolling sea.

It was stormy water, and a surface that must be crossed by the druid sent on this quest.

A rocky promontory dropped sharply a hundred feet or more into the foaming surf. The steady cadence of the sea came to them from below like a booming tempo that marked away the minutes remaining to them. Danrak felt, with a cold shudder, that those minutes had become all too few. Perhaps not the entire time of his life had been good, but he surprised himself by realizing, when faced with its possible and potentially imminent end, how much he wanted to keep living, to sample many more minutes of existence.

Closing his eyes, Danrak offered a quiet prayer to the goddess. Though he felt no response to his act of faith, the litany soothed him, and he felt better prepared to face the challenge implicit in Meghan's remarks.

"Here, Danrak," said a softly female voice. "I made this for you—just the way it was in my dream." Petite Isolde, her black hair framing a round and very serious face, held an object in her hand.

"Thank you, sister," he said, clasping the small feather in his hand.

"And here, brother," offered Kile, extending a small curved object, the crossed talons of a great wolf's paw.

"You, too, Kile?" Danrak could not help asking. "You had this dream?"

"Aye, and I carved the claw as it was in the dream."

A young druid called Lorn gave Danrak a shiny pebble,

which he said had come from a shallow streambed. Danrak saw that it bore a circular spot, like the pupil of an eye. Forn had smoothed and polished the bauble until now it glowed more brightly than gold.

One by one the others gave him the gifts they had made—things of animal, or plant, or earth. With each bestowal, Danrak felt a flowing of love and a slowly growing sense of power. Each of the druids had spent months in the preparation of the talisman, and now all of their might, limited though it was, flowed together into one. All of them had made the objects of their dreams, and in those dreams, they had given them to Danrak.

Only Danrak had had no dream, had seen no token. Yet he couldn't ignore the combined will and prescience of the others.

"I will go on the quest as the goddess commands," announced Danrak, when they had finally finished. He carried the talismans about his person, in belt pouches and pockets and, in some cases, pinned to his woolen tunic.

"May her benevolence watch over you," said Meghan quietly, her voice catching. Danrak was surprised and touched to see tears gathering in her eyes.

The others stood back, forming a loose ring around him. Trying to suppress the trembling in his knees, Danrak stepped to the edge of the promontory. He didn't look down, yet he remained acutely conscious of the surf pounding against the jagged boulders far below.

It had been decades since any druid had gained power from the goddess, either to cast a spell or to employ the innate abilities of their order. This had been the reason for the talismans, but none of them knew if their hopes had any basis in truth.

Now Danrak took the pebble from Lorn. He looked at it and stroked it with his fingertips. Finally he touched it to his forehead, and then cast it into the distance, watching as it soared to the north and then suddenly veered to the right, to the east. He felt a strong sense of destiny and purpose and now, with the flight of the stone, he knew where to go.

Still, it took an act of faith to see if his intuition—indeed, the hopes and plans of all the druids—had been correct. They didn't know if the years of toil and craftsmanship had indeed

DOUGLAS NILES

been able to impart to them some sense of the old art, the old skills that had gained for the order mastery over the wild places of Moonshae.

Slowly, reverently, Danrak took the feathered token given him by Isolde from a pouch at his side. He looked at the woman and saw her as she had been twenty years ago, a red-cheeked girl bursting with the faith of nature, then confused when that faith had seemed to desert her.

Now she smiled, and once again Danrak saw her as that girl. He tried to remember some of his own faith when the goddess had been real, her power accessible to any druid of serious nature and righteous virtue. Surprising himself, he felt the memories flow into him, bringing a surge of joy the like of which he had never known.

He held the feathered token lightly between his fingers, feeling the wind carry the plumes away as he slowly toppled forward. An image came into his mind, of a white gull dipping along the shore of a sea. Wind rushed into his face, roaring in his ears, and the shoreline whirled below him, rushing upward terribly fast.

And then, instead of striking the rocks, he flew.

* * * * *

From the Log of Sinioth:

My princess, you tantalize me with your dreams. Soon— very soon now—you shall make your pledge, and we will share the same master. Then the secrets will be yours and mine to share.

And then, too, will we share the land of your people.

❧ 14 ❧

Gnarhelm

The northman capital of Gnarhelm was, to Alicia, disappointingly small and rustic by comparison to Callidyrr. The city centered around a hundred great log buildings, which Brandon proudly indicated as the lodges of Gnarhelm's sea captains. Many houses of drab, weatherbeaten wood dotted the shoreline and pastures around the lodges. Tracks of dirt led to them, and sheep and goats grazed on the scruffy patches of grass that browned the yards.

Beyond these great lodges, across the grassy moors that spread inland for miles and reminded Alicia of the rolling country of her parents' home in Corwell, hundreds of small farms dotted the land. The barns and pastures looked brown and withered and much less prosperous than those of the Ffolk. Sheep and goats and occasionally cattle or horses managed to eke out a survival from the harsh terrain.

The streets seemed empty, almost deserted. The princess enjoyed the bustling market of Callidyrr, with its crowds, music, jugglers, and booths. Of course, the rain, steadily drumming since her arrival, discouraged such activity here. In Callidyrr, the buildings along shop streets were lined with overhanging arches, sheltering the walk down either side of the road. Gnarhelm offered no such amenity. Still, she had accepted Brandon's offer to tour the town, and she knew it would be fruitless to wait for a cessation of the rain.

"These are the smithies and the wainwright!" the prince explained as they walked along the edge of the main street of mostly hard-packed dirt. The center of the avenue was a morass of ruts, mudholes, and pools of brown water.

Brandon pointed out several great barnlike buildings. Sounds of hammering emerged from one where the doors stood open, and Alicia saw a craftsmen pounding an iron rim onto a spoked wheel. The princess realized that these, the great centers of this capital, were no larger than any of a dozen such shops that could be found throughout the mercantile quarter of Callidyrr. She refrained, however, from speaking of her conclusions, since the prince's pride in his realm was obvious and she had no wish to offend him.

Finally Brandon led Alicia to the waterfront, and here she saw real fire come into the northman prince's eyes. Salmon Bay jutted like a stabbing finger of sea into northern Alaron, and Gnarhelm occupied the shoreline of a sheltered cove near the southern end of the bay. Alicia marveled at the many graceful longships at rest in the dark, gentle waters of the large, natural harbor.

She counted more than a score of the vessels, each nearly a hundred feet in length, with sweeping lines and proudly curved prows. On some, she saw figureheads, many of women, though others depicted great beasts such as an eagle-headed griffon, a bear, or even a leering dragon. The princess watched a crew haul in the anchor of one sleek longship several hundred yards from shore. The sail of the vessel unfurled with a sudden billow, revealing the image of a crimson hawk, wings spread wide. With practiced ease, the helmsman turned the prow toward the mouth of the harbor, and the ship fairly sprang into the bay.

Among the anchored longships, gathered like dogs slumbering among horses, bobbed a number of fishing craft, some with sails hoisted, others tacking out to sea, where they swiftly vanished in the gray haze. Like the longships, these sturdy knarrs were deckless. Crates, nets, buoys, and baskets filled the hulls of the smaller fishing vessels. Great sheds at the other end of the dock emitted the unmistakable smell of fish, and Alicia felt a sense of relief when Brandon led her in the other direction, along the length of the solid wharf.

Beside the long pier stretched an area where the princess saw the bony outline of a new longship, the keel formed from a trunk of a gigantic mountain fir. Even in the partial state of the vessel's completion, she recognized a grand ship, larger than any of those currently within the bay. Hull boards ran partway up the ribwork, but she saw that the gunwales lay far above the unfinished section.

Piles of logs lay nearby, and shirtless northmen, their hair constrained by long braids down their backs, labored at shaving these into planks. Other men carried the lumber to the skeleton framework, where still more workers skillfully formed the boards to fit the sleek shape of the hull.

"She's beautiful," Alicia said sincerely.

"And she will be mine," Brandon replied. For once, the pride that had filled his voice with boasts faded into the background, replaced by a reverent sense of awe that the woman found very compelling.

"What's her name?"

Brandon smiled, his eyes distant. "I haven't chosen one yet. It will be an important decision."

The princess sensed the pride in his voice, and it seemed to soften the warrior in her eyes. She remembered Mouse and Brittany and her own fast chariot, and she understood how Brandon felt about his ship.

"Look out there," said the prince, indicating one of the largest longships currently floating in the bay. The ship's prow curved into the sweeping figure of a long-beaked bird. "That's the *Gullwing*. She's been my ship for five years now, and a proud vessel she is."

"The hulls are so low," Alicia observed. "It's amazing the waves don't pour inside!"

"We have to bail now and then," Brandon laughed, stepping so close to her that she could feel the heat of his body beside her through the damp chill of the air. The princess had a sudden desire to board the ship, to feel the smooth hull slide over the waves of the wide sea. With the prince of Gnarhelm at the helm, nothing would be safer—or more exciting.

As if reading her mind, Brandon turned to her. "Perhaps when our business is concluded you'll allow me to carry you back to Callidyrr in the *Gullwing*."

"I'd like that."

Alicia looked at the waterfront again and realized that she saw the heart and soul of Gnarhelm here. No wonder the streets had seemed so plain, the shops and houses mere structures of log, with little adornment and no sense of permanence, entirely unlike the great stone edifices of her own home city. Why should these people devote such efforts to their landbound dwellings? Now she sensed, for the first time, a thing she had long been taught but had never really understood: The northmen looked to the sea for everything—for their homes, their sustenance . . . even, in times past, for their wives. As a daughter of the Ffolk, Alicia had been reared with tales of young women, during her mother's day, seized by northern raiders and carried away to lives in lodges just like these.

Finally she began to understand the neighbors of her people, and in that knowledge, there was no fear, but rather an exciting kind of anticipation.

* * * * *

Yak, Beaknod, and Loinwrap made their gruff farewells to the rest of the tribe and then started for the shore. The great war chief, resplendent in his cat's-head cape with its grinning, fanged helm, desired to depart with little formality.

"Where do we go once we get in the boat?" asked granite-faced Loinwrap, none too enthusiastic about the impending voyage. Yet, as the strongest giant in the band, Loinwrap was indispensable to Yak's mission should they be received with other than open arms.

"To a place where men live," Yak replied. "There we tell them what has happened, so that they know it is not firbolgs who make war upon them!"

Earlier, Yildegarde had found a fishing boat of the northmen stored between concealing rocks. It had escaped the notice of the sahuagin, and thus the hull remained intact. Now the trio of males made their way to the little craft.

"This will carry us? In those waves?" inquired Beaknod, with an anxious look at the gray swells beyond the shore.

"Quit whining. You two come in case we fight, not so I have conversation, just like at my own hearth. Now let's go."

Awed by the leering skull of the beast and also by the knotting muscles in Yak's shoulders, the other two firbolgs complied. In moments, they cast the boat away from shore, and it was immediately seized by the wind.

Perhaps the goddess smiled slightly from the depths of her

long sleep, for though the gales and storms raged around them, with swells rising like mountains on all sides, the three land-dwelling giants ran before the wind, riding a following sea to the southwest.

* * * * *

"I'm off to Callidyrr," announced the Earl of Fairheight as he broke his fast with his sons. "I depart before noon."

Hanrald, though he had overheard his father's plans the previous night, feigned surprise. "You'll carry word about the northmen, I presume?"

"What? Oh, of course," said his father, avoiding the knight's eyes. "Also I'll have a word with the queen regarding the excavations of Granite Ridge."

Hanrald wanted to shout his accusations, his suspicions, at his paternal lord, but he forced himself to hold his tongue. In the first place, he didn't know what accusations to make, and secondly he judged that the time was not yet right.

"I leave the tending of the estates in Gwyeth's care," continued Blackstone. "See that the dwarves don't slack off. They've been grumbling about the hours and the wages again! Enough of this and I'll send the whole bunch back to the Sword Coast and hire myself a new batch of engineers!"

Hanrald knew this to be an empty boast, for the Blackstone mines employed the most skilled tunnel-working dwarves found anywhere along the coast, or a thousand miles inland, for that matter. The trouble, in any event, was that the dwarves realized their worth and insisted on being compensated accordingly.

"And the Moonwell," said Blackstone, turning to address Gwyeth. "Send a squad of men up to that accursed pond. Have them log the cedars and burn the brush. I want these rumors of a miracle stopped!"

"Aye, Father," Gwyeth agreed, his eyes flashing.

"And you, Hanrald—the cooks tell me we have no venison. Go and slay us a stag."

"Certainly." The knight admired his father's ruse. Because of the disappearance of the cantrev's hounds, the hunt for deer would be a challenging and time-consuming one. The request would have kept him from Blackstone for some time— if he had had any intention of making it.

Hanrald found the discussion an interesting charade, since the pair had already made their plans the previous night. The knight's mind clicked through plans of his own, events to occur as soon as his father departed the cantrev and his brother began the task the earl had assigned.

"See that you tend to your duties, especially as regards that Moonwell. This sorcery disturbs me. It must be disposed of quickly. Pull some of the guards off the mine crews to take care of it. I can spare a few men-at-arms."

The earl blotted egg from his beard and rose from the table, still addressing Gwyeth. "Get out to the foremen's stand this morning. I want you to understand what's happening up there."

Hanrald, already forgotten by his father, turned to Gwyeth. "And how fares my brother? I trust that your wound heals cleanly?"

"Don't worry about him," grunted the lord, scowling. "You've enough of your own to tend to."

As the earl returned to his chambers, Hanrald went to the stables himself, but instead of taking a light archer's mount for the hunt, he found his loyal groomsman and told him to quietly ready his war-horse for a journey, letting no one know his intent. Then Hanrald returned to his own rooms, there to gather the few items he would need for his ride.

He had debated about his destination, for first it had seemed to him that he must go to Callidyrr. But several factors had changed his mind.

For one, his father rode along that same road, to the same place, and the son intended to keep his mission a secret from the earl—in the same manner, he reflected, as Blackstone himself sought to deceive Hanrald. But Hanrald also knew that the king was absent, and the queen, according to his eavesdropping, slumbered in an unnatural trance, not knowing what occurred around her.

The ranking member of the royal house, he knew, would thus become the princess Alicia, and she would not be found in Callidyrr. Instead, as far as Hanrald knew, she was still up in the Fairheight Mountains. Perhaps she and her companions had been captured by northmen—a thought that chilled him to the bone. The knight of Blackstone felt clear in his purpose: He would go to the High Princess with his tale of treachery.

Some hours later, the earl and a party of guards trotted from the manor, on the road to Callidyrr. Shortly afterward, Gwyeth rode into the cantrev to assemble and detach a small party of men to the Blackstone Moonwell.

As soon as they had left, Hanrald completed his preparations. He donned his armor of burnished steel and even his heavy helmet, though he would ride with the visor of the faceplate raised. His groom had prepared his steed and stood waiting beside the war-horse, holding Hanrald's lance and his stout shield. A cloak of blue cloth covered the horse, matching the knight's silken overshirt.

"Good luck, my lord!" stammered the youth, his face beaming with pride.

"I have gone to hunt a very large stag," he told the lad, adding a wink. "At least, that's what you'll say to explain my departure."

"Aye, Sir Hanrald!" The fellow saluted sharply as Hanrald hoisted himself into the saddle by means of a wooden step. The knight took his lance and raised it. From the tip fluttered a pennant bearing the Blackstone emblem of two swords crossed over a square shield.

On impulse, Hanrald reached up and tore the silken flag away. He cast it to the ground and grinned at the shocked look on his squire's face.

"From now on," he said, "I ride under no banner but my own."

Then he kicked his armored heels, and the ground in the courtyard shook as his massive charger trotted through the manor. A ray of sun somehow poked its way through the tiniest gap in the clouds, and in the squire's eye, Hanrald's armor glinted like silver for a moment before the fog and the rain closed in again and buried him in the haze.

* * * * *

A full day passed before King Svenyird could find time in his busy schedule to interview the princess from Callidyrr. Alicia had enjoyed the time, the morning spent with Brandon, walking through the town. In the afternoon, she went for a stroll along the shore with Tavish and Keane prior to the meeting with the king.

"I wonder what happened to Newt," Alicia said to them. "I haven't seen him since that first night in Brandon's camp."

"I think the little fellow's gone back home," suggested Keane, his tone indicating that for once the mage thought very highly of the faerie dragon's intentions.

"He'll do that," Tavish agreed. "He's not much for large groups of people or journeys to cities and the like."

"He's not the only one. I haven't had a good night's sleep since we left Callidyrr," complained Keane as they wandered among great trunks of pine, beside the rocks that lined the shore of Salmon Bay. "They gave me some boards and a pad to sleep on, but the straw had gone to mold, and I threw it away!"

"It's good for your spine," teased Alicia. "You get too hunched poring over your tomes all the time."

Keane looked down, his face flushed, and the young woman realized that her remark had truly stung him. Why? She didn't know; it was the kind of thing she said to him all the time.

"To the King of Gnarhelm," said Tavish smoothly but firmly. "What will you say to him?"

"I'll tell him about the golem . . . and I'm sure Brand has already told him about the attack by the archers. I hope to learn if he knows of any other enemies that might deserve the blame for this mischief!"

"Is there no different reason we have come here, then?" inquired Keane, an edge to his tone.

"The princess knows her mind, I expect," said Tavish, gratifying Alicia. "Now let's get to the lodge. It's not too many hours until sunset."

But they found, as they returned to Gnarhelm, that the town was already in an uproar. Rumors raced through the streets, reflected in the looks given to Alicia and her companions as they approached the royal lodge.

"What is it?" she demanded, confronted by the scowl of a warrior from Brandon's band.

"You Ffolk!" he replied, his tone surly but his eyes downcast. "Word has just arrived. An army, under your king's banner, has invaded Gnarhelm!"

* * * * *

Danrak soared to the north in the body of a white gull, not quite believing that he actually flew, or indeed that his body had changed shape. Gradually, however, he accepted the fact that the talisman of Isolde had worked magic upon him.

He shrilled his delight, a harsh cry that swiftly vanished into the limitless expanse of gray sea. He dove, skimming nimbly above the wave tops, bobbing over each restless, foam-crested swell and then swooping into the troughs, racing with dizzying speed over the deep, gray-black water.

For a time, he flew northward, realizing that he simply needed to extend his wings to glide effortlessly along the eddies of the storm-tossed air. For many hours, past the sunset and through the blackest part of the night, the druid glided and sailed, leaving the coast of Gwynneth as a distant memory.

Dawn came, gray and stormy as ever, and Danrak flew through squalls of rain. Once hail pounded him, but he dove away and escaped with nothing more than bruises along his wings and back.

Finally he passed a rocky shore and veered slightly toward the east. He remembered the talisman from Lorn, and the way it had marked his path when he threw it. First north for a long way, but then the stone had veered to the right. Now, as the coastline passed below him, he understood and banked his own course from north to northeast.

Soon crags of granite marked the ground below him, and these grew and expanded like the tail of some horned reptile merging into a broad, plate-studded back. By midday, the gull reached a range of mountains that loomed high enough to challenge his presence in the sky, rending the overcast with their stone-edged crags.

Now, Danrak knew, he was getting close. He dove, darting along a sheer crest and surprising a snow fox in its deadly pursuit of a quail. The gull swept over a final ridge, and there below him he saw it—the thing he had never seen before in his life, but to which the will and power of the goddess now brought him: a Moonwell, in the verdancy of life.

The small vale in this gray and apparently lifeless range fairly burst with vitality. A grove of tall, lush cedars shaded the lower shore of the pond, where a crystalline stream splashed outward, sparkling even under the cloudy skies.

Silently, reverently, the druid-gull descended through a series of wide circles. Now that he had reached his goal, Danrak was reluctant to land and abandon the magic of Isolde's talisman, for the feather had vanished in the casting of his shapechange, and like the eye of direction, it could not be used again.

Instead, for a time, Danrak soared and watched. His keen gull's eyes allowed him to see details in the vale: the blossoming violets and daisies in the meadows, the lush lilies along the shore. He looked into water as clear as glass and saw plump trout swimming lazily below the surface.

Only then did he notice the people. Several of them knelt by the pool, their hands clenched in prayer. He saw several more humans walking steadily up the dusty track that led to the vale. Some of these hobbled on crutches, and one wore a bandage across his face, concealing his blinded eyes. A slowly growing band collected around the restored well, here to share the miracle of the Moonwell's rebirth.

Danrak himself felt a choking swell of emotion. He could no longer doubt the vision that had gathered the druids and had sent him on this quest, for here was the proof before him. A small, subtle sign it was, but it gave clear indication that the power of the Great Mother was not entirely gone from the world. He squawked, the only noise he could make in his current form, but it was a profound cry of joy.

Finally he came to rest on a rock, well up the valley side, away from the pool. As his human form returned, Danrak dropped prone behind the rock and continued to watch the humans he had spied around the shore of the well.

The druid felt a surprising vitality in his arms and legs as his body nestled in the scant shelter. He clenched and unclenched his fingers, relishing their wiry strength. Stretching, he felt the power in his wrists and his shoulders. Indeed, Danrak felt more alive than he ever had before.

A commotion caught his eye, and he looked down the rude

trail that began, or ended, at the shore of the well and followed the descending stream, eventually, Danrak assumed, to flow past some mountain community of the Ffolk. Now he saw a party of men-at-arms ascending that trail, roughly pushing the hobbling pilgrims out of the way.

A half dozen of the warriors marched toward the Moonwell, each wearing a black tunic over his chain mail shirt. On the breast of the tunics was emblazoned a crest, and as the men drew closer, Danrak identified the symbol as a shield, with a pair of crossed swords below it. But then something else caught his eye, and his blood chilled: Each of the armed men wore a sword but carried over his shoulder a stout double-bladed axe—not a battle-axe.

A woodsman's axe.

Shuddering in fright, the druid looked at the massive cedars that towered above the pool. Instinctively he knew that these were the targets of the axemen.

As he watched, some of the pilgrims tried to stand in the way of the men-at-arms. The leading warrior bashed them aside with his steel-gauntleted fist, while drawn swords encouraged the unarmed pilgrims to stay back.

Now the druid's mind raced. He had to do something! Stealthily he crawled from behind his boulder and darted to a nearby shrub. From here, he advanced another twenty feet to the concealment of a great pile of boulders. As he moved, however, he saw the men approach the nearest of the great cedars. The pilgrims watched in horror, gathered in a circle but fearing to intervene.

In moments, the *crack-crack* of sharp blades biting into wood echoed through the vale as three of the men wielded their axes in fast cadence. The other three stood, with swords drawn, warily watching the bedraggled onlookers. The latter, Danrak saw, numbered more than twenty, but most were very old or crippled, and a few were children.

Chips flew from the broad trunk in a yellow shower, swiftly gathering in a pile surrounding the foot of the tree. Belatedly it dawned on the druid that the soldiers would think him but another scruffy-looking pilgrim, and he rose from his hiding place and walked boldly toward the thin crowd.

Still his mind churned, examining and discarding several of

the varied talismans he carried about him. One, he knew, would be helpful, a dried powder made from the stingers of a hundred hornets, if he could only find the final ingredients for the spell.

"This'll make a fine blaze for the earl's hearth!" boomed a guard, taunting the Ffolk who watched dumbly.

"Aye," agreed another, brandishing his sword, his voice an evil chuckle. "We'll kill us some farmer's ox and have steak for the manor tonight!"

Danrak joined the Ffolk who watched, taking the arm of a withered crone and aiding her to sit on a flat rock. Her feet, he saw, bled from many sores, for she had climbed the rugged mountain trail without shoes.

Then, beside her foot, he saw the things he needed: bees, several of which buzzed from blossom to blossom amid a patch of plump clover. Danrak stood, trying to appear casual, and realized that the great cedar was near to toppling. He saw that it would fall away from the onlookers and was satisfied. Patiently he watched and waited.

An awful, mourning creak shot through the vale, and the top of the tree swayed. The giant trunk leaned, almost imperceptibly at first. The three axemen scampered away and stood with their backs to the pilgrims, looking up as the huge cedar slowly gained momentum. The guards, too, stared upward, all attention focused on the tree.

The creaking grew to an earsplitting shriek as the trunk broke free from its stump. The massive timber gained momentum until it struck the ground with a pounding smash that shook the earth.

At the same time, Danrak pinched and released his talisman, the fine dust fluffing through the still air, then settling across the clover where the bees labored so diligently. The men of Blackstone still looked at the colossus they had felled, clapping each other on the shoulders and boasting as if they had slain a dangerous giant.

Immediately, as the dust touched the striped hairs of their backs, the bees darted upward, buzzing angrily. Three of them zoomed toward Danrak.

But the druid turned and looked at the six armed men who had already begun to select their next victim. He had faith in the talismans now, faith that he admitted he lacked when first he had embarked from Myrloch Vale. Now his attention focused on the target, and his word, though he did not shout, reached the primitive hearing of the insects.

"*Attack!*"

The crone looked up in astonishment as the shadows flashed overhead, and the high-pitched buzzing of the insects quickly became a deep, resonant drone. One of the men heard it and turned to locate the source of this annoyance.

He screamed in a voice taut with panic. The bees darted toward him, full of singleminded fury and armed with sharp, venomous stingers, no longer the tiny insects the druid had observed among the clover. Now each was more than two feet long and flying as fast as a diving eagle.

In another second, the men fought wildly, swinging their axes and swords at the giant insects. The bees darted past and then separated, each diving toward the six humans from a different angle. The droning sound of their wings resonated from the rock walls of the vale, filling the valley with the deep, unnatural hum.

"Look out!" cried one of the men, and then his voice became a strangled cry for help as a huge insect struck him full in the face.

The force of the blow pounded the man to the ground. He lay, stunned and groaning, as the great bee settled to his chest, its stinger poised over the unprotected abdomen. A pair of his fellows leaped at the creature, and one stabbed with a sword, brushing the stinger aside at the last moment.

The bee rose angrily into the air and darted toward the swordsman, who struggled desperately to hold the creature at bay. His companions fought the persistent approaches of the other two bees and could offer him no aid.

"Run!" cried Danrak. "Run to safety!"

The words were like a rope thrown to a drowning man. The swordsman turned from the bee, leaped over the trunk of the felled cedar, and raced down the path, away from the Moonwell. The bee dove after him but quickly turned to join its two companions in harassing the other men.

The remaining guardsmen needed no further encouragement. In a mass, they scrambled away, casting their axes to the ground and sprinting down the trail. The bees followed for a hundred paces before abruptly losing their rage. Instead, they bobbed and drifted lazily across the meadows, which still burst with an array of blossoms.

The crone looked up at Danrak, squinting wisely. Her face was withered, and one of her eyes was missing, the socket grown shut behind crude stitchwork. When she smiled, she revealed two bare gums, with not a tooth to be seen.

But she smacked her lips and cackled, relishing the delight of a secret shared. Danrak offered her his arm, leading her to the Moonwell, and when she washed her feet there, they no longer bled.

* * * * *

"What charges are these?" Alicia demanded, storming toward King Olafsson's throne. "Who claims that the Ffolk have attacked you?"

The great lodge had fallen silent when the princess, flanked by Tavish and Keane, entered the building. Nevertheless, the trio had heard the furor from well beyond the walls. Keane had tried to hold Alicia back, but she had insisted on confronting the situation before it got out of hand. Her arguments had prevailed.

"*Serious* charges." The King of Gnarhelm spoke with great solemnity. "Made by my cousin, King Dagus of Olafstaad."

Alicia's eyes flicked to Brandon, who stood on the king's left. The prince's mental anguish showed plainly, but his chin was set in a line of stone. Next she turned to the king's right.

There, she guessed, stood King Dagus. The grizzled warrior was older and larger than his cousin from Gnarhelm. The visiting king's face was covered with scars, his posture crooked. He glared at Alicia with ice-blue eyes over a frost-colored beard, and she had to suppress a shiver. She noticed that the monarch's left arm ended at the elbow.

Rumbles of anger rose from the packed lodge of northmen. Feeling a sense of growing helplessness, Alicia saw Knaff the Elder's face twist in fury. King Svenyird himself regarded her with hostility.

"An army of knights, flying the standard of the Great Bear,

attacked northward along the west coast of Alaron!" shouted King Dagus, his tone full of accusation.

"From where?" Alicia demanded.

"They march north from Callidyrr, sacking and looting as they go. They butchered an entire village in the dark of the night, another in the gray haze of dawn! They burn and they rape and they kill! Aye, and I fought them myself—killed one and watched another slay my son! They spoke your language, they wielded your weapons! Do you dare to say they were other than the Ffolk?"

"I dare to say they did not fly my father's flag in his name!" Alicia declared, unflinching before the northman's anger. "They are my enemies as surely as they are yours!"

"Too many lies!" bellowed Knaff the Elder. "My son dead . . . good people slain in their beds . . . how long do we delay our vengeance?"

"Don't you see?" cried Alicia. "Someone *wants* us to do this—to fight, to turn on each other!"

"Words—where is the proof?" demanded King Svenyird, his face flushed with anger.

"Wait!"

The single word, barked by the Prince of Gnarhelm, somehow penetrated the great lodge, and the bellicose northmen settled back to listen amid continuing rumbles of discontent.

"Sire! My people! Face this enemy with your minds as well as your might! Listen to the princess and think: Why should the Ffolk make war upon us? If they do, for some reason we cannot guess, we'll fight them. But if they don't, and we've been deceived, then we'll hurl ourselves into a war without cause!"

"But where is proof either way?" asked Brandon's father. Alicia noticed, with relief, that the king's face had returned to its normal ruddy complexion.

"I will sail tomorrow, in the *Gullwing*, to confront these knights. They are near Olafstaad, on the coast. I hope to bring them to battle within two days. And when I do, we'll get the answers we seek."

"I sail with you!"

"And I!"

A chorus of cries greeted the prince's declaration, but he

gestured with both hands, calling for silence. Slowly the bois-
terous northmen quieted.

"When I return, I suspect that the outcome will not be war
between the Ffolk and ourselves. No! Instead, I shall sail the
lady princess to Callidyrr and meet with the High King of the
Ffolk. There I will gain a peace that will continue for many
years ahead—years of profound happiness and joy." Brandon's
eyes, shining with emotion, came to rest upon the princess.
He continued, speaking loudly, but Alicia sensed that he was
talking directly to her.

"For when I meet him, I intend to ask King Kendrick to
grant me the greatest treasure in his realm—the hand of his
daughter in marriage! Let Gnarhelm and Callidyrr be linked by
the blood of their king and queen!"

Great shouts, bellowing accolades and frenzied whoops
thundered around Alicia, but somehow the noise seemed to be
very faint, as if it came from someplace far away. Her mind
tried to shake itself, to think, but she could not.

And then, as the noise began to intrude, driving against her
temples and threatening to press her to the ground, her temper flared. It began with disbelief, and then shock, and quickly
progressed to outrage. How dare he! She looked at him, furious, as he smiled back at her, somehow oblivious to the emotion contorting her expression.

The princess stepped forward, anger sweeping through her
body, tensing her muscles and bringing fiery words into her
throat. Alicia barely sensed Keane's hand on her arm, restraining her, and she whirled on her tutor.

But at the look on his face, she paused, her fury slowly cool-
ing. Keane's expression was shocked, his skin pale. He glared
at Brandon, his face twitching with ill-concealed hatred, but
still he held the princess back from verbally attacking the
Prince of Gnarhelm. Abruptly she shook him, off but the inter-
val had been enough. Harsh words against the prince's arrogant self-assurance that would certainly have ended hopes of
peaceful cooperation, remained unspoken.

For a moment, the entire lodge seemed to whirl about Alicia, a mass of confusing noises and sights. Knaff the Elder still
railed about treachery, while many of the younger northmen
shouted approval of Brandon's brave words and cast envious

eyes over the princess's face and body. Alicia felt Tavish's arm around her shoulders and leaned against the older woman, grateful for her strength.

Then the tumult settled for a moment as the lodge door burst open with an implosion of wind and rain. A bedraggled warrior stood, sopping wet from his post on the waterfront. He raced toward the throne and cast himself on the floor.

"Sire!" he cried, raising his face to his king. "Firbolgs! They attack Gnarhelm even as I speak!"

"The giant-kin!" cursed Svenyird, leaping to his feet. "Do they come from the highlands or along the shore?"

"Neither, Your Majesty! I swear on the honor of my father, they do not march by land! Nay, lord—these firbolgs attack us by sea!"

* * * * *

Musings of the Harpist

This is one of those times when the gentle bard must sit back and quietly reflect upon the pace of events around her.

First we shall have a war, then we will not—at least, not for now. I never tire of the lively debate around a strong monarch's throne, but this matter is too confusing for easy settlement.

Next a royal marriage, proposed for the dear child of my king and queen! Alicia's face flushed at the announcement— the strong-willed young woman is indeed her mother's daughter! Though the proposal wasn't made in the most romantic of fashions, I still wonder if the princess objects more to the manner of the question than to its substance.

And finally an invasion of firbolgs! Firbolgs? By sea? Very strange indeed! The next thing you know, it will stop raining and the sun will shine again!

❧ 15 ❧

A Knight and
a Champion

"Fools! Imbeciles! I send you to do a simple task, and you fail because of pestering *insects!*" Gwyeth sputtered at his men-at-arms, his fury flecking spittle from his lips.

The six guardsmen quailed in the face of his rage, but none of them preferred a return to the onslaught of the giant bees, which had become hornets in their slightly exaggerated version of the incident.

"My lord!" objected a burly veteran, Backar. "They were the size of eagles, and they set upon us unnaturally!"

"Indeed, lord!" protested another. "And we fought like heroes, but the venom dripped from their stingers! They numbered in the hundreds, to be sure!"

"Only when we fled the vale altogether did the bewitchment cease!" Still a third guardsman spoke up, striving to divert the nobleman's rage.

Gwyeth stalked back and forth in the earldom's hall. He was glad that his brother was absent, but he desired his father's counsel. Unfortunately, the earl had ridden to Callidyrr several days ago, and thus his son would have to make the decision.

Then he remembered: Pryat Wentfeld, the cleric of Helm who had tended his arm. He barked an order to summon the good priest, and then he sat before the great fireplace and fumed while he waited for the man to attend him.

"Your lordship requested my presence?" asked the cleric less than an hour later, as he humbly bowed and entered the Great Hall. He wore a rich gown of gold-embroidered silk, and his round face was clean-shaven and well scrubbed. His eyes were small, but they sparkled with curiosity as he regarded the young heir to the duchy.

"Indeed. First I thank you for the skills you employed in

tending my wound."

"It is always an honor to serve the house of Blackstone," replied the Pryat smoothly. Gwyeth knew full well that, after Wentfeld's second visit, his father had sent the cleric away with a bulging sack of gold. "I trust your shoulder has returned to full strength, or will soon?"

"Aye," grunted Gwyeth, raising his arm and passing it through a swing forward and rear. "As good as ever, I'll swear."

"Splendid!" The priest waited, sensing that the young nobleman had other business on his mind.

"I would speak with you on a matter you brought up with my father the night you first tended my wound."

"Indeed." The cleric smiled thinly. "You speak, I presume, of the pond, the so-called 'Moonwell' that has undergone some kind of—obviously illusionary—transformation?"

"Yes, precisely." Gwyeth was relieved that the cleric understood, and he poured out his frustrating tale. "I sent six veteran guardsmen there to begin the destruction as my father ordered—orders grown from your suggestion, to be sure. They were to fell the cedars and form a pile of the brush, burning what was not useful and sending horses to drag the good lumber back to the cantrev. I know them all to be steady men, courageous in battle.

"They reached the pond and encountered pilgrims who, as you suspected, accredited the place with some kind of miracle. The rabble did not stand in their way."

"Naturally not."

"However," Gwyeth continued, his tone dropping grimly, "the guardsmen claim to have been set upon by a giant swarm of stinging insects, creatures that drove them from the valley with great violence, though none of the cowards could show me so much as a bee sting!"

"There must be some germ of truth to the tale," observed the cleric, "else they would not have invented it, knowing there to be witnesses."

"That thought had occurred to me as well," Gwyeth agreed unhappily.

"But that proves nothing, save that magic is at work in that mountain vale," continued the pryat, undaunted.

"And how can we combat such a presence?" demanded the lord, exasperated.

"I'll prepare a salve that will render the men proof against the attacks of insects and like creatures," mused the cleric. "Though who knows if they will be threatened in a similar manner again. . . ." His voice trailed off and his face tightened, as if he was deep in thought.

"I was hoping that you could accompany a band of men, led by myself, to the place," suggested Gwyeth.

Wentfeld looked shocked. "Begging my lord's pardon, but a day away from my ministries is a burden to impose upon my apprentices," he explained, shaking his head firmly. "And a costly one, since the oafs do little more than to squander the donations that I strive so diligently to collect." The pryat sighed heavily, the picture of dejection.

"Perhaps the loss to your coffers could be . . . compensated," Gwyeth said, galled but pragmatic.

He gritted his teeth to hide his anger as he saw the cleric's aspect brighten. Someday, he vowed silently, when the earldom was his, he would see that this gross imbalance of power was rectified. The clerics should *serve* their lords, not extort from them. Trying to keep his face blank, he listened.

"Oh, my lord—of course it is not necessary, but if in fact the financial health of my temple could be maintained, I should be only too willing to embark upon this task with you and remain until the work has been done."

"Very well," said the young lord, relieved in spite of himself to have the cleric's help. "Go and make your arrangements. We'll journey to the well tomorrow—myself, you, and half a hundred of my men-at-arms!"

* * * * *

The war-horse trotted up the mountain track. Each huge, white-fetlocked hoof plodded forward with strength and determination, as if the great steed did not acknowledge the hampering effects of weather or terrain. Astride the deep saddle, the knight held his lance high and cast his dark eyes this way and that, in search of any sign of the princess or her companions. The blue silk trappings of both horse and rider were now muddy and soaked, dripping with the steady rain that continued to drench them.

Hanrald had ridden for two days, combing the most rugged country on Alaron. Alas for him, he was no ranger. He crossed the trail of the princess and her escort of two hundred northmen on several occasions, but in each case, he mistook the spoor for a goat track.

For hours, the huge stallion cantered along high crests or thundered through wide, shallow valleys. Hanrald reined in at the highest places, and, his visor raised, peered into the distance in all directions, searching to the limits of his vision across the mist-obscured highland. When nothing moved within his field of view, he spurred the steed onward, lumbering through the next valley at an easy gait and then charging up another ridge, where he paused and again searched the land to the far horizons.

Finally, atop a grassy rise that dropped gradually into a pastoral vale, Hanrald caught a glimpse of something moving. A greenish shape dropped behind a rock, as if something had caught sight of the knight at the same time as the rider looked below. Bordering the grassy expanse, a shallow stream meandered with bucolic contentment.

Urging the horse into a gallop, he lowered his lance and set it to rest in the crook of his arm. The hackles of his neck bristled with an instinctive sense of warning. He felt an unspeakable menace in this hulking shape that had so swiftly taken shelter.

Nearing the rock, he reined in, and as the horse reared backward, he shouted at the mass of granite. "Ho, varlet! Come out from there or face the steel of my lance!"

The knight didn't flinch at the horror that arose from behind the rock, but he recognized immediately that he was about to fight for his life. The thing stood more than eight feet tall, covered all over in green skin that was slick with slime in some places, in others grotesque with patches of great, hairy warts. Vaguely humanoid in shape, though the arms and legs were unnaturally long and gnarled, the beast glared at Hanrald, its visage grotesque. Two eyes, sunk deep into shadowed sockets of black, stared outward at him, as emotionless as the gaze of an adder.

A troll! The vicious predator was worthy prey for any knight. Hanrald's heart pumped with the prospect of action.

Raising its two hands, each of which ended in four long, wickedly curving claws, the creature stepped from behind the rock. Its jaw gaped slightly, a caricature of a gleeful grin, revealing rows of needlelike fangs.

"Come, monster!" shouted Hanrald, flipping his visor down to cover his face. "Come and face your death!"

He seated his lance comfortably at his side and urged the stallion forward. With a powerful kick, the mount lunged into the charge. Hanrald sighted down the wooden shaft to the gleaming steel head. He knew that his first blow would have to tell, for the troll was a formidable opponent and only the force of a charging war-horse might give Hanrald the opportunity to prevail.

But as he thundered closer, the knight saw another flash of movement, a clue that told him he had made a terrible mistake. Another troll, every bit as big as the first, lunged onto the boulder, looming overhead.

Desperately Hanrald raised his lance as the second troll launched itself into the air. The keen head met the creature in the chest, skewering its belly and emerging from its back in a shower of black blood and green gore. The jolt knocked the knight back into his saddle, and then the weight of the monster pulled the head of his lance downward.

The troll hissed an inhuman screech as the cruel barbs ripped through its innards, but even impaled it struggled to crawl up the shaft of the lance. Sharp claws raked across Hanrald's armored chest as the tip of the lance struck the ground. Instantly the charger's momentum knocked Hanrald from his saddle.

The knight crashed to the ground with a gasp of pain but immediately rolled to the side and struggled slowly to his feet. He could see little through his eyeslits, but the terrified screams of his horse told him something. Drawing his sword and raising it in his hands, he turned to seek his enemies.

Kicking and shrieking pathetically, his war-horse tumbled to the ground, dragged down by the leap and grasp of the first troll. The monster sank long fangs into the faithful steed's neck and ripped out the windpipe with a gush of air and blood.

In another instant, the horse's struggles ceased, and the monster lifted its gore-streaked face to glare malevolently at the knight.

Closer, the second troll writhed on the great skewer of Hanrald's lance. Before the knight's horrified eyes, the creature began to pull the weapon through its body, forcing the wide hilt into the wound with ragged gasps of pain.

Retching in horror, Hanrald stepped forward and brought his sword down with all the might of his arms. The keen edge slashed through the troll's neck and sent the green, grotesque head rolling onto the ground. The body continued to writhe, pressing the lance through the gaping slash.

The deadly shaft emerged, streaked with green ichor, as the beast slowly worked the weapon free. Horrified, Hanrald raised the mighty sword again and chopped brutally downward. Again and again he hacked, until little more than a fetid pile of gory troll parts littered the heather. And even then, some of these continued to twitch and to move.

But now Hanrald was forced away from this victim as the other troll, the one that had slain his horse, leaped over the corpse of the steed and charged, fanged maw smeared with blood, gore-streaked claws raised in ominous threat.

The knight met the charge with a powerful blow of his sword, and though the troll tried to duck away, the keen edge bit into the green, wart-covered shoulder, knocking the monster to the side. Hanrald lunged in for the kill, but the beast sprang to its feet with shocking agility, smashing a clawed fist into the side of Hanrald's helm.

The knight fell, momentarily stunned, and he felt the pressing weight of the monster land on top of him. Squirming desperately, he twisted his blade upward and pressed, feeling it tear through tough skin. The beast howled, and something warm and slimy splashed onto Hanrald's once-shiny armor.

Gasping for breath, the man scrambled back, away from the wounded beast. It took all of Hanrald's concentration to remember to keep a grip upon his sword, so intense was his horror. He had fought men before, but never had he faced something as vile and unnatural as these monstrous, regenerating beasts.

Finally he stood again and saw that the wounded troll had

also risen to its feet. Now it loomed over him, shaking its head as if to clear away the effects of Hanrald's deep, slashing blows. Yet even as the knight watched, the deep gash in the beast's shoulder slowly closed, the slimy effluvium drying on the lumpy skin. Whole again, the troll advanced in a crouch, reaching forward with those long, deadly arms.

Grunting from the exertion, Hanrald swung his blade once more, lopping an arm off at the elbow. The beast hissed and recoiled as the blade swished past it again, the retreat causing the blow to narrowly miss the grotesque belly.

Hanrald stepped forward, but then he gagged in shock as he felt the dismembered hand seize him around the ankle. Hacking and chopping in a frenzy, he mangled the limb beyond all recognition, but by the time he again pursued the retreating troll, the creature had already begun to sprout a new hand. Nubs of claws formed on the gruesome member, and he saw them begin to grow.

His strength failing from the exertion of the deadly battle, Hanrald had to make a killing blow, and quickly, else the inevitably regained strength of the monsters would give the fight a grim and unavoidable close. Now, with his horse dead, escape wasn't even an option. Angrily he chastised himself for the thought; escape had *never* been an option! A knight did not flee from a fair fight once it was engaged!

"Stand, villain, and face me squarely!" Hanrald shouted taunts at the creature, but it only grinned evilly and backed away, beyond the reach of his keen, gore-drenched sword.

The knight realized that he lacked the endurance and, because of his plate mail, the speed to pursue the creature. Gasping for breath, he stood and watched the thing as the new arm slowly extended into fingers, and then those deadly claws curved, wickedly sharp, to gradually complete the limb.

Suddenly remembering his first foe, Hanrald looked at the ground, toward the once-mangled remains of the first troll he had slain and then slashed into pieces. Already it had begun to reform, though as yet the thing's regenerating legs remained too frail to raise it up. Immediately he stepped to its side and hacked brutally, again and again, ignoring the creature's screams and desperate blows until it had once again been reduced to a grotesque mass of chopped bone, meat, and ichor.

A sense warned him of danger, and he spun on instinct to see the second troll springing through the air at him, arms extended, face split wide in a gruesome, horrifying grin. Gasping, the knight placed all of his strength into a single blow, using both of his hands to bring the great blade around in a whistling, murderous arc.

The slimed steel met the troll's midsection as it neared the end of its lunge, and all the power of the knight's muscles, backed by the spiritual force of his faith and, so he thought, his virtue, drove the keen edge through wart-covered skin and tough, stringy muscle. The momentum of his swing pulled him through a complete circle, but when he again faced his attacker, Hanrald saw two pieces of the troll, both writhing furiously on the ground.

In the next instant, he leaped forward, driving his blade over and over again into each of the troll's halves, knowing that his only hope was to inflict the damage faster than the thing could heal itself. Finally, groaning and staggering with exhaustion, he leaned back, seeing that no piece of either troll moved.

Lifting his heavy helmet from his head, Hanrald gasped great lungfuls of air and felt the cool breeze start to kiss the sweat from his brow, but he knew that his task remained unfinished. He stumbled to the saddlebags of his fallen steed and quickly lifted out several flasks of oil that he had carried, fuel to light his lamp or even to coax a fire from wet kindling.

He returned to the corpses, pausing only long enough to chop at a hand that had once again begun to twitch. Pouring the syrupy liquid over the grotesque masses of gore, he kicked random pieces of the trolls onto the corpses. Then, with a spark from his tinderbox, he struck a flame from each oil-sodden mass.

In moments, orange flame crackled upward, and thick, black smoke wafted into the air. The parts of the trolls vanished with an evil hiss, devoured by the one thing that could destroy them permanently. Even as they burned, Hanrald retained his watch over them, to insure that no living piece could escape the fringes of the blaze.

Only then did he remember his quest and realize that he still had no idea where the princess had gone. And now, without a horse, his current circumstance seemed to be more than a slight disadvantage. He grimly cleaned and sheathed his sword, then picked up his helmet, selected a pouchful of provisions and supplies from his saddlebag, and slung the heavy sack across his shoulder.

On foot, weary and bruised but still alive—and, more important, still a knight of the Ffolk!—Hanrald started across the rugged highland terrain, his body clinking heavily as he marched in his rigid metal boots.

*　*　*　*　*

The invading army of firbolgs numbered three, and this trio now stood before a battered sailboat, their broad backs to the bay, facing a suspicious and growing ring of belligerent northmen. It was to King Svenyird's credit, Alicia decided, that his warlike countrymen did not attack these traditional enemies immediately.

As usual, it rained steadily, and though it was merely afternoon, the dockside was shrouded in an evening-like cast. The Princess of Callidyrr accompanied the King of Gnarhelm and his son as they approached the giants. Alicia took care to keep the monarch between herself and the prince. She didn't think she could keep her composure if he talked to her.

The three firbolgs were hulking brutes, ten feet tall or more, with craggy faces and dark, scowling eyebrows. They wore crude garments of linen, and their feet were bare. The one in the center of the group, however, was distinguished by a huge black cape. The cloak was tied around his shoulder, with the hood thrown back to hang down his back.

"We seek the king," said the largest of the firbolgs.

"I'm the king," declared Svenyird. "What do you want?"

"No." The firbolg shook his head defiantly. "We seek the true king."

"What?" The monarch's eyes bulged. "You insolent castaways! I'll see you flogged at the post. You won't insult my—"

"Excuse me," said Tavish, smoothly sidling past the sputtering King of Gnarhelm. She eyed the cloak as she addressed the center firbolg. "Is it King Kendrick of Corwell you're looking for?"

The giant looked at her, his brows deepening into a scowl

that carved gullies and ravines across his stony face. Alicia gripped Keane's arm as she saw the firbolg's expression.

"Is she in danger?" she whispered.

Keane, studying the giant, disengaged his arm and raised his hands before him—ready with an instant spell, Alicia realized.

"I think," the firbolg said finally. "King Tristum?"

"Yes, Yak—Tristan Kendrick!" Tavish stepped forward and gave the firbolg a hug around its broad midriff, surprising no one more than the giant himself, who stumbled backward and would have fallen into the bay if not for the saving reach of one of his fellows.

"Bard lady?" said Yak, his brows lowering still further as recognition came.

"Yes—I'm Tavish!"

"Good music," remarked the giant in a softer tone. "I still dream your harp sound."

"Why, Yak, you old charmer," replied Tavish, nudging his hip with her elbow.

"You *know* this firbolg?" Alicia demanded, asking the question that was on a thousand tongues. "*How?*"

"It's a long story," she explained. "He helped your father in the final battle against Bhaal."

"Enough!" barked the giant, his voice surprisingly harsh. The topic obviously annoyed him. "We bring news."

His words, in crude Commonspeech, were barely understood by the listeners. Nevertheless, the gist of his tale was clear to those close enough to follow.

"Many humans killed on Grayrock by dragon with firebreath and fish-men from the sea. They slay and then they go. Make it look like other humans did killing. Or firbolgs. We come to tell you not us."

"Sahuagin?" asked Brandon, initial disbelief quickly converting to certainty.

"With a dragon," Tavish observed. "*That's* an unnatural pairing if ever I heard of one! I don't suppose you know where it lairs?"

Yak shrugged. "Flew away, over sea."

"And so there are more even than these in alliance. Those were *human* knights who masqueraded as the Ffolk, sacking the villages of Olafstaad," Alicia added.

"That's a lot of enemies," Keane noted. "And evidence of conspiracy, if they all serve one master."

"But finally we have an enemy before us!" Brandon proclaimed. "And now we know where to start—with the bandits of Olafstaad! We can hoist sail with the dawn and be there in a day and a half. Even if they're on horseback, we shouldn't have trouble picking up the trail!"

"Proof," noted Alicia grimly. "We'll find out what's behind this." Privately she reminded herself that the matter of Brandon Olafsson was not settled, but perhaps she could postpone its resolution until this matter was concluded.

"Tomorrow before sunrise!" cried the Prince of Gnarhelm, throwing up his arms and addressing the hundreds of men who flocked forward, pledging to serve as his crew. "The *Gullwing* sails for Olafstaad and the start of our vengeance!"

The cries of the men of Gnarhelm rang across the shore, and for once, the people were so loud that they drowned out the steady beat of the rain.

* * * * *

Robyn, High Queen of Moonshae, lay in a stillness little distinguished from death. Her second daughter, raven-haired Deirdre, looked down at her mother with a certain sadness. Nevertheless, the young woman was surprised at the remoteness of her feeling, as if a wall had grown around the softer portions of her heart, and so she felt emotion through a gray, stony filter.

Some emotions, she reminded herself, as her eyes drifted to the window. Others burned as hot—or hotter—than ever they had before.

Her thoughts turned to Malawar, as they often did when she took even the slightest moment for reflection. Many days had passed since she had last seen him, and despite the long hours of concentration required for her meditation and studies, she couldn't get the images of his golden hair, his benign smile and shining eyes, out of her mind.

A tapping at the door to her mother's chambers broke her reverie, and she opened the portal to reveal a steward.

"Lady Deirdre, a visitor has come to the castle and would

desire an audience at your convenience. He is Earl Blackstone of Fairheight."

Her heart quickened, for she knew from Malawar that the earl was a confidant of the golden wizard's, and Blackstone's visit here, she hoped, might bring her news.

"See that he is fed and given rooms in the keep." This would place him close to her should they desire a surreptitious counsel. "And tell the Lord Earl that I shall attend him . . . in the throne room, in two hours."

"Aye, my lady."

The servant withdrew, and Deirdre cast another glance at the queen. Robyn, of course, had not moved. The princess felt a moment of guilt. She had intended to sit with her mother throughout the morning, but she shook off the feeling easily, for she was now called to an important matter.

Two hours later, dressed in a gown of emerald silk trimmed with a ruby broach and a stole of white fur that set off her hair dramatically, Deirdre entered the Great Hall. It was midafternoon, but the light that spilled through the high windows was dim, filtered by cloud cover, and the room remained cloaked in various levels of shadow.

The Earl of Fairheight bowed deeply, and Deirdre raised her hand, which he kissed gallantly. He wore a black cloak with a silver clasp, and his heavy leather boots had obviously been polished since he had reached the castle, for they gleamed with an inky shine that seemed more willing to absorb light than to reflect it. His dark mane of hair and beard had been brushed into a semblance of control.

Deirdre felt mature, older than her years, and yet a small part of her tingled with excitement as she embarked on matters generally reserved for rulers and their trusted and noble advisers.

They exchanged formal pleasantries, and she sensed that the earl studied her, as if he looked for some response that would key the matter that had brought him to Callidyrr.

"And the matter of the Moonwell?" Deirdre inquired after a few minutes. "Did my sister render a verdict consistent with the king's wishes?"

"Alas, lady, she did not," said the black-bearded lord with a sigh. He related his version of Alicia's visit to the Moonwell, including the mysterious creature that the princess said attacked her, but of which no clue could be discovered.

"Now the place remains ensorcelled, and I've had reports that herders and woodsmen are calling the thing a miracle! Of course, the good men and dwarves of the Fairheight Earldom put no stock in the stories."

"It seems she may have been rash," Deirdre agreed. Privately she wondered at the tale of the transformation. To her, it bespoke more than mere illusion, and she wondered what power might lie behind it.

"To be sure," added the earl. "I left my older son, Gwyeth, in charge of the cantrev, with instructions to burn the cedars and remove any other indications of this so-called miracle."

"A wise precaution," the princess agreed. She was tempted to countermand her sister's order and tell the earl to begin mining in the Moonwell's vale. Then she hesitated. Such a move would be too contentious, she decided, given the tenuous state of rulership in the currently king-and queenless realm.

"And my sister? I thought she would return to Callidyrr when she finished the mission."

"That's another strange tale," explained the burly nobleman. "She embarked, with her two companions and my son Hanrald, into the Fairheight Mountains to meet with a party of northmen that were observed there. My son returned, with word that the men of Gnarhelm were not hostile, and reported that the princess would meet with them further. There has been no word from her since, though I trust she is in safe hands."

"Northmen?" Deirdre asked. "There have been reports over the last few days of northmen raiding the coast of Callidyrr. I'd thought them exaggerated, but now I wonder."

Blackstone's perennial scowl deepened at the news. "It could be that the danger is more severe than—"

At that moment, a figure moved beside the hearth and the two, who had thought that they were alone in the Great Hall, whirled in surprise. Deirdre's mouth snapped open, but then she recognized the intruder and cried out in delight.

"Malawar! Come and meet the Earl of Fairheight." It slowly dawned on Deirdre that finally he had come to her in a chamber other than the library. The earl, meanwhile, looked at the visitor with mingled shock and suspicion.

"We are acquainted," said the earl, with a stiff bow. "Though not by that name. And, sir, our acquaintance does not give you leave to startle me into old age!"

"I am sorry, My Lord Earl," said Malawar, his hood thrown back and his eyes sparkling. "But necessity requires me to enter with stealth."

"We were discussing the Blackstone Moonwell," said Deirdre. "My sister has ordered the earl to refrain from his excavations. Should I—?" She stopped, catching herself. "I was considering ordering the mining to proceed."

"Alas," said Malawar, his expression wistful. "I fear it is too late for such a course." He addressed both of his listeners as he sat on one of the large chairs. "There is great menace afoot here—menace that threatens the very survival of the Ffolk!"

"You!" he declared, turning on Blackstone, his face twisted in sudden anger. "You *know* of the imminence of war, and yet you dismiss your information as irrelevant! Won't you believe the danger until a column of northmen batter down the gates of your home?"

Blackstone flinched visibly before the verbal onslaught but quickly found his tongue. "My son assured me—"

"Your *son?*" Malawar's tone was heavy with scorn. "You mean Hanrald, do you not?"

Now the earl scowled more darkly than ever, but Deirdre noticed that he didn't reply to the question. Instead, he glared at the cleric in impotent hostility.

"And you!" Malawar turned on Deirdre, his voice harsh, and the princess felt she had been whipped.

"What?" she asked, frightened. "What is it?"

"Your country has been invaded!" Malawar barked, not loudly, but still the words struck her like a blow across the face. "You're in command now. You must defend it!"

"What can we do?" the princess asked. A sudden enormity of responsibility threatened her, leaving her vulnerable to great doubts. "My father's gone, and my mother lies unknowing!" Even her sister, or Keane, she thought, would be comforting presences now.

"Send out your father's army! Strike back before it's too

late! Mount the cavalry—patrol the borders! Be prepared to send a force into Gnarhelm to punish the insolent savages!"

So many commands! Deirdre's heart quailed at the magnitude of her challenge. But then, as quickly as it took her mind to focus on the thought, she remembered the presence of Malawar, and her fears vanished. With him beside her, she could do anything!

"But there is another part to this danger," said the priest, his tone modulating. Deirdre heard affection in his words again, and she felt a feeling of profound relief. "There is perverted magic at work, corrupting power that seeks to deceive your people into believing that their dead goddess returns to life! That is the menace of this Moonwell."

"My son Gwyeth addresses that problem!" Blackstone objected.

"It may be a task that is beyond him," Malawar replied noncommittally.

"But what can we do about it?" the princess inquired.

"If we have to, we can journey there," replied the golden-haired cleric. "To the place where the war will be decided. There we can make sure that we triumph."

"Where's that?" demanded Deirdre. "How can you know?"

"I don't know yet," replied Malawar. "But the knowledge will be given to me."

"Given to you by whom?" the princess persisted.

"By the power of my god." For the first time, all the lightness was gone from the cleric's voice. Deirdre was silent in the face of his solemnity.

"When do we go, then? And how?" inquired the earl.

"I'll tell you when. As to how . . ." The cleric's voice trailed off, and he looked at Deirdre. Once more he smiled. "Deirdre will take us," he concluded.

"Me? How?" she gasped, thrilled even through her amazement.

"Your power will take us far—and quickly, for we will neither sail nor ride," Malawar said levelly, his eyes meeting the woman's. "You will transport us by the power of sorcery."

Deirdre's heart pounded again—*she* had the power! Yet somehow she was no longer surprised at his remark. Instead, it seemed to provide a solid confirmation of suspicions she had begun to develop, ideas of her own powers and abilities that she had thus far been afraid to try.

Their attention suddenly was drawn to one of the great windows that marked the walls, too high for observance into or out of the hall but useful for admitting light.

A figure stood there, silhouetted against the gray sky. It was a man clad in a brown robe, his two hands upraised as if he would call some lofty power down upon the trio in the Great Hall below. At first Deirdre thought he stood outside the window, perched on the narrow ledge above the courtyard, but as she stared closely, she saw that the man was inside the Great Hall with them.

"Who are you?" she shouted angrily. Her first thought was that one of the servants, with colossal insolence, had chosen this time to clean the glass in the throne room windows, one of the few chambers in the castle equipped with the luxury of windowpanes. In the next moment, her suspicions grew. She felt that this visitor was a far more sinister harbinger.

"I bear witness to a congress of *evil!*" shrieked the stranger, in an old man's voice that was full of fury. He leaped from the windowsill, dropping twelve feet to the floor of the hall to land lightly and stride toward the trio.

"No!" Blackstone's tone was horrified, and Deirdre looked at him, shocked to see that his face had blanched in terror.

"Leave us, old man," demanded Malawar, his own voice soft. He rose and regarded the intruder, his expression menacing, but the trespasser marched resolutely closer.

Deirdre studied the approaching stranger, finding something oddly familiar about his appearance. The top of his head was bald, his robe tattered. His white hair trailed in a fringe to each of his shoulders, and a full white beard was matted upon his chest. His eyes blazed with a light that seemed wholly unnatural.

"Get away from me!" howled Blackstone, almost tumbling over his chair as he scrambled behind the stout wooden furnishing. "You're *dead!* I saw you die!"

"You plan your *own* doom, you who would seek to doom the earth!" cried the intruder, pointing his finger at the quailing earl and then at the princess.

"Leave here now!" Deirdre shot back, "or I'll summon the

guard and have you put to the sword!"

The white-haired man's laughter mocked and infuriated her. Though she felt no fear of this intruder, his appearance enraged her beyond any capacity for reason. She opened her mouth, ready to shout for the castle guards, but a gesture of Malawar's held her command, and she paused.

"You have the power," said the golden-haired mage quietly. "You have no need of guardsmen to banish this impudent rogue."

"What do you mean?" she demanded, her anger turned even on the man that inspired such passion in her heart.

"Use it—use the power," Malawar said, his voice still soft. "Remove him!"

Deirdre whirled back to the old man. He had ceased his advance and stood watching the three of them, his hands planted on his hips, his mouth twisted into an expression of derision that served to madden her still further.

Abruptly she sensed the rightness of Malawar's suggestion. She raised a finger, pointing it full into the chest of the old man. He laughed, his tone still mocking, and her fury grew to volcanic heights.

"*Go!*" she shrieked, her voice sounding like a distant, shrill wind in her ears. Deirdre stood motionless, her finger aimed at the intruder, all her concentration, fueled by her massive rage, directed at him.

For a moment, the Great Hall settled into an awful, poignant stillness. Then the shrieking that Deirdre had heard moments earlier came back, as if a groaning, howling maelstrom of wind sought to form within the huge building. The princess felt like a statue, locked motionless in the grip of her own power.

She began to tremble, to feel an awful heat building within her, but still she couldn't move! Her finger remained fixed, and the stranger stared, as challenging and insolent as ever.

A dull rumbling shook the great tables, and chairs bounced and vibrated on the floor. Dishes rattled against the hearth, and the windows shivered in their frames. Deirdre felt as though she would burst.

Then the explosion came—a massive release of tension that ripped outward from the woman's finger in the form of a great bolt of energy. Red lines of power pulsed, etching themselves in the air, sizzling toward the wild-eyed prophet, striking him full in the chest and smashing him backward to the floor, battering his body with crushing force.

The rumbling continued, but now Deirdre could lower her hand. She felt weak, but suddenly Malawar was at her side, catching her when she would have fallen and lowering her gently into a chair.

The intruder, meanwhile, lay upon his back, the expression of awful gloating still fixed upon his face. Crimson flame outlined his body as his back arched and his legs jutted stiffly, raising him into an arc over the floor.

Then the hellish light pulsed brightly, so intense that Deirdre had to shield her eyes against the flash. When she looked again, the body of the stranger was gone.

* * * * *

The stream of pilgrims trickled to the Moonwell, Ffolk from small farms and highland pastures, remote from even the modest-sized town of Blackstone. A few came from the town, while others were drawn from farther cantrevs.

A woman from Blackstone told Danrak that Sir Gwyeth had proclaimed the Moonwell bewitched, forbidding travel to it until he and his guardsmen had had the chance to break the spell. He posted men-at-arms beside the foot of the trail, but those pilgrims coming from Blackstone immediately started bypassing the trailhead, following a treacherous goat track over several steep foothills.

Danrak talked to one young man who had carried his crippled bride all the way up the sheer and rocky trail. The fellow said Gwyeth had recruited a cleric of Helm into his plans and that the knight and his men would come to the vale of the Moonwell on the following day.

Not all of those who journeyed to the small pond had come with some need for healing. Some made the trek from curiosity, others because they had inherited a knowledge of druidical teachings from their parents or grandparents and wished to see the power of the goddess incarnate on the world. This, in fact, was what they believed: that a miracle had restored the Earthmother, and this well was simply the first sign of her coming. The faithful represented all ages, men and women and boys and girls, and though they were destitute, the miracle of the Moonwell gave them great joy.

All those who sought cures for ailments, it seemed, were miraculously healed by the magical waters. They came with limp and twisted limbs, with great scars on their skin, or with ears or eyes that failed to sense. They came, they bathed in the waters that—though they flowed directly from mountain heights—seemed as warm as a bath, and they emerged from the well healed and whole.

Some of them remained, resting or praying, around the water, while others started back to their farms or homes. They would spread the word to their neighbors, and soon the truth would carry across the isle. For a time, Danrak meditated with contentment on the miracle worked before his eyes. None of the pilgrims, except for the crone whom he had aided to the water, took any notice of him. The old woman took the time to gather a pouchful of sweet, dark raspberries and offered them to the druid. Danrak realized, with surprise, that he was famished, and he ate the simple meal with warm gratitude.

But as he ate and considered the steady stream of humanity, he realized that he could not become complacent. The young man whose once-crippled wife even now danced in the shallowest part of the pool had provided fair warning of the mischief intended by Blackstone's acting lord.

Danrak knew that the pilgrims, none of whom were armed, would be unwilling or unable to defend this place against the band that Gwyeth would bring on the morrow. He expected that group to be much larger than the half-dozen men he had routed on the previous day, and they would also be supported by the religious powers of a cleric.

Against them stood only Danrak of Myrloch, with his bare hands and the talismans he carried. Yet a week ago the prospect of such a struggle would have depressed and disheartened him—though, of course, he would still have faced it resolutely. Now it presented a challenge that inflamed his determination. He began to form a plan.

He selected several talismans and decided to begin his discouragement of the lord's party some distance away from the valley. If they became confused and demoralized during the half-day march into the mountains, he reasoned, they would be less likely to stand firm against him here.

Still, the question tickled the back of his mind even as he refused to consider it: What, in truth, could he hope to accomplish against a score or more of armed men and the magical abilities of a cleric who had known his god for his entire life?

Danrak's deity, after all, had so far been around for no more than a few days.

* * * * *

From the Log of Sinioth:

The Moonwell! That is the key now. The armies are poised to spread chaos across the isle, sweeping Talos to his proper position of power and domination. The princess yields herself to me, and in our union, we shall prevail.

But that is why the destruction of this vestige of the Earth-mother's power must be accomplished with all haste. If the young knight of Blackstone proves incapable, then the matter shall fall into my own hands.

And I will not fail.

❧ 16 ❧

The Sea of Moonshae

Sir Gwyeth felt considerably heartened now that he was clad in his suit of plate mail, mounted atop his eager, prancing charger, and trailed by a column of more than one hundred men-at-arms. He had doubled the size of the party he had originally planned in order to make certain they could deal with any threat.

The presence of the cleric Wentfeld, riding beside him, did much to enhance his confidence. Whatever the nature of the ensorcellment transforming the Moonwell, the knight of Blackstone felt certain they would make short work of it. Even the rain, beating against his armor and trickling in icy rivulets down his skin, couldn't dampen his enthusiasm.

The column, which included the cantrev's ready men-at-arms plus more than threescore hastily recruited troops from the militia raised in the town itself, marched out of the manor's gatehouse several hours past dawn. Most carried swords or axes, though some two dozen carried heavy crossbows. Sir Gwyeth was taking no chances.

The sky remained gray, and a chill wind blustered, bringing frequent squalls of rain. All in all, it was miserable weather for a march, but even that didn't seem to dampen the enthusiasm of the footmen. Perhaps Gwyeth's enticement of ten gold pieces for each member who remained with the expedition through the completion of its task served to warm the souls of these avaricious guardsmen—or perhaps they all sensed the danger that the resurgent Moonwell and its attendant faith presented to the mines that were their means of living.

In any event, the men raised a crude marching song, which the cleric pretended not to hear. Gwyeth felt as bold as any general who had ever embarked upon a war of conquest.

"Have you any clues as to the nature of this enchantment?" he asked the pryat as they made their way along the broad trail that preceded the narrow, steeply climbing path leading directly to the Moonwell's vale.

"Dark magic, undoubtedly," noted the cleric, who had given the matter little thought once he had received his pouch of gold. "But with the faith of Helm behind us, we'll make short work of it, I'm certain."

The good pryat knew that Helm, as one of the New Gods of the isles, was inherently superior to the primitive Earthmother the Ffolk had once cherished. Though Helm was not an evil god, he was ambitious, and a resurgence of any rival was something that ever vigilant deity regarded with little pleasure. Therefore it pleased Wentfeld doubly, for the profit and for the knowledge that he served his master's will in this endeavor.

"What can we do to reverse the effect?" inquired the knight. "It seems to be potent sorcery."

Pryat Wentfeld reflected. "Polluting the pond will be the most effective tactic, I believe. It was done successfully to a Moonwell many years ago with coal, but I should think a mountain of ashes would serve as well."

"The trees—we burn them and dump the ashes into the pool!" Gwyeth liked the idea.

"Correct. If we have to, we persevere until the thing is nothing more than a patch of grimy muck!"

"Hold—what's this?" demanded Gwyeth as the trail curved around a steep foothill.

"Where goes the path?" inquired Pryat Wentfeld, also puzzled.

The valley floor, which they remembered as a bare and rocky expanse, vanished behind a choking growth of forest. Oaks and pines, tangled with trailing creepers and densely packed among bristling thornbushes, filled the expanse from one steeply sloped side of the valley to the other.

"This is the trail, as the gods are my witnesses! It follows the stream! Backar—come here, man!" Gwyeth called to the sergeant-at-arms who had led the abortive expedition to the Moonwell two days earlier.

Backar, who marched near the head of the footmen, hastened forward at his knight's command. "Yes, my lord! What is it?" He saw the wooded tangle before them and gasped. "Curses to the Abyss, sir—this was plain and clear two days ago!"

"Are you certain you came this way?"

"Aye, lord. There is no other good way!" Backar, still stinging from his previous failure, swore his sincerity.

"Go and seek a path, then!" commanded Gwyeth. The man, with several assistants, hurried forward to examine the wall of dense growth. From his position on his proud charger, the knight could see no suggestion of a break that would have allowed a small child to pass through the overgrowth, much less a band of armed men.

The sides of the valley, to the right and the left, rose unusually steep at this point to form a pair of rocky bluffs standing like gateposts. The forest formed the gate, and Gwyeth had the unsettling impression that the wood had been *placed* here, where it would form the most effective barrier. The clouds capped the valley, covering the heights with oppressive weight and yielding their steady wash of rain over the increasingly disheartened humans below.

Backar and the others hunted across the face of the tangle, pressing back branches, hacking away creepers, and trampling thorns. After some minutes, during which Gwyeth grew increasingly restless with the delay, the man trotted back to report.

"There's no path, sir. It's solid as a briar patch. From the size of the trees, it could have been here for years, but I *swear* it—"

"I know!" snapped the knight. "Well, stop making excuses. Get out your axes and hack us a path!"

The song of the men had faded away when they discovered the inexplicable barrier, and now the knight and the cleric heard muttered curses as a dozen men shouldered axes and advanced to the wall of the thorny forest. They began to chop at the wood that closed over the path, slowly carving a tunnel-like path.

"Wider!" demanded Gwyeth. "I've got a horse to get through there, imbeciles!"

In the meantime, Pryat Wentfeld dismounted and advanced

to the edge of the wood. He removed a small pinch of flour from a pouch at his side and muttered a short, arcane command. At his words, the particles of flour whisked forward with magical speed and stuck to the nearest leaves, sticks, and trunks, outlining a small area in white.

"As I suspected," he reported, returning to Gwyeth's side and remounting. "The forest is magical in nature."

"That helps a lot," growled the knight sourly. "Can you make it disappear the same way?"

"I have an enchantment that will dispel magic," the cleric responded, ignoring his companion's tone. "But I can cast it only once per day. I fear it would be unwise to expend it here, when we don't know what other obstacles might be placed in our path farther up the trail." The priest didn't add another disturbing thought in his head: that the power behind this enchanted forest might well be too great for his own magic to dispel.

Gwyeth had to agree that the priest spoke the truth, though his men chopped their way into the forest with agonizing sluggishness.

Two hours passed before a drenched Backar trudged back to the knight, who had dismounted and paced beneath a few stunted cedars that grew beside the trail.

"Sir Gwyeth, we can see light through the trees now. It would appear that we near the end," reported the obviously fatigued guardsman.

"Redouble your efforts, then!" snapped the knight. "We've wasted more than enough time here already!"

"Aye, my lord." The man headed back to the work party as Gwyeth and the cleric mounted, urging their horses forward. They waited with growing irritation as yet another half an hour passed before the men finally broke through.

The knight saw gray daylight at the end of a tunnel of verdant darkness, and though he had to duck his head beneath the trailing vines overhead, he spurred his steed forward in his eagerness to press on. The column of men fell in behind him, and in another minute, he had passed through the barrier, which proved to be no more than a hundred feet thick, though in width it was sufficient to seal off the valley.

"Press on! We'll make up the time lost. Double march!" He

turned to command his men to follow and practically fell off his horse in astonishment. The men of the column gasped and shouted in consternation at the same time.

The forest had disappeared! Even as the footmen worked their way through the narrow tunnel, the tangled shrubbery blinked away. Making no sound, leaving no sign of its previous presence, everything from the greatest trees to the smallest thornbushes simply vanished, as if it had never been there at all.

"By the gods, man! What deviltry is this?" demanded the knight, pointing for the cleric's benefit.

Wentfeld looked momentarily nonplussed as he studied the transformation, but then the priest turned and squinted around the valley ahead of them. He saw no one—only a small ground squirrel that scampered out of the path of the approaching humans.

"It's not only sorcery, as I told you," Pryat Wentfeld explained, "but someone *controls* it—someone within our sight, for the dispelling was cast as it occurred."

"Find the varlet!" shouted Gwyeth, drawing and waving his sword over his head. "Form a skirmish line. Take him alive!" he shouted at his men.

The footmen drew their swords, except for the two dozen with crossbows, who held back from the others and covered their advance. Next the footmen moved into a well-spaced line across the narrow valley and partway up the steep and rocky sides. The formation slowed their progress considerably, but no person could have remained concealed in the path of the diligent search. Gradually they probed and prodded, combing the valley without success.

"He may well be gone already," said the cleric. "Or lurking on the heights, above our reach."

Gwyeth looked at the craggy slopes looming above them to either side and realized that Wentfeld spoke the truth. Still, having ordered his men into the search, he would not embarrass himself by revoking the order. Instead, he urged them forward with curses and abuse, trying to hurry them over the rough terrain.

A shout came from the far right of the line, and he urged his charger there at a gallop, hoping to find some sorcerous wretch in the grip of his men. Instead, he saw that the cry had come from a clumsy oaf who had scrambled too far up the steep wall in his search. He had fallen into a clump of rocks and now lay there moaning, with his leg jutting to the side at an unnatural angle.

"Fool!" roared Gwyeth, incensed at the further delay. "I am surrounded by idiots!"

Pryat Wentfeld went to the man and cast a healing spell, which straightened the broken leg enough that it could repair itself properly.

"It will be too weak for him to walk," the priest explained when he returned to Gwyeth. "And it would be premature to expend my healing magic for this accident."

Reluctantly Gwyeth agreed and ordered two men, both of whom accepted the assignment with obvious relief, to carry the injured man back to the cantrev. Already, he knew, it was well into the afternoon, and yet they had progressed only a quarter of the way up to the Moonwell.

"Now, move!" he bellowed, spurring his horse into a trot that would easily outdistance the trudging footmen. "Pick up your feet and march!" Wentfeld, the only other horseman, followed his brisk pace.

Several of the veterans among the men-at-arms added their own curses to the nobleman's orders, and slowly the column picked up speed, worming along the trail, the footmen marching with collars raised against the chill and wet. Many of the Ffolkmen cast headlong glances back at the place where the forest had stood. Those who had chopped their way through the tangle looked at the blisters on their hands where they had grasped axes and remembered their keen steel blades hacking into firm and unyielding wood, and they muttered under their breath about unnatural dangers.

For an hour, Gwyeth maintained the brutal pace, reining in when he got too far ahead and exhorting his troops with insults and invective. Finally the cleric drew up beside him and spoke, in a voice that carried to the knight's ears alone.

"My lord, they will be no good to you if they all collapse from exhaustion before we reach the well! We must allow them to rest and then resume at a more humane pace."

It took a supreme effort of Gwyeth's will to suppress his

sudden anger toward the priest. After a moment of enforced, cool reflection, however, he realized that the man spoke the truth. In frustration, he looked before him.

The rocky valley curved to the right, and the gray clouds scudded past the granite tors that loomed to either side of the trail. The path here was smooth, albeit narrow. In several places, herdsmen in years past had cleared the brush on either side, and one of these clearings lay a hundred paces ahead, beside the valley's clear, shallow stream.

"We pause for water and a few moments rest!" Gwyeth announced, leading his men to the spot. "Check your weapons, here. Our next march will conclude at the Moonwell!"

Most of the troops flopped to the ground, while some of them knelt beside the brook that ran through the center of the valley. A number of men sat beside a great pile of sticks that had been piled at the edge of the clearing by whatever shepherd had cleared it in the past.

Gwyeth himself dismounted, removing his helmet and gauntlets to stretch and pace. The men-at-arms avoided him as much as possible, which suited the knight well.

A shout of alarm whipped his head around. He heard multiple screams of terror and saw a full score of his men leap to their feet and flee in panic, leaving their weapons on the ground. They were the men who had sat beside the pile of dried sticks.

But now that brush moved! Gwyeth gaped in shock as he saw a stick bend down with liquid suppleness and crawl onto the ground where the men had been sitting. Other sticks, too, slithered across the ground in a distinctive motion.

One man, who had lain flat on the ground with the chance to rest, now screamed and stumbled backward, a whiplike form lashing at his throat. He pulled it free and cast the hissing thing aside, then pitched forward onto the ground, gasping and gagging.

"Adders!" cried one of the men, stumbling as he fled and madly crawling away from the venomous serpents.

"Snakes—from sticks!" shrieked another.

"Cowards! Don't flee them! Fight!" cried Gwyeth, drawing his own sword and stepping to the nearest snake. The viper whipped itself into a menacing coil, hissing, its forked tongue flickering toward the knight, but the great broadsword chopped downward across the center of the coil, instantly slicing the snake into several pieces. The segments twitched and flailed for a moment, then grew still.

"They die if you strike them! Kill them, you curs!" he shouted, attacking and decapitating another of the serpents. A few of his men seized their own weapons, and in moments the snakes, which had numbered no more than a dozen or so, lay in many bleeding pieces on the ground.

Pryat Wentfeld rose from the still form of the man who had been bitten in the throat. "I can do nothing for him," the priest said grimly. "He is already dead."

"All gods curse this unnatural place!" growled Gwyeth as his men cast fearful glances among themselves. The armored warrior felt heat surge into his head as he struggled with the frustration of not knowing who attacked them and being unable to strike back.

Blood flushed Gwyeth's face as he looked at the rest of his shamefaced troops. His eyes bulged, and the force of his rage strangled his throat so that he couldn't shout, or else he would undoubtedly have invented new volumes of curses as his legacy to the tongue of the Ffolk.

"A *druid* seeks to stop us!" hissed one of his men, hiding behind a cluster of his fellows.

"Aye," grunted a seasoned veteran who had been a young man in the days when druids still had power in the land. He ignored Gwyeth's look of fury and continued courageously. "A forest that doesn't exist . . . sticks that become snakes. These are the powers of a druid, my lord."

"He speaks the truth," said the cleric, placing a hand upon Gwyeth's shoulder. With the touch, the knight felt the fury drain from his body. Again he had control of his mouth and his tongue. Though he remained angry, rage no longer held him in full control.

"This is part of the charlatanry!" Gwyeth said firmly. "Whatever power has created the illusory restoration of the well now seeks to make us believe that a druid has returned to menace us!"

"It's also true," said the priest, addressing the men in support of their captain, "that other clerics may gain powers similar to these in many respects. This is no proof that a druid has returned!"

The cleric lowered his voice, however, when he concluded to Gwyeth. "Still, this is evidence that we face someone of more than ordinary ability."

Gwyeth cast a scornful look over the sullen faces of his men. Many, he saw, gazed mournfully down the valley, and he knew that they regretted their presence here and longed to return home. One lost to a broken leg, and now a man killed by an Abyss-cursed viper! And not a blow struck in their own defense!

"The first man who deserts me will suffer the sting of the lash!" he blustered. "And the next one will be hanged for cowardice! Now form a column, you craven dogs. We'll march up to that stinking pond and see this curse removed!"

Gwyeth mounted quickly, but even propelled by the kicks and curses of the veterans, his men-at-arms were slow to take their formation on the trail. Gwyeth tried to ignore the dark looks of anger and fear that he saw on their faces. He didn't care how they felt about this mission, only that they remained with him until its conclusion.

Finally the men were ready. The cleric rode behind the knight, since the trail was too narrow for more than one horse, and Gwyeth drew his sword as a precaution. Then, peering suspiciously into the heights around them and up as much of the length of the trail before them as he could see, he urged his charger forward and led his men along the next stretch of the march to the Moonwell.

* * * * *

The light of dawn barely penetrated the rainy shore of Salmon Bay. The city of Gnarhelm bustled, however, with lanterns and torches sputtering in the dampness. Crates and barrels, plus a cluster of humanity, occupied the dock and the longship moored beside it.

Brandon directed his crew with precision, and the loading of provisions into the *Gullwing* was quickly completed. The prince had selected some sixty warriors for the voyage, with Knaff the Elder to man the helm. The firbolgs Yak, Loinwrap, and Beaknod willingly joined the crew. Alicia, Tavish, and Keane would also accompany them. Brandon had found it necessary to roughly overrule some superstitious grumbling from men who feared the presence of the women would bring bad luck.

"Well, I'm ready for a little salt air," announced Tavish, winking at Alicia. The bard busily tuned her harp while the pair boarded the vessel and stood near the stern.

The princess frowned, irritated. "Still, they let the firbolgs sail without complaint! I'm annoyed that it took an order to get them to accept you and me!"

"We're here, anyway—and who knows, maybe they would have done us a favor by leaving us behind," replied the bard in that confounded good humor. "Perhaps there's something else that's bothering you."

The princess sighed, casting a look at the commanding figure of the Prince of Gnarhelm. "Aye, Auntie, indeed there is. He probably assumes I agree with his 'proposal' because I haven't said anything. Proposal? It sounded like he was talking about a diplomatic treaty!"

"Relax, child," Tavish noted, her eyes glimmering with amusement. "It probably hasn't occurred to him yet that you have anything to say about the matter."

"He'll find out otherwise when this is all over," the princess noted grimly.

Keane, his expression glum, climbed over the gunwale and took a seat beside the mast. Quickly the crew scrambled aboard. Alicia avoided Brandon by going to sit beside the mage as the young prince ordered his men to oars and rigging. She knew, however, that sooner or later she and Brandon would be forced into proximity. She found that her anger over his arrogant proposal had soothed somewhat, but she didn't want to risk conversation on the topic until their mission was concluded.

The ebbing tide carried them silently away from the dock, where the king and many other bearded captains and warriors watched solemnly. The oars dipped in smooth cadence, propelling the sleek vessel through the choppy waters of the bay.

After a time, Tavish strummed a tentative chord on her harp, and then another. In a few minutes, her fingers began to bounce about the strings, and powerful music filled the air. Yet, the princess knew, it was more than music flowing from the unadorned instrument. Indeed, a feeling of celebration and joy surrounded the ship.

The bard herself looked surprised as the sounds of power rang through the *Gullwing*.

"The harp from Cymrych Hugh," murmured Keane.

"An artifact of magic," Alicia agreed.

"In the hands of one who can work its sorcery very well."

The crewmen, hearts swelled by the song, strained at their oars. The longship raced across the bay, easily breasting the high waves that indicated the nearness of the open sea.

As soon as the *Gullwing* passed beyond the sheltered waters of Salmon Bay, the relentless and powerful Sea of Moonshae began its assault. The storm winds of Talos heaved against the surf, and rain swept from the skies, backed by the force of a developing gale.

"Can you make headway in this weather?" Alicia asked of Brandon, who had come to stand beside her at the mast. Above them, the sail remained furled, while the oarsmen strained at their benches. In the stern, Tavish still played, and the music gave the men strength.

"It's no worse than any summer storm," he reassured her, but she detected something in the narrow set of his eyes.

"But it's not just *any* storm, is it?"

The prince met her eyes shrewdly. "You sense it, too, then?" he asked.

"There's a power behind it that seeks to thwart us—that much I can feel. But what power? And can we prevail?"

Brandon nodded his head slowly. "The *Gullwing* is the finest ship in Gnarhelm, and I've picked the most able crew. If the force of the gale doesn't increase, I'm confident."

"And if it does?"

"We'll make our prayers to Valkur the Mighty and sail all the harder!" he exclaimed. Alicia sensed little bravado but much determination in the northman's words.

Alicia looked at the expanse of surging sea and wished for a moment that she had faith enough in some deity to allow her to pray. Though she remembered the sudden vitality of the Moonwell, that transformation seemed remote and irrelevant now. It hadn't changed her life; she had seen no further evidence that the goddess was a real presence in the world. She shivered and looked at the twin silver bracers spiraling about her forearms. The metal chilled her skin uncomfortably.

Keane joined her, catching himself on the mast to keep his balance in the pitching, rolling hull. The mage came from the gunwale, where he had just deposited the remnants of their previous evening's dinner over the side. His thin face was cast in a sickly shade of green, but Keane had impressed Alicia by his lack of complaint thus far into the voyage.

"I've always enjoyed a pleasant cruise on a sheltered sea," he informed them, trying unsuccessfully to conceal his chagrin.

"Splendid sailing weather!" boomed Brandon, clapping the slim Ffolkman on the back, a gesture which almost sent Keane lurching back to the rail.

Despite the northman's heartiness, which seemed somewhat forced to the princess, even Alicia's unpracticed eye could see that the swells grew higher and higher as they pressed toward the south. Gray mountains of water loomed over the bow, seemingly ready to swamp the craft, yet somehow the sleek figurehead rose into each precipitous crest and carried the ship smoothly to the top.

There the *Gullwing* teetered on the breaking summit, white water foaming all around them, and then she tipped forward to career with dizzying velocity into the trough between the heaving swells. Though the vessel stretched nearly a hundred feet in length, the waves rose or lowered her as if she were a mere cork bobbing in the brine.

"Stroke, you fainthearted wretches!" called Knaff from his position at the stern. The oarsmen redoubled their efforts, and Alicia saw the old warrior turn and bark something to Tavish, who sat beside him. His words were inaudible over the pounding of the sea, but the princess heard the music of the bard's harp, louder than ever, fill the ship with renewed strength and determination.

A gray wall of water rose suddenly, and tons of the icy sea poured over the bow, soaking Alicia and the others as it thundered the length of the hull. The ship wallowed and slowed, growing sluggish, as yet another, higher, wave loomed before the sea gull figurehead.

All the northmen not straining at the oars seized buckets and frantically started bailing the water over the side. Alicia joined them, while Keane clung to the mast, his teeth clenched, his greenish cheeks taut with determination.

The mage fumbled in his pouch as the wave began to break, reaching with greedy fingers of foam to embrace the craft as the vessel nearly foundered. Keane finally removed that which he sought—two tiny squares of crystal. He raised them, pinched between his fingers, as the water crashed downward toward the open hull of the *Gullwing*.

"*Dividius! Arcani—tuloth!*" He cried the enchantment as the crew bailed and Brandon looked fiercely upward at the angry spume that threatened to doom his ship.

Keane shattered the two crystals with a snap of his fingers, and abruptly, magically, the frothing barrier parted before the *Gullwing*'s prow. A trough appeared, slicing as if a knife divided the great wave, and the longship slipped through while the swell collapsed into a maelstrom on either side.

Brandon turned to regard the passenger, his face a mask of shock, but Keane took no notice. Instead he stared forward, where gray swells—all of them capped with angry caps of foam—stretched to the far horizon.

And as the mage concentrated, the waves before them parted, and though heaving swells still tossed and smashed on each side of them, a narrow, straight gap had been carved in the sea.

Along this sleek highway, the *Gullwing* sprang forward as if the ship herself felt the exhilaration of the wizard's triumph.

* * * * *

"Lady Deirdre! Earl Blackstone! What is the trouble? Are you hurt?" The demanding questions were accompanied by persistent pounding on the doors of the Great Hall. The princess recognized the voice as belonging to young Arlen, the castle's burly sergeant-at-arms.

Deirdre blinked, looking quickly from Malawar to Blackstone. The latter still gaped at the place where the intruder's body had disappeared. The former looked mildly at the confused, hesitating princess, and finally he spoke.

"You must send him away, my dear, but reassuringly."

She nodded dumbly, but then her mind began to work.

"All is well, Sergeant," she called, pleased that her voice sounded level and calm. "It was a mild commotion, but the matter is concluded." She crossed to the doors and lowered her voice. "And please, Arlen, I would desire that you keep this matter in your confidence. No harm has been done."

"As you wish, my lady." The sergeant's voice quite clearly indicated that the resolution was not as *he* wished. Nevertheless, she heard him order several other men-at-arms away. She pictured the strapping warrior taking the position as door guard himself, and she knew that she could trust him not to intrude.

"He—he was dead! It's the same man . . . but I saw him die! I *killed* him!" Blackstone recovered his voice, but the brawny earl's tone quavered as his words groped for some kind of understanding. He pointed at the spot where the man had vanished, and they all saw that no spot—no mark of any kind—indicated the place.

"He seemed to be quite alive," said Malawar dryly. "Perhaps you are confused as to his identity."

"But . . . he *sounded* the same, said the same sort of things!" Blackstone shook his head, then looked up. "Of course, though . . . you must be right. He *was* dead. . . ."

The earl turned to look at Deirdre, his eyes wide. "How, lady, did you slay him? What power do you have?"

For the first time, the princess recalled the explosion of might with which she had taken a life. The memory frightened her, yet the sense of triumph gave her a strange thrill as well.

"It—it comes from within me," she stammered.

"You have summoned the Bolt of Talos, an enchantment controlled by the will of a very potent sorceress," Malawar explained. The priest turned to Deirdre and placed his hands upon her shoulders. "Now, my dear," he declared, "you must tend to your country."

"Raise an army?" she asked reluctantly.

"Any further delay could be disastrous," he observed. "You know that the northmen are on the march!"

"I'll notify the lord generals," she said. "They'll have all the cantrevs mustered. It'll take a few days."

"The captains will do quite well," the priest noted. "You can be certain that the war will begin with a vigorous attack."

"I'm concerned about my cantrev," Blackstone announced. "I have to be there in case that column comes over the mountain."

"Yes," agreed Malawar. "You should go."

"Can you stay here for a time?" Deirdre asked Malawar. "As a guest of the castle? I have chambers that are ready even as we speak. You'd be very comfortable."

"I don't doubt that in the least, my lady. But, alas, comfort is not a luxury I can currently afford. No, I have to leave you. There are other matters to which I must attend. I will return to you before the moment of decision."

"As you will," Deirdre concluded unhappily. Before she had completed the last word, her mysterious companion had faded to nothing before her eyes.

"I hate it when he does that!" growled Blackstone, gesturing at the place where Malawar had disappeared. "It gives me the shivers, thinking he might be anywhere, whenever he wants to be there!"

Deirdre paid little attention. Instead, she stared at the place where Malawar had been and thought about the eternal hours that must pass before she would see him again.

* * * * *

Darkness of his second night in the highlands found Hanrald seeking shelter in a low vale protected from wind and rain only by the craggy tors on all sides. During his wanderings since the death of his horse and the fight with the trolls, the knight had realized that he was totally lost.

A small, dark pond indicated the possibility of fish. Hanrald, who had grown up in country well-laced with trout streams, was able to tickle a fat rainbow from the water by lying very still above an overhanging bank and holding his hand in the water. When one of the trout unknowingly swam across his fingers, he flipped it out of the water and quickly bashed its head on a rock.

No trees grew in his rocky vale, but he found enough dried

brush to build a small fire. He decided that if his fish could not be called cooked, neither was it entirely raw—and never had he enjoyed a meal so much.

Leaning back against the rock that he would use as his pillow, the knight placed his drawn sword across his lap, where he could raise it with an instant's notice. He stared at the fading embers of his fire, and his mind turned—as it did so often—to the Princess Alicia.

Where was she? During his days of wandering, Hanrald had become convinced that she would no longer be found in the highlands. Nevertheless, he had no regrets about making his impetuous search, for during this time, he had clarified much in his own mind. Solitude, he decided, did that for a man. It allowed his mind to look at things with a clarity that was often denied by the bustle of society.

Foremost among his realizations had been a full understanding of his own loyalty. He was devoted to his king, and if this meant a betrayal of his own family, then so be it. Such a betrayal could only come about because of treachery on his father's part, and Hanrald felt fairly certain that such treachery figured prominently in the earl's plans.

The knight's thoughts turned to his father, the Earl of Fairheight. Since Hanrald's first awareness, he remembered striving to please the man, but always he fell short of Blackstone's harsh goals. The older Currag and Gwyeth, dark and brooding like the earl, had been his father's favorites in everything.

Gradually, however, the young knight had realized that the differences between them ran much deeper. Of course he had heard the rumors spread by the servants and old guardsmen, the claims that the earl's wife had been unfaithful and Hanrald was not his true son after all. But he had always dismissed that speculation as mere gossip, else he couldn't imagine why Blackstone would have raised him in the manor. His wife, after all, had died in the act of bearing Hanrald.

Now he wondered if the tale might not have some credence after all. The differences between himself and his brother and father seemed so profound that perhaps they required an explanation such as this. Not in a physical sense, of course— Hanrald had inherited his fairness and blue eyes from his mother—but morally. How could they be men of the same stock?

His musings were interrupted as he caught sight of a sudden brightness in the night, a gleaming spot of light that appeared and then as quickly vanished. Hanrald's hands clenched around the hilt of his massive sword, and he slowly rose to his feet. He could see nothing through the darkness, and even his fire was now a mere bowl of cherry-red embers.

But he felt something out there, and a shiver passed along his spine. There! He saw it again, this time a pair of spots, yellowish green and glowing dimly in the faint, reflected light of his pathetic fire. The glowing points were close together, unmistakably the eyes of a large animal.

Hanrald bent his knees, holding the sword before him in a fighting crouch, expecting momentarily that some horror would come lunging from the darkness to tear at his throat. He intended that the beast would meet its death on his blade before its slavering jaws ever got close to his neck.

He heard a movement behind him and looked around, but all was darkness. Nevertheless, his senses began to confirm that he faced more than one of these creatures. Indeed, by listening and remaining perfectly still, he slowly discerned the truth.

He was surrounded.

Dark shapes moved on all sides of him, more than he could count. He heard heavy breathing, sensed stealthy footpads approaching. Slowly, deliberately, he raised his sword.

If he had come here only to die, so be it. None would say that he had not fallen like a man and knight, with his sword in his hand and the bodies of his enemies scattered around him.

* * * * *

Beneath a heavy cloak of dark cloud, soaked by chill, persistent rain, Danrak plodded the last few steps back to the Moonwell. Finally the milky glow of the enchanted pool rose in the night before him, and he collapsed on the rocky ground, exhausted. Several children—pilgrims, like their parents and the hundred others who now rested here—approached and offered the druid a hatful of ripe berries, which he ate with relish.

Gwyeth and the column from Blackstone wouldn't reach the well tonight, he knew. The young lord had called a halt to the march after darkness completely masked the trail. Nevertheless, they were only a few miles away, and it wouldn't be long after daylight before they reached the Moonwell.

The druid had to admit that he was at a loss as to how he could further delay them. The spells he had cast today had each come from his talismans, and he knew they had been effective in delaying the men. But how could he expect to do more?

The hallucinatory forest and the sticks-to-snakes castings had demoralized the force early in its march. Then he had used a heat metal spell, which had caused the knight and his leading warriors to cast down their weapons and tear off their gauntlets before their skin burned. Finally he had employed a raise water enchantment, which had caused the stream to flood the men's camp just after they built their supper fires, while their long-awaited dinners cooked. He knew that it was a very wet, cold, and disgusted group of men that now bedded down in the mud.

But still he didn't see how he could stop them in the morning. His remaining talismans gave him abilities that could frighten or injure some of them, and he might even slay one or two, but with a hundred men-at-arms marching this way, he may as well have faced an unstoppable tide.

"Here, my son. Have some broth."

The voice was faint, but he looked up to see the stooped figure of the crone he had helped earlier. His troubles felt less burdensome as she sat beside him and handed him a chipped cup containing a hearty soup of vegetables and fish.

"Thank you, Grandmother," he said, and she beamed at the term of affection and respect.

"You will stop them," she said softly. Again he saw those toothless gums as her face split into a wide grin. "*I* know you will, even if you do not believe it yourself!"

He laughed and allowed the warmth of the soup to flow through his body and revitalize his muscles. As he leaned back to sleep, he found himself hoping that the old woman was right.

* * * * *

Hanrald stayed awake through the long, dark night, sensing the presence of the creatures lurking just beyond his vision. His hands grew cramped around the hilt of his sword, but he dared not release the weapon for fear he wouldn't have time to snatch it up again in the event of an attack.

Above the clouds, the moon glowed full, though no trace of its light seeped through to the ground. The creatures surrounding the knight sensed it, however, and as the bright orb reached its zenith, they greeted its ascendance with their song.

As the howling of the hounds rose around him, some of the man's tension eased. He knew the sound, and now he knew the nature of his nocturnal visitors.

And no longer did he fear them.

* * * * *

King Sythissal crawled reluctantly onto the shore. He ignored the wind-lashed rain that spattered against him, for his displeasure had nothing to do with physical discomfort. Indeed, to one used to the depths of the sea, the climate here was uncomfortable more for its dryness than anything else.

Rather, the sahuagin king bemoaned the fact that he must present himself to Gotha and report an initial failure. Even as he reached the mouth of the great cave, the huge shape of the dracolich loomed before him.

"O most iniquitous master!" cried the king, prostrating his scaled body on the rocks of the cavern mouth.

"Speak, fish!" commanded the serpent.

"Our task on Grayrock was incomplete," reported Sythissal. "The day following our attack, a boat set sail from the island."

"Your warriors intercepted it, I presume," replied the dracolich softly.

"We discovered the craft when it reached the line of my scouts."

"And it was attacked there?" inquired the monstrous undead figure.

"Alas, execrable one!" wailed Sythissal. "They sailed with great speed, as if some sorcery propelled them! My scouts could not match their pace, and so the ship passed our first line of defense!"

"They could not reach the hull?" wondered Gotha, his voice calm but his tone skeptical.

"Through the Deepsong, they sent word that the ship passed by before they could even draw close. I hastened here with all speed to let your mightiness know of this news!"

"What course do they sail?" inquired the dragon, puffing a blast of flame over the sahuagin's head that singed uncomfortably close to the spines bristling along the piscine monarch's back.

"They mark for Alaron," explained the cringing creature of the deep.

"Then I shall go to Alaron and kill them. Return to your brine, fish, and gather your warriors! We attack with all haste! Further failure will not be tolerated!"

"But of course, loathsome lizard!" The sahuagin wasted no time in scuttling down from the rocky hill and diving into the sheltering sea.

In the meantime, the great dragon body emerged from its lair, and the decayed wings stretched wide. With a powerful spring, the creature hurled himself into the air, ignoring the rain that lashed at him and the wind that would have driven a lesser creature back to earth.

With sweeping strokes, Gotha gained altitude until the gray mist surrounded him. He flew through a blinding fog, but the evil of Talos guided him. For hours, he soared to the southeast, breasting the storm clouds and ignoring the frequent squalls of rain that doused him. Finally his instincts told him to descend.

As the great serpent emerged beneath the clouds, dusk had begun to darken the already storm-shrouded ocean. But the creature saw a foaming wake before him, and at its head, propelled by driving oars, a sleek longship pressed through the sea along a straight, unnatural trough in the water.

But not for long, the dracolich reflected, with an evil chuckle. Tucking his wings, Gotha nosed forward into a killing dive.

* * * * *

From the Log of Sinioth:

No! The truth comes to me now, in the depths of my meditation: It is the Moonwell! There is where the threat to Talos lies, festering subtly while my master sends his agents hastening to their tasks!

I see it: The gold-bedazzled cleric of Helm knows the truth when I, the eyes of Talos himself, am blind! Real power grows there, and it looms as a threat to all our plans, for if the Ffolk know of the rebirth of their goddess, all our efforts will fail. My crop of chaos needs a spiritually weakened, angrily divided people as its sowing ground.

Kaffa serves me well, bringing his longship up the western coast of Alaron. He nears Olafstaad, and he may serve as my sentinel there, proof against the intrusion of the northmen. I am pleased at my own foresight. The tri-bolt charm protecting his ship will render him invulnerable to attacks of magic.

I need to summon Larth and his riders and the great dracolich. They must make for the Moonwell with all haste. Finally there is the young princess of Callidyrr. She is power, waiting to erupt.

And it is time for me to light the fuse.

❧ 17 ❧

Undeath from Above

"Look!" Alicia pointed upward from the *Gullwing*'s hull. The vessel still raced along the trough in the sea carved by Keane's spell. Now the princess wanted to scream, but her voice remained level and firm. "Dragon!"

The huge beast dropped from the gray overcast, dimly visible in the fading light of day. Wings as broad as the *Gullwing*'s length spread across the sky, and a horrific head drooped at the end of a sinuous neck. Scales of dull red, crusted over with rot and mold, formed a patchwork of skin, gaping to show white bone. Gleaming red eyes compelled attention, glowing spots of fire that burned within the black chasms of their sockets. Jaws wide, the monster plummeted toward the sleek longship.

Keane's head whipped around to follow Alicia's gaze, and immediately the concentration of his part water spell broke. Waves heaved around the vessel, though not so violently as those that had threatened to swamp her earlier in the day.

"Archers! To arms!" cried Brandon. The prince himself seized a long harpoon from the hull and raised it to his shoulder, turning to face the creature that swooped toward them from the rear.

Tavish immediately changed her song, striking a series of martial chords that filled Alicia's heart with savage courage. The princess drew her sword and stood beside the prince, uncaring that the weapon would be of little use against the monstrous presence in the sky.

"Let fly!" shouted the prince.

A dozen northmen launched arrows, but as the missiles soared upward, they all realized the futility of the attack. Most of them fell short, and those that struck the great snout seemed little more than slivers in the face of the monstrous foe.

Staring at the beast, Alicia felt the awe-inspiring presence of the great serpent strike terror into her heart. Her knees weakened, and her vision blurred as she reached out to grasp the mast for support. Even Brandon, she sensed, grew numb at the sight of imminent, diving death.

But then Tavish struck her harp again, and the magical strings sent notes of heroism and pride through the air. Alicia heard them and shrugged off her fear, to be replaced with a cool anger that brought her to a peak of fighting efficiency. All around she felt the northmen reacting to the enchanted harp and the spell woven by the skilled bard, a spell that vanquished their fear and cleared their heads for battle.

Beside her, Brandon grunted as he hurled his harpoon. The heavy missile soared upward to bury its barbed head in the monster's chest. The dragon's mouth gaped as it bellowed its rage, and then a rumbling roar assailed them. Smoke belched forth, and staring into that hateful maw, Alicia saw a billowing inferno of fire start to erupt.

"*Frigidius! Karythi!*"

Keane pointed his finger straight into those murderous jaws and shouted the command of a spell. As the dragon's fireball breath erupted, a blast of white light exploded from Keane's hand, meeting the fiery cloud in midair. The princess felt a blast of frost—the icy effect of the wizard's spell.

The two arcane forces, one of unnatural hotness and the other of equally extreme cold, met in the air with a sound like a thunderclap. The force of the explosion rocked the *Gullwing* in the water, sending Alicia tumbling.

The pressure of the blast surged outward as wind, smashing the diving serpent to the side. The monster, struggling desperately to stay aloft, nearly struck the tops of the gray waves. Veering wildly, pressing powerful strokes downward with its vast wings, the creature barely stayed above the water. Striving to fly, it slowly gained altitude as it flew away from the ship, trailed by another volley of arrows that fell well short of its scaled tail.

"Well met, my hearties!" Tavish's voice, full of cheer and confidence, boomed from the stern. Surprised, Alicia saw that even Knaff the Elder looked at the bard with respect from his position at the helm.

"Did we drive it off?" Alicia wondered, looking at the gray cloud where the serpent had disappeared.

"I doubt it," Keane said sourly. "Though perhaps we surprised it a little."

"*You* surprised it," Brandon said, looking at Keane with frank appreciation. "Sorcery or not, that was well done!"

"Look!" Giant Wultha, in the center of the longship, pointed skyward and shouted. "It comes again!"

"And here, to port!" Knaff added his own cry to the alarm. Unlike everyone else, the grizzled veteran had not confined his attentions to the flying creature. Now he pointed to the left, across the storm-tossed surface of the sea.

"Another longship!" Alicia cried, feeling a momentary delight. "Friends?" A ship emerged from the haze, rising and falling across the rolling swells. Its red sail, emblazoned with the dark image of a great bird of prey, swelled in the wind.

"Not likely," Brandon replied, quashing her hopes after a quick glance. "I don't know that black eagle sigil, and I know who my friends are."

But they couldn't afford to spend time in deliberation. The other ship, tacking against the wind, was still several miles away as the flying monster skimmed at them from the starboard beam, racing just below the pressing blanket of cloud. They could see no sign that it had been injured by the attack. Indeed, the creature uttered a bellow of rage that seemed to indicate it attacked with more fury than ever.

"Archers ready!" cried the prince as the beast nosed into a shallow dive.

Alicia clenched her sword, and much to her surprise realized that her other hand grasped Keane's arm quite firmly. Embarrassed, she released him, knowing that their only real hope of besting the creature rested with him.

The dragon seemed to sense this, too, for it dove directly toward the magic-user. The monster's red, glowing eyes, floating like amorphous spots in its great vacant sockets, sought out and locked onto Keane.

"*Bulterus!*"

The man spat another spell, this one a hissing bolt of lightning that crackled upward straight into the face of the monster. Like the force he had unleashed against the iron golem, the blast of electricity smashed into the serpent and filled the air with the sizzling odor of its force.

The dragon shrieked and veered, knocked from the path of its dive by the explosion. But this time it did not soar away over the wavetops. Instead, the monster crashed into the bow of the *Gullwing*, cracking away the figurehead and rocking the vessel crazily in the rough water. The beast perched at the prow of the ship, its hindquarters balanced on the hull while its tail dragged in the water.

"Attack!" shouted Brandon, seizing his great war hammer and charging toward the bow. Alicia ran at his side, so propelled by the mighty cadence of Tavish's song that she forgot the fear that would normally have locked her, or indeed any other person, in place.

The dragon's neck darted forward, and a seaman screamed as the awful jaws closed over his head and torso. When the monster reared, it left only the wretch's legs spurting blood from the severed midsection. A savage, taloned forefoot raked, ripping the faces from two more northmen.

Yak and Beaknod attacked. The firbolg chieftain wore, as always, his displacer beast cape, but now the grinning cat's skull rested on his head, snarling in hatred at the dracolich. Driving his stout club against the monster's shoulder, the firbolg struck with bone-crushing force.

Beaknod drove at the beast's other side, the huge giant-kin bellowing a battle cry. Gotha met the firbolg with a slash of his claws that sent the giant stumbling backward. Then the awful mouth struck down and daggerlike teeth closed over Beaknod's shoulders and head. With a strangled cry, the giant twisted reflexively and then drooped, dead.

The beast cast the body aside as Brandon's hammer crashed onto a monstrous foot, and Alicia drove her blade into the tendons of its leg. Screaming in pain, the dracolich reared back, the force of its motion carrying the splintering bow of the longship deeper into the rolling sea. Huge jaws gaping, the creature belched another cloud of smoke, and then Alicia felt the impending heat of its fiery breath.

In that instant, she lost hope of living and became a whirlwind of battle. She chopped with all her might, hacking deep into the decayed flesh of the monster's thigh. At the same time, she saw that horrible fireball emerge and shouted her disdain at the beast even as she thought that she died.

But Keane stood beside her, and he brandished his fist upward at the beast, while with his other hand, he pulled Alicia back into the ship. Brandon fought next to the mage, his hammer clenched in his hands, his face glaring upward in mute frustration as the inferno rained down.

Something, however, held the deadly force at bay.

For a moment, Alicia couldn't believe that she still lived. Hellish flame surged around her. She saw the bow of the *Gullwing* engulfed in fire as the orange blossom of death filled the air. Yet she and the men who were near her remained safe, as if wrapped in a blanket of protective air.

"The *ring!*" Keane shouted, exultant, and she knew that he was as surprised as she by their survival.

Indeed, as she looked at the hand where he wore the plain bronze ring from the tomb of Cymrych Hugh, she saw that the artifact glowed brightly. Lines of brightness swirled outward from the ring, forming a spherical cocoon around the half-dozen or so humans who survived in the bow of the ship.

For a moment, the battle paused as the dragon started back, astonished at the ineffectiveness of its deadliest attack. The humans, though equally shocked, recovered first.

"Die, wyrm!" shouted Brandon, his voice rich with savagery. He sprang to a bench and swung his hammer over his head. The heavy maul crashed into the monster's breast with a splintering of bone. Alicia leaped to his side and sank her own blade to the hilt into the monster's rotted flesh.

The serpent bellowed again, a gout of flame blossoming into the air over their heads. Above, the sail, still furled atop the mast, burst into flames, and the greedy tongues of fire licked their way down the long shaft of timber.

Sailors screamed and groaned behind Alicia, and she knew that not all of the crew had benefitted from the protection of Keane's ring. Again she stabbed the creature.

A claw reached toward her and she stumbled, falling as the vicious talons barely missed her head. The sinews in his back taut with effort, Brandon bashed his hammer onto the foot of the beast, and the snapping of bone cracked through the ship. The dragon howled again, and its jaws darted toward the northman prince.

Alicia screamed in terror, remembering the sailor who had perished so brutally at the outset of the fight. She struggled to rise, but splintered boards and broken bodies lay around her, trapping her where she was. Instead, it was Keane who leaped forward to the northman's side. This time the mage raised both his hands in the air and shouted something that sounded to the princess like an oath.

Before his upraised hands, a shimmering wall appeared in the air, like a slightly imperfect pane of glass that had been cast across the vessel's bow, separating the crew from the monstrous attacker. The dragon's snout crashed into the barrier, and the beast toppled back, howling in surprise. The noise of its cries shook the ocean, drowning out even the eternal crashing of the waves.

The serpent sprang again at the wall of force, only to bounce back with more shrill cries of outrage. It smashed with its unbroken forefoot, and that, too, was deflected.

"Back!" shouted Keane, grabbing Brandon's arm as Alicia struggled to her feet. "Back to the center of the ship, before the beast comprehends the spell!"

Alicia saw what he meant. The shimmering wall extended only a short distance overhead and was barely wider than the hull of the *Gullwing*. Soon the monster must realize that it could easily go around or over it. Indeed, the dragon suddenly lunged upward, pausing to hover over the bow of the stricken vessel while its glowing eyes sought a target.

She risked a glimpse to the side and saw that the other longship had raced much closer. Armed men stood along the hull, and the vessel had begun a wide turn that would run her alongside the stricken *Gullwing*.

Again the fiery breath erupted as the beast spewed its hellfire over the top of the invisible wall. The spume, crackling and hissing in its hunger to devour flesh and wood, spilled downward and quickly blossomed into a great cloud.

But once more Keane raised his fist, and the ring met the fireball with its own irresistible force, glowing like a tiny sun, casting warmth into the face of inferno and somehow holding the maelstrom away. The dragonbreath was deflected over each side of the *Gullwing*, hissing like a mass of burning oil as it spread across the stormy waters.

"*Keer—heesh!*"

Keane shouted, and this time a web of blue sparks blossomed into the air, expanding like a whirling spiderweb of light. The net flew toward the dragon, and the great creature bellowed in frustration. Finally, with a lash of its tail that caved in several planks along the longship's bow, the serpent surged up into the air. The crackling web of sparks sailed after it, until both the dragon and the arcane force that pursued it disappeared into the low overcast.

"Alert—to port!" cried Knaff, and the crew immediately turned to confront the other longship. The hawk-winged sail loomed close as the vessel carved through a tight turn and commenced the last leg of its tack, a course that would take it straight into the Gullwing's shattered prow!

A moment after the alarm, a volley of arrows arced toward the *Gullwing*, striking several men of Gnarhelm. Shouts of war rang from the dark-sailed ship. Though the crew were obviously northmen, their intentions couldn't have been more clearly warlike.

"By the Abyss!" cursed Keane. "This is *enough!*" His face twisted in fury, the mage barged past the astonished Alicia and leaped onto the rail of the wallowing *Gullwing*. The enemy vessel, the *Vulture*, slipped past them two hundred feet away, and the princess caught a glimpse of a huge, one-eyed helmsman leering at his foes in triumph.

Keane pointed a long, steady finger at the center of the mysterious vessel's hull. His eyes narrowed into staring points of anger. "*Dissidius!*" he cried, barking a single word. The force of his magic wasn't visible, but Alicia sensed a pulsing in the air as a great force reached for the enemy's hull, seeking to rend the beams and nails into splinters.

But then Keane cursed. The princess felt the pulsation of magic rebound from the target, as if the longship was protected by some sort of proof against sorcery. The mage fell into the hull of the *Gullwing* and lay still.

"Keane!" Alicia cried, quickly kneeling beside him.

"Port helm! Hard!" Brandon shouted.

Knaff leaned against the rudder, and the stricken longship slowly veered, finally facing the oncoming vessel head-on.

"Hold on!" bellowed the prince, then ignored his own advice by raising his axe and charging toward the bow of the *Gullwing*. Yak, Wultha, and a dozen of his crew followed.

The collision wracked both ships with splintering violence. The sturdy *Gullwing*, despite her damage, wallowed with her bow only slightly lower in the water. The attacking *Vulture*, however, reeled to the side as several planks broke away from the weatherbeaten hull. The two bows snagged together for a moment, and Brandon led the charge across the pitching, splintered boards. The Prince of Gnarhelm leaped into the midst of his enemies, slashing with his huge axe. Yak waded into the fray behind him, picking up his human foes and throwing them over the side.

Alicia rolled forward from the force of the impact, slamming into an oarsman's bench. Cursing, she sat up and saw that Keane's eyes had opened. The mage blinked, squinting in pain.

"Wait here," the princess told him, relieved beyond words to see that he lived. At the same time, she knew that a battle for the survival of their ship raged only a few yards away.

But when she reached the bow, she saw that the two ships had drifted apart. Brandon, Yak, and Wultha battled furiously in the stricken, hawk-sailed ship, the bodies of a score of their foes lying around them. The mysterious ship foundered as gray water poured through the wounds in her hull.

"Ropes!" cried Alicia, and several northmen raced to obey. "Brandon! Over here!" she shouted as lines were pitched into the water. "Jump!"

Without hesitation, their three compatriots hurled themselves into the tossing sea, desperately grasping the ropes that trailed before them. In moments, they were hauled, sputtering and chilled, into the *Gullwing*. At the same time, the black-sailed *Vulture* slowly rolled onto her side and then vanished, along with her crew, beneath the waves.

For a moment, the crew of the *Gullwing* stood rapt, as if the sea itself had gone silent around them. Eyes searched the mist and the clouds, expecting the horrors to return any instant . . . but the sky remained still.

Not so the sea.

"Bail!" cried Brandon as great spurts of foaming sea burst through the cracked planking of the bow. His crew leaped to their buckets, while others returned to their oars. Alicia, Keane, and Brandon kept alert for a return of the monster from the skies, but it didn't reappear.

"You—you scared the dragon away," the princess said to Keane in amazement.

"The monster will be back sooner or later," the mage assured her. "As to the loss of that ship, it is a matter of sadness. I'm certain those men were just the pawns of the power that seeks to send us to war."

"My friends, the wizard and the princess," said Brandon, coming up to them with a weary smile. "We would all be dead now if not for you," he told Keane. "And for this, you shall always have the gratitude of me and my people. And you, dear princess—you fight like a dervish! I'm more glad than ever that we battle as allies and not foes."

Alicia shook her head, disparaging the comment. In her mind, she thought of the blows delivered by Brandon, the sorcery wielded by Keane, and even the benign magic of Tavish. Her contribution seemed paltry indeed.

Water splashed around their ankles. The *Gullwing* foundered, and they all wondered if they would be here to greet the monster upon its return.

* * * * *

For Gwyeth of Blackstone, the dawn was shattered by the screams of twoscore of his men as the wretches awakened trapped within a twisted mat of creepers and vines, plants that had sprouted during the night to entangle the unfortunate warriors who slumbered in their path. Howling, they struggled to escape, but all of them remained pinned to the ground by their arms, legs, necks, and torsos. Unhurt but terrified, they pleaded for help from their comrades.

The rest of the troop set upon the thicket with knives and shortswords, chopping and hacking at the verdant bonds imprisoning their compatriots. Soon they freed all the trapped men, though several had suffered nicks and cuts from blades wielded by their overzealous comrades.

Morale had reached a nadir as the men started up the last few miles of the trail to the Moonwell. Gwyeth, in the lead, mounted upon his charger, was in as bad a humor as the troops of his company. Pryat Wentfeld rode well behind the knight as the armored man muttered and cursed his way up the rock-strewn mountain track. But the entanglement, it seemed, was the last obstacle in their path. Less than two hours later, the mounted knight saw the tops of the tall cedars waving in the breeze. Shortly afterward, the pond came into view.

A hundred Ffolk or more, raggedly dressed and unarmed, scattered from the path of Gwyeth's column as he led them into the vale. The knight dismounted as they drew near the pool, and he made a point of ignoring the rabble that had ceased its flight at a respectful distance.

"There, lord. That's the one we dropped," explained Backar, indicating a great cedar trunk stretched along the ground. "You see the stump, right th—"

The man's voice trailed off in shock. Gwyeth, too, stared in disbelief. The tree, he could see, had obviously been felled recently. Its needles were still green, and moist pine sap gummed on the exposed end.

Yet the stump could not be seen. Where it should have been, another great cedar grew into the sky, nearly equalling the others in its lofty height.

"I *swear*, Sir Gwyeth!" Backar was nearly blubbering in confusion and chagrin. "There! Where that tree grows! Two days ago we left it a ragged stump!"

"Never mind!" snapped the knight, angrily scowling at the assembled peasants. "It's no more than I would have expected from this bespooked place. It makes it more important than ever to have done with the curse!"

Pryat Wentfeld had also dismounted. Quietly he performed another casting with the pinch of flour, the same he had used to examine the hallucinatory forest. This time the white powder flew away from him, dusting into the crowd of pilgrims to settle across the garments of one man—a man, the cleric noted, who seemed remarkably young and, though thin, possessed of a wiry strength that belied his appearance when compared to the ragged lot around him.

"There!" hissed the priest, pointing at the marked man, who had begun to sidle away. "*That* is your druid!"

"Seize him!" cried Gwyeth, who would have chased the varlet himself, except that his heavy plate mail practically immobilized him. "Bring him to me!"

The thin bearded man identified by the cleric turned and sprinted away, but a dozen men-at-arms, led by Backar, quickly overhauled and tackled him. They dragged him back to Gwyeth as they bound his hands behind his back.

"So you're the charlatan who pretends to practice the arts of druidhood!" the knight said, sneering. The man remained silent. Looking more closely, Gwyeth saw a hard determination in the druid's green eyes. His insolence annoyed the knight, who cuffed the prisoner across the face.

"The goddess shall prevail," hissed the druid, spitting out a broken tooth. "It's too late for you to stop her!"

"Silence, knave!" Gwyeth slapped him again before he could speak more of his treasonous drivel. The knight saw that already some of the more superstitious men looked at the prisoner with expressions of wonder, even awe. He knew he had to put a stop to this, and he drew his dagger, ready to slit the man's throat without further ceremony.

"My lord," said the cleric, anticipating his act. "Perhaps the deed would be better done with formality—an example lest anyone else presume to impersonate a member of that forgotten order."

"What do you suggest?" Clenching his dagger, Gwyeth held his blow long enough to listen.

"You say you shall burn the brush after you fell the trees. Why not affix yon charlatan to a stake in the midst of that fire? Such a death would be only suitable for this murderer, and the spectacle would also make a far better tale than to hear of him slain by your dagger while bound before you."

The image of the druid burning at the stake flamed in Gwyeth's imagination. The cleric was right.

"Very well. Detail six men to guard him," he told Backar. "Bind his feet and gag his mouth as well. He shall die by fire before this day is out."

Quickly he instructed fifty of his men to scatter the crowd of pilgrims who had sullenly watched this proceeding. The men-at-arms went about their task with relish, using clubs and the flats of their swords. The last of the ragged onlookers soon fled for the safety of the high rocks around the vale, where they looked down with unconcealed dismay.

The rest of Gwyeth's men hefted axes even before the pilgrims had been driven away. They started toward the grove of cedars, and soon the ringing of twoscore axemen sounded a cadence of death in the valley of the Moonwell.

* * * * *

Orange flames crackled upward from the weatherbeaten barn. The pyre marked the destruction of a season's precious straw and grain and the livestock that would have survived on the fodder. The farmer and his family had been butchered in the yard as the five pitiful figures had tried to defend their home from twenty-five mounted, armored knights.

"Valiant but stupid," Larth announced as his own black charger reared back, kicking anxiously at the flames. With the remark, the brigand dismissed the lives and deaths and all the hopes and aspirations of his victims. It was a mental tactic he had begun to use with increasing frequency as his reign of terror swept along the coast of Gnarhelm.

The thickset knight preferred not to remember the details of faces and forms that marked the bodies in his wake. By all measures except the nagging voice of his conscience, the mission had been exceptionally successful. He had lost only five of his riders, and the survivors had claimed enough treasure to make them all rich men.

The losses had come during a skirmish with hundreds of northern axemen, led by the King of Olafstaad. The armored knights, all mounted, fought the northmen on a grassy moor, and the horses had inflicted horrible losses on the footmen.

Larth's charger reared back suddenly, and the knight gaped in astonishment at the man who had abruptly materialized there.

"You!" he gulped, steadying his prancing mount.

"You have served me well," said the hooded priest. "Now I bring further instructions."

"I remain yours to command," Larth pledged as cold terror

gripped his gut.

"You must ride with all haste into the Fairheight Mountains, to the Moonwell near Cantrev Blackstone."

"Why?" the knight had the audacity to ask.

"This entire island will explode in chaos if we can but maintain the pressure. Talos and his faithful will be richly rewarded! But there is a threat to his might found in this Moonwell. I need you there. My auguries show me that there is where the issue will be decided!"

"We ride with all haste," promised the warrior as his men gathered silently around them. The burning farm hissed as rain fell into the flames, but the dried wood crackled and burned as hot as ever.

"See that you make no delay," the cleric commanded. "I need you there in two days." As quickly as he had appeared, the robed figure vanished.

Larth and his warriors disappeared as well, swallowed by the dark, wet night as they rode away from the fire.

* * * * *

Danrak watched the preparations of Gwyeth's men in mute despair. His arms ached, bent as they were around the stake driven into the ground behind him. The dirty gag nearly choked him, but the cleric had ordered his eyes unmasked, doubtlessly so that the helpless druid could observe the destruction being wrought on the valley of the Moonwell.

Eight men stood near Danrak with swords drawn. They were taut as bowstrings, as if they expected him at any moment to turn into a viper and slither away. Now he was as helpless as any prisoner could be. He watched as cedar after towering cedar slowly gave way to the axes, each seeming to shriek in protest as it toppled in doomed majesty, then slammed into the ground with earthshaking force.

Other men hacked with their swords—they had neglected to bring sickles—at the berry bushes and the roses and other flowers that had blossomed throughout the vale. The brush they piled around Danrak, and the druid felt a bitter irony as the fragrance of the aromatic buds wafted around him, marking the impotence of his last moments on earth.

After a few hours of work, the once beautiful place already resembled a wasteland. The men cleared the near shore of the well first, and then slowly began to work their way around the pond. They reached the halfway point on either side, and the circle of destruction slowly started to close.

Danrak wanted to close his eyes, to shut out the images of disaster, but his mind compelled him to watch. Despair grew to a raging storm within him, but he could do nothing.

A sudden sound pulled his head around. He saw a flash of blue and thought at first that a bluebird had flickered past, further mockery of his plight. Then he saw the movement again and realized that it was larger than a bluebird, though the thing now fluttered before him on wings as faerielike as any butterfly's.

The watchmen beside the druid stumbled backward, shouting in alarm. The strange creature, who looked something like a flying lizard with a wide, toothy grin, seemed to smile at Danrak.

"Hi," said the serpent. "I'm Newt. What are you doing tied to that pole?" Danrak gaped in astonishment, but before he could make a sound, the creature had disappeared.

* * * * *

The night lay thick across the isles, but nowhere was the cloak of darkness more dense than over Caer Callidyrr itself. Here the High Queen Robyn slumbered in her unknowing, deathlike trance, bound by the power of chaotic Talos. And here the Princess Deirdre awaited the summons to the greatest challenge of her young life.

She lay awake, tossing on her bed, until finally she rose and went to her high window. Casting open the shutters, she looked across a world of ultimate, desolate blackness. The aperture faced away from the town, so she saw only the occasional torches of watchmen or hearthfires glowing in some distant herdsmen's huts.

The sky above remained thick and impenetrable, clouds masking the moon, which, unknown to her, rose before sunset, only a day away from the fullness of its cycle.

Then she felt a tremor in the air, and she stepped back from her window, catching her breath and hoping it was *him!* Malawar came into her room, and for the first time, he swept her into his arms. She felt a fierce, exultant joy as he kissed her.

"Now," Malawar murmured, his voice a soft music in Deirdre's ear. "The oath. It is time for you to pledge."

"The oath to Talos," she replied, softly and unsurprised. "I could feel that the time was coming. The power has been growing rapidly within me. Day by day I feel its intensification."

"Good—very good."

Malawar's smile was dazzling, and his hair gleamed like spun gold as he removed a wax figure from a pouch of his voluminous robe. From another place, he pulled a small, tightly rolled parchment.

He touched a finger to the wax figure, which bore a crude resemblance to a maiden—it might have been Deirdre. The image burst into flame, and he unrolled the scroll and gave it to the princess to hold.

"Read the words," he instructed, "while holding it over the flame. As the fire consumes the vellum, the power of Talos shall flow into your veins."

The sigils on the sheet were strange to Deirdre, but as she stared at them, the fire making the material glow in her hands, they began to form themselves into sounds. They were strange noises, things not intended to issue from any human throat, but somehow they came to her naturally, brimming with a deep, guttural joy. As she made the sounds, the vellum grew hotter and hotter in her hands. When she reached the final sound, the sheet popped brightly, disappearing except for a trace of perfumed smoke that hovered in the air between her hands. The wax figure, she saw, had burned to a pool.

For a moment, time froze. The princess felt a heightened awareness, as if she could feel the blood pulsing in her veins, the guards patrolling the castle walls beyond—even the moisture, slowing gathering into rain, that lurked in the clouds overhead. She saw Malawar's smile, and her joy expanded to impossible heights.

Deirdre barely noticed when Malawar picked her up and carried her to the bed.

* * * * *

"What purpose do you take me to, Warlock?" asked Hanrald, wishing that the great hound could talk. The powerful animal had always led the Blackstone pack, and even now, among the fifty or so dogs that escorted Hanrald, he stood out as alert, quick, and cautious. For the most part, the moorhound led his pack across the highland plateau at an amble, tongue lolling, gait steady. The knight had labored to keep up for all of this long day.

Suddenly Hanrald paused and held up his hand. As if sensing his purpose, the moorhounds stopped panting so that they, too, could listen.

"Chopping—that's the sound of someone chopping wood!" declared the knight, delighted with the discovery. "That means there's *people* up there—people with food and drink and perhaps a horse that could get me back to Blackstone!" He started forward at a lumbering trot.

But as he came to the high bluff that overlooked the activity, he realized that he was wrong. He recognized the place immediately as the Blackstone Moonwell, and for the first time in days, he knew where he was. He remembered all the details of the miracle Alicia had described and knew that Gwyeth had done his work well.

Hanrald saw a man tied to a great stake driven into the earth. The brush and tree limbs stacked about his feet left no doubt as to his sentence.

Beside him, Warlock growled, his hackles raised, and suddenly Hanrald's task gleamed in front of the knight like a holy beacon: The hounds had brought him here so that he could stop this desecration.

Ignoring caution, Hanrald started to pick his way down the steep slope leading toward the pond. He saw a great stack of cedar trunks and the stumps where they had grown only hours before.

Alicia! In his mind, he pictured her, and he knew that she had performed a miracle here. Hanrald vowed his life to the preservation of that miracle, and he would fight in the name of his princess.

The knight saw the pilgrims who had been driven from the

well. They squatted here, high on the rocky slope, and studied Hanrald with mute suspicion. Soon the clanking noise of his passage—he still wore his plate mail, though he had discarded his helmet—attracted the attention of the men in the valley. Some of them gathered in a semicircle to greet him as he reached the bottom of the bluff, though they regarded him suspiciously, with upraised axes. A circle of hounds gathered around the knight, growling and holding the men-at-arms away.

A helmeted warrior, clad in armor similar to Hanrald's, approached. Hanrald recognized his brother Gwyeth.

"What are you doing here?" demanded the latter as his men opened their ring to their leader. Gwyeth stopped twenty feet from Hanrald and scowled through his opened visor, planting his hands firmly on his hips.

"I come to send you away," Hanrald retorted, "and to let nature take the course that she will."

Gwyeth laughed sharply. "You would disobey our father?"

"Only because he—and you—show treason to our king!"

The older man glowered even more darkly. The men-at-arms looked among themselves—treason to the High Crown was not something lightly contemplated or loosely charged.

"It's fit that we find you in the company of curs. You're a lying dog and a disgrace to the family!" snarled Gwyeth, his hands on the hilt of his broadsword.

"A family I would as soon be rid of," retorted Hanrald, his voice calm but his own hands ready to loose his weapon. "For it has lost all sense of honor in its undying quest for gold!"

Warlock growled and stepped before the knight, but Hanrald called him back. "This battle is mine, friend."

Gwyeth, however, stared at the dog. "That's Warlock!" he exclaimed. "The dog who fled the manor on the night of Currag's death! And these others—all the hounds of Blackstone!"

"Aye, Brother, and they are here because of the offense you give to the earth!"

"Enough!" Gwyeth's rage took hold of him, and his sword burst from its scabbard to gleam in his hands. "Steel can silence your treasonous tongue."

Hanrald barely had time to draw his own weapon and meet his brother's assault with a clash of sharp steel. The two knights bashed at each other again, then circled warily. Once more they closed in, exchanging blows from the right and left, high and low, but each time one sword met the other, and the ringing notes of the conflict echoed through the vale.

Some of the men-at-arms fidgeted with their own weapons, as if they would help their lord, but they found themselves confronted by slavering hounds, baring white fangs and standing in stiff-backed, bristling readiness.

The two knights chopped and parried, asking and giving no quarter. Their blades cut silvery arcs through the air, and the momentum of their attacks slowly carried them down the gentle slope toward the shore of the pool. The man tied to the stake watched them impassively, as did the ragged pilgrims around the fringe of the vale, while the men-at-arms stayed well back from the menacing hounds.

One man, however, did more than watch. Unseen by either of the combatants, Pryat Wentfeld, devout cleric of Helm, slowly withdrew something from his pouch. Carefully, surreptitiously, he prepared to cast a spell.

* * * * *

Musings of the Harpist

She is here, and alive, though just barely. I have seen an essence in my dreams these past nights, and I curse my old brain that it did not understand more quickly. But now I am certain.

The Earthmother has returned. A glimmering of her might was born in the Fairheight Moonwell, and now that fragment struggles for life, as a sapling struggles to raise its leaves to the sun.

She has floated through a long night, and her awakening is not yet assured. It remains to us to give her that chance.

☙ 18 ❧

A Focus of Might

As usual, dawn was an obscure moment in the dark, gray hours of early morning, yet Deirdre sensed it was just at that moment she awakened. She knew that somewhere, above the leaden clouds and beyond the icy, stinging rain, the sun had just crested the eastern horizon. Languorously she stretched, the events of the previous night coming back to her bit by exhilarating bit.

The oath of worship! The memory of that experience awed and moved her as much as had the ceremony itself. Now, as she met her first day following that pledging, she felt as though she had moved in a few hours from a child to some stage far beyond adulthood. The power pulsing within her animated Deirdre's body, compelling her to full alertness, tingling her nerves with suppressed tension.

And the oath had only been the first part, for then there had been Malawar. He had taken her to her bed, and for the first time, he had remained with her through the night.

She sat up in the bed and looked at the form beside her, covered by the heavy quilt. A smile played with her lips as she recalled the forbidden delight, the glorious culmination of their love. Now he still slumbered, and she cherished her private moment of joy.

Gently, tenderly, she reached out and pulled the coverlet away, longing for just a glimpse of his straw-colored hair, his fine-chiseled features. The quilt flipped away—and Deirdre gagged in shock.

Biting back her scream of terror, she threw herself from the bed, pulling the covers with her and wrapping them around her nakedness as she backed toward a corner of the room. The *thing* that had lain beside her stirred and then sat up—slowly,

and stiffly, as befitted the wrinkled figure, withered and wizen-
ed with age.

Cold eyes, as dark as the Abyss, stared out at Deirdre from
lined sockets. A bald pate of blotched skin covered the man's
scalp, and his ears lay back against his skull as if they were too
tired to support themselves. His mouth was almost lipless, his
cheeks and chin creased with a multitude of lines.

It was a man, she knew, but a man who was extremely, impossibly old.

"Where is Malawar?" she demanded, finding her voice.

"My dear," cackled the ancient shape through toothless
gums. "I'm disappointed you do not recognize me."

"No!" Deirdre moaned, unaware that she slumped against
the corner of her room and slowly sank to the floor. "You—
you're *not!* It's impossible!"

But even as she spoke, she knew that she lied to herself.
How else had he come to sleep and awaken beside her?

The stooping figure rose stiffly from the bed and pulled
Malawar's robe over his scrawny form. "Must serve the
needs of dignity," he noted, with an obscene edge to his laugh.

Suddenly Deirdre's stomach heaved in revolt. She turned
away from the grotesque form and vomited onto the floor,
retching until she could barely breathe.

"I hope you're quite finished," announced the now-hooded
priest, his tone acid, "because we have a lot of work to do."

But Deirdre could not bring herself to rise. Instead, she
turned toward the window, curling herself into a protective
ball. The world swam around her, and then it felt as though she
was swallowed up by blackness.

*　*　*　*　*

King Sythissal drove his finned legion with all the brutal authority of his command, yet he knew that the sahuagin could
never match the pace of the flying dracolich. Still, the fish-men
slipped through the sea a hundred feet below the surface to
avoid the turbulence of the storm.

Yet by the time the Army of Kressilacc reached the coast of
Alaron, the sea battle was over. The ravenous sahuagin discovered, much to their delight, the wreck of the *Vulture*. The

bodies of her crew served as splendid sustenance in restoring the creatures' stamina.

Beyond this wreck loomed rainswept Alaron. Here Sythissal would not go. Too often in the past his warriors had ventured upon land, only to meet with gory disaster before they could reach the protective refuge of the sea.

Instead, the sahuagin turned back from the battle, swimming to their deep home in Kressilacc. His forces intact, the King of the Deep would await a more opportune time to work the will of Talos.

* * * * *

"Hey! That's not fair!"

Pryat Wentfeld started backward, interrupted in the casting of his spell. He had attempted to summon an air elemental in order to set the creature against Hanrald and quickly end this duel between the brother knights. But now this high-pitched voice from nowhere distracted him, and the spell was wasted.

"Who speaks?" he demanded. "Show yourself or face the vengeance of Helm!"

"It's not *fair*, I told you!"

The priest gaped in astonishment, for the speaker was a tiny dragon, bright blue and hovering on wings that belonged more appropriately to a great butterfly.

"How dare you destroy my spell!" snarled the pryat, lunging toward the creature, who instantly blinked out of sight as the man stumbled through the place he had been.

"I didn't destroy your spell!" The now invisible dragon was indignant. "I just made it more *interesting!*"

Staring in shock, which quickly blossomed into mind-numbing horror, the cleric saw that the diminutive dragon spoke the truth: The spell had in fact already begun to work.

The summoning and control of an elemental by a spellcaster is a two-stage procedure, and it is always dangerous. These beings, representing the fundamental forces of air, water, earth, and fire, are called only reluctantly from their respective home planes. Vengeful and mighty, they constantly seek a way to release themselves from the bondage of their sorcerous masters.

Once summoned, the caster must maintain careful concentration in order to shape its unwieldy slave to the controller's will. Pryat Wentfeld had successfully concluded the summoning portion of his enchantment, but Newt had distracted him at the very moment when he should have been asserting his control over the invoked being.

In the case of this air elemental, it had been dragged summarily from a windy display of exuberance with hundreds of its kin, the usual pastime of the creatures on their home realm in the Inner Planes. Now, alone, confused, and compelled to enter a hateful world of unpleasant solidity, it reacted with forceful resistance. Then it suddenly found itself freed of its summoner's will.

The full vengeance of the air elemental swirled into the vale. Immediately it saw the two knights bashing at each other, the hounds and the men-at-arms all awaiting the outcome. It sensed the druid staked to the pole, and even the pilgrims who watched the fight from above. But most of all, the air elemental detected the cowering cleric—the one who had forced the creature to come here but now held no power over it. The tenuous form became a howling vortex, swirling upward into a funnel-shaped cloud of destruction. Furiously the mighty wind surged toward the cleric, casting limbs of trees and piles of wood chips into hailstorms of splinters.

Wentfeld screamed and raised his holy symbol, a medallion depicting Helm's ever-vigilant eye, in a desperate attempt to ward off the monster. When this failed to deter its advance, he ducked away from the whirlwind and scrambled toward the imagined shelter of a cluster of cedar logs.

Danrak, like the others, stared in astonishment at the airy form. Only after a few moments did he notice another figure in front of him, but then he grunted through his gag when he saw that the tiny blue dragon had returned.

Newt, for his part, scowled at the druid. "What is it? If you've got something to say, spit it out! Can't you talk?"

Danrak strained against his bonds, furious with the dragon's failure to understand.

"Oh—*ropes!*" the creature said, seeing his arms flex. "Well, why didn't you *say* so! I untied Tristan once when he had to fight a monster but he couldn't because he was all tied up. He was grateful, too. He gave me some cheese to eat. As much as I wanted!"

Danrak sputtered, chewing on the rancid cloth. The guards forgot their duties as they nervously watched the elemental, which now tossed cedar limbs aside like matchsticks in an attempt to reach its desperate victim.

"Say, should I untie *you?* You're all bug-eyed . . . does that mean yes?"

Newt dove behind Danrak and started chewing on the ropes that bound him. Beside the Moonwell itself, the two knights continued to hack at each other. Hanrald bled from a gash on his ear, and Gwyeth's breastplate and helmet bore several slashes and dents. Still, neither had seriously injured his foe.

The younger knight struck his brother a ringing blow to his helm, twisting Gwyeth's visor across his face and blocking his vision. Cursing, the brutal warrior pulled the iron headpiece away as Hanrald held his blows until his brother could once again see.

"Fool!" Gwyeth spat, sneering. "You should have taken me when you could!"

"I shall take you," replied Hanrald calmly, "but it will in a fair fight."

Their blows became less frequent, their gasps of breath more strained. Steel rang against steel as each stumbled over the rough ground, struggling to remain standing. On wobbling legs, the two men struggled against exhaustion.

"Surrender your blade, bastard of my mother's house!" demanded Gwyeth, lunging at his brother.

"Better a bastard," retorted Hanrald, with a desperate twist to the side, "than a traitor!"

Still the hounds held Gwyeth's men at bay, and Danrak, aided by the desperate nibbling of Newt upon his bonds, slowly worked his way free of his bonds.

* * * * *

The night seemed endless to the forlorn crew of the *Gullwing*, who battled tirelessly to keep the graceful vessel afloat. But the damage was severe, and whereas the sea could maintain its pressure for hours and days, the muscles of the humans aboard the ship could only labor for so long. Inevitably the sea must prevail.

Alicia bailed until her arms grew leaden, until her back creaked and ached like an old woman's, and still the water rose. The bow of the longship had been punctured by the onslaught, and though the firbolg Yak and the northmen Wultha and Knaff the Elder waded into the foaming leaks and stuffed rags and cork plugs into the worst of them, the rolling swell placed additional stress on the vessel.

Finally, as dawn colored the gray sky with its own grim cast, the princess collapsed. Brandon hoisted her from the watery hull and held her exhausted form by the shoulders.

"Here, now—you must rest!" he ordered her, and she was too tired to rebuke him.

"But the ship!" she said, shaking her head. Her rust-colored hair hung in an unruly mat across her face, and she pulled it aside to look at him.

"You've done as much as any sailor—more than most," he assured her. "Others can take over for a time. You'll do none of us any good if you work yourself to death!"

"No!" she cried, suddenly frantic. She took him by the arms and stared into his face. "I have to—don't you *see?*"

"I see one who has worked herself to exhaustion. Here, sit for a moment." Gently he guided her to a bench, and she slumped there, feeling all the fatigue he described. A feeling of utter hopelessness and dejection sapped her.

"Is there any hope? Of saving the ship, I mean?" she asked.

Brandon appeared to think before answering, but she saw the answer in the pain reflected in his eyes. "The hope we have is that we can reach the shore of Olafstaad before she goes down."

In the stern, Tavish didn't hear the conversation between the prince and princess. Indeed, she knew little at this point beyond the blistering pain that wracked her fingers and the cramps that threatened to stiffen her arms into locked positions around her harp.

Yet she had strummed the night through, and now, with the coming of dawn, she once again wanted to raise her voice in song. The magical harp had given strength to the northmen for many hours; indeed, it seemed likely that they never would have kept the *Gullwing* afloat without her.

"Lady bard!" cried Yak, straining to hold a plank against the hull while two sailors lashed and nailed it into place. "Give us a song to make us laugh!"

Tavish chuckled, albeit hoarsely. "I know just the one! It's called the 'Ballad of the Murderous Maid,' " she announced, strumming the first chords.

" 'A farmer saw a maiden; he took her as his wife. She didn't know her pots and pans but surely liked her knife!' "

Tavish bounced through the chorus, the pain in her fingers forgotten.

" 'The maiden, she was willin', the menfolks she dismayed, for it was her taste for killin' to which this maiden made!' " She sang heartily.

" 'The wedding night was cloudy as the couple rode away, and when they fin'ly found him, he was smilin' in the hay! His britches, they were missin', and his tunic and his bibs, but not his bride's stiletto: That was stickin' from his ribs!' "

Tavish played and sang more loudly, her pain forgotten. The music drowned out the noise of the pounding seas, ringing above the grunting and cursing of stone sore, staggering men. As the rude song unfolded, the bailers bent to their tasks with renewed energy, while the oarsmen labored to keep the stricken vessel nosed into the wind, grinning despite their weariness at the raunchy lyrics.

For a time, it seemed that new life had come to the *Gullwing*, and indeed the prow forced its way through the swells proudly once again. The song ran through many verses, for the maid had lived a long and productive life, and all through the choruses and notes, each time the sea swelled before them, the longship rose to meet each looming crest, foaming its way through the dark, frothing caps.

And when the song of Tavish finally faded away, the sound of the combers had changed, becoming deeper, somehow more substantial. In the bow, Alicia instinctively looked at Brandon and saw him listening carefully to the sound.

"That's surf pounding against the rocks," he said after a moment. "We'll make our landfall, perhaps more quickly than we desire."

"Headlands!" The booming cry came from Knaff, who

gripped the tiller firmly on the raised deck at the stern. The old man pointed over the bow. "A rocky bluff, dead ahead!"

Brandon leaped upward, seizing the cracked remains of the figurehead and staring over the rolling swells into the mask of gray. "Starboard helm!" he cried.

Immediately the *Gullwing* veered to the right. Then, with shocking quickness, Alicia saw a dark mass of rock looming high above them. Waves bashed against it, exploding in chill clouds of spray. In the gray mist, they hadn't see the menace until they were upon it.

"Row! Row for your lives!" cried the northman prince. The *Gullwing* leaped ahead, carving a sharp curve through the storm-tossed sea. Perhaps if she had been a whole ship, she would have made it.

As it was, the weight of the waterlogged bow, coupled with the drag of splintered planks, slowed her down just enough to doom her. A heaving swell raised them high into the air, and Alicia had a sickening image of a shore lined with massive, brutal rocks.

Then the longship crashed onto the boulders, and the sound of splintering wood and shouting men filled the air. Alicia felt herself tossed upward, and she tried to curl herself into a ball to lessen the inevitable shock of landing. Nevertheless, she crashed into a solid surface of stone with stunning force and lay motionless—still conscious, but unable to move. Icy water doused her, covering her completely as she feared that she would drown. Finally the brine receded, and she gasped and choked as it washed away.

All around her, Alicia heard cries of pain and the groans of the injured, even over the smashing of the waves and the splintering, tearing sounds of the *Gullwing*'s destruction. Crying in agony, she tried to sit up, but collapsed after raising her head an inch off her rocky pillow. Explosions of pain whirled in crimson torture through her mind. She closed her eyes, but that only made the torment worse.

Then, where her body contacted the ground, she felt a strange thing, as if a soothing balm caressed her, washing away her pain. As she lay still, the feeling of warmth spread throughout her body, the rocky ground forming a soft and well-cushioned bed beneath her.

Finally she dared to look around, and her blurred vision slowly cleared. The princess couldn't locate any members of the crew, but she tried to convince herself that that didn't mean they had all perished. She had landed among huge boulders, and they blocked her view to either side.

By the time she had forced herself to a sitting position, relieved that she could do so without pain, several men came into view. Brandon led the group, and they cried out with relief when they saw her.

"Lady Princess!" gasped Brandon, his voice thick. "By the gods, if you had been—"

"I'm not," she said quickly, not wanting him to go on. "Can you help me up? What about the others—Tavish, and Keane, and your crew?"

"Your companions survived," Brandon said, assisting the woman to a grassy knoll above the reach of the waves where the ragged castaways had gathered.

In addition to the three Ffolk, only Yak had survived of the firbolgs, the one called Loinwrap drowning in the wreck. A dozen of Brandon's crew had also perished, leaving the prince with fewer than twoscore warriors. Many had suffered broken limbs or other injuries. Now the healthy members of the band tended the wounds of their comrades while Keane and Wultha went to make a reconnaissance of the area.

"We've landed at the right place, in any event," announced Keane, upon their return. "We found a village that was ransacked by horsemen. No one is alive there now, but the hoofprints were still visible."

"Going which way?" demanded Brandon, his hand instinctively seizing the hilt of his axe.

"Inland."

"But how can we catch them now?" groaned the prince in sudden and complete dismay. Alicia had never heard him so disheartened. "Even if they continued to follow the coast, without the *Gullwing*, we couldn't hope to pursue!"

"I know where they went," Tavish said suddenly. "And that dragon, too. It explains why it hasn't attacked us before!"

"Where?" demanded Alicia, Keane, and Brandon.

"The Moonwell—the Fairheight Moonwell! May the goddess forgive my ignorance, I should have seen it *days* ago!"

Tavish cried, shaking her head in frustration.

"Why would they go there?" demanded the Prince of Gnarhelm.

"The goddess!" Alicia exclaimed. "The power of the Earthmother returns, and these knights go there to destroy the hope that was born!"

"I—I meant to speak of this earlier. Now I regret the fact that I didn't," the bard stated with unaccustomed solemnity. "But I've dreamed of the well each time I sleep these last few days. A power awakens there that offers tremendous hope for the isles, but it's a frail thing and menaced by great danger. I believe that it's imperative we go there, with all speed!"

"I remember your tale of this well, and your description of its location," interjected Brandon, addressing Alicia. "It's at least four days' march from here!"

"But less than that for horsemen or for a flying beast," the mage observed grimly.

"Keane!" Alicia said suddenly. "Do you have some way you could get us to that well quickly?"

"I wish, Princess, that I did," replied the sorcerer with a shake of his head. "I have a spell—teleportation—that will take *me* there in an instant. But it will not benefit anyone else."

"Isn't there *something* you can do?" demanded the princess.

"As I said, I can go there myself," he said curtly. "And it may be that we have no other tactic available to us."

"Not good enough," grunted Brandon. He seemed to have shaken off his despair. Once again his voice was commanding and controlled. "You have great power, but alone you could fall to a single arrow, or even a well-thrown rock. No, we must travel together."

"Those who can march, at least," Tavish noted, with a look at the dozen or so injured men who were having legs or arms splinted by their companions.

In another hour, a bedraggled band of castaways shivered under a steady rain. The injured had been moved to the village, quartered in as much comfort as possible. Finally those who could walk started across the lowland moor. In minutes, the buildings of the tiny community had vanished into squall and murk.

Surrounded by the storm, the companions marched on.

*   *   *   *   *

Larth and his twenty-five mercenaries rode as if all the beasts of the Abyss pursued them. The ponderous war-horses lumbered across the rough country of the highlands, carrying the knights to their mountain goal. The captain allowed them four or five hours of rest during the night, but cursed and kicked them back into the saddle before first light. Fear gripped Larth, a fear such as he had never known. He feared that he would be too late—that he would fail his master.

The thought of facing that softspoken robed figure, the Nameless One, and suffering the brunt of his wrath as penalty for Larth's blunders sent cold daggers of ice into the knight's belly. So he drove himself, and he drove his men.

And they rode through the rain toward the Moonwell.

*   *   *   *   *

"Hold thee, beast!" shrilled Pryat Wentfeld, brandishing the Eye of Helm as he crawled from beneath the felled trunk of a massive cedar.

The whirlwind of his air elemental subsided into a great humanoid-shaped being of translucent gas. Now the thing pushed and ripped its way through the huge woodpile in search of the cleric who had summoned it here.

Finally the priest shouted a command word, even as the animated mass of air loomed before him, ready to pull the stout body apart in a cyclonic death swirl, and this time the force of his magic held the beast in check.

The clang of swords against steel still rang from the shore as the two knights battled both each other and ever-increasing exhaustion. But neither could gain the edge that would allow him to win the fight. At the stake, an invisible Newt busily chewed at Danrak's bonds, and slowly the druid tried to work himself free.

"There!" shouted the cleric, his voice shrill with bubbling fright as he tried to control the being from another plane he had summoned. Pryat Wentfeld pointed at the staggering form of Hanrald. "Kill him! Destroy him!"

The air elemental, subject to the pryat's will, swirled toward the battle at the same moment that Danrak finally pulled his hands free. Swiftly he untied his feet, grateful that his guards still gaped at the fight. Then abruptly the druid sprinted toward the well, breaking past the surprised men-at-arms who had ignored their presumably helpless prisoner in lieu of the spectacle of battle around the pond.

Danrak took out a talisman, a round, grape-sized object that he squeezed between his fingers. He saw the whirlwind waver, pausing in its single-minded pursuit of Hanrald. Obviously the cleric had seen the druid, for the elemental now veered toward Danrak.

"*Aquais!*" cried the druid, popping the tiny vessel, which contained a small amount of pure water. The droplets sprayed into the surface of the Moonwell, and Danrak chanted the rest of his summons: "*Portille, condarus equae!*"

Instantly a whirling column of water began to rise from the middle of the well, like a living creature formed of glutinous liquid. Foam sprayed from the watery monolith's flanks as it grew more stable and upright. Circles of waves flowed outward in perfect rings until the liquid being began to move. Then it cast a frothy wake in an expanding wedge behind it. Danrak concentrated, pulling the elemental of water from the Moonwell and directing it against the creature from the plane of air. The being swiftly spun toward shore, a moving column of frothing water casting a cloud of spray around it.

As Wentfeld sent his air elemental howling toward the druid, Danrak's own elemental of water surged ashore to meet it. Amid the background of clanging blades, snarling hounds, and frightened observers, the primal forces of gas and liquid clashed in an explosion like a thunderstorm.

* * * * *

The massive form of the dracolich curled sinuously around the mountaintop. For the first time since he had been called to the service of Talos, Gotha knew pain. The wizard's magic had wracked his body and finally driven him to land. Here he lay for a night and a day resting his battered bones.

Gotha spread his wings to the accompaniment of biting pain. Nevertheless, the command of Talos had been compelling, drawing him toward the Moonwell, and finally the monster knew he could no longer delay.

Bellowing in frustration, he coiled his great legs beneath him. Aiming his head like an arrow, Gotha sprang into the air, extending his battered wings but relying on the power of his god to sustain him.

* * * * *

Hanrald staggered, desperately trying to lift the leaden weight of his sword. Finally he did, but not before his brother's blade darted forward, reaching for the perspiring flesh of his face. Once again the ringing of steel echoed from the walls around the Moonwell.

"By all that's holy and sacred," groaned the younger knight, lifting his sword again. He saw Gwyeth stumble backward, and he lunged forward. "You will yield to me!"

Hanrald smashed his sword downward, driven with all the fading strength of his body, and this time Gwyeth's parry failed, twisting the defending knight's sword from his hand. The weapon clanged to the ground as Gwyeth stared sullenly at Hanrald's blade, which was now held to his throat.

"Very well, Brother," he spat. "I yield."

"The fight is finished," grunted Hanrald with a sigh of relief. Wearily he lowered his sword.

Quickly Gwyeth pulled a dagger from his belt and lunged at his brother. Keen steel flickered toward Hanrald's face, slashing his cheek and narrowly missing his throat.

Staring in astonishment, Hanrald stumbled backward, falling heavily to the ground.

The great moorhound Warlock sprang at Gwyeth as the knight crouched above his brother, sneering. The hound's jaws closed over Gwyeth's face, twisting it to the side. Howling in maddened terror, the man went down as the rest of the snarling pack closed in to pin his armored body to the earth. They tore at his face, ripping away his eyes, his ears, his flesh—and finally his very life.

In the well, the elementals of water and air contested, controlled by the druid and the cleric. Mist swirled upward from the pond in a raging cyclone, howling like a gale and obscuring the entire Moonwell beneath a blanket of fog.

The clash of elements continued to rage within the obscuring cloud, surging waves foaming against the shore, across the meadow, and around the stumps of the felled cedars. Winds circled with growing force in the little valley.

The fog closed completely around the pond. The air became almost liquid, full of spray that soaked and blinded everything in its path. From this concealment, Danrak concentrated his will upon the water elemental, the being the druid himself had summoned. By the force of the goddess, he drove the water elemental away, vanquishing it to the plane of its own kind.

In the confusion of the gale, the water being's departure was not immediately apparent, since the magical creature of air still whirled under the pryat's control. Under the cover of the fog, Danrak crept toward the cleric. Wentfeld, focused upon the whirlwind, didn't notice the druid's stealthy approach.

Danrak pushed the cleric suddenly, knocking the man to the ground. Immediately the cyclone roared toward them, freed once again from the cleric's absolute control.

"Stop!" shrieked the priest, scrambling to his knees.

Danrak stood frozen, shocked at how quickly the raging funnel cloud swept toward them. His talismans . . . he had no time!

"I banish thee in the name of the goddess!" shouted the druid, standing firm before the cloud. "Go from here and return to your rightful place of being!"

Immediately the magic of his command swept outward, seizing the whirlwind in its arcane grasp. The creature of the plane of air howled as a gap opened in the fabric between the worlds. Pressure, invisible to the humans but compelling to the elemental, sucked the being against this gap.

Then a great vortex of air swept outward, like a finger of black cloud swirling at an impossible speed. It reached out like a solid thing, a tentacle that wrapped around the pryat's leg. The pressure of its suction raised to a howling crescendo, and the cleric's scream was lost in the sound.

Then abruptly silence came to the valley, like a soothing,

warming breeze. The elemental and the horrified pryat were gone. Gentle waves lapped in the pond, the fog and mist dissipating as quickly as they had arisen.

"Look! The trees!" gasped one of Gwyeth's men-at-arms, pointing to the stumps of cedars that had already begun to sprout upward.

Hanrald looked around in amazement. Flowers began to blossom before his eyes, and the trampled foliage stretched and extended itself with renewed vitality.

Then his eyes fell upon the heights where, shortly before, he and his hounds had descended to the well. Arrayed there now, he saw, was a line of mounted knights, some two dozen or more in number.

As he watched, they urged their horses down the steep slope. Though they moved at a walk, they brandished lances and swords.

* * * * *

Musings of the Harpist

The Harp of Cymrych Hugh! It has proven itself twice now, in the strength it shared with the Gullwing's oarsmen, allowing them to row tirelessly through the rough seas; and again in the courage it disseminated when the great dragon attacked— courage that allowed men to stand and fight when all mind and muscle turned to jelly in the face of the monstrous threat.

Now a third use occurs to me. It can enhance endurance and courage. Perhaps, with the right resonance, it might enhance magic as well.

I shall have to speak with Keane.

☙ 19 ❧

Convergence

Slowly Deirdre opened her eyes. At first she saw nothing but dark, foreboding clouds, hanging so low in the sky that they seemed to press downward against Caer Callidyrr. Then she realized that she stared at them through her bedroom window, and finally the memory of the true Malawar came flooding back to her, and she wished that unconsciousness would claim her again.

Instead, the opposite occurred. Malawar himself—or the thing that had disguised itself as Malawar—approached Deirdre's slumping form. His withered face crinkled into an expression of amusement, an effect resembling a grotesquely grinning skull.

"You have flattered this old priest with your affections," he chortled, drool flecking from his narrow lips. " 'Tis not often that one as old as I samples the pleasures of such a temptling!"

The princess gagged in horror and struck out at him, but his veined hand easily caught her wrist and held it in a tense and wiry grip.

"Come," Malawar hissed in a voice like the dry rasp of a file against coarse wood. "Our master summons us!"

"No!" she moaned, turning her head to the side, away from the horrible visage. But there was no escape to be found there, save perhaps a desperate and fatal leap from the high window. Even in her anguish, Deirdre gave that possibility no consideration.

"You have no choice." The withered creature spoke, his voice deep and rumbling. "You have taken the vow." A sneer curled the tight lips, and the hellishly dark eyes flared with an eagerness that Deirdre knew was hunger.

She tried to resist but felt her muscles drawn by a summons

that came from beyond her mind. Unwillingly she turned back to the hideous priest. She wanted to struggle and pull away from him, but her own mind would not respond.

"Now," Malawar snapped, obviously losing patience with his recalcitrant recruit, "you will perform the magic that will remove us from here."

"Me? How?" Deirdre asked. She felt her willpower return to her own control.

"That's better," crooned the superannuated priest. "You will find that Talos bends you to his will only when you yourself are reluctant to meet the terms of your vow."

Deirdre remained silent.

"You will take us to Caer Blackstone," continued Malawar. "There the earl will join us as we proceed to our final destination."

"Which is where?" she asked sullenly. Now she regarded the priest in a different light. She knew that she *did* have power—perhaps not as great nor as subtle as Malawar's, but true might nevertheless. The use of her power, she began to understand, would not be only his to control.

"The Fairheight Moonwell, of course," he said with a bare-gummed grin. "Where this resurgence of the Ffolk's goddess shall be destroyed for once and all!"

The goddess of the Ffolk? Deirdre winced at the phrase, for she was of the Ffolk, and the Mother had once been her goddess as well. But then a grim rage possessed her. She knew that she had chosen a different path, a different god. As fury gnawed at her soul, she understood one of the names of Talos—the Raging One.

That is how I shall know you, she vowed, a silent statement between herself and her god. And that is how my enemies shall know me!

"Hurry!" growled the priest, scowling at her like a glowering mask of death.

"What makes you think I have the power to take us there?" she asked.

"I *know* you have the power!" Malawar continued to cackle. "For I taught you myself!"

"Why don't you perform the magic?" demanded the princess.

"There is the difference between us, my child. I am a cleric of Talos, and my powers are those of the priesthood. You, however, have demonstrated an astounding aptitude for sorcery, a prodigy such as I have never encountered."

"I don't know how to do this magic—I don't understand!" she protested.

But he took her soft hands in his own bony claws and stared into her liquid eyes, and she understood.

* * * * *

The baying hounds, led by Warlock, raced to meet the armored riders coming down the slope, but the dogs couldn't slow the progress of the dark knights. Snarling, the pack attacked savagely, only to meet the swords and lances of the riders and the sharp hooves of the war-horses. Many of the moorhounds fell, mortally wounded, and the others backed away, licking their wounds.

The men of Gwyeth's company, leaderless and demoralized, stood in a group near the trail. The horsemen turned toward them, trampling through the few dogs foolish enough to continue the harassment, pressing their steeds into a lumbering charge.

"This isn't *my* fight!" growled Backar, the unfortunate sergeant who had led the first expedition and had witnessed the problems of the second in all their unnatural horror. Now he faced a charging company of horsemen with his supply of fortitude exhausted. "It's back to the cantrev for me!"

The hefty axemen ran for the trail leading from the Moonwell. The rest of the band needed only this example of leadership before they were quick to follow.

The horsemen looked for other foes. Hanrald and Danrak stood at the shore of the well, while the pilgrims had retreated to the crest of the valley. The knight raised his sword and started along the shore of the pond, the druid beside him. The two of them, on foot, stood before the steady advance of twenty-five heavily armored riders. The horsemen came at a walk, straight toward the pair.

"Hey—here's *more* of them! And these have *horses!*" A third ally popped into view on the knight's other shoulder as

Newt buzzed forward, eager for a little more excitement. "But don't you think it's *still* kind of unfair?"

"Indeed I do," Hanrald remarked wryly. He stopped and raised his sword, staring at the leading rider, a huge black-armored man with a longsword and great metal shield. "Halt!" cried the third son of Blackstone.

Ignoring the command, the rider spurred his horse to a trot. His company followed, and the ground in the vale rumbled under the heavy impact of hooves.

"He said *halt!*" Newt snapped, darting ahead of his two compatriots. "That means you're supposed to *stop!*"

As the dragon spoke, a massive chasm appeared in the earth before the startled riders. Horses screamed and kicked, rearing back in the moment before their forehooves plunged into blackness.

"Sorcery!" cried one of the mounted warriors.

"Around it, then!" shouted another, spurring his horse toward the edge of the chasm, coming around the corner and breaking into a charge toward Hanrald and his companions.

But the knight of Blackstone stepped forward and raised his sword. He felt supremely confident now—the power of the goddess flowed within him. As the charger lumbered forward, Hanrald suddenly dodged to the side. The rider tried to pull his horse around, but the knight saw a potentially fatal gap in the man's armor.

Hanrald thrust for that opening, between the breastplate and armored back. The sliver of steel that was his blade sliced into flesh. With a shriek of agony, the mortally injured rider tumbled from his saddle. Hanrald seized the reins, pulling the steed to a halt by sheer strength. The rest of the riders raced toward him, intent on following the fallen warrior, as the knight swung into the saddle.

"Go this way!" shouted Newt, gleefully flying past. As the faerie dragon darted toward the yawning gap, the chasm suddenly vanished, as Hanrald had suspected it might.

Instantly the mounted knight urged his horse across solid ground. Hanrald's charge carried him into the last two riders of the long file, who like the rest of their company, had been riding along the edge of a barrier that no longer existed. The knight's sword cleaved the head from one, while the other's horse tumbled, throwing its armored rider to the jagged, rock-strewn ground with bone-crushing force.

Cries of consternation and rage burst from the mounted company as they whirled, trying to close with the lone knight. Exploiting his momentum, Hanrald rode full into the midst of them, hacking to his right and left. Shieldless, he relied upon quickness and audacity for protection, and as he fought, these traits served him better than steel plate.

The mass of horsemen milled and lunged about as one after another they tried to strike at the swordsman, only to find that Hanrald had broken away. One hulking rider wearing black plate slashed at the Blackstone knight, striking a ringing blow against his chest and then evading Hanrald's return thrust. The man bellowed commands at his fellows.

Moments later, Hanrald burst from the other side of the band, but his seconds of savagery had left no fewer than five more of the riders groaning or bleeding on the ground. He spurred his horse along the shore, back toward the druid.

Danrak, meanwhile, drew another of his talismans, a tiny piece of charcoal that had been coated with phosphorus, from his pouch. The druid ran toward the fight, watching as Hanrald evaded his enemies by leading them on a long, curving ride around the fringe of the well. Half the attackers broke off, reversing direction, charging around the opposite side of the circular pool so that Hanrald would be caught in a deadly pincer.

The latter group, some ten riders, thundered past Danrak, ignoring the unarmored and apparently unarmed footman. As the first horse reached Danrak, however, the druid threw the coated coal onto the ground, directly in the mount's path.

Immediately red tongues of flame exploded upward from the earth, searing the legs and belly of the first horse and then surging higher, a fiery wall of death in the path of the following riders. Fingers of hissing, murderous heat lunged outward, grasping for and seizing the unfortunate men and horses, whose momentum carried them inevitably into the inferno. Hideous screams, from riders and mounts alike, rang through the vale of the Moonwell, but only for a moment.

Then the flames towered higher, a wall of fire touching the shore of the pool and extending away from the water for fifty feet. Grotesque shapes, charred black and outlined in flame, marked the places where the horses and their warlike riders had perished.

Meanwhile, Hanrald whirled his own horse about, charging full into the faces of the riders who still pursued him on the far side of the pool, including the huge black-armored man who seemed to command them. Again Hanrald rode into his enemies, hacking and bashing, ducking away from each return thrust. Another man fell, stabbed in the throat, before Hanrald broke free. A thundering gallop carried him back to Newt and Danrak, while the surviving horsemen halted in confusion, staring in awestruck horror at the fiery pyre where their companions had perished.

Their captain berated them, but they cast nervous glances at the charred shapes of their comrades. The riders remained reluctant to ride against the supernaturally aided Hanrald.

The taut equilibrium was broken, not by the renewed charge of the riders but by a darkness that dimmed even the gray light of the cloudy day. The humans looked upward, while the horses shrilled in fear.

"Hey, look!" Newt shouted as he looked upward, oblivious to Hanrald's and Danrak's horror. "Here comes a *big* dragon!"

* * * * *

"It might be worth a try," Keane said, his tone skeptical.

"What's that?" asked Alicia, marching with numb stoicism behind the mage and Tavish. The latter pair had been engaged in a long, quiet conversation.

"Tavish wonders if the power of her harp might enhance my teleportation spell," Keane explained. "It's a powerful artifact, certainly, and that power has aided us before. But this is something new, and I can't tell you if it's going to work."

Brandon, at the head of the ragged column, halted the march and joined the discussion. "We've *got* to try," he argued. "Look at us—after six hours, we've lost ten men who couldn't continue because of their wounds, and the rest of us, if we reach the Moonwell after four days of hiking, won't be in any shape for a fight."

"There's something else to consider, too," Tavish observed quietly. "I doubt that, even by tomorrow, there'll be anything left to save."

"All right," Keane agreed. "Weave your music, bard lady, and I'll prepare to cast my spell."

"If—if it fails," Alicia said tentatively, "what will happen?"

"Most likely I'll teleport there myself and the rest of you will stay right here," Keane explained.

"Can you come right back, then?" inquired the princess.

The mage shook his head. "The spell is gone when cast. I would have to get back to Callidyrr and restudy my spellbook before I could teleport again."

Despite the risk of dividing the party, they realized that they had to try. Yak found a cluster of rocks that concealed a sheltered grotto where they could all gather with at least minimal protection from the weather. Here, Keane and Tavish prepared to work the enchantment.

Their ragged group numbered fewer than fifteen now, still including Wultha, Knaff the Elder, the firbolg Yak, and the three Ffolk. Gathering in a rough circle around Tavish and Keane, they waited with rapt attention.

Tavish handed the Staff of the White Well to Alicia. The bard raised her harp, and for a moment, her fingers caressed the strings without drawing sound. Then she touched a high, trilling chord, and slowly allowed her fingers to descend through a series of bright notes.

Next the bard held that chord, strumming her fingers faster than the watchers could see. The music expanded, swelling into a powerful cocoon, building to a crescendo and stretching the listeners' nerves taut.

When it seemed that Tavish couldn't possibly sustain the pressure of sound for another moment, Keane closed his eyes in concentration. He reached out and took Alicia's and Brandon's hands, and the others joined their hands around the great circle.

Then Keane barked a word, so short and abrupt that Alicia didn't even hear what he said. She blinked reflexively.

When the princess opened her eyes, Keane—and *only* Keane—was gone.

* * * * *

"This is the Circle of Transport," said the decrepit Malawar, showing Deirdre a ring of gold about a foot in diameter. "It is mine, but it can only be activated by a sorcerer—or sorceress!" He cackled at his addendum.

The princess stared at him. In the hours of this darkest of mornings, her emotions had run a gauntlet from guilt, to disgust, then to anger and self-loathing at her previous naivete. Finally she had returned to anger. Grimly determined not to let her fury show, she waited with taut attention for the priest to explain.

"How does it work?" she asked finally, hating him.

He showed her, and they both grasped portions of the ring with both of their hands. "You will take us to the hall of Caer Blackstone," he concluded.

Deirdre nodded, then gasped as a whirlwind of pressure swirled around her. Quickly she realized that the gale was a storm in sound only, since no wind gusted past her skin or disturbed her hair.

Yet in the next instant, she recognized the dark-beamed ceiling and the array of stuffed animal heads that were the prominent features of the Earl of Fairheight's Great Hall.

"By the gods!" sputtered the earl, leaping to his feet in astonishment, knocking his chair backward, and dropping the half-eaten remains of a pork haunch to the table. A nearby maidservant dropped a crystal tray, and the crash of ceramic rang through the hall with shocking violence.

"Leave us!" Malawar barked at the maid, who cast a frightened look at the earl, then ran for the door.

"What is the meaning of this?" demanded Blackstone, still standing. "Who are you?"

"It is *I!*" The withered cleric spat the word, and the earl stepped backward as if he had been slapped. Recognition mingled with horror in his face.

"How did—?"

"You're coming with us. Now." The venerable priest's words were driven home like nails into soft pine.

"What? You can't—why? Where are you going?"

"To the Moonwell—where one of your sons has failed to perform your instructions!"

"Gwyeth? He *failed?* But how? Did he—"

"He's dead," snapped Malawar. "Slain by the hand of your third son, who even now threatens to disrupt all of our plans and ambitions."

"Hanrald, a traitor? The *bastard!* I *knew* he couldn't be a true Blackstone!" The earl, his voice verging on hysteria, bellowed his anger.

"Take a weapon and let's *go!*" the priest ordered.

"Yes, of course," the earl declared, his voice dropping grimly. He took a huge dark-bladed battle-axe from the trophy wall, the same axe he had used to slay the prophet.

The three of them seized the golden circlet, and Deirdre's brow wrinkled in concentration. She heard that same cyclone, but this time it didn't distress her. In another moment, the three of them stood among the stumps of the ruined cedars, looking around the battle-scarred vale of the Moonwell.

A wall of fire crackled beside the pond, slowly dying, while several armored horsemen stared at them in shock. As Deirdre's eyes swept upward, she beheld the grotesque image of the dracolich Gotha, perched on a rocky bluff above. Blackstone shouted in alarm, while the princess pressed her hand to her mouth in shock.

"No need to worry," said Malawar, noting the source of their fright. "He, too, is a devoted servant of Talos!"

"Keane!" cried Deirdre, stunned on top of her surprise to see her tutor suddenly materialize before them, about fifty feet away.

"Deirdre! Beware!" shouted the mage.

"*He* is your worst enemy!" Malawar hissed at her. "You must destroy him—quickly!"

"Keane? No!" she cried, appalled.

"Else he will destroy us and the hopes of our master along with us—you *must!*"

Keane, his angular face perplexed, stepped toward Deirdre.

Anger surged within the princess, a hot fury directed at Malawar, who would twist all of her being to his own ends if she gave him the chance. She whirled on him, but somehow her rage changed its focus. Reluctantly she looked at Keane. She remembered all of his smug arrogance when, many years ago, she had struggled with her studies. She recalled his stubborn refusal to aid in the development of her powers as a sorceress. The princess didn't feel the looming presence of Talos, but that dark god now used her own indecision as an opportunity to steer her anger and her will.

In that instant, Deirdre knew her path. All her fury exploded to the surface. She raised her hand, invoking the name of her god, and directed the force of her power. Remembering the raving prophet who had come to her in the hall of Callidyrr, she called upon the same deadly magic she had unleashed against him—the Bolt of Talos.

Now that same force erupted against Keane. Waves of crackling magic surged outward as Deirdre's target raised his long arms up to protect his face.

It was no use. The blast picked him up and drove him backward, smashing his lean body to the ground, hissing and popping around him as the magic-user's eyes closed. In moments, he lay still.

* * * * *

Alicia sobbed, the bitter taste of defeat rising like bile in her throat. She leaned on the Staff of the White Well while Tavish held her, the bard's own tears falling on the shoulder of the younger woman. Around them, Yak and the northmen stood in mute, angry frustration. Keane was gone, and it seemed that all hope of success had gone with him.

"To come so close!" Her voice caught as she whispered to Tavish. "And to fail!"

"We haven't failed yet," the bard replied softly. "It's not over."

"But what can we do?"

"We could pray."

Alicia blinked in astonishment. Impatiently she wiped away a tear and thought. "We could, couldn't we? And perhaps now the goddess will hear us!"

"We have to try," agreed the bard. "Hold the staff, my child."

Alicia stood with the Staff of the White Well in her hand, one end of the long shaft resting on the ground. For the first time in days, she felt a sense of joy, a feeling that approached elation. It was so simple, but Tavish was right! She closed her eyes, without trying to articulate her thoughts for the Great Mother, the earth. But she made a pledge to the goddess that she would serve as her own mother had served and offer her life, labor, and love as willingly. And as she pledged, a sense of ultimate tranquility flowed from the ground into her feet and legs, pulsing through the staff she held in her hand, and flowing through her fingers into her wrists and her arms.

Tavish was the first to notice. "Look," she said quietly, indicating Alicia's bracers.

The princess had almost forgotten the spiraled rings of silver that she had placed on her forearms in the tomb of Cymrych Hugh. Now she saw that they glowed with a pale blue light, a color like that of a clear sky, half an hour or more after the sun had set.

"The talismans of a druid," Tavish said, her voice calm. "Now they receive the favor of the goddess."

The illumination spread swiftly to the wooden staff that the princess still held in her hand. Then the color spilled onto the ground and swept outward in wide strips of brilliance. They saw other hues—green, yellow, a dark, rich violet. Still more colors exploded overhead, cascading like a fountain: red and orange spilling as cool light, not fire.

The northmen grumbled superstitiously and began to back away. The giant firbolg held up a restraining hand. "Wait," Yak said. "This is goodness."

Indeed, the colors flowed together, swirling on the ground and then spiraling upward, seven clear bands that ranged from red to violet. The gray clouds parted silently, and the bands of color arced into the heavens. Blue sky framed the long lines, and sunlight washed around the group on the ground.

"A rainbow," Alicia breathed reverently. The sun struck the shades with brilliant, incandescent glory, a brightness that would have been painful to the eyes of the watchers had they not been overwhelmed with awe.

"More than a rainbow," Brandon observed, studying the solid-looking surface that rose from the ground, disappearing into the distance. "It looks like a bridge."

"To the Moonwell!" Tavish cried, immediately understanding. She hurried to the foot of the sloping, ramplike rainbow and, without hesitation, placed a foot upon it.

"It's solid!" reported the bard, beginning to climb upward.

"Hey!" cried Tavish, from far above them. Though she had taken but three steps, she was more than a hundred feet in the air.

"It *carries* her!" shouted Brandon triumphantly. Without further hesitation, he followed the bard, and in moments, the northman, too, was a distant figure.

"By the goddess!" breathed Alicia, as the rest of the party started to climb the miraculous bridge. "We may yet arrive in time!"

* * * * *

In the depths of darkness, High Queen Robyn started, struggling against the cloak of evil that enwrapped her. She felt the power of the goddess like a kiss of warm wind that restored breath to her lungs.

Chaos remained a thick fog, blocking all light and knowledge and memory. Yet now that fog dissipated somewhat. She felt a warmth and brightness beyond the fog, a hope and a promise that she hadn't felt for twenty years.

Slowly, with great determination, Robyn started upward, toward the sun.

* * * * *

"A dragon!" groaned Hanrald, his eyes riveted to the monstrous beast on the knoll above him. The horse he had claimed in the battle danced skittishly beneath him. The surviving riders of the twenty-five were gathered in a tight knot across the pond and seemed to be waiting for something.

The knight looked around and noticed behind him the prostrate form of Keane and, farther away, the trio of Deirdre, Malawar, and his father.

"Hanrald!" cried the Earl of Fairheight. "I command you to lay down your sword and yield the well to me!"

"I cannot," the knight stated simply.

"Treachery!" shouted the earl. "Upon the evil you have already wrought as slayer of your brother!"

"I would have shown him mercy," protested Hanrald, "but

he betrayed me—and it was not I that struck the fatal blow!"

"Surrender—*now!*" demanded the earl.

"I refuse."

"Kill him! Strike him quickly!" Malawar's cracked voice was a rasping hiss in Deirdre's ear. She stared numbly at the knight, her mind still reeling from the knowledge that she had just slain her teacher, a man who trusted her and would have been her friend. "*Do* it!" shrilled the priest.

"No!" The voice of refusal was a deep rumble, and it came from the knoll above the Moonwell. Gotha, the dracolich, spoke. "The knight is *mine!*"

Hanrald turned, with no display of fear, to observe the great wyrm. The beast coiled its great legs beneath it, spreading its great skeletal wings to the sides. Crouching, it prepared to spring.

But then a sound like thunder rocked through the vale, and the darkness was split by a bright wash of sunlight. The heavy overcast broke apart above them, revealing an expanse of blue.

And a rainbow streaked down from the sky.

* * * * *

Musings of the Harpist

We cross meadows with a single step, mountain valleys in a few strides! Landscapes spread below us, exposed to the sun as the clouds flee the glory of the Earthmother's rainbow. We feel glorious warmth, we see expanses of forgotten beauty— indeed, it seems that vitality begins to return to the land.

Thus the power of the goddess carried us across moor and mountain to the heart of her life—and of our hope.

✿ 20 ✿

Rainbow

The clouds parted below as Alicia and her companions walked swiftly along the avenue of the rainbow. A sky of glorious blue swelled above them, and the warm sun felt like a kiss of life on the woman's brow. A sense of faith propelled her, filling her with joy. The goddess lived! The gray vapor rolled back away from the iridescent spectrum to reveal sodden moors and rain-lashed mountains. All the landscape glistened in the brilliant rays of the sun.

The great ramp of the rainbow curved downward, splitting the overcast and finally spilling with a rain of color into the valley of the Fairheight Moonwell. Gleaming like a roadway, the smooth path of the goddess invited them to step down to the ground. Alicia, Brandon, and their companions descended in long, easy strides, watching the valley rush upward with dizzying speed. The magic of the Earthmother's power carried them smoothly to the bottom, where the rainbow met the shore of the well, and in moments, they stood among the familiar rocks at the tiny lake's shore.

The first thing Alicia saw was Keane, lying still and apparently lifeless. Her mind filled with whirling impressions: Her *sister* was here, as well as the Earl of Fairheight and a robed stranger. She saw Hanrald, with another man beside him. The pair faced a dozen riders, who watched the newcomers warily. Nearby, several dozen hounds stood in a pack, bristling with tension.

Then the shadow of the dracolich blotted out the sun, and the princess looked up to see the monster dive. Horrendous wings swept across the sky, while the fanged maw gaped, and Alicia well remembered the hellish power lurking within that grisly cavity.

The princess, in a moment of sheer panic, knew that Keane's ring had been all that protected them from the dragon's killing breath, and even that was only when he had brandished it against the monster's fireball. Now she felt terribly exposed, vulnerable to a blast that could kill her in a second.

The monster veered abruptly, belching a ball of hot gas into the air. The sphere exploded in the sky, far above the watchers in the vale, and then a tiny form ducked away from the dracolich. A bellow of rage exploded from the grotesque mouth, the sound rumbling back and forth in the bowl-shaped valley as the monster reached, trying to seize something too small to be identified from below.

Roaring mightily, swerving this way and that in its flight, the wyrm slithered furiously through the air. The sound of the massive bellows broke rocks free from the cliffs, adding the clatter of small avalanches to the chaotic scene in the air.

"Newt!" Hanrald guessed.

Alicia, squinting, spotted a tiny shape bobbing and weaving before the huge serpent. The faerie dragon dove to the side, disappearing for a moment only to materialize behind the dracolich, squealing in laughter that only inflamed the monster further.

The monstrous wyrm ducked and lunged in enraged pursuit, whipping the great body through a series of airborne contortions and several times filling the air before it with an orange-red cloud of intestinal hellfire. The fiery emissions quickly dissipated in the clear air, though the thunderous noise of the their eruption rumbled ominously throughout the vale. Back and forth the two dragons—one tiny and maneuverable, the other huge and immensely powerful—soared in their desperate game of tag.

The princess felt the power of the goddess warming her bracers, and the Staff of the White Well felt smooth in her hands. Above, the monster breathed again, and this time Newt yelped in pain. Fluttering awkwardly, he started to descend in a staggering spiral, though he vanished before Alicia could see whether—or where—he fell.

"Goddess of my mother and my Ffolk," breathed the princess softly, "give me the strength to face this challenge!"

She felt herself become part of the earth, an extension of the

Earthmother's power. Giantlike strength filled her. She recognized the dracolich for the hateful abomination that it was, and she knew that her duty compelled her to destroy it.

"Serpent!" cried the princess, stamping the staff on the rocks before her.

In the sky, the dragon turned from its now invisible opponent. With a rumbling snort, it tucked the massive wings and nosed into a hurricane dive straight toward the Princess of Callidyrr.

* * * * *

"Now take *her!*" commanded Malawar, pointing to Alicia with a skeletal finger. Deirdre didn't have to look at the priest to identify the indicated target.

Alicia stood out like a golden statue, backlit by the brilliant hues of the rainbow behind her. Her coppery hair gleamed in the sun, and brilliant circles of pale blue light spiraled around her forearms. The staff of her mother she held vertically, in both hands, and where the shaft rested upon the earth swirling lines of light flowed outward. Alicia's attention remained rapt, focused entirely upon the serpent above her.

Colors swirled, ranging from a bright crimson on the outside to an inner violet so deep that it verged upon black. Beams of light spiraled into a funnel, with the Princess of Callidyrr at its vortex, flashing upward higher and higher, expanding in a cone that gaped before the plummeting dracolich.

The Earl of Fairheight stood, awestruck, beside Deirdre and Malawar. The nobleman took no note of his two companions. Instead, Blackstone gasped at the dragon, and then fixed his wide eyes on the proud figure of Alicia, barely visible behind the translucent screen of bright hues.

"*Kill* her!" screamed the ancient priest. He squeezed Deirdre's arm until his clawlike fingers bit into her flesh.

Then suddenly she broke free, knocking his hand aside. He reached out to block her way, and she punched him solidly in the chest, driving his surprisingly frail form backward several steps.

"*Treachery!*" he cried. "You betray your own god!"

"Treachery only against a betrayer," Deirdre shot back. "I

am yours to command no longer!"

"Talos will punish—"

"You yourself clarified it for me," spat the princess, her black hair flying around her head as she stepped toward the priest. "I am *sorceress*—not *priestess!* The power of Talos can aid me, and I can work his will, but he will not *bind* me!"

"What are you doing?" demanded Blackstone plaintively, looking at the dragon. "What about *them?*"

"Stay out of this," snapped Deirdre, casting a look that withered the earl's courage, sending him staggering backward in search of cover.

"Harlot!" shrieked the cadaverous cleric, sputtering at Deirdre. "You will pay for your perfidy!" He reached a withered hand into a pouch at his belt, but the younger, faster Deirdre lashed out with a foot, tripping the priest and smashing him backward into the rocky ground.

"No," the princess said, quietly and grimly. "*You* are the one with a debt to pay, and soon it will be time for me to claim my restitution!"

* * * * *

Gotha hurled his horrid body toward the princess, impelled by all the hatred wrought by his long decades of undeath. Moments ago, the insolent faerie dragon had infuriated the monster beyond all reason, tormenting Gotha with tiny pinpricks of icy cold magic. Each attack reminded the dracolich of his centuries encased beneath the ice, and each drove him to further heights of rage. Compelled by this fury, he had pursued the thing with berserk intensity.

Now, finally, the buglike annoyance was gone, either scorched or frightened away by Gotha's flamebreath. All of the serpent's hatred and loathing focused on this bright figure of a woman in the path of his dive.

The princess glowed with a brilliance that seared the monster's vision, burning into his brain. He knew it to be the power of the resurgent goddess, the direct foe of Gotha's own master. He plunged faster, a monstrous engine of death plummeting earthward at breakneck speed. The woman, in her arrogance, did not flee. Instead, she stared upward, as if she would meet the dracolich in battle.

If she did, thought Gotha grimly, she would die.

* * * * *

Alicia knew that it was not she who faced the diving dracolich—at least, not entirely so.

The power of the goddess burned within her, soothing her fears and making the princess strong. Whatever the horrible effects of the monster's attack, Alicia felt that she could face the onslaught with more than courage. She possessed the might to meet the monster on its own terms.

The moment of collision came and passed, and the princess felt no impact. Instead, she knew the strength of her own massive embrace, reaching outward to envelop the hateful image. Alicia's body was gone, though it waited for her, somewhere safe, she knew, and her will controlled a force that was far greater than a mere mortal form.

She was a physical presence in the air, in the water, in the ground—she was one with the goddess herself! Constricting the squirming beast with the power of her clasp, she melted downward into the soothing, cloaking waters of the well.

* * * * *

Deirdre watched in awe as the power of her mother's goddess arose from the earth to clasp the deathbeast and carry it to its end. The dracolich disappeared within the whirlwind of color as the water frothed like an erupting fountain of multicolored liquid. Slowly the rainbow-hued funnel settled into the swirling waters of the pool.

The Moonwell sparkled, tiny wavelets reflecting the sunlight as if the surface was coated with diamonds.

Malawar recovered his balance and scrambled to his feet. Now he regarded Deirdre, squinting in tight caution. Obviously he feared her—for he made no move to attack.

Blackstone stalked in agitation toward the priest. "By the gods, man, what do we do now?"

"*She* is the cause of this disaster!" spat Malawar, gesturing toward Deirdre. "She and her accursed sister!"

A sound pulled their attention away from the pond, and the trio gasped in unison as a figure lurched toward them. His wide-set eyes fixed upon Blackstone as his voice boomed, an all-too-familiar sound.

"Disaster? Nay! Behold the glory!" howled the prophet gleefully. His white beard, the long, wispy hair straggling around the bald pate—all were familiar. He raised his arms and staggered toward the Earl of Fairheight, as if to embrace him, to share the miracle of the Earthmother's resurgence.

"Where did you come from?" demanded Malawar, his voice a taut hiss.

"The well . . ." Deirdre breathed the reply. The white-robed figure was soaking wet, and the trail of water led straight to the shore of the pond.

"She returns!" cried the prophet, his tone rich with glee. "Know the truth and the glory!"

"No!" shrieked Blackstone. "You're *dead*—you *must* be— you *are!*" The nobleman, spittle flecking his lips, stumbled backward.

Princess Deirdre, alert, tried to watch neither the earl nor the prophet. Instead, her gaze stayed riveted upon Malawar. But then as the raving lunatic came closer, she darted a glance at the white-bearded stranger, seeing the man's face locked in that expression of fierce joy.

In the instant Deirdre turned her eyes away, Malawar snatched his clawlike holy symbol, three lightning bolts of steel, exploding outward from a gem-studded nut, from his pouch. He brandished the thing as if he himself was a storm cloud, whirling toward Deirdre, raising the artifact menacingly. The movement caught her eye, and the princess instantly turned back to face him.

The earl continued to jabber, and the white-bearded man advanced farther. Blackstone spun, darting away from the apparition, lunging between Deirdre and Malawar.

At that exact moment, the priest invoked the name of his god in killing magic. A fatal word triggered the spell, and the power of Talos lashed out, hissing through the air with flesh-rending force. The fatal force intended for Deirdre struck the fleeing earl full in the chest, enveloping him in light and fire that spit and crackled with power.

Lord Blackstone, Earl of Fairheight, died in supreme agony, his body wracked by the fatal power of Talos the Destroyer. His black-maned head flew backward, his mouth locked open in soundless horror. His fingers clenched desperately at the air, clutching for some hope of survival.

The robed priest of Talos stood transfixed behind the earl, his hood thrown back and his withered, balded pate spotted with sweat, staring wide-eyed at the misdirected power of his god. At last the sputtering died away, and a grisly corpse fell stiffly to the ground before the princess.

The cleric dodged backward, away from the princess, as he raised his holy symbol to ward off her attack. The corpse of Blackstone smoldered on the ground between them.

"Glory! Rejoice!" The prophet raised his hands, shouting at Deirdre, though it seemed as if he looked right through her. Then he turned toward Malawar as the cleric crouched defensively, ready to meet Deirdre's return spell.

"Know the *truth!*" cried the strange man, and he suddenly lunged at Malawar. His hands wrapped around the holy symbol clutched by the cleric, and then the prophet pulled the talisman away. "Throw down the idols of false gods!" he expounded.

"*No!*" The priest shrieked in horror, desperately grabbing for the artifact. But the prophet shouted, as if in pain, and stumbled away from Malawar.

And Princess Deirdre raised her hand.

* * * * *

The arc of color spanned the skies. Fueled by the glory of the reborn Moonwell, it blasted a path through leaden clouds, spearing shafts of sunlight breaking to the sodden land below. Yellow rays spilled across the ground, sweeping over rock and forest and marshland alike. Grassy moors, the trees of the woodlands and hills, all cast thin plumes of steam into the air as the moisture melted away.

The great arc rocketed from place to place, always gleaming pristine and bright in the sun, extending across the middle of Alaron Isle. From the rugged western shore, where it began, the great bridge spanned mountains and moors and finally arced over the fertile coastlands to the east to center upon

Callidyrr, and when it plummeted to land again, it touched in the very courtyard of that alabaster castle.

The High Queen of the Isles sat up in her bed, energy pulsing through her. Darkness, like a deep and ill-remembered dream, passed from her consciousness into the farthest corners of her mind.

Vitality sang in her muscles, pulsed in her bloodstream, as she sprang to her feet and stepped to the window. She felt a childlike joy at the advent of a beautiful day.

Throwing open the shutters, she felt the warm air caress her skin, while once again her eyes beheld the glorious orb that was the sun.

* * * * *

"*No!*" The shriek of Malawar's horror stretched beyond the limits of the human voice into an ululating screech that reverberated from the surrounding walls of the vale. His mouth stretched wide, wider than any man's jaw could bend.

Skin peeled back from his lips, tearing away like sheets of paper ripped from an enclosed package. The tissue itself looked like human skin, but the stuff that lay beneath it was neither bone nor flesh. Instead, beneath the skin of Malawar lay a green, pulsating mask of ichor that oozed and changed shape as more and more of the outer surface tore away.

Before the gruesomely altered thing, Blackstone's twisted carcass lay, and beyond that stood Deirdre—vengeful, potent Deirdre, ready at last to exact retribution for the abuses of her corrupt mentor. Her hatred inflamed by loathing and horror, she stared dumbstruck, but she resisted the nausea surging in her stomach. She saw Malawar's true nature, but also she understood her own power. The princess employed that strength with resolute determination and even, she admitted, with a fierce joy.

She pointed her finger at his scrawny chest and let the Bolt of Talos fly. The magic came from *her*, not from the god, and the sorcery exploded savagely in the air. The power of her enchantment erupted in a bright, jagged spear, scoring straight at the cringing figure, which by now had thickened and shortened considerably. Malawar raised the podlike limbs that had been his hands, and the blast struck the remnants of his fist.

A thunderclap of sound knocked Deirdre backward and echoed over and over in the vale. The princess saw a space, like some kind of opening in the air itself. An aperture yawned about the decrepit creature, and through that hole, she saw a smoking, fire-colored sky beyond a landscape of soot-blackened hills. Flames surged into the sky, and crimson lava spilled across ash-covered slopes.

And then the oozing figure of Malawar and the space that gaped around him were gone.

*   *   *   *   *

Princess Alicia swam upward, feeling warm and alive. All around her, the water caressed her in a greenish-blue hue that she thought must be the most beautiful color in the world. Finally she broke the surface, and when she stepped onto the shore, it was to enter a place of surpassing grace.

Once again lofty cedars towered overhead, and flowers bloomed in abundance on the shore of the pool and the steep slopes surrounding it. The scent of pollen was heavy in the air, and sunlight washed the entire valley in warmth.

"Keane? Are you there? Speak to me!" Alicia saw the bard stroking the mage's head while Keane blinked and worked his jaw. His voice, when it emerged, was a faint croak, his question directed at Deirdre.

"Why?"

The princess, who stood beside her sister and the prostrate magic-user, returned his gaze coolly. Somehow she had combed her black hair back from her face, and it fell in smooth cascades down her back.

"It was a mistake," Deirdre said. "I was . . . misguided. I have punished the one who was responsible. I'm sorry." The words rang stiffly resentful to them all, and Alicia gave her sister a sharp look. But the mage held up his hand in restraint and gestured to the plain bronze ring.

"The ring—it blocked the magic, partially. It saved my life. But what about the dragon?"

"Gone," said Alicia. The princess indicated the well, and at once Keane took notice of the lush verdancy of the surrounding valley.

"The goddess has returned," Alicia concluded. "None can deny it now!"

"And you have brought her to us," Tavish said, throwing an arm around Alicia's shoulders. "The daughter of a Great Druid—and now a mighty druid herself!"

"My Lady Princess!" cried Hanrald, his face flushing with emotion. He knelt before her. "I pledge my life and my labors to you and the goddess Earthmother and to any cause you name!"

Alicia was touched deeply by his sincerity. She knew of the knight's valiant defense of the well. "You have already fulfilled the needs of devotion," she said. "Without your fight here, before the rest of us arrived, all our efforts would have been too late."

"And the goddess has given us another druid of power," observed Tavish, smiling at Danrak. "Hanrald told us of your role in the defense of the well."

"And she sent her prophet," added the druid, "that we might know of her coming."

"The prophet!" Tavish exclaimed suddenly. "Where *is* he?" None of them had seen any sign of the figure since he had seized Malawar's holy symbol and broken away from the priest of Talos.

"More to the point, *what* is he?" Deirdre interjected. "He appears and disappears like no man!" She made no mention now, or later, of her encounter with the stranger in the throne room of Caer Callidyrr.

"We have also witnessed a sorceress of note emerging," Keane observed. His tone was neutral, but he regarded Deirdre with cautious eyes. "Lady Princess, I would query you on that topic some time very soon."

"Perhaps," Deirdre said, still guarded.

"Such power can be dangerous to the wielder as well as the target," Keane noted.

"Hey, everybody—flowers! And fish—the pond's filled with fish!" A bright blue figure appeared above the shallows of the Moonwell. Newt dove into the water with a great splash and emerged, sputtering but empty-clawed. "I had a trout right in my paws!" he boasted. "It was *this* long, but I almost pulled it out!"

"Good fishing, Newt," said Tavish. "You've earned it." In another moment, the dragon blinked out of sight, but a pattern of dripping water speckled the surface of the pond, marking his location for the onlookers—and the trout—very well. Several times the invisible serpent splashed into the water, but the fish remained a little too smart for him.

"My lady." Alicia turned at the quiet voice behind her, seeing Brandon. In that instant, the matter lingering between them came to her mind.

"Walk with me, will you?" she asked, taking his arm and leading him away from the others, across a meadow studded with columbine and wild roses.

Behind them, Keane and Hanrald cast anxious glances at the pair. Then, spying the concern on each other's faces, they turned away with feigned nonchalance. The Prince of Gnarhelm and the Princess of Callidyrr strolled on, quickly out of earshot.

"I'm proud of what we've done together," Alicia began, slowly and awkwardly. "And knowing you has brought a richness to my life that makes me very grateful."

"Aye," Brandon agreed, squeezing her hand. "This I feel, too—and more." He stopped and turned to face her, placing his hands on her shoulders. "My Lady Princess, I know that I love you!"

"But I—"

He silenced her with a finger to her lips.

"Enough," said Brandon softly. The northman's lips smiled, but his eyes were sad. "I have come to know you, too, my princess—and in knowing you, I see many things differently than I did before. You're not a bride to be given like some prized treaty or diplomatic coup. Your father is not the person I should ask for your hand."

She smiled, grateful for his understanding.

"And so I ask it of you yourself. Will you marry me and be my queen?"

"No, Brandon—I won't. At least, not yet." She tried to speak gently as his face fell. "That's not to say I never will. If you still feel the same way about me, we'll talk about this again in the future. But for now, too many things have changed too quickly. What the future holds I can't imagine. I need to find out."

He smiled feebly, restored to some measure of hope. "I had promised, I recall, to carry you to Callidyrr in the *Gullwing*. I should still like to see your home, but I no longer have the ship to carry you."

"I think we should all go back to Callidyrr," Alicia agreed as they rejoined the others. "Perhaps the new Earl of Fairheight would provide us with horses."

Hanrald, accompanied by Danrak, had returned to the group after burying his father's body. Now he started, as if the thought was new to him. "If my lady will have it so, I would like to accompany your party to the castle, there, perhaps, to make my claim to the queen!"

"Of course!" exclaimed Alicia. At the thought, she turned to her sister. "And how is mother?" she asked. "Well, I hope!"

The younger princess stared at her sister. For a moment, Deirdre thought of the truth—of the state in which their mother had lain for all these days. Of course Alicia knew nothing of that.

But then the knowledge came to her, like a presence on the wind, that the danger was past—that the High Queen of the Isles was healthy again, and vital. There would be time enough to tell the full tale later.

"Yes," she replied simply. "She's very well."

* * * * *

From the Log of Sinioth:

Talos welcomes the return of me, his special pet. My master's vengeance is harsh, my soul wracked by fire, tormented by the justly deserved fruits of failure. But in the end, knowing that they did not learn my name, he graciously allows me to survive.

And with that survival comes strength—the power to return and work my lord's will. Soon the tools of that dream will fall into our hands. We have been bested for now on the land, but always, as we reach for these island lands, we have the pathway of the sea.

I know not the form nor the shape that my being shall take when Talos sends me again into the world, but once more I shall go namelessly and work my evil in his cause.

Coss-Axell-Sinioth

Epilogue

High Queen Robyn welcomed the Crown Prince of Gnarhelm as a royal guest of her court. Brandon's presence amplified the already sumptuous festivities surrounding the ascension of Hanrald of Blackstone to the Fairheight Earldom.

Feasting on boar and beef, dancing—highlighted by a new ballad from the Greater Bard Tavish of Snowdown—and revelry lasted far into the night. Wrestling matches between champions of the Ffolk and Wultha of Gnarhelm provided entertainment, though the great northman bested all challengers. The tale of his match against Keane was greeted with amused skepticism by the Ffolk who knew the royal tutor.

It was after midnight when the great doors opened to admit the agitated figure of the city harbormaster. He hastened to the royal table and leaned over to speak to Robyn. The raucous celebration faded to a roar around them.

"Tidings, Your Majesty, from a ship just in from the Sword Coast." The harbormaster looked at the floor, the walls—everywhere but at the queen.

"What is it?" Robyn's face had gone pale.

"I fear to tell you, My Queen, so grievous is the news!"

"Speak now!"

"The dying gales a few days since—they swept around the south of the isles, whipping for the mainland. There they caught a galleon in their fury, capsizing the vessel in moments. She sank like a stone, my lady, with loss of all hands."

"Finish." Robyn, pale but upright, gestured to the man to speak. The gaiety slowly faded around them, stricken faces all staring at the royal wife.

"It was a ship bound for Callidyrr, Majesty, returning King Kendrick to his home!"

FANTASY ADVENTURE

Druidhome Trilogy

Douglas Niles

The Coral Kingdom   Book Two

King Kendrick is held prisoner in the undersea city of the sahuagin. His daughter must secure help from the elves of Evermeet to save him during a confrontation in the dark depths of the Sea of Moonshae. Available October 1992.

The Druid Queen   Book Three

In this exciting conclusion, the forces of the Earthmother are finally united, but they face the greatest challenge for survival ever. Available Spring 1993.

Other books by Douglas Niles
The Moonshae Trilogy

The Maztica Trilogy

Darkwalker on Moonshae
Black Wizards
Darkwell

Ironhelm
Viperhand
Feathered Dragon

The ultimate struggle
of good and evil . . .
At stake, the survival of
the Moonshae Isles and
the peaceful Ffolk. High
King Tristan Kendrick
and the druid Robyn
confront an evil that
has invaded the land,
manifesting itself in the
form of an army of giant
firbolgs, dread
Bloodriders, and
the beast, Kazgaroth.

Tucked into a farflung
corner of the Forgotten
Realms lies the savagely
beautiful land, Maztica,
where vengeful gods battle
in an epic struggle for
supremacy, with human
pawns as gamepieces.
Pitted against these warring
titans are Erix, a former
slave girl, and Halloran, a
mercenary. Will they be
able to save the land–or
themselves?

FORGOTTEN REALMS®

Fantasy Adventure

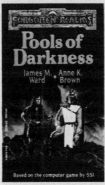

Pools of Darkness
James M. Ward & Anne K. Brown

The entire city of Phlan has vanished, ripped from the surface of Toril by dire creatures and magical forces. While the minions of the evil god Bane bicker over the spoils, the denizens of Phlan mount a stubborn defense.

A ranger thief named Ren seeks his missing friends, Shal and Tar, spellcasters nonpareil. Ren bands together with a mysterious sorceress, Evaine, her intrepid shapeshifter cat, a couple of droll druids, and a fearful knight who is absolutely, positively dead.

The novel *Pools of Darkness*, also a best-selling computer game by SSI, revisits the heroes of Phlan ten years after the city was saved in *Pools of Radiance*. Available now.